EQUINOX

a novel

Neil Barratt

with Allan Taylor

Trafford
PUBLISHING

Order this book online at www.trafford.com/07-2572
or email orders@trafford.com

Most Trafford titles are also available at major online book retailers.

© Copyright 2007 Richard N. Birnie

All rights reserved. No part of this publication may be reproduced, stored in a retrieval system, or transmitted, in any form or by any means, electronic, mechanical, photocopying, recording, or otherwise, without the written prior permission of the author.

Note for Librarians: A cataloguing record for this book is available from Library and Archives Canada at www.collectionscanada.ca/amicus/index-e.html

ISBN: 978-1-4251-5719-7

We at Trafford believe that it is the responsibility of us all, as both individuals and corporations, to make choices that are environmentally and socially sound. You, in turn, are supporting this responsible conduct each time you purchase a Trafford book, or make use of our publishing services. To find out how you are helping, please visit www.trafford.com/responsiblepublishing.html

Our mission is to efficiently provide the world's finest, most comprehensive book publishing service, enabling every author to experience success. To find out how to publish your book, your way, and have it available worldwide, visit us online at www.trafford.com/10510

Trafford PUBLISHING   www.trafford.com

North America & international
toll-free: 1 888 232 4444 (USA & Canada)
phone: 250 383 6864 ♦ fax: 250 383 6804 ♦ email: info@trafford.com

The United Kingdom & Europe
phone: +44 (0)1865 722 113 ♦ local rate: 0845 230 9601
facsimile: +44 (0)1865 722 868 ♦ email: info.uk@trafford.com

10 9 8 7 6 5 4 3 2

for my father

"It needs doing, just do it right!" JC

Part One

The drive north was marred by two things; the weather which was wet and windy, and the persistent squeal of the windscreen wipers as they tried to keep pace with the heavy rain. The distance the driver and his mate had to cover that day was less than 120 miles, but the nature of Ireland's road network meant that they had allowed over three hours for the journey. They hadn't even been driving an hour and the continuous squealing was already beginning to wear their patience thin; God alone knew what they'd be like if it kept raining for the whole drive. The van was nearly eight years old and it showed; the interior was tatty and the air freshener that hung from the rear view mirror did little to disguise the bad smell. The one thing that could be said in its favour was that it was mechanically sound, but that was only due to the ministrations of the "Big House's" mechanic.

"Where did you dig up this piece of shit?"

"Munn's Car Auctions, down on Sir John Rogerson's Quay."

Sir John Rogerson's Quay was on the south side of the Liffey near the city centre. Despite its proximity to the bustling hub of Dublin it was, like all too many dockland areas, somewhat depressed and seedy – just the place to find a beat-up old Transit van saleable for cash – no questions asked.

"Well you really picked a winner."

"Look, the order was simple; a van or a truck, something that wouldn't attract attention, and something cheap. I didn't exactly have a lot of choice – it was this or a knackered old Bedford. I was on my own if you remember, and I didn't have time to run all over Dublin looking for the best. Buy the van and get a set of plates off a similar wreck, then have Morris give it the once over and help him out with any repairs – it's a lot of work at short notice."

There was a measure of truth in what the driver said, but he hadn't been the only one with a lot on his plate – people had been making travel plans, booking tickets, booking accommodation, in one case a set of plans had been requisitioned and copied at the planning offices of a local council – so he hadn't been acting alone, it had just felt that way. He'd had a busy Friday and Saturday what with locating a suitable vehicle, getting a new set of number plates, and then helping with the servicing. The only major work that Geoff Morris, the mechanic, and he had had to undertake was the stripping and rebuilding of the brake system; a time consuming and dirty business. Other than that the white Ford Transit was reasonably sound despite the tatty appearance. The driver had spent Sunday morning road testing the van around Dublin, and thankfully it hadn't missed a beat. After the test drive the only other work was the fitting of a new set of tyres, after that the van was ready for the delivery.

"Well you got the job done. If Morris reckons this old banger's OK then I suppose it'll do."

"Thank you so much for your vote of confidence. I'm glad you're here to correct any mistakes I might make."

The sarcasm was not altogether lost on the younger man, but he kept on pushing to see how much needle he could give.

"Don't worry, I'll keep you right. You know, an old man like you needs looking after much as you may like working on your own."

"Aye, and the more crap I have to put up with from you the more I wish this was a solo job."

That was that. One more jibe would probably be one too many. The passenger decided a conciliatory approach would smooth the feathers he had ruffled.

"Seriously though it could've been worse. At least this time you got some notice. It's usually stop what you're doing and be, well, wherever, in two hours time. I was in Cork until last night and I only got the word on Friday evening. Otherwise I'd have been around to lend a hand."

"Then I have to be thankful for small mercies."

"Oh very bloody funny. At least you got something worthwhile, me on the other hand had two days in Cork for no good reason – the bugger never showed up."

"No uncertainties on this job, so let's just get it right."

"Looks OK so far and with me on the team it's bound to go as planned. By the way, where'd you get the plates?"

"I was lucky there, first place I tried, a car breakers on South Circular Road. An early '72 Ford Transit – same colour and everything."

"So if we get stopped the van passes scrutiny?"

"Yeah, but let's just not get stopped, not with that stuff in the back."

They drove on in silence through the small town of Slane continuing along the N2 towards Ardee. If it hadn't been raining the drive north would have been reasonably interesting; the scenery along the way would at least have proved a distraction, but the rain and the poor visibility just made the drive a trial. Spray thrown up by passing vehicles made life difficult as the windscreen wipers only managed one speed. At times it was all Crawford could do to keep the van safely on his side of the road. Even with the new tyres the van was only just maintaining a positive grip on the road. Kavanagh was getting fed up with the miserable driving conditions and the periodic skids as the van aqua-planed and Crawford fought for control of the steering. His gloved hands actually slipped on the wheel at one point and this was more than enough for Kavanagh.

"For Christ's sake pull in at the next service station and take a rest."

"Are you giving me orders now?"

"No, I'm just suggesting that you take a break before this bloody weather does for us both."

"Yeah, you're probably right. Look we'll be in Ardee in about ten minutes, we'll stop then."

Less than a quarter of an hour later Crawford brought the van to a halt at the roadside, across the street from a newsagent's shop. He had driven through Ardee, stopping on the far side of the town on the road leading to the N2 and Carrickmacross. Both men needed a snack and Kavanagh was deputised to go and get something. He stepped out of the van and ran across the road as the rain continued to fall heavily.

Linehan's was a typical paper shop, unchanged for a couple of generations and selling a little of everything. The ill-lit interior was made even darker by the overcast day outside and the fact that the windows hadn't been cleaned in God alone knew how long. Kavanagh had to be careful of his footing as it seemed that every available inch of floor space had been given over to stock. He went to the chill cabinet and retrieved two cans of Coca-cola and then made his way to the counter that housed the till and the formidable cashier, a woman in her fifties. One look at her told Kavanagh that Linehan's didn't suffer from much in the way of shop-lifting. He lifted a copy of the Irish News and the Sun from the pile of papers that covered the front of the counter.

"Have you any crisps, missus?"

"Aye, son they're just over to your right."

"OK, I see 'em, thanks."

Kavanagh left his cans and newspapers on the counter and walked over to the boxes containing packets of crisps and picked out four. He went back to the counter and picked out a couple of Mars and Marathon bars. The cashier, who was in fact the owner, Mrs. Pat Linehan, had given Kavanagh the once over and deduced from his work-boots and overalls that he was a labourer.

"Are you working in that weather today, son?"

"Aye, missus. Me and the boss have a job up near Castleblayney. Mind you, I don't think we'll be up to much today.

"Sure, that rain's fearful altogether", as they had spoken she had totalled up Kavanagh's purchases, "That's one, thirty-nine, son."

He handed over two single punt notes and received his sixty-one pence change. Taking the plastic bag that Pat Linehan had put the newspapers and so on into, Kavanagh moved towards the door.

"I hope the weather breaks for you and your boss. It'd be miserable having to work in that."

"Thanks missus. 'Bye now."

Kavanagh left the newsagent's thinking that appearances could be deceptive – she hadn't been a holy terror after all. Pat Linehan was also considering her perception of the young labourer – a good looking boy and polite too, a pity that there weren't a few more like him. If she had known the truth about Kavanagh she would have changed her mind.

Even though it was only a short distance from the shop to the van Kavanagh still managed to get wet. He clambered into the cab and shook his head sharing the effects of the downpour with Crawford.

"Thanks a lot, you stupid bugger."

"Ah, piss off! Next time go yourself", he rummaged in the bag and took out the crisps and cans of Coke, "Here, those are yours, and I got papers as well."

"What d'you get?"

"The Irish News and the Sun."

"Give me the Irish News. You can keep the Sun. I don't know how you can read that rag, there's nothing in it except a pair of tits."

Crawford's reference to the Sun's page three girl brought a smile to Kavanagh's face. He opened the paper to take a look and was happy to discover a big busted blonde, then he held it up to let Crawford get an eye full.

"I'd sooner look at her than your ugly mug."

There was no reply to that so Crawford shrugged his shoulders and sighed deeply and then gave his attention to the front page of the Irish News. Kavanagh leafed through the Sun and both men ate and drank as the rain continued to fall unabated. The short break from the hazards of driving in the rain had relaxed them considerably. Crawford had taken his gloves off to eat his crisps and the Marathon bar; now that he was finished he put all the rubbish into the plastic bag and then put his gloves back on. Kavanagh did the same when he finished his snack, and with all the cans and empty packets in the bag he once more got out of the van to dump them in a litter bin which was happily close by. Crawford started the van as Kavanagh got back on board.

"I think the rain has slackened a bit."

"I hope so, 'cause driving this thing in the wet is no fun. These new tyres may have been a necessity but they aren't gripping well at all."

"Just take it easy then", Kavanagh checked his watch, "It's coming up on ten to one, we've got plenty of time."

Crawford looked in his wing mirror, signalled and moved back into the flow of traffic. The rain had eased somewhat; the windscreen wipers were no longer fighting a losing battle.

Traffic was mercifully light and they covered the twelve miles between Ardee and Carrickmacross in under twenty minutes. One thing that both men had become aware of during the drive north was the fact that the further they got from Dublin the worse the general condition of the road became. In the last five miles leading into town the van had hit a couple of nasty potholes forcing Kavanagh to look into the cargo space to make sure that everything was secure. The last thing they needed was their load breaking free and rolling around the back of the van. Thankfully the lines tied to the anchor points were holding fast.

Carrickmacross had a wide main street with more than its fair share of bars. To have embarked on an inclusive pub crawl would have been to attempt suicide. The dull, wet day added to a pervading atmosphere of depression – Carrickmacross had seen better days. Crawford thought that maybe the number of bars was symptomatic of this depression – if he lived in Carrickmacross he'd probably seek solace in a glass. What else was there to do? Kavanagh, who had been looking around the main street too, brought himself out of his reverie.

"There's a famous poet from this neck of the woods."

"What's his name?"

"Patrick Kavanagh."

"You don't mean to tell me that you're a long lost relative do you?"

"Wouldn't that be a laugh? Somehow I don't think the family would be too quick to claim me as one of their own. No, I don't think there's a connection; my people are originally from Limerick, and that's going way back. What about you?"

"I don't know for sure."

"You must have some idea?"

"To be honest I've never given it much thought."

"Well aren't you the inquisitive one."

"As far as I'm concerned all that family history is a distraction, it's who you are yourself that counts. Suppose all your ancestors were total bastards, does that make you one? No it doesn't; you make your own choices and those choices define you."

"Here endeth the lesson according to Crawford."

"It's just the way I see things. If people don't like it – tough – I'm not going to change to suit them."

"No wonder you like working on your own – you'd never get anyone to measure up to your standards."

"You'll learn."

"No I don't think I will, not from your point of view anyway. There'd be too many let-downs if I was that rigid."

"Then it looks as if you're going to be one of those let-downs. Oh well, you're young yet; there's still time to avoid expediency."

"Is that what you really think? Jesus, are you ever in the wrong trade to be an idealist. How'd you ever get in in the first place?"

"Because I'm bloody good at what I do."

Both men felt they had said enough, any more and they would have risked serious offence, so they dropped the subject. Their conversation had carried them through and beyond Carrickmacross; once again they were driving through the Monaghan countryside and once again the road surface became a pre-occupation. The old white van periodically lost grip, skidded and then hit a pothole. Crawford would have slowed down to compensate for the state of the road but felt that even though they were still running to schedule it was better to keep to it and risk the bumpy ride than to accept the luxury of a smoother passage. As long as he kept it between the hedges and didn't hit anything, well, it would have to do. Kavanagh on the other hand was less philosophical and was feeling extremely pissed off with the jarring ride he was having in the front passenger seat.

"When are those useless buggers in the government going to do something about the state of these bloody roads?"

"How the hell would I know? Anyway, you just sit there and read your paper; we'll be in Castleblayney in about five. After that it's only another hour at most."

"And then it's time for work."

"You're not wrong there. It'll take us the best part of three hours to bury that lot."

"Just hope you're up to it."

"I could take you any time I felt like it."

"Is that so?"

"That it is, kiddo, that it is."

Crawford reflected on this – how long would he be up to the task? The job itself and the possibility of having to face off someone like Kavanagh? There were no answers to his questions. One good thing had come from the exchange, however, the good nature had returned to the van after the awkward moment they'd had in Carrickmacross. This was their third job together, and potentially the most important. Personal differences could only prove obstructive, and anything that got in the way of a smoothly planned operation would only create friction that they didn't need.

The outskirts of the town became apparent as the rural gave way to the urban. Crawford gave even more scrutiny to the streets and traffic of Castleblayney than he had to the open road – an error of judgement and the ensuing accident would result in the involvement of the police, the Garda Siochana, and that was a problem they did not need. Vigilance was particularly important given the somewhat eccentric driving habits of the locals. Kavanagh kept his eyes open too, and was rewarded with some quite bizarre examples of roadcraft. Signalling was unnecessary, observation of road signs for fools, and where better to stop and chat with a friend than in the middle of the road?

"Forget what I said about the state of the roads, they'd do better teaching this lot to drive."

"It keeps you on your toes, that's a cert. Oh well, we'll be out of the town soon enough."

They had come to the crossroads; left would take them to Monaghan, right to Keady. Crawford turned the van left and followed the N2. They cleared the town quickly and were soon back on the open road. They both breathed a sigh of relief – less traffic meant less likelihood of an accident and the difficulties that would bring. They were still running to schedule with a little over 20 miles to cover. Traffic was light and the road was fairly straight so any slow-moving agricultural vehicles were quickly overtaken. The hamlet of Castleshane was about 12 miles from

Castleblayney; it was here that they made their turn due north for Tamlat, and it was here that the road surface took a distinct turn for the worse.

"Should have got a four wheel drive; this road's a frigging disgrace. I mean, the main road was bad, but this is a fucking donkey track. My backside is…"

"For Christ's sake Sean, change the bloody record. I can't wave a magic wand and fix the roads. If your arse is so bloody sensitive next time bring a cushion."

Kavanagh was about to reply, but thought better of it and held his tongue – Crawford had a point. They sat in silence as they made their northward progress, both men concentrating on the task at hand. Kavanagh checked his watch – nearly ten to two. By the time they had carried out their security check at the site it would be around three o'clock – the latest time they had allowed for the start of the dig. They came to Tamlat and took the left turn for New Mills Bridge. The van's front suspension took a real battering from the latest series of potholes, and from the noises in the back of the van it sounded as if their cargo had broken free.

"Take a look in the back, would you Sean."

Kavanagh clambered into the rear, and from the noises Crawford could tell that he was securing the containers to the anchor points. After a couple of minutes he resumed his seat in the cab of the van.

"That's it, that is fucking it! I'm looking for a new line of work after this job. I'm not some bloody navvy."

"No you're not, but there are times when you sound like one. Get a grip, would you. Let's have this as smooth as we can – roads permitting, OK?"

"Yeah, OK."

They were both feeling tense. Crawford knew from experience that tension was both a blessing and a curse; it sharpened the wits, but too much of it could be a distraction. Another turn, leading them through Glaslough brought them to the dismantled railway line that had once carried passengers and freight between Armagh and Monaghan. This was to be the site of their excavation. The van bounced along the access track that ended beside the railway cutting. When the van came to a halt Crawford and Kavanagh sat with the engine running for 10 minutes. No vehicles, no Garda officers – nothing disturbed the concentration of the two men, except the windscreen wipers, but even they ceased to be an irritation when the rain suddenly stopped. They got out of the van and began the onerous task of checking the surrounding area on foot. Both men had stiffened up in the van after the three hour drive, and were glad of the opportunity to stretch. The sky was clearing after the rain and the temperature would certainly drop – at least the physical activity of the dig would keep them warm.

There were no fresh vehicle tracks, no footprints, nothing to indicate a disturbance in the surroundings. They moved into the wooded area on the north side of the cutting and checked for broken branches on the trees and shrubs – again there was no sign of any unusual activity. They paid particular attention to the burial site to make sure that there were no overhanging branches that would obstruct the dig, and no signs of tree roots on the surface that would interfere either. When both were satisfied with the site and the overall feel of the area they returned to the van to collect the "packages". Crawford considered the use of the term "package", and like so many of the codes and acronyms that he and others like him used he thought it escapist. They were just labels that allowed him to forget what he was really involved in. The two "packages", in fact two plastic water butts, weighed around 65lbs each. It was not the weight but the bulk that made them awkward to carry. Thankfully it was less than 100 yards to the burial site, so the two men's fitness was not put to a severe test.

"Sean, I'll stay with the "packages", you go and get the rest of the stuff."

"I thought you were starting to feel the strain. Take it easy now. You know at your age you should be more careful."

"Bugger off, get the stuff, and less of your lip."

"Anything you say, you're the boss."

Kavanagh went back to the van and retrieved the trowels, shovels, and groundsheets that they would need to accomplish the task. The older man watched Kavanagh retrace his steps; pleased to see the attention he paid to the surrounding area, obviously taking care to make sure that they were still alone. "All clear. I suppose we can get going", Kavannagh checked his watch, "It's just shy of five to three."

"Fine, let's get started. Give me a hand with this groundsheet, and be careful not to trample any of the plants."

They selected the nearest clear area to the burial site for the groundsheet and spread it out. The next task was to lift the turf covering the area they wanted to excavate. The two men went to great lengths to ensure that the surface was as undisturbed as possible; they hoped to leave no signs of their work. The turf was cut in small sections, and these were gently lifted onto the groundsheet. Now came the hard manual part of the job. Even with something as simple as digging a hole they had to take exaggerated care with the freshly dug soil. This was bagged up and transferred to the groundsheet, emptied out, and the bags taken back to the growing hole for yet more soil. The two men worked steadily for an hour without incident. The soil was heavy clay, but other than that they encountered no rocks or roots to impede their progress. Crawford surveyed their work and decided it was time to take a breather – there was after all no sense in overdoing it. The digging had loosened their muscles and both men felt the warm inner glow that prolonged activity produced. They were both used to exerting themselves, although that might not have been apparent from their physiques; they were both wiry men with a stature that did not command attention.

The hole was finished and the break in work was welcome. Sean opened the small haversack that he had brought from the van with the other kit and picked out an orange. He leaned up against a tree, took his gloves off and ate it, sucking the juice from each segment before swallowing the pulp. He put the peel in his pocket. Crawford took the opportunity to give the area another check. He went back to the van and surveyed the track that would take them back to the road – nothing was amiss. Once he was satisfied he returned to Sean and the hole.

"OK Sean, back to the grind. Give me a hand and let's get all this stuff shifted into one container."

"Right, you hold it steady and I'll get the gear."

The older man gripped the side of the water butt as Kavanagh reached for the lid.

"Jesus Sean, how long have you had your gloves off?"

"As long as it took to eat my orange."

"You haven't taken them off at all since we started this morning?"

"Only when we stopped in Ardee, and so did you. Anyway I was careful, for God's sake!"

"Well, put them on again before you touch anything, understood?"

For transportation purposes there had been the two "packages", but for burial only one was really necessary. That was good news for Sean and Crawford as it meant that they had a smaller hole to dig. They opened the butts and began transferring the contents of one into the other. Sean let out a low whistle as he examined the equipment he was handing to the older man.

"This is a pretty interesting set of gear; I wonder what the job is."

"I wouldn't ask any questions about that if I were you. Better off not knowing if you ask me."

"Yeah, but this has got to be important, I mean…"

"I'm serious Sean, forget about it. That's my last word on the matter."

Kavanagh's thoughts were set aside and they addressed themselves to repacking the container. It was a tight squeeze but they managed to get all the gear into one water butt. They resealed it, gently lowered it into the hole and filled out the spaces around it with soil retrieved from the groundsheet. Lastly they replaced the turf. By the time both men had finished, the site looked unaltered. Some leaf litter and a few broken twigs and branches scattered judiciously finalised the effect. The remaining soil was either bagged up or shovelled into the second water butt. The two men carried the bags, the tools and the butt to the van in three shifts.

"Sean, bring the haversack with you, and we'll give the site a final once-over."

When all the gear was safely locked away they returned to the burial site. The area did not appear to have changed since their arrival nearly three hours ago. Even the closest scrutiny failed to show any deficiencies in their work – if they hadn't known they wouldn't have known.

"God, but we're good."

"Maybe so, but before we get carried away by our artistry let's finish the job."

"Yeah, you're right; I suppose we'd better mark the site so the lads know where to dig."

"Which is why you're carrying the haversack. You'll find a can of yellow marker dye in it. Give it to me."

Sean tossed the small can of spray to the older man who then walked to the nearest large tree and painted a ring around the trunk. Then he faced the excavation and once more turning to the tree he sprayed an inverted U facing the hole.

"Is that enough?"

"It's the agreed signal and it shouldn't attract attention – the Forestry people mark trees for cutdown like this all the time and this is their property. Satisfied?"

"Not quite. Let's leave them a little extra."

Sean reached into his pocket and retrieved the orange peel which he carefully placed at the bottom right hand corner of the camouflaged hole.

"Nice touch Sean", he glanced at his watch, "its quarter to six, time to go."

After one final sweep of the area they were back in the van. Crawford took his place behind the wheel, started the engine and slowly drove them away from the railway cutting. No sirens, no floodlights, no armed Garda officers, no reception of any kind awaited them as they returned to the road. They turned left and then right before they were back in Glaslough. The road now led to the border crossing at Annaghroe Bridge. They had driven about a mile when Crawford pulled over to the roadside. Again they got out and opened the back of the van. There was no point arousing the suspicions of the troops or police at the border crossings so the evidence of their excavations had to go. They dumped the water butt, bags of soil and the groundsheets in the ditch that ran alongside the road. They also stripped off the boiler suits they had been working in, but rather than dumping them along with the other gear, they hung them in the back of the van. Muddy work boots were replaced by training shoes and the jeans and sweatshirts they had been wearing under the overalls would do in the meantime as a change of clothes.

It was still dry even though the sky had clouded over; they would hopefully have a clear drive through to Belfast. First things first, they had to get across the border. It was just gone 6 o'clock when they pulled up at the checkpoint. Neither man was in the least concerned by the formalities. The usual questions were asked – "Could I see your driving licence, please sir", "Where are you coming from", "Where are you going to", "Could you step to the rear of the vehicle and open the doors". If the replies were polite and what were expected then there was no trouble. Crawford did not want any hassle so he accommodated the young soldier performing the routine inspection. Kavanagh played his part, answering those questions directed at him in a similar manner. Neither man's name was listed, nor was their vehicle, both men had been compliant, so with no reason to detain them further the young soldier waved them on.

They were now in Northern Ireland. It was 6.21pm, Monday 19th March 1979, they still had to get to Belfast, dump the van and get to the bed & breakfast where they were booked for the night. Crawford followed the road to Caledon from where he took the road north to Dungannon and the start of the M1. After the rural roads, both north and south of the border, the motorway seemed a driver's paradise. The motorway and the fact that the rain, which had been forecast, had held off allowed them to make good time and it was just before 8 o'clock when they arrived on the outskirts of Belfast. They turned off the M1 and took Kennedy Way which led to the junction with the Falls Road. They turned right and took the Falls Road city bound. It was dark but the republican graffiti stood out on the walls illuminated by the streetlights – BRITS OUT, VICTORY TO THE IRA, FUCK THE QUEEN – it was all depressingly familiar.

It was obviously a quiet night in Belfast; there were no queues of traffic at vehicle checkpoints, no British Army foot-patrols on the streets, then again, it was only the middle of the evening, time enough for the soldiers to come out from their barracks. Crawford drove carefully along the Falls Road still aware of the fact that even at this late stage of the operation an accident was the last thing he wanted. Just ahead of them at the junction with Broadway the traffic lights changed, and the van had to come to a halt. Crawford started to indicate a right turn.

"No, it's not this one – it's the right turn after these lights."

"You sure?"

"Yeah, they said dump it after the Broadway junction, but not in Broadway – it's too open. We want Thames Street."

The lights changed again and they moved off with Crawford indicating his right turn as soon as they passed through the junction. Thames Street was a short red-brick terrace, poorly lit. There were several spaces where they could leave the van and the one Crawford selected was on the left-hand side about half way down the street. The two men got out of the van for the last time, each taking a grip containing fresh clothes, toiletries and shaving tackle. They closed the doors and walked away. Crawford had taken the keys but left the van unlocked.

They moved in the direction of the Royal Victoria Hospital at an unhurried pace. As they walked they kept their eyes focused on the surroundings of the Falls Road. Nothing drew their attention as being out of place – the scene around them was surprisingly ordinary. If it hadn't been for the graffiti and the occasional sight of Army Landrovers patrolling the area the Falls Road would have looked pretty much like a part of any big town.

"Wait a minute Sean. Need to tie my shoelace."

As he crouched down to tie his lace Crawford dropped the van's keys down the drain in the gutter at the curb side. There was now nothing to connect them to the van. They moved on to the taxi rank outside the main Falls Road entrance to the hospital and waited their turn. After around five minutes an old black taxi pulled up and they got in.

"Where are you for, lads?"

"We're in a B&B off Botanic Avenue."

"Just visiting?

"Aye, should be just a couple of days."

"Somebody sick?"

"Yeah. We've just been in to see our auntie. She had a coronary two days ago."

"Jesus, that's rough."

"The doctor says it was a warning. She'll be alright in a day or two, then we should be able to head home."

"You lads aren't local then?"

"No, we've been on the sites in Manchester for a couple of years now. Just casual, you know, but the money's good."

"I'd sooner stay close to home. God knows there's enough Brits over here without going to live with them."

The taxi was coming up to the junction of Tates Avenue and Lisburn Road. The driver's concentration went back to the job of negotiating the left turn down the Lisburn Road. Sean was glad of the break. The cover of the sick aunt had been part of the operation but it hadn't been thought vital. Those involved in the planning stages hadn't considered talkative taxi drivers. Crawford had kept silent throughout the conversation – for form's sake he thought he'd better say something.

"I was just thinking, you know, that ward Maggie's in is bloody depressing. Like, I hate hospitals anyway but you'd think they'd do something to lift them a bit."

"I know what you mean. When the wife was in having our latest it was all you could to get me through the door. And the noise – Jesus, one baby crying's bad enough but a whole bloody ward of them!"

For the remainder of the journey, which thankfully wasn't long, the two men were given the taxi driver's colourful views on the National Health Service and child-rearing. He was still complaining when he pulled up outside the guest house on Botanic Avenue.

"…the price of kids' clothes these days. If you ask me it's a bloody rip-off. Well, enough of that – here you are lads, that'll be £1.70", Sean handed him two singles and told him to keep the change, "Thanks, and I hope your auntie is feeling better."

"Aye, well I hope so too. Take it easy, mate."

Sean closed the taxi door and followed Crawford into the bed & breakfast. When he got through the front door he saw the landlady already handing over the keys as the old man signed the register.

"What time would you like breakfast?"

"Sean and I have an early start in the morning, so we'll say quarter to eight if that's not too much trouble."

"No trouble at all. Is there anything else that you'll be needing?"

"Yeah, there is actually. Could you phone a taxi for us in the morning, please? It'd be a great help."

"Certainly. Are you moving on tomorrow?"

"Yeah, it'll be just the one night in Belfast."

"Well, the room's the first on the left at the top of the stairs – number 2. The bathroom's just down the landing on the right. So, if there's nothing more I can do for you, I'll see you both in the morning."

"Just one last thing. I hate to be a bother but could we get a cup of tea?"

"There's tea and coffee making facilities in your room."

"Oh, that's grand. Well, goodnight then."

"Goodnight gents."

Kavanagh took the lead up the stairs to the room with their bags. Crawford followed him up to the spotlessly clean twin room and sat down on the bed nearest the door. He breathed in and out deeply for a couple of minutes while Kavanagh stowed his gear. He checked his watch, nine twenty-five, time for a shower, a cup of tea and then bed.

"I'm going to get cleaned up and then I'll have a cup of tea before I get my head down."

Sean turned from the chest of drawers where he was putting his clothes and held up a half bottle of Hennessy.

"I think we can do better than a cup of tea."

"Yeah, I have to agree with you. What's more, I think we deserve it after the day we've put in. Give me ten minutes and I'll be back for a nip of that."

The shower was not that powerful but at least it was hot. Crawford let the water work its magic and loosen the tension that had built up in his shoulders and lower back. He washed the sweat of the day's labours away – he felt clean. When he had finished he stood in front of the full-length mirror which was fogged up with condensation. After wiping it clear he looked at his reflection. There he stood, an old man to some, an experienced one to others. He looked himself over – physically he was in good shape for a man ten years younger, it was only when he took a closer look at his face that any signs of aging were apparent. The lines around his eyes and the deep furrows on his forehead gave him a careworn appearance. He looked as if he was weighed down by responsibility. How long could he keep up with the likes of Kavanagh? He was thirty-two years old, and starting to push himself a bit harder than he used to. Sean had jokingly said that he was going to look for a new line of work after this job, maybe that wasn't such a bad idea. A change might be for the best, yet, this was the life he had chosen and what did he really have to offer away from it.

He unlocked the bathroom door and walked back to number 2. Sean now took his turn in the shower, leaving Crawford with some wise crack about "age before beauty". He was still considering his options or rather the lack of them when Sean returned. He looked up at Kavanagh with an expression that reflected his thoughts.

"Jesus, did your best friend die or something. Cheer up; we can have that drink now."

"We should have glasses for Hennessy, are there any over at the wash-hand basin?"

"No. We'll have to make do with the cups for the tea, unless you'd prefer the bottle?"

"The cups'll do", and Crawford held them out for Sean to pour two large measures of brandy, "Here's to a job well done."

Both men drank and both felt the tawny liquid leave its fiery trail from mouth to stomach. The worries of the day were receding – they were far from the excavation site, in another country, nothing they possessed could tie them to any illegal activity, ahead of them was the prospect of a good night's sleep followed by a good breakfast and then they would be on their way. The plan had unfolded with nothing more than minor irritations to upset the schedule, they had performed flawlessly, they should have been feeling the satisfaction that was their due, but both men only felt an odd sense of anticlimax.

It was Kavanagh who first gave voice to his concerns, and the older man realised that the questions he had posed earlier in the day were still requiring answers.

"You know, the gear we buried today, I was wondering what's the job?"

"Sean, I told you before don't ask those sort of questions. The answers would only get you into a lot of trouble. Seriously you're better off not knowing."

"But we took risks today and I just want to know why."

"Sean, listen to me – you and I are just a small part of a much bigger picture. An important part, granted, but don't ever overestimate that importance."

"Don't you ever get curious about what we're up to?"

"I learned to bury that curiosity in much the same way as we buried that water butt this afternoon. You'll learn, believe me."

"Suppose I don't want to learn?"

"Now you're just being bloody stupid. If you take that attitude to someone in charge he'll jump all over you. Look, you're tired, and if you ask me not making a whole lot of sense. Get your head down. We've still got a lot to do tomorrow to finish this job off properly."

"Yeah, you're right. Here, give me your cup and I'll rinse it for you."

"Don't you want to finish the bottle?"

"To be honest, no. Do you?"

"Give it here. It'll help me sleep."

Kavanagh passed the bottle to Crawford before going to the wash-hand basin to clean his teeth. As he got into bed he reached up to the switch above him.

"Do you mind if I turn the lights off?"

"No, go ahead."

Crawford sat in the darkened room with his cup of brandy. He listened to the younger man's breathing as it became more regular. After a quarter of an hour had passed he was sure that Kavanagh was asleep. There he lay with a head full of questions and he had managed to fall asleep without any difficulty. How could he do that? Crawford knew that he would be up half the night if he were to consider all the possible consequences of their actions today. What was done was done – better to give consideration to the action tomorrow. They'd be out of Northern Ireland by lunchtime, after a couple of days rest they would be ready for the next job. The next job, what would it be? Would he be working alone or as part of a team? What would be the result of his involvement? God! He was getting as bad as Kavanagh. Enough of this, it was time he got to bed.

He stretched out on the narrow single and tried very hard to put the events of the day and the possibilities of the future to the back of his mind. It was a struggle he nearly lost, but just after 1.00am he finally managed to triumph and succumb to sleep.

His internal clock told him to wake up just as Sean's alarm went off. It was six-thirty, there or thereabouts – he'd got a little over five hours sleep which was going to have to be enough, and anyway he could sleep on the plane.

"Do you want to go to the bathroom first? And none of your cracks about age before beauty."

"OK, I'll go first."

"Right. I'll pack my gear."

Packing his gear was the work of a minute. He reached into the inside left pocket of his jacket, which was hanging on the back of the door, and brought out the tickets for their flight to London. The departure time was ten o'clock which meant that they should get into Heathrow about an hour later and be clear of the airport for midday. If he got a taxi and the traffic wasn't too heavy he'd be back in the flat in Greenwich sometime after one-thirty.

Sean came back into the room, a towel wrapped around his waist.

"The bathroom's free if you want a shower."

"I don't think I'll bother. I just need to clean my teeth and have a quick shave."

"Not only a miserable bastard, but a dirty one as well."

"Look, I had a shower last night and I'll have a long soak in the bath this afternoon. In the meantime I reckon I'm clean enough."

He stepped over to the wash-hand basin and took off the tee-shirt that he had slept in. He got his shaving kit out of his sponge bag and lathered his dark stubbled face with foam. With deliberate strokes he removed the two days growth. When he was satisfied with the result he rinsed his face with cold water and then cleaned his teeth. He re-packed his toiletries, put them in his grip, and got dressed.

Sean had towelled himself dry and put on the fresh change of clothes that he had unpacked the previous night. The effect of the outfit he now wore was pronounced to say the least. The Sean Kavanagh who stood in front of Crawford was a very different young man from the one who had walked into the B&B the night before.

"Jesus, look at you. You look like a shop-window dummy. That lot must have set you back a packet."

"I know the value of good clothes. Where's the harm in that?"

"None at all, but take a look at what you've got on and then think about who you're supposed to be."

"So, I like to dress well."

"You don't get it do you? Your shoes, where'd you get them?"

"John Lobb's on Jermyn Street and before you ask they were off the shelf not bespoke. I couldn't afford bespoke."

"Poor you. How much were your off the shelf Oxford brogues?"

"Two hundred and seventy."

"Really, is that all? Think on this, Sean Kavanagh, casual brickie wouldn't spend two hundred and seventy pounds on clothes in a year. You've blown that on a pair of shoes. What about the rest of it?"

"The jacket's a Bladen which I got in Cordings on Piccadilly. The cords are Cordings own and the shirt's a Hackett of Jermyn Street."

"So you bought your shoes in Lobb's and went next door for your shirts – how convenient."

"How'd you know that Hacketts and Lobb's are side by side?"

"Never mind that. Nothing but the best. You must spend a hell of a lot on your wardrobe. All told you've got half a grand on your back."

"I didn't pay that much."

"Nick some of it did you?"

"No, I wait for the sales."

"I admire your economy but let's face it who are you trying to impress?"

"No-one in particular, but at least I make an effort. You on the other hand look like something the cat dragged in."

"Like me, it's all clean. It's non-descript and won't attract attention, it fits the character and that's the way I like it."

He was wearing a pair of grey trousers, a white shirt with a cheap polyester tie and black shoes that could have used a polish. The whole outfit had been acquired in Marks and Spencer with the exception of the shoes which were Hush Puppies. The effect was altogether uninspiring and as Crawford had implied instantly forgettable. Both men checked their personal gear and gave the room a quick once-over to make sure that they had left nothing behind. Happy with the condition of the room, Crawford took his jacket off the hook on the back of the door, and they went downstairs for breakfast. They took their seats in the dining room, each with a morning paper that they had retrieved from the desk in the hall. Tuesday 20th March was not offering much in the way of news. Mostly it was economic doom and gloom with Callaghan's Labour government being blamed for yet more disastrous inflation figures.

"Morning gents, did you sleep well, nice to see you down bright and early, would you like tea or coffee?"

The questions had come in a well rehearsed cheerfulness that was somewhat lacking in sincerity.

"We slept just fine, the pair of us. And Sean and I would both like tea, thank you."

"Tea it is then. I hope a full fry is to your liking?"

"Oh aye. That's one thing we miss across the water – a full English breakfast, as they call it, isn't a patch on a good Ulster fry."

And that was precisely what Sean and Crawford got – sausage, bacon, fried egg, soda bread, potato bread, fried tomato and mushrooms. While they were enjoying their breakfasts, the lady of the house phoned a taxi firm based just down the road in Botanic Avenue.

"That's your taxi sorted gents. The dispatcher says there'll be one here at half eight."

"That's grand, thanks. Could we have some more toast please?"

"Of course you can. I'll say this; you wouldn't half know you were working men, the way you've both packed that fry away. It's good to see men enjoying their food."

She hurried back to the kitchen to make them more toast.

"God, I'll not be able to move if I eat any more. Mind you that was a super fry, best I've had in ages."

"Yeah, I'd have to agree with you, but bear in mind we ate next to nothing yesterday", Crawford looked at his watch, "What time have you got Sean?"

"Eight-oh five. Has yours stopped again?"

"Forgot to wind it last night", and he took his "Everite" off to readjust and wind it, "There's nothing wrong with this old watch."

"Oh come off it! When are you going to enter the 20th century and get a quartz? That thing is a bloody antique."

"Old it may be, but it's reliable as long as I remember to wind it."

"If you had a quartz you wouldn't have to remember. One less thing for those old grey cells to worry about."

With that the landlady returned with fresh toast. She put it on the table along with a receipt.

"I made up your bill to save some time, what with your taxi coming and all. It's seventeen pounds for the pair of you."

Crawford reached for his wallet and took out a twenty.

"I'll just go and get your change."

"Never mind the change. That breakfast was smashing, wasn't it Sean?"

"Aye, it was. Next time we're in Belfast we'll definitely be staying here."

"I wish all my guests were like you two gents, it's been a pleasure having you."

As she spoke a man and a woman came into the dining room and she was off. Crawford watched as she went into the same routine that she had greeted them with. He reckoned it was all part of the hospitality business and was glad that he would never be in such a position. He was about to say something to Sean on the nature of duplicity when a car horn sounded outside the B&B.

"That'll be your taxi. I hope you have a safe trip, and I look forward to seeing you in the future."

Before they could reply she was away into the kitchen. They picked up their bags and walked out to the taxi. As soon as they left the warmth of the guest house the wind caught them. It was a bitter wind coming from the north-east and it had brought heavy clouds promising rain or even sleet. They were glad to find the interior of the taxi was warm. Sean shivered as he settled into the back seat of the car, and the driver saw it as he glanced in the rear-view mirror.

"Aye, its bloody cold today and it's going to get worse if you believe the forecast. Anyway, where are you for?"

"Aldergrove."

The driver put the car into gear and drove off towards the city centre. He was the opposite of the cabby they'd had yesterday because other than his observation on the weather he remained silent throughout the duration of the 20 mile drive to the airport. It was only when they came to the security check-point on the airport road that he spoke again and this was only in the course of showing his driver's license to the policeman. He dropped them off outside the terminal entrance, took his fare plus tip, and that was that.

Both men went inside and joined the queue for yet another security check. Again they had nothing to worry about – neither of them was carrying so much as a pen-knife to cause offence. They checked in for their flight, which was on time. The flight was called at ten-oh five and after a short walk across the wind-blown tarmac they took their seats in the British Airways Trident. Everything had gone to plan, except now as they took off, it started to snow.

* * *

The crossing on the Stranraer to Larne ferry had been quite rough with the Ailsa Princess pitching and rolling severely at times. The three men were very glad when the purser's metallic voice came over the PA and told car drivers and their passengers to return to their vehicles in preparation for disembarkation. After a wait of about ten minutes the boat finally stopped manoeuvring and was secured to the dock. The bow doors opened and the crew signalled to motorists to drive their cars off the ferry.

Once they had left the calm interior of the boat they became instantly aware of the nasty change in the weather as a gust of wind blew into the side of the car.

"Great, that's just fucking great. All we need is bad weather, and look what we've got, fucking snow!"

"We've got three days before show-time, so to be honest the weather is not a problem just yet. Even if there is snow we can still do what we're here for. In other words, Mike, calm down!"

John Colquhoun reinforced his point with a glare before Mike O'Brien could raise any further objections. There was just the formality of the police check-point at the harbour exit to negotiate and then they could be on their way. They fully expected to be flagged down – the fact that their car had English registration plates and that they were all men in their early thirties should have made them of interest to the police – but surprisingly the officer on duty waved them on. Colquhoun waved back and drove out of the harbour complex. Maybe the nearly new silver BMW and the fact that all three men were respectably dressed had helped. They by-passed Larne town centre and drove up the hill that led away from the port taking them along the main road to Belfast. Colquhoun glanced behind him at the third man in their group, Jim Mathieson, and saw that he was checking over the route that they had selected.

"Jim, you don't need to worry about the route, Mike's perfectly capable of reading a map."

"I just like to know where I'm going that's all. No offence Mike?"

"None taken. Are you happy enough with the drive through Belfast, John?"

"Yeah, seems easy enough, just keep following the signs for the M1."

"You could do that, but it's quicker to go along Oxford Street to Cromac Street, up the Ormeau Road turning right onto the embankment, then along Stranmillis Road…"

"Hey, you've lost me at Cromac Street. Just tell me which way to go when we get there."

The road was clear of traffic so Colquhoun was able to make good time. He gave in to the temptation to open the BMW up to see what the performance was like. The car had plenty of acceleration and when he took it through a series of fast left then right corners the road-holding was more than adequate.

"Slow it down a bit John. A speeding ticket wouldn't be good."

"Take it easy Jim; I was just having some fun. Let's face it; I don't get to play with a beemer that often."

"Maybe so, but I don't like getting bounced around here in the back for no good reason."

"Quit moaning, you've got more space than Mike or me."

"Yeah, but at six three I need all the room I can get. Besides you've got seatbelts to hold you in place – I don't."

Mathieson was the tallest of the three but of a slim build which allowed him to give the impression of being somewhat loose-limbed, uncoordinated and even clumsy. The reality was completely at odds with the impression – Jim was capable of the most precise and delicate manoeuvres and had a stamina that didn't know when to stop. Mike O'Brien was six feet tall and of the three the obvious athlete. He looked fit, and given the amount of physical training he did for rugby and his other love, middle distance running, he had every right to. John Colquhoun was an inch or so shorter than O'Brien and slightly more heavily built with a physique that was capable of bursts of extreme energy. The confines of the car didn't really suit any of them but they all regarded it as the necessary evil which it was.

It was just coming up to one o'clock when they came off the M2 and onto Corporation Street. At this point O'Brien took over the navigation and to his credit they drove through Belfast to join the M1 at the bottom of Stockman's Lane without a hitch.

At about the same time Crawford was getting out of the cab that had brought him from Heathrow. The flight had got in about ten minutes early and as Kavanagh and he had no baggage to reclaim they were able to leave Terminal One without any delay. The two men had parted company at the taxi rank without exchanging a word – they'd see each other soon enough. The drive in from the airport had been uneventful except for the persistent questioning of the cabby about the perils of Belfast. Crawford really hadn't been in the mood and had discouraged the driver from pressing the issue with a few well chosen words. He reinforced his irritation by not tipping the cabby when he finally reached Greenwich.

He opened the door to his flat beside the entrance to the newsagents on Hoskins Street and climbed the stairs. He unlocked his own door and stepped inside. After he had collected the various items of mail from the floor and sorted through them he lifted the handset of his telephone and dialled a number from memory. It was answered on the fourth ring.

"This is Crawford. I thought you'd like to know the funeral went without incident. There were no unexpected guests and everything is ready for the removal men."

The voice at the other end of the line expressed its thanks and told Crawford to drop by the following day to give a full account. With nothing else to say Crawford hung up.

"So what's the next turn?"

"If you take the road for Craigavon and then follow the road on to Armagh that looks our best bet. What do you reckon, Jim?"

"Aye, that looks OK to me. You're doing a grand job young Michael, so, if you pair don't mind I'm going to get some kip."

"You sure you don't want to take a turn behind the wheel? Or maybe just keep an eye on things?"

"No thanks, John. Anyway, you can always wake me up if you get lost."

"We'll bear that in mind you lazy sod."

It stopped snowing as they approached the Craigavon turn, but other than that the day showed no signs of improvement. The new town of Craigavon looked hard and grey as they followed the ring road around its outskirts. Like all purpose built urban experiments it lacked character, seeming unfriendly in its newness. Large numbers of people had been transplanted from Belfast to this oasis of peace in a troubled land – sadly the effort appeared to be wasted judging from the graffiti. The only apparent difference between Craigavon and some of the ghetto areas of Belfast that they had driven through earlier was that this was all new.

"What's the road number from Armagh to Keady?"

"It's the A29, I think. Hold on, I'll just check the map. Yeah, it's the A29. After that it's a straight run through to the border."

"The A29, right. Do we still have a sleeping beauty in the back?"

O'Brien twisted around in his seat to take a look at Mathieson.

"Yeah, he's out for the count. D'you want me to wake him?"

"No, never bother. There's nothing for him to do except enjoy the scenery."

There was precious little scenery to enjoy as they by-passed the town and continued towards Armagh. The cloud cover was unbroken and hanging very low in the sky, the wind was still blowing hard even though they were by now well inland, and had they been outside the warmth of the car they would have felt the bitter cold of a March day that had forgotten it was early spring. The only saving grace was that the snow that had already fallen was not lying, but that could change if the temperature dropped another degree or two.

"I'm glad we packed that cold weather gear – there's nothing worse than hanging around in the cold."

"Mike, I hate to tell you but this isn't exactly cold. Unpleasant, maybe, but cold, no. The arctic, now that's cold."

"Yeah, but we're not in the bloody arctic."

"My point exactly."

"There's no such thing as winning an argument with you."

"Then don't try. Changing the subject, have you got our reservation for the hotel?"

"It's in my pocket."

"What's this place like?"

"The Carnagh Lodge Hotel – it's an old estate house, although it's only been open as a hotel for about five years. It can't be very big – we got the only three single rooms they have. All in all it's meant to be quite good, and I was told that the food is excellent. So, at least we'll eat well."

"I hope so, I don't know about you, but I could do with a decent feed. Talking of which, is there anything to eat?"

"Would a Mars Bar do you?"

"That'll do fine."

O'Brien opened the glove compartment and retrieved two Mars Bars, passing one to Colquhoun. Right on cue, Mathieson woke up, yawned, and stretched as best he could in the confines of the rear seat. Without saying a word O'Brien re-opened the glove compartment, got another Mars Bar, and passed it over his shoulder. Mathieson took it without voicing his thanks. Once all three men had torn open the wrappers, they ate in silence as they approached the cathedral city of Armagh.

As Crawford soaked in the bath he was thinking over the job he had just completed, the jobs to be undertaken in the future, and his place within the "Department". The one conclusion that he reached was that as long as he continued to perform a useful role he was secure. To do that he could not afford to question the morality of not only his own actions but also that of the organisation as a whole. He would give a complete report on his actions over the past five days and get the necessary details of the next job and he would keep his mouth shut. That was settled – no more damn fool questions. He got out of the bath, put on a towelling robe and after pulling the plug to let the water drain away he went through to his bedroom.

He needed to get out and be around ordinary people with ordinary concerns. He opened his wardrobe and made a selection. If Kavanagh had been present he would have been calling Crawford a few choice names; inside the wardrobe were neatly hung suits, sports jackets and trousers. The sharply dressed Crawford was an entirely different proposition from the character who had flown out from Aldergrove that morning.

The blazer and flannels were from Jaeger, the crisp white double cuff shirt was from Turnbull & Asser and the highly polished black brogues, while not nearly as expensive as Kavanagh's, were from Crockett & Jones. Thirty-two years old, single, no mortgage, no car – Crawford felt more than able to indulge himself. He decided to take a cab up west and do just that – he'd take a look around town and then go for dinner. He looked out his first floor window and saw that it was raining so he shrugged on his raincoat and lifted his umbrella before going down to the street to look for a taxi. He was in luck, no sooner had he reached the street than a cab came towards him with its For Hire light on. He flagged it down and got in.

"Where to, guvnor?"

"Jermyn Street."

The miserable weather did not add anything to the impression made by what was in reality a small town. The colours that picked out the signs of the shops and pubs seemed drained of vibrancy; even the graffiti, that had stood out in bold colours in Belfast, was limited to black and white. There was no effort at decoration here, no marking of territorial colours, just a bald statement of fact – IRA LAND. The two cathedrals made Armagh the ecclesiastical capital of Ireland for both Roman Catholics and Anglicans, and it seemed that after that the two sides could find little to agree on. Recent history certainly seemed to indicate the truth of this, but more careful consideration opened a can of political worms that went beyond the simplicities of "Taigs" and "Prods".

There was no ring road to by-pass the centre of Armagh, so Colquhoun took the most direct route through the town. They passed the Observatory and the Planetarium, Armagh's other claims to fame. At least the secular nature of these two educational establishments left them free from sectarian labelling. The drive through town was uneventful and only took them about ten minutes. Once they rejoined the A29 on the south side of Armagh they only had about 12 miles to go. Colquhoun had made good time all along the drive from Larne; O'Brien had given the receptionist at the Carnagh Lodge an arrival time of four o'clock, but it looked as if they were going to be a little early.

A mile outside Keady and three miles short of the hotel they encountered their first vehicle check-point. Colquhoun had just brought the car around a sharp right-hand bend and there in front of them was the Stop Police sign. He slowed the car and joined the short queue. The RUC officer waved several cars through, but signalled that Colquhoun should stop.

The well wrapped RUC man stamped his feet to try and spread some warmth through his legs as Colquhoun wound down his window.

"Lovely day for it. You must be bloody frozen mate."

"Beginning to feel that way, sir. Could I see your driver's license please?"

John reached inside his jacket for his license, under the watchful eye of the police officer. O'Brien and Mathieson said nothing as Colquhoun handed over his license.

"Could you tell me where you are coming from?"

"Well, we just arrived on the Stranraer – Larne ferry this afternoon, and we've driven straight here."

"And where are you going to?"

"We're staying at the Carnagh Lodge for a few days. We're over for a week's fishing."

"Could you step out of the car and open the boot, please?"

When the boot was opened it was clear that John wasn't joking about this being a fishing expedition. Apart from their personal luggage, which didn't amount to much, the boot was full of fishing tackle.

"If you don't mind me saying sir, you gents could've picked a better week to come over – the weather's been bloody awful and the forecast isn't much better."

"To be honest the fishing is incidental", the RUC man looked puzzled, "We're escaping from our wives for a week. Anyway if the weather is lousy there's always the hotel bar."

"I see what you mean sir. Have you been to the Lodge before?"

"As a matter of fact I haven't. None of us have. Why, is there something wrong with it?"

"Oh no sir it's a grand place. I was just wondering if you knew how to get to it, that's all."

"It's just off the Castleblayney Road – a couple of miles through Keady, isn't it?"

"That's right sir. I had to ask, it wouldn't do to have visitors from the mainland getting lost. Anyway sir, sorry for the inconvenience, but you can blame the terrorists."

"That's alright – it'll give us a story for the pub back home."

Colquhoun got back into the car, started up and drove off.

"Did you give him our National Security numbers, John?"

"Very bloody funny, Jim. He was just being thorough. Did you see the rest of the check-point crew though?"

"Yeah, a total of six, carbines and sub-machine guns."

"I wonder if they've got wind of something?"

"Mike, they've always got wind of something. This is the South Armagh border for Christ's sake!"

Another five minutes saw them through Keady and taking the right turn onto the driveway of the Carnagh Lodge. The hotel was set well back from the road, a distance of some 300 yards. The tree-lined avenue that led to it was planted with elm and beech trees, but did not look at its best as the trees were still budding. They rounded a final bend and there stood the Lodge in all its glory, a stone-built Victorian Gothic house.

Colquhoun parked the car in front of the hotel entrance and all three men went inside to register. The interior was wood panelled with a heavily carpeted floor and gave a distinct impression of comfort. The receptionist, a pretty brunette in her early twenties, showed them up to their rooms. Mathieson made a point of being first in line; the receptionist's skirt was just a little too tight and he was enjoying the view. The rooms were well appointed, each equipped with its own shower. When they had all seen their rooms, the men came back downstairs to retrieve their luggage from the car. There was that much fishing tackle between them that it required two trips to the car before they had emptied all of their gear. Once it was all safely deposited in their rooms they came down to the hotel bar for a drink.

The receptionist was on hand to take their drinks orders when they arrived. She seemed to be the only member of staff on duty. Mathieson ordered for everybody.

"Could we have three gin and tonics, please? It seems you're being kept busy; is it just yourself running things?"

"Oh no, not at all. It's just that the season has hardly started yet, so we have to double up on our duties until the number of guests increases and we take on the summer staff."

"Is there anyone else staying at the moment?"

"There is an American couple, but you'll probably not see much of them. They're trying to trace their Irish roots and they're doing a lot of travelling. I think they were going up to the county registrar's office in Armagh today, but they've been all over the countryside. Every cemetery in the.... here I am, talking too much as usual and you gents haven't got your drinks yet – it was three G&Ts wasn't it?"

"It was indeed."

As Mathieson studied the receptionist, as she walked back to the bar, Colquhoun studied Mathieson.

"Steady, Jim. We're not here to eye-up the local talent."

"Give me a break. There's no harm in looking."

"As long as that's all you do."

Before Colquhoun could develop the point their drinks were brought over from the bar.

"There you go gents. I'll leave you in peace but if you need anything just call."

"And who should I call for?"

"Oh I'm sorry, Maureen, my name's Maureen."

"I'll be sure to remember that, Maureen."

After she had got out of earshot Colquhoun finished what he had to say.

"Like I said Jim, no skirt chasing."

"I don't think I'd have to chase that too hard."

"Christ Almighty, I'm not kidding."

"OK, OK. I'll behave."

O'Brien, who had been hunched over a map of the local area, sat up, placed it on the table and turned it around so the other two could see. All the good fishing lakes had been marked, north and south of the border. There were several other annotations, but to the casual observer they didn't amount to very much. He tapped the map at Keady and made a circular motion with his hand.

"I reckon we could start with the local lakes tomorrow – that's Clay Lake and Tullynawood Lake. They're both meant to be good for bream and roach."

"Yeah, that should be OK, but I do want to take a closer look at some of the southern stretches of water – Glaslough is said to be really good for pike."

"You're the boss John. When do you want to take a look, tomorrow?"

"Yeah, I think we should familiarise ourselves with the roads so we can get about without any hassles. We can take all the gear with us and do the other thing while we're in that neck of the woods."

O'Brien folded the map, reached for his glass, and raised it.

"Here's to a successful trip."

Colquhoun and Mathieson raised their glasses and nodded their assent. They knew what they had to do and now all that remained was to put the intervening time to the best use. Right now that time was best served by having another drink and seeing what was on offer for dinner. O'Brien got up and went to the bar returning with three more G&Ts and a copy of the menu. The conversation had moved on from the business of fishing and which lake to try first to the altogether more pressing topic of this season's FA Cup. O'Brien put down the tray of drinks but didn't sit down.

"If you two are going to talk football I'll take my drink upstairs and unpack. The dining room doesn't open for dinner until six-thirty so there's plenty of time for you to talk crap, but I don't have to listen to it."

He picked up his drink and left the bar just as the merits of Arsenal were being weighed up against Manchester United; the two teams that looked most likely to contest the final. He'd heard it all before and could do without the repeat performance. Once in his room he closed the curtains and started to unpack – the clothing only took a couple of minutes, it was the more interesting items amongst his fishing tackle that consumed his time and concentration. He worked through the equipment methodically – making sure that there had been no breakages in transit. Satisfied that everything was functioning as it should, he turned off the main light, took off his shoes and stretched out on the bed. The gin took its effect and in minutes he was asleep.

Downstairs in the bar the debate raged on, only by now they had moved on to the superiority of individual players in their chosen positions. It was the sort of conversation only the true enthusiast could enjoy. They were now arguing over who was better in the air, Young or McQueen.

"Jim, it's no contest, Young's taller, stronger and a cleaner header of the ball, end of story."

"You must be watching different soccer matches from the ones I've seen. McQueen's by far the better player."

The telephone rang at reception and Maureen left the bar to answer it. She came back into the bar within a minute.

"Mr. Colquhoun, there's a call for you, a Mr. McFadden. Would you like to take it at reception or would you prefer to have the call transferred to your room?"

"Reception is fine, thank you."

He got up and left Mathieson to ponder his next point on the skills of Manchester United. It was a short call, lasting less than a minute. Colquhoun came back to his seat. Mathieson looked at him, the subject of football, for now, forgotten.

"Well?"

"They're here."

Liam McFadden replaced the handset in the cradle of the payphone and walked back across the tiled floor of the airport terminal to rejoin the three men by the exit.

"We can get going. Colquhoun knows you're here."

They made their way outside and used the pedestrian crossing to get to the car park. Tom Bennett pushed the trolley that carried two sets of golf clubs and the personal baggage belonging to both himself and Martin Bradley. Chris Gatland led them to a silver Ford Granada estate. He opened the tailgate and helped Bennett to load the gear into the back of the Granada. It was a tight enough squeeze as McFadden and Gatland had their own sets of golf clubs as well as a couple of grips. When they had finished Bennett took the luggage trolley over to the collection bay as the other three men got into the car. McFadden took the driver's seat with Gatland joining him up front, leaving the rear seats for Bradley and Bennett. McFadden started the engine and eased the big car from the confines of its parking space. They came to the main junction leading from Dublin International and they turned left and north on to the N1. Bradley, who had been under the impression that they would be staying the first night in Dublin, which was to the south, allowed his curiosity to get the better of him.

"OK fellas, where we making for this evening?"

"As I'm driving and you two got the earlier flight I thought we could best use the time by heading north. The reservation has been brought forward a day and we're staying at the Slieve Coolan Hotel outside Belturbet. Chris, would you reach into the glove compartment where you'll find a manila envelope. Pass it to Martin."

Gatland did as he was asked. Bradley opened it and examined the contents. There were several receipts including one from the Shelbourne, Dublin's best hotel.

"What are these for?"

"They establish your whereabouts for the last two days. You've been over for a series of business meetings and now you're going to play some golf before you fly back home."

"Receipts are one thing, but what if someone was asked about us, you know, faces to names, that sort of thing."

"The Shelbourne is always busy. Two suits more or less shouldn't be a problem. Anyway we've had two fellas staying there since Sunday. It was the easiest way to get the receipt."

"Very slick. It's nice to know we're working with professionals."

"Chris and I have been back since Sunday setting things up. I think you'll find that we can take care of ourselves and you lads as well."

"Hey, I wasn't saying that you couldn't. Everything we've seen since we got the call on Friday says you fellas know what you're up to."

"I'll take that as a vote of confidence. You can do us a favour, spread the word when you get home – we're not an ignorant bunch of Paddies."

"You got it."

"Oh by the way, did they feed you on that flight?"

"No."

"I thought not. We'll eat when we get to the Slieve Coolan."

O'Brien woke with a start. For a couple of seconds he wondered where he was and then he realised as the day's events crowded his consciousness. He swung his legs over the edge of the bed and bent over to put on his shoes. He walked into the shower room and looked at himself in the mirror above the wash-hand basin. There was a distinct five o'clock shadow that would have to go before he went down for dinner. He brought his electric shaver in from the bedroom, plugged it in and quickly removed the light stubble. Then he cleaned his teeth to remove the stale taste of gin. He finger combed his sandy coloured hair until it took on a more controlled appearance. He looked at his watch and noted with satisfaction that his body clock was running almost in tandem with real time; it was six-twenty. He went back into his room and opened the wardrobe from which he took his rugby club tie and the tweed Dunn & Co sports jacket that he had hung up earlier. He carefully knotted the tie, slipped on the jacket, and with one last look in the mirror for re-assurance he went back to the bar to join Colquhoun and Mathieson.

There were a few more people in the bar when he arrived back. Holding centre stage were the American couple Maureen had mentioned. They were both in their mid-sixties and sadly doing nothing to improve the image of Americans abroad. At present they were extolling the virtues of the county registrar's office in the "quaint" little town of Armagh. Rather than go to the bar for another drink O'Brien resumed his seat beside Mathieson.

"Were you ever right not to go to the bar Mike. Jim tried to get a round and it took him a quarter of an hour. In that time he became an expert on Mr. & Mrs. Sullivan, didn't you Jim?"

"Yeah, they like to talk, mostly about Mr. Sullivan. I didn't think I was going to get away from them. As it is they've asked us to join them for dinner."

"Oh shit, you didn't accept, did you?"

"I'm afraid so, old son. I couldn't see any way of avoiding it."

"That's just great. So what's the story on the three of us, John, same as before?"

"Yeah, same as before, three mates in the haulage business escaping the wives for a week's fishing and drinking. Although from what Jim says we'll probably not even have to tell them that. Look, Jim and I need to change, so we'll introduce you, you keep them amused, and we'll see you all in the dining room at seven – how's that?"

"Perfect."

"Do I detect a note of sarcasm?"

"John, fuck off."

Introductions were duly made and Mike spent the next half hour in the company of the Sullivans. Surprisingly, he found himself warming to the couple and their tales of Boston, Mass. Donald "call me Don" Sullivan was sixty-four and an infantry veteran from WW2; he'd seen action in Sicily and France. He'd married Jeanne, his high-school sweet-heart, on his return from Europe, and they had been devoted to each other ever since. He'd worked in local government as a union representative until his early retirement two years ago. Jeanne had taught elementary school, and she too, was retired.

"Let me tell you, young Michael, Boston's full o' sharks. God knows I tried to make a difference, but that town'll just swallow a man whole."

"Yeah, I know what you mean, Don. Some of the back-handers we have to pay to keep our trucks on the road would make your hair curl."

"For sure. Same all over – the working Joe can't get an even break."

Mike was really beginning to enjoy himself when John walked into the dining room. He, too, had shaved and put on a jacket and tie.

"Come on over, John, take a seat. We were just putting the world to rights."

"You haven't got a hope, Don, it's a rotten place. Any sign of Jim, yet?"

Just as he asked, Mathieson appeared at the dining room door. Don Sullivan spread his arms wide and called out to him.

"Talk o' the devil, here he is. Jim come on over!"

And that was more or less that for the evening. Don's irrepressible bonhomie was infectious and the three men found themselves carried along by it. The conversation was lively and the food was excellent. They really could have been three friends taking a week off from their work and their wives. Don was enjoying the opportunity to hold court with a receptive audience. He'd just finished telling a long story about attempted union corruption by a certain Italian family from New York and how they had been put to flight by the combined forces of the police and City Hall; both institutions dominated by the Irish.

Just as the plates from the main course were cleared away, Colquhoun glanced at his watch, got up and excused himself. He walked to the public phone located beside the gent's lavatory. He went into the booth, closed the door, and took a small notebook from his inside pocket. He flicked through the pages to the phone number he wanted and dialled. His call was answered on the third ring and he pushed his coin into the slot.

"Good evening, Harper's Hotel, can I help you?"

"Yes. Can I speak to Mr. Alex Roper please?"

"Mr. Roper has just checked in, I'll see if he's in his room. Can I ask who's calling please?"

"John Colquhoun."

"Just one moment please, I'll connect you."

After a few seconds the call was put through.

"Hello John. Everything is OK. No problems at the airports and no problems getting here. The car was where we were told it would be, so no complaints about the scheme. Any news from your end that we should be aware of?"

"None, see you all on Friday."

Colquhoun hung up and walked out of the phone booth straight into Don Sullivan.

"And there was me thinking that you lads were getting away from the little women, ha! Calling home to check that she was coping without you?"

"Yeah, something like that."

"And?"

"And what?"

"Is everything OK?"

"Oh yeah, sure, sure."

"Did Colquhoun have any news?"

"No. He just said that he would see us all on Friday."

"Nothing else?"

"No. He doesn't bend your ear does he?"

"Not his way. I'll get Pearson and then we can go and get that nightcap."

Dessert and coffee were served just as Don Sullivan returned from the gents. Jeanne had been talking of their success at the registrar's office – it seemed that they had found details of Don's great-grandfather. This was their first visit to the North – she'd been put off by all the violence, convinced that they would be shot or blown up the second that they crossed the border. It came as something of a surprise that it wasn't really like that.

"I said to Jeanne that it would take more than some hoodlums to put me off coming back home. Anyway, I've only seen police and army activity since I got here. Why don't they just go home and then all this trouble would stop."

"We'll be sure to leave when our week's fishing is up."

"Hell, I didn't mean you guys. I thought you were coming home, same as me."

"Not quite. Jim and I are Scots. Only Mike can claim to be Irish."

"Well, you're not English, that's the main thing."

"I suppose it is, and on that note we must be bidding you goodnight. Jeanne, Don, thank you both for a great evening."

"Surely you guys can stay up for a few drinks?"

"Maybe tomorrow night, but we had an early start this morning and we want to be up first thing tomorrow."

Don's protests went unheeded as they once again expressed their thanks and took their leave. Each one of them was glad of the early night; they'd need the rest for the day ahead.

As they left the restaurant they passed reception where they were surprised to see Maureen still hard at work. She looked up from the desk and asked the three men if they would like to make their breakfast orders now to save some time in the morning. She handed them a menu each on which they merely had to tick the appropriate course for breakfast. Once they had made their orders Mathieson couldn't resist a little flirtation and stayed behind as the other two went upstairs to their rooms.

"You know Maureen you should be tucked up in bed. It's obvious that they work you too hard."

"Oh, I'm just finishing up for the night and then, you're right, I'm going to bed."

"Do you have far to go to get home?"

"Not far at all. I live here; this is my uncle's hotel."

"Is it now, that's interesting. We'll be seeing quite a bit of each other this week then."

"I'm sure we shall."

They bid each other goodnight and Mathieson headed upstairs. As he got undressed he thought about Maureen; enough eye contact, enough smiling, a slight rise in her colour, almost a blush, all in all the signals looked good. Colquhoun could go to hell; what harm was there in making a play for the girl, it just made the whole trip a bit more interesting.

Crawford was settling into his armchair with a glass of Hennessy. He'd had an enjoyable if somewhat damp afternoon calling in the shops along Jermyn Street; he'd bought a couple of shirts and a tie. Then he'd gone to Bellini's, a small family owned restaurant on Vigo Street, for dinner. He had a relaxed evening with each course arriving just at the right time. He'd sat at a corner table at the rear of the restaurant, a position he was familiar with. He was able to watch the world go by and nobody bothered him, not even the staff, even though he was something of a regular, it was just that he didn't seek conversation and therefore none was offered.

He'd left at around ten-thirty, again finding a taxi with no difficulty. Even under artificial light London looked clean and fresh after the day's rain. The sky had cleared and there was the promise of a good day to come. Tomorrow he'd have to make his report and with that thought came all the details of the past five days. His return that day had reminded him of the normalities of life and the pleasures that could be derived from good food and the freedom to do as he pleased. Tomorrow would reinforce the penalties he paid to enjoy those pleasures. He drank his brandy and thought of ways out.

* * *

The following morning at around seven thirty ten men awoke separated only by distance. By 1.00pm the full complement of sixteen men would be on the island both North and South. It was Wednesday March 21st.

Colquhoun, Mathieson and O'Brien assembled in the dining room for breakfast at eight-fifteen. They had slept well and were all ready for a full day's fishing. O'Brien had brought his map to the table and was looking over the various lakes that they had selected last night in the bar.

"Do you still want to check out Glaslough, John?"

"Yeah, I still think we should go and see if the pike are biting. You're navigating, Mike, so tell me what's our best route? We wouldn't want to get lost now, would we?"

"The easiest way is to go back into Keady and take the road for Middletown, cross the border at Ardgonnell Bridge and I'll keep you right from there. It should take us forty minutes at most."

As they discussed the plans for the day, breakfast was served just as they had ordered it the previous evening, and at that point the conversation stopped as all three men turned their attention to the important matter of doing the considerable meal justice.

At the Slieve Coolan the golfing foursome were enjoying a leisurely breakfast before taking their first round on the course. The weather looked as if it was going to be kind – there were some breaks in the cloud with only a light breeze blowing from the north-west and best of all it was dry.

It was dry in Dublin as well and that was the best thing Roper, Lauder and Pearson could say about the start of their day. They were unlucky with their breakfast – Harper's was a hotel that relied on a fast turnover of travellers both to and from the airport and was sadly not too concerned with giving those guests the best of everything. The most that could be said of breakfast was that it filled a gap. When they had finished they went back upstairs to retrieve their belongings before checking out. Once they had loaded the red Vauxhall Cavalier, Roper took his place behind the wheel and they made their way north following the same route that McFadden had taken the previous day.

It took about ten minutes for the gangplank to be secured to the ferry; ten minutes that dragged by at a ridiculously slow pace. Alan Scott had never claimed to be the best sailor in the world but the night crossing from Liverpool had tested the mettle of even the most seasoned traveller. The smell of vomit was still heavy in the air no matter how much bleach was used to clean the floors of the lavatories, no matter how much air freshener was sprayed to deaden the odour. If anything the crew's best efforts had only succeeded in making things worse. Dave Armstrong and Peter Osborne both sympathised with Scott – they were nearly as pleased to be leaving the boat as he was.

Once on dry land all three men experienced the strange sensation of lost equilibrium. The ground seemed to move under their feet and they couldn't take their balance for granted. By the time they left the passenger terminal and walked to the taxi rank things had more or less returned to normal. After a couple of minutes wait they got a cab to the Europa Hotel. Once they had checked in and left their bags up to their rooms they went to the main residents lounge and had coffee. They had plenty of time to kill before they contacted Colquhoun at the Carnagh Lodge so it was agreed to take a walk into Belfast city centre. The three men walked the short distance down Great Victoria Street until it joined Wellington Place; from there it was less than three hundred yards to Donegall Place that marked the city centre. The security barriers with their overt police and army presence showed Belfast to be a siege town.

By lunchtime their appetites had returned and Osborne suggested that they go to Thompson's restaurant on Arthur Street. He'd been in Belfast before and assured them that it really was the best the city centre had to offer. At around ten to one they went into the restaurant and joined the ranks of the professional classes who frequented it. Three well dressed men in their early thirties attracted no more than the most casual attention.

The Cairnryan to Larne ferry docked on time at one-fifteen and the car deck was cleared at one-twenty-five. The long wheelbase Landrover was amongst the last vehicles to move off the exit ramp. The police officers on duty at the checkpoint stopped the Landrover and gave the three occupants and all their fishing tackle thorough scrutiny. Nothing untoward was discovered and as the three men all had valid means of identification there was no reason to detain them further.

John Davison drove them out of the harbour complex and onto the main road to Belfast. Stephen Todd sat in the front passenger seat with an identical map to the one Mike O'Brien had used the previous day. Graeme Hart was in the back with enough room to stretch out his long legs; like Jim Mathieson he was tall – around six-two. Davison and Todd were both smaller around five-nine or ten but they all had plenty of space – the Landrover had room to spare. The route that they planned to follow was virtually the same as O'Brien's except that it took them across the border to Castleblayney and the Glenmore Hotel. They could afford to take the drive slowly and still arrive in time to check in with Colquhoun.

By the time they had finished breakfast and packed all their fishing tackle in the BMW it had been well after nine. O'Brien had been right about the drive time and they arrived in the village of Glaslough just before ten. The guides that O'Brien had brought with him indicated that permission had to be obtained from the local post office before they could fish the lake.

"Jim, you and Mike wait in the car and I'll go in and see what the score is."

Colquhoun went inside and approached the only window that was open for business. The counter was occupied by the post-mistress, a jovial looking woman in her fifties.

"Can I help you sir?"

"Well I'm rather hoping that you can. My friends and I are here for a spot of fishing and the guide we have said to call at the post office about permission."

"That's right sir. It's Glaslough itself that you'll be wanting is it?"

"Yes. We were told it's a good lake for pike."

"Indeed, indeed. How many days is it you're wanting?"

"Just today for starters, then we'll see how it goes."

"Aye well, I can give you the permit for the day. You see the post office acts as agent for Mr. O'Dwyer who owns the rights. How many of you are there?"

"Three."

"Well that comes to six pounds altogether."

Colquhoun took out his wallet, handed over the money and was given three slips of paper that showed themselves to be day permits.

"May I wish you luck sir. It's a grand day for it."

"Thanks very much."

Colquhoun got back in the car and handed the slips to O'Brien. He turned the car around and drove back out of the village. They parked the BMW just after ten-fifteen near the parish church which was but a stones throw from the lake. All three men carried assorted rods, tackle boxes and nets down to the lake shore and set about the business of finding a likely spot from where to cast their lines. By midday they were all studiously hunched over their rods with not a bite between them. The pike that they had seemed so hopeful of yesterday were obviously lying low. Colquhoun stood up, asked Mathieson to watch his line, and announced that, as he was starting to get cramp, he was going to take a walk to loosen up.

He walked eastward until he came to a track that led down to what had been a railway cutting, long since disused. There was a light breeze blowing from the north-west but other than that nothing to disturb the quiet of the scene. Colquhoun stopped to massage his right leg and as he did so he took a look around the location. Nothing appeared out of place. He resumed his walk and moved into a wooded area on the northern side of the cutting. Even with the wet weather of the previous couple of days it was quite dry underfoot because of the overhanging trees but Colquhoun moved carefully anyway, stopping now and again to look over the ground and the surroundings. He had been in the woods for nearly ten minutes when he found what he was looking for; on the far side of a small clearing was a large tree with a ring painted around it. The ring had an inverted U sprayed above it. Colquhoun walked over to the tree and stood with his back to the trunk; then he moved slowly forward coming to a halt after six or seven yards. He crouched over the ground and gently disturbed the covering of leaf litter; as he did so he uncovered an orange peel. He'd seen enough.

Mathieson and O'Brien were drinking coffee when he got back. The remains of the packed lunches that they had got from the hotel were neatly bagged up at their feet.

"I hope you greedy buggers have left me something?"

Mathieson poured a mug of coffee and passed it to him,

"Don't worry John, there're a few scraps left for you. How's the cramp?"
"I walked it off. It's OK now. Everything's OK."
O'Brien lifted his rod and started to reel in his line,
"If that's the case we can pack up."
"And where do you think you're going?"
"Oh come on John, you don't expect us to sit here all day, do you?"
"That's exactly what we're going to do. If anyone sees us we'll look like three fishermen out catching a cold. We'll pack up around five and go back to the hotel. I've got some calls due after six but we're staying here in the meantime."

Crawford had slept in after having sat for several hours the previous night contemplating his future. Having reached no conclusions he had gone to bed just after three. He never suffered from such indecision on a job so the quandary which he had placed himself in was to say the least unnerving.

He had had a late breakfast in a small coffee house round the corner from his flat and after that he had taken a cab to "the Centre" in Leinster Gardens off Bayswater Road where he now sat waiting to see one of his superiors so that he could make a full report. A door opened down the hall and the dishevelled figure of a man in his late forties came towards Crawford holding a mug in his right hand.

"Bear with me Crawford, I'm just going for coffee. Do you want one?"
"I'll pass."
Harry Lynch returned from the kitchen with a refilled mug
steaming in one hand and a packet of digestive biscuits in the other. He gestured for Crawford to follow him and went back into his office. Once inside, Crawford was surprised to see that the room was immaculately tidy. The only things that were out of place were a camp bed folded in one corner and Lynch himself; the man had obviously been working long hours, the bags under his eyes bore testimony to a lack of sleep. Lynch sat behind an uncluttered desk and watched Crawford take a seat opposite him. Crawford was as always too well dressed for Lynch's liking; truth be told Crawford made him feel inadequate, but then again he had been up for two days with virtually no rest and no change of clothes. He sipped his coffee and took a bite from a digestive before speaking. Crawford knew better than to interrupt Lynch's train of thought so he waited. At last he spoke.

"How was your trip?"
"The whole time in Ireland or just the job details?"
"The job itself will do for starters. Then I want a report on young Kavanagh."
Crawford started with the outline hitting his desk on Friday all the way through to the taxi ride from Belfast and the flight from Aldergrove yesterday. It surprised him that he was able to cover all the details in a matter of minutes. The five days had gone very quickly and amazingly without a hitch.

Lynch sat impassive throughout Crawford's description of events. Only once did he show any signs of interest and that was when Crawford detailed the actual burial of the water butt. When he had finished his description of the conduct of the job Crawford paused to allow Lynch to question him. Lynch laced his hands, leaving both index fingers straight, which he now pointed at Crawford.

"You say that you transferred the contents of one "package" into the other. Whose idea was that and did you look at the make-up of those contents?"

"It was my idea to transfer the contents so as to cut down on the excavation time and when it came to looking at the gear we didn't have much option did we? I was going to raise that issue when I gave my report on Kavanagh."

"And what were you going to say?"

"He displayed a natural curiosity about the contents, who was going to use them and what for. I told him that those were matters that didn't concern him and that he would be best advised to put such thoughts out of his head."

"And did he?"

"As far as I am aware he realised very quickly that it was not in his interest to pursue the matter, so, my answer would have to be yes."

"What about you? Are you not curious and in need of answers?"

"I just do as I'm told. I'm not paid enough to ask questions like that."

"Fine. Anything else about Kavanagh's performance?"

"He's getting better. I would say that with a little more polish he'll be first class. He's methodical and attentive to detail and those aren't qualities that can be taught. I've got no complaints."

"Good. I'm giving you some time off. Be back here in two weeks to get the details of your next job. Your interest in this one has come to an end. Am I understood?"

"Absolutely."

Crawford got up and left. Two weeks off? What the hell was he going to do with two weeks off?

Mike O'Brien was at his wits end – the boredom of fishing, particularly when it was as he saw it unnecessary, was giving him a headache. Colquhoun had checked the area so why couldn't they just call it quits and head back to the hotel. All those thoughts disappeared when something took his bait and the line began to race.

"Christ, I've caught something! Jim give me a hand. Hurry before I lose the bugger!"

Mathieson put his rod down and came to O'Brien's assistance.

"OK, he's stopped taking line – reel in some of the slack and let's see if you've got a fighter."

"What do you reckon I've got?"

"With the dead bait you were using you've got yourself a pike and it could be a fair size."

The task of landing the pike took O'Brien nearly half an hour and the physical effort amazed him. Having never fished before he had no idea of the size of the fish and he had no concept of the power a determined pike could bring to bear. He was also surprised by the total concentration he had to give; he found it faintly ridiculous that he was having to out think a fish. The pike fought hard at times and at others seemed to play dead. One thing was for sure, the hook had been well bedded, and the fish wasn't able to free itself of the torment.

"My bloody arms are killing me. Jim do you want to take a turn?"

"Your fish, you land him. Don't let him run again whatever you do. Your line could get fouled on something and then you'd lose him so keep his head up."

The exertion was showing on O'Brien's face – he was starting to sweat and his colour had risen. He could feel the burn spreading from his arms across his chest and shoulders down his back. He wasn't going to be beaten by a fish and again the funny side of the contest struck him. As his rod bucked in his hands a broad grin spread across his face.

"Enjoying yourself are you?"

"I don't want to lose this fish Jim!"

"You're doing fine."

At that point the pike broke the surface and O'Brien got a clear look at the size of the fish he had hooked.

"Christ Almighty! Did you see the size of that?"

"Aye, you've got a nice fish there Mike. Now keep calm."

Colquhoun, who had reeled in his line so he could watch, stood on the lake side enjoying the struggle; envious of O'Brien as the pike was obviously a big fish. The pike was beginning to show signs if tiring and O'Brien was able to take advantage of this as he brought the fish into the shallows and Mathieson, who was wearing waders, stepped from the bank into the lake with a net. The pike made one last attempt to break free and thrashed at the end of the line determined not to cooperate. Even at this stage it was no foregone conclusion and it was with some difficulty that Mathieson was able to net the fish.

Even out of the water it tried to fight and Mathieson had his work cut out.

"Mike reach in the tackle box and get me the priest."

"The what?"

"The priest", there was only a blank look on O'Brien's face by way of reply, "Oh for Christ's sake, it's like a sap."

O'Brien quickly rummaged through the box and came out with a short wooden club.

"Is this it?"

"Aye, give it to me."

Mathieson took the priest and dispatched the pike with several sharp blows to the back of the head.

"Jim, why the hell is that thing called a priest?"

"'Cos you give the fish the last rites. I thought that would be obvious. Well, it's dead now; you know they never do look as impressive when they're landed. I suppose that's where the saying comes from."

"What saying?"

"'A fish out of water'."

Mathieson had a point. Now that the struggle was over they could see just how big the fish was – a little over three feet long and somewhere around 28lbs – yet it looked sad somehow. Mathieson didn't want to spoil the moment so he clapped O'Brien on the back.

"First fish?", O'Brien nodded, "Well, there's nothing like starting at the top, is there John?"

"No there's not. Take my word for it Mike, some men wait a lifetime to catch a pike that size. It's a stunner and you did well to bring it in. Many's a one would have lost it."

O'Brien's grin returned with the praise and both Colquhoun and Mathieson could tell that Mike was going to be hard to stomach for the rest of the day.

It was to be their only fish that day. Come five o'clock they packed up their gear and drove back to the hotel with one brief stop at the border checkpoint where they had to show the pike to the soldier on duty who was a keen coarse fisherman. He voiced his appreciation and told them that he would much rather be out with the rods than standing on duty in the cold.

Once they were back at the hotel O'Brien asked Maureen, who was on duty as ever, if the pike could be put in cold storage. She said that they could put it in the walk-in refrigerator at the back of the kitchen. Mathieson and Colquhoun went to their rooms to shower and change leaving O'Brien to carry the pike through to the cold store. Maureen showed him the way through the kitchen to the fridge.

"Before you put it in the store would you like to weigh it?"

"Aye that's a good idea. We didn't have any scales with us so we were having to guess."

As it turned out they had underestimated the weight by 2lbs 2ozs. O'Brien lifted the fish from the scales and followed Maureen into the cold store

"From what the lads have been saying that's a real brute of a pike."

"So you're not a fisherman then?"

"Not really. Too be honest this is my first trip."

"Call it beginner's luck then."."

"Aye, that's for sure. I don't suppose you'd know of anyone local who does fishing trophies?"

"I don't but I can find out for you."

"That'd be great! Thanks! Anyway, I don't want to take up any more of your time and I'd better go and get cleaned up."

Maureen was flicking through the Yellow Pages without success, it seemed trophy making was something that wasn't advertised, maybe someone at the hotel would know. Before she could go and ask any of the kitchen staff the telephone rang and she forgot all thoughts of fishing and trophies.

"Carnagh Lodge Hotel, can I help you?"

"Hello, I'd like to speak to John Colquhoun, please. My name's Alan Scott."

"Thank you, I'll just connect you to his room."

Colquhoun had just finished shaving when his phone rang. He walked into the bedroom and sat on the bed, answering the call on the fourth ring.

"Yes?"

"Mr. Colquhoun, you have a call from a Mr. Alan Scott. I'll just connect you."

The phone clicked as Maureen put the call through and he heard Scott's unmistakeable Glaswegian accent.

"John, its Alan. Just to let you know we'll be able to take care of that removal for you on Friday. We're still up north but will be heading south as soon as we've got the vehicle sorted out. How's things with you and the lads?"

"We had a good day today, at least Mike did. He caught an absolute beauty of a pike – two stone at least. We're going to take it easy tonight and have a few drinks."

"Sounds like you're having a cushy time of it."

"Yeah, it could be worse, but you know me, Alan, if everything is as it should be then you've got nothing to worry about."

"Make the most of it; you'll soon be back, having to earn a living like the rest of us."

"God preserve me from that. Anyway, thanks for the call and I'll see you soon."

"OK, John. All the best in the meantime."

Colquhoun replaced the handset when the line went dead. He only had one more check-in call coming and with it he would have a complete team. So far this was the best organised job he had worked on; if only it would stay that way, would that be too much to ask?

He towelled himself dry and got changed for dinner. As he sat on the bed lacing his shoes the phone rang again. This time it was John Davison confirming that he would be available for the removal job at the weekend and that he expected to meet up with Alan Scott on or before Friday. Other than that he had nothing to add and cut the call off before he could be asked any questions. This annoyed Colquhoun, who made a mental note to have a word in Davison's ear to remind him just who decided when contact should be broken. He looked at his watch to see that it was six-thirty – time for a drink before dinner. He put his wallet in the back pocket of his trousers, slipped on his jacket and went down to the lounge.

Mike O'Brien had beaten him to the bar and had already ordered drinks. John walked over to pick up his gin and tonic just in time to hear O'Brien finish telling the story of his fishing exploit to the Sullivans, who had just arrived back from a gruelling day at the registrar's office in Armagh.

"Hi John. Young Michael was telling Jeanne and me all about his struggle with the monster from the deep. Must have been some fish."

"Oh it was a big one alright. It's on ice in the kitchen, I think Mike's going to have a trophy made. Enough of the fish, what sort of day have you had?"

"Not as exciting as yours, that's for sure. Jeanne and me have been going through a lot of old papers at the records office. Who'd' a' thought there were that many

Sullivans in such a small place. I tell you John I must have hundreds of relations roundabouts."

"I hope for your sake you don't."

"What makes you say that?"

"Well if they find out about you and Jeanne in Boston they'll all want to come and stay."

"Gee, I hadn't thought about it like that."

"I think John's pulling your leg. I wouldn't worry about an invasion of Sullivans."

For once Jeanne spoke up in an effort to reassure her husband.

"I think Michael's right dear, John's only making a little joke. Besides where would we put them all? Our little house just couldn't cope with a lot of visitors."

"Is that right John?"

"I was only kidding Don. I see we need another round of drinks. What'll it be Jeanne, Don?"

"We were just going to get washed up before dinner, but we'll hold you to that drink later. See you in a while. Oh, I almost forgot – you guys still on for dinner tonight?"

"Definitely."

The Sullivans left the bar and O'Brien and Colquhoun moved to a table and sat down.

"Did you get the calls?"

"Yeah, everyone's here more or less. I've got to call McFadden at the Slieve Coolan later on and that's about all we can do today."

"So it's a case of make the most of tonight is it?"

"Why not – live each day as if it were your last. My round I think, same again Mike?"

"Please, and you better get Jim one while your at it, he should be down by now."

Colquhoun went to the bar with their empties and had just placed the order when Mathieson walked into the lounge.

"Well aren't you looking sharp tonight. What's her name Jim? And it better not be Maureen."

"You don't have to make such a bloody issue of it!"

"For God's Sake! Lighten up would you, I was only having a laugh."

"Very fucking funny!"

"OK, that's enough."

"Just because I've got an eye for the ladies you think…."

"I said that's enough. Just drop it Jim!"

They took their drinks over to the table and joined O'Brien. To avoid any further ugliness the conversation was turned to fishing and the catch of the day. O'Brien gave Mathieson the good news about the weight.

"You'll be pleased to hear that my fish tipped the scales at thirty pounds two ounces."

"Congratulations, that's a hell of a fish. You should get it stuffed or something."

"Aye, well, Maureen's seeing if there's someone local who does that sort of thing."

"Good. You could put it up in the bar as a testament."

"What d'you mean?"

"It would stand as a reminder to what you can be doing when you're supposed to be working – a sort of tribute to skiving."

"Thanks a bunch Jim! You know, landing that pike was bloody hard work!"

"All I meant was that it'll be hard explaining it to anyone else. It'll make a grand trophy and a bloody good story. Look, I wish I'd caught it, now I can't say fairer than that, can I?"

"I suppose not."

Colquhoun had followed the exchange with a growing sense of wonder.

"You know something, you two are like a pair of old women. I'd hate to see you argue over something important."

Mathieson and O'Brien looked at one another and as hard as each of them tried to be serious the funny side of the situation prevailed and their good humour returned.

"So what's the plan for this evening, John?"

"Well let's see. We're having dinner with the Sullivans and a few drinks afterwards. You can tell the Moby Dick story again, Jim and I can keep you right on the detail, the Sullivans will be spellbound and it should be a good night."

"What about tomorrow?"

"Jim, I think you or I should get the chance to net a monster and I'm sure Mike would like another crack at it. So fishing again, agreed?"

Neither Mathieson nor O'Brien raised any objections so the agenda was set for Thursday.

A similar discussion was taking place at the Slieve Coolan Hotel. The days golf had gone well, with fine weather making the two rounds the four had played a pleasure. As players they were evenly matched and no-one felt hard done by. After a couple of pre-dinner drinks it was agreed that they would play another four tomorrow, the only difference being a change of partners, as today had been an Irish v American affair.

They had arranged to go into the dining room at seven and were just leaving their table when McFadden saw Colin Lauder. They had only met briefly last week, but even though he was now wearing a suit rather than the jeans and sweatshirt that he'd had then, his short black hair and stocky frame picked him out. He glanced at his companions and confirmed with a nod that they had also noticed the arrival.

Lauder had spotted the Irish/American group as they left the bar and with their presence confirmed he returned to his room. He was unpacking his gear when there was a gentle tap at the door; opening it he found Alex Roper waiting in the hall way.

"Did you see them?"

"Aye, they're here."

"Right, Pearson's gone down to the bar. I suggest we join him."

"Yeah, I'll be right with you."

Dinner had gone well with several tales of fishing prowess and the inevitable 'ones that got away'. The fact that some of the stories were downright lies didn't spoil the telling. Don capped them all with the story of a three and a half hour battle with a black marlin off Key West. Everyone looked to Jeanne for confirmation but she explained that it had been a union trip and strictly stag. Colquhoun wanted to know what was done with the fish. Don explained that the cost of such a trophy was beyond him and that the boat charter company had kept the marlin for display at their dockside office. To pursue the truth further would have been churlish so Don left the dinner table top fisherman.

As they moved back to the lounge Colquhoun excused himself and went to the phone kiosk. He dialled the number for the Slieve Coolan and asked for Liam McFadden. When the receptionist failed to locate him in his room Colquhoun asked her if she could page him. After a couple of minutes McFadden came to the phone.

"How's John?"

"Fine. Just checking to see if everything's alright."

"Aye, can't complain."

"Have our friends arrived from Dublin?"

"Aye."

"But you haven't spoken to them?"

"No, that wasn't the arrangement."

"Good, keep it that way."

"I'll see you on Friday then."

"That you will."

Colquhoun had one more call to make but that one would have to wait until Friday. Satisfied that everyone on the team was where they should be and that there had been no mishaps he rejoined his companions in the lounge.

No sooner had he taken his seat than Jeanne announced that she was tired and was going to bed. The men all stood as she took her leave with a final instruction to Don not to stay up too late. When she had gone he gave them a conspiratorial wink.

"Well guys, we can have that drink now, what'll it be?"

Everyone settled on whiskey, and the barman was asked for four double Black Bush and a jug of water which each man added according to his taste. The conversation took no particular direction – politics, the rising cost of oil and the effects, the Russians and the Cold War – Don had an opinion on all of them. By the time the mantle clock above the fireplace chimed midnight Don had drunk more Black Bush than was good for him and Colquhoun signalled to O'Brien that it was time to call it a night and give the old man a helping hand up to bed.

When they made their move to help him, Don protested and managed to get to his feet unaided. He was a little unsteady but walked to the staircase under his own steam. He was closely followed by Colquhoun who at this point insisted on providing a degree of support as Don began climbing the stairs. O'Brien followed the pair as they progressed slowly to the first floor landing.

Mathieson remained in the lounge nursing the last of his drink and cursing his luck. He was pretty sure that he'd got on the wrong side of Colquhoun despite the apparent good humour. There was no doubting who was the boss on this job and he had a feeling that he could suffer for making Colquhoun raise his voice. He knew that authority should never be questioned but sometimes he felt he had to stand up for himself. All this possible trouble because he had a roving eye. God, he was only looking! Maybe the disagreement would be forgotten if the job was a success and there could be no question that Colquhoun had run things pretty smoothly since they had got the call the previous Friday, maybe too smoothly. The whole fishing trip story had worked well but he was getting the distinct impression that O'Brien was beginning to forget what he was here for; to lose the focus was always dangerous. He hoped that the rest of the team, wherever they were, had kept their eyes on the prize. That had been his main objection to coming early; if a task was not undertaken immediately when people were sharp it could get sloppy. He'd raised the issue last week but had been in the minority. One thing was certain, now that they were here they had to make a success of it.

He raised his glass, made a toast to success and finished the last of the Black Bush. He looked at the mantle clock again just as it chimed the quarter; time to turn in. He made his way upstairs, stopping at Colquhoun's room where he knocked the door. The voice inside, muffled by the heavy panel door, told Mathieson to come on in.

"I just wanted to check a couple of things before calling it a night, if you don't mind."

"That's OK Jim. What's on your mind?"

"Well, is everyone in place?"

"Let me worry about that."

"But are they?"

"As a matter of fact yes, and before you ask everything's still a go for Friday. Happy?"

"Better than I was, but I would appreciate a bit more involvement."

"What do you want?"

"The contact number for Friday night for the check-in will do. No offence, but giving it to one man was just a bit narrow. What would we do if something happened to you?"

Colquhoun tore a sheet of paper from a notebook and wrote down a nine digit number before handing it to Mathieson.

"You've got a point, and now you've got the number, anything else bothering you?"

Mathieson rubbed his chin between thumb and forefinger before answering.

"Do you think O'Brien's up for this?"

"You're worried about his concentration aren't you?"

"Just a bit."

"Don't be. I'll make sure that Mike is running one hundred percent come Friday. Now, if you don't mind I'm going to bed."

"OK, goodnight John."

Mathieson wasn't the only one to have doubts about O'Brien. The man himself was sitting on his bed weighing up the pros and cons of his place on the team. If he cried off at this point he would face the judgement of men he considered to be his friends, but worse than that he would have to face his own judgement. That was more than he was prepared to do. Come Friday he would be asking difficult questions of himself; he'd better have the answers, for everyone's sake.

* * *

During the course of the night it snowed, worse than that it froze and when the team members looked out their respective bedroom windows it was on a landscape covered with a thin blanket of snow. It was Thursday March 22nd.

Mathieson slid out from under the bedclothes and went into the bathroom to pour himself a glass of water. He walked to his window and looked out between the curtains. The view made him swear.

"Shit, oh, shit!"

It had snowed during the night, the end of bloody March and it had snowed!

Mathieson was the last down for breakfast and his late arrival did nothing to improve Colquhoun's foul mood.

"Good afternoon Jim. Glad you could join us."

"For Christ's sake John, it's five past eight. Who rattled your cage?"

"You've looked outside, I take it. That snow could bugger things up."

"I thought it was agreed that the opportunity was too good to be missed and that we went regardless."

"Yeah, it was, but I want clearance for this. You know what's likely to happen in the aftermath and I don't want neat size tens all over the bloody place to make life easy for someone looking for detail."

"So what's the plan for today?"

"Mike and I were talking that over before you came down. We're going to drive up to Armagh and I'm going to make contact. We'll take it form there."

"You don't think that they'll pull the plug do you?"

"I don't know what to think, that's why we're going to Armagh."

Alan Scott finished the last of his coffee and put his cup down. David Armstrong and Peter Osborne were still eating as he got up from the table and made his way through to reception where he gave his name and room number and asked if anything had been left for him.

"As a matter of fact, Mr. Scott, a set of car keys and a car park ticket were left earlier this morning. The man who left them said you would know where the car was parked."

Scott took the keys and returned to the dining room.

"OK fellas, we're mobile."

Davison, Todd and Hart unpacked their gear from the Landrover and spent the best part of an hour setting up their fishing stand at Muckno Lake. They had only come about a mile and a half from the Glenmore Hotel to the spot on the lake shore that had been recommended to them the previous night in the hotel bar. The hospitality had been warm and it had been with some difficulty that the three of them had managed to get to bed. The cold crisp air at the lake speedily cleared their heads of the Guinness that they had over-enjoyed. All three men were grateful for the cold-weather clothing that they had packed – the air temperature never crept above freezing.

Golf was out of the question at the Slieve Coolan but fortunately there were other diversions to occupy the time. Bennett and Bradley were introduced to the pleasures of snooker, which for them proved to be something of a disaster. Both men were reasonable pool players but the increased size of the table was their downfall. Chris Gatland had a very successful morning; taking somewhere in the region of twenty pounds from the Americans, both of whom felt that an increase in the stakes could improve their game – they were both wrong.

The weather didn't prove a problem to the three recent arrivals at the Slieve Coolan either; Alex Roper and Colin Lauder were able to make use of the squash courts, having brought racquets and sports kit with them. Marcus Pearson, sensibly as it turned out, sat in the lounge with the day's newspapers and a cafetiere which his attentive waitress replenished more than once.

After an uneventful drive to Armagh Colquhoun parked the BMW near the Planetarium. Mathieson and O'Brien stayed in the car as he went to the public phone box to make his call. The phone box was a mixed blessing – happily the phone itself was working but someone had used the booth as a toilet and it smelled strongly of urine. Colquhoun dialled the number and was connected on the fifth ring. He gave his name and the number of his phone and then hung up. Less than a minute later the phone rang and he answered on the fifth ring.

"Just what the hell do you think you're doing calling this number today?"

"The weather has become a bit of a problem and I wanted clarification."

"Unless it's the return of "The Great Flood" I don't want to know."

"It's worse than that, it's snowed."

"You're not in the arctic circle you know. You mean to tell me that you and yours can't deal with a little snow?"

"It's a case of what we leave behind us."

"Let us worry about that. This is an opportunity too good to miss."

"I know, I heard that at the briefing last week."

"Well, I'm not calling this one off."

"And I wouldn't expect you to. It's just…."

"It's just what? Come on!"

"I don't know."

"No, that's obvious. Tell me what you want and I'll get it for you."

"Well, we need some assurance. Can you put a watcher in for us?"

"It's very short notice but I'll see what I can do. Will that suffice?"

"Yeah it gives us a safety net I suppose."

"Right, well you run along and check in as arranged tomorrow night. Unless you hear the contrary everything is still on."

Before Colquhoun could add anything the connection was broken. He hung up and returned to the car.

"Everything's still a go. I asked them to put a watcher in tonight if at all possible and they've agreed."

O'Brien shivered at the thought.

"Poor bastard. He'll freeze his tits off in this weather."

"Not our problem Mike. I think it's necessary so let them put one of their own in. It'll spread the labour a bit and to be honest it's high time they took some responsibility. Anyway, we've got time to kill – I'm open to suggestions."

"Why don't we go home?"

"Very funny Jim."

"OK, since we're parked outside it, why don't we go to the Planetarium. Who knows we might learn something."

"Wouldn't we look well going to the Planetarium. It's for kids Jim."

"Well, it seems to me that we either go in here or back to the hotel, collect our tackle and find somewhere convenient to, as Mike so delicately put it, freeze our tits off. I vote for the central heating and the comfy chair."

"He has a point John. I'll go along with it."
"OK, but we're paying for this ourselves, I'm not putting in for expenses."
"I think we can run to the cost of a ticket, can't we Mike?"
"Yeah, come on let's go."

Harry Lynch sat in his office looking at the telephone. Damn Colquhoun and damn his worry over a little snow – he was creating difficulties that Lynch didn't need. He reached into the middle drawer of his desk and brought out his personal telephone directory, opening it at 'B'. Picking up the receiver he dialled the number on the list – it rang as the connection was made and was answered on the fourth ring.

"Yes?"

"It's Lynch, is Walsh there?"

"He is, but he's sleeping."

"Well go and wake him up. I've got a job for him."

The receiver at the other end was put down and Lynch could hear footsteps receding down a corridor. After about three minutes, more footsteps, and the handset was picked up again.

"Walsh."

"Get down to the "black hangar" at XMG, there'll be a lift for you to the Spur Hill hide. You're going to be watching again."

"That's just marvellous. I was meant to be going in to tidy up afterwards."

"And you still can, you'll just be walking to the site rather than driving."

"So what's changed?"

"I want a first-hand weather check."

"You've got to be fucking joking."

"Do you hear laughter? I'm reliably informed that there's been a change in the weather and I don't want to pull the plug because of some snow."

"You wouldn't. This is down to the heroes isn't it?"

"The team leader, yes."

"Boy scouts, fucking boy scouts."

"Easy Walsh, you'll be meeting them later. I don't want any unpleasantness. Is that clear?"

"As crystal."

"Well, put your gear together and get down there. Any further details will go through thirteen's shack; so call in with them to see if anything has arrived for you."

"OK. I'll see you next week."

"Remember Walsh I want this one done right."

"You can rely on me."

Lynch returned the handset to the cradle. He had two more calls to make – one to arrange Walsh's lift and the other to check the status with thirteen; he didn't want just anybody handling Walsh's transmission.

It was probably the lack of an adequate warm-up that led to Lauder's injury. In the second game, just when the two men were starting to loosen up, he stretched for a ball that he really should have left and wrenched his knee. He dropped to the floor of the court, his racquet falling with a clatter beside him.

"Fuck!"

Roper didn't realise that Lauder had injured himself and offered no sympathy or assistance.

"That'll teach you. Why don't you just admit that you're up against a better player."

When he didn't get up straight away, Roper went over to him and knelt down.

"What's the problem mate?"

"I've twisted my bloody knee. Here, give me a hand up."

As Lauder limped his way back to the changing room, Roper regarded the way that he transferred his weight and realised that the injury could prove awkward.

John Davison reckoned that if he stayed at the lake shore any longer he would become a permanent fixture. The cold climbed up his legs through the soles of his boots and along his arms from his gloved hands so that by now only his midriff felt warm. The conversation had stalled and the only noise was the sound of lines being reeled in and cast. Their luck had been poor with a small catch of bream and perch.

"Bugger it fellas, I'm bloody freezing. What do you say we pack it up?"

"And then what?"

"Back to the hotel and hot whiskeys all round I think Graeme."

Hart nodded and started to reel in his line.

"What about you Steve?"

"Yeah, I've had enough and a hot whiskey sounds good."

It took Davison, Todd and Hart about half an hour to pack up and it was close to four o'clock when they got back to the Glenmore.

"OK, I'll be the first to admit it, that was interesting."

"Comfy seats weren't bad either."

"Yeah, I noticed how soundly you were sleeping through the tour of the universe. God, but you are one lazy sod, Jim."

Mathieson smiled not so much at the name calling as at the memory of the warmth and comfort of the Planetarium.

"Let's get back to the Lodge, I'm buying the first round."

"That's awfully decent of you Jim, you're on. Do you want to drive Mike?"

"Sure, give me the keys."

On their way back to the hotel they ran into the vehicle check-point again just outside Keady. The same officer whom they had encountered on Tuesday was on duty and recognising the car he waved them on.

"Must be a regular thing. John be sure to tell the cleaners not to come through Keady on Saturday – not in this car anyway."

"Yeah, I've made a note of it Jim."

Five minutes saw them back at the hotel and they went straight to the bar.

Scott and Armstrong were still up in their rooms dropping their bags off; so Osborne was left to his own devices in the residents' lounge. The drive from Belfast had been tedious with many drivers creeping along because of the snow. The 2 litre Ford Cortina that they had picked up from the car-park on the Dublin Road would ordinarily have made short work of overtaking the slower vehicles, but not today, today they had to be cautious. It was still freezing and the temperature was showing no signs of rising. The comment had been made on the way south that it was just as well that the cold weather gear had been packed. Osborne sipped his whiskey and hoped for a change in the weather.

Roper returned from the hotel bar with a second bucket of ice and some fresh drying clothes. Lauder had spent the last two hours with ice packs on his left knee, attempting to minimise any swelling.

"How's it looking Colin?"

"Not good. It's starting to puff up a bit. Of all the stupid fucking things."

"Maybe so, but there's no point getting pissed off about it. D'you think it'll be right for tomorrow?"

"It'll just have to be."

"I'm serious. Can you do the job with that leg?"

"Get me some decent pain-killers and some crepe bandage and I'll be fine."

"Well, we'll see tomorrow. I don't want any heroics from you. If it's bad we leave you behind."

"Understood, but that's not going to happen. Believe me Alex, I'll not be missing the show."

"If you're OK on your own I'm going down to join Marcus in the lounge. What about dinner?"

"I'll see how this looks later and if it's OK I'll join you. Otherwise it's room service."

"Right, see you later."

"OK, and thanks for the ice."

The Americans wouldn't quit and only lost by an ever increasing margin. Gatland and McFadden were beginning to get embarrassed, but not to the point where they were prepared to throw a game. As a means of softening the blow of defeat they had started playing doubles but Bennett and Bradley still couldn't win. The break for lunch hadn't helped the losing streak; the Americans returned to the table with new determination but no improvement in their game. Fortunately boredom intervened before tempers were strained to breaking point.

"You guys sure can shoot snooker. Tom and I know when we're beat, so how about we go get a beer?"

"Who's buying Martin?"

"Hell, you guys took enough of our money, you can afford it."

"Aye, I suppose we did. Come on Chris let's buy these losers a beer."

"That'll take us up to dinner. The time's gone real quick today but I think we'd have preferred being out on the course; at least that's a game we can beat you at. Do you think that snow's going to last?"

"I hope not Martin. Life would be much easier without it."

The phone rang once, stopped, then rang again three times and stopped – he hadn't been expecting a call but when the phone rang for the third time Hugo Robinson was ready. He picked up the receiver on the third ring.

"Crusoe."

"It's Finn."

"What's on your mind Finn?"

"I've been tryin' to get out of this fuckin' meetin' and I can't. I don't want to be there – these people you have comin' how can I trust them? I trust you Crusoe, but I don't know these fuckers."

"Finn, you go to the meeting, you behave just as normal, you keep your eyes and ears open. What's the problem in that?"

"Suppose someone's on to me, suppose that, you know what happens to touts. I should never have started this…"

"But you did, so don't start whining now. Haven't I said that you'd be taken care of? Haven't I always been fair with you?"

"Yeah you have, but…"

"But nothing Finn. After Friday you'll have your own patch – think of the money for God's sake."

The thought of his own gain gave Finn pause; Robinson could guess what was going through his mind – all the greedy little possibilities.

"I've got to go. I'll phone you tomorrow before I pick up the lads I'm takin'. This is all fucked up."

"Calm down Finn. You're not helping anyone behaving like this. Why do you need to call tomorrow? Everything's all right."

"Just you be there. Oh fuck….what have I done?"

Finn hung up with the question unanswered. The resignation in his voice typified a man with no options. Robinson had his man and the measure of him – Finn had nowhere to run, he'd stick to his end of the deal – what Robinson had to be sure of was that others would stick to theirs.

Lynch lay on the camp bed in his office, if not trying to sleep at least trying to relax. With the exceptions of Colquhoun's whinging and the fact that he could happily sleep for a week everything was shaping up well. He'd had the working brief on his desk for the best part of three years and this was the first occasion he had had all the pieces to play with. There was a bottle of Scapa 10 year old malt that he had set to one side – if Friday night went as planned he'd open it. He lay thinking of malt whisky; vastly superior to anything distilled in Ireland and as for what the Americans cooked up – well really – dreadful stuff, and then his phone rang. He wasn't expecting any calls; looking at the desk clock he saw it was ten to six, he shouldn't even be at his desk. He struggled off the bed and lifted the handset from the cradle. The line was poor but there was no mistaking the voice, the accent and the obvious disdain.

"Lynch? It's Robinson. I need to talk to you."

"What can I do for you Robinson?"

"I've just had a call from an excitable young man who may be preparing to tear your little party to pieces."

"What does he want now, more money?"

"Oddly enough no. He wants to know if he can trust Friday night's visitors."

"I've told you that he'll be taken care of. I take it that he'll be in contact again, so, when he is, you can tell him that everything is settled. I can't say fairer than that."

"I hope you live up to your word. Just remember the quality of the material he has passed to us to date."

"I won't forget, but maybe you should try to remember just whose side you're on."

"Let's not get into an argument about sides – that sort of thing is for the school quadrangle."

Point scoring as bloody usual – where had he gone to school – somewhere like Eton or Harrow, no doubt.

"I will call you when I hear from Finn."

"You do that."

The line was broken and Lynch replaced the receiver. Conversations with Robinson were always a pain – the public school superiority – how the hell did the arrogant bastard know that Lynch's school didn't have a quadrangle? He shouldn't let Robinson get to him like that. He consoled himself with the fact that he was responsible for Robinson's security and that they both knew it. He wondered how bloody superior Robinson would be if he needed the cavalry. He got up from the desk and stretched out again on the camp bed. Thoughts of agent/handlers were soon replaced with those of malt whisky and good food. When this job was over he was going to enjoy some time off – really enjoy it.

The snow was the main topic of conversation in the residents' lounge back at the Carnagh Lodge. The fact that there was no sign of a thaw was causing concern; it wasn't so much the cold, more the visibility problems. With a white background they would stand out like sore thumbs; nobody had built a contingency in to deal with snow.

"If they pull the plug, what then?"

"Then we go home like Jim said and wait for the next opportunity."

"Do we stay out the week or pack up tomorrow as planned?"

"I think we go tomorrow whether the job's on or not, talking of that I'd better go and announce our change of plans so to speak."

Colquhoun went out to reception to pass on the news of their early departure. Mathieson regarded O'Brien – his responses to the potential difficulties had been measured and had displayed none of the warning signs that had given Mathieson cause for concern – it looked as if he was coming into line after all. Colquhoun returned to his seat.

"That's settled then – we check-out tomorrow."

"What's the reason?"

"I'd have thought that was obvious Jim. All the calls I've taken in the last couple of days have been about problems back at the firm. We've got to go home on a rescue mission."

"Not that far from the truth. Let's have that drink, like I said I'm buying."

Mathieson signalled to the waiter who came over and took his order for three gin and tonics. Their mood was not lifted by the arrival of the drinks; each man was considering the day ahead and his own place within the set-up. Thoughts briefly turned to the sense of relief that would come if the job was called off, but these didn't last long – it was not their place to walk away. They sat in silence, periodically looking at each other, by turns seeking reassurance and offering it. The spell was broken by the arrival of the Sullivans. Don took one look at the sombre threesome and came over.

"Hi guys, what's up? You look as if someone just died."

"We got word that a deal we've been working on has been brought forward and if we don't get back pronto we'll lose it; so we've got to go home tomorrow."

"Jeez, that's too bad. What with the weather an' all you guys haven't had much of a break."

"It's not been what we'd hoped but we've had a good time for all that."

Mathieson and O'Brien nodded their assent.

"Well, Jeanne and I would be real pleased if you joined us for dinner tonight to say goodbye."

"Don thanks, we'd be happy to join you. I'm just going to have a quick shower and get changed and I'll see you in the dining room at seven."

Mathieson and O'Brien also expressed their wish to get cleaned up so they parted company. Once they had gone upstairs Colquhoun reminded them to give their gear another check and re-pack it for tomorrow.

Once he had locked the door Mathieson went to the wardrobe and began removing his gear. The items of clothing that he hadn't worn yet were set to one side. He gave his boots a quick once-over, satisfied that they would be alright he put them back on the floor of the wardrobe. Next he lifted his canvas grip and checked the last of his gear. Everything was as he had packed it and he knew better than to start pawing over everything. Nit picking at this stage wouldn't help, so he put his kit back in the wardrobe with what he'd need tomorrow within easy reach.

Lauder limped down to the dining room and then with considerable effort strode purposefully to Roper and Pearson's table. He sat down, picked up the menu that had been left for him and began to look at the table d'hote.

"You're leg doesn't look bad at all Colin. Alex told me you'd really knackered it. The ice must've helped."

"Yeah, it's eased up a bit, but I think I'm still going to need some painkillers and bandage."

"Aye, Alex said you'd need something so I've dug out some Co-Codamol and Brufen and some crepe and elastic bandage. When we've eaten come up to my room and I'll take a look and see if you need strapped up."

"Thanks Marcus."

Their waiter arrived to take their order and each man made his choice. There was a disagreement over red or white wine so a bottle of each was selected.

"We'll be putting in for expenses so what the hell."

"I hope you're right Alex. Those pen-pushing bastards in accounts might take a dim view of it."

"For appearances sake what are we meant to drink, water? Doesn't sit well, anyway, it's not as if we chose the most expensive wines on the list."

When the wines were brought to the table, tasted and poured, they raised their glasses and Roper proposed a toast.

"Here's to your leg and its speedy recovery and here's to a successful job tomorrow night."

Similar rituals were taking place at the other hotels where the various members of the team were staying. The one thing that wasn't mentioned was luck – it was never a matter of luck – they would never put their trust in a commodity they couldn't quantify. The abilities they possessed would either be enough to see them through the job or they wouldn't – simple as that.

After another excellent meal, Don suggested that they retire to the lounge for a drink. Colquhoun had discussed this possibility with Mathieson and O'Brien and they had decided to limit themselves to a couple of drinks before they got to bed because of their supposed 'early start' in the morning. They hadn't wanted to offend Don and Jeanne by refusing, but it was more than that – they genuinely liked the retired couple from Boston and had enjoyed their company over the past couple of days.

"Jeanne, Don on behalf of Jim and Mike I want to say thank you for being such good company. It's been a real pleasure meeting you both and we all want to wish you a happy conclusion to your holiday. So, once again thanks."

"Well, Jeanne and me were saying the same thing earlier today. We sure are glad to have met you guys and we want to say that if any of you are ever in Boston be sure to look us up. We would love to have you come stay with us."

At this point addresses were swapped but as is usually the case no-one seriously considered the possibility of having guests as a result. Drinks were finished and O'Brien made his excuses, signalling an end to the evening. It took nearly a quarter of an hour but with the farewells finally exchanged the three men made their way upstairs for one final check of their gear and then bed.

* * *

The wind changed direction during the night. It blew from the west and the warmer air started the thaw that had been prayed for. It also brought rain clouds that speeded the process along. Some of the men were aware of the change as they had not been able to sleep. The last vestiges of their anxiety were washed away with the snow. By one-thirty everyone was asleep. It was Friday March 23rd.

"Sir, time to wake up, sir. Your lift's ready."

The corporal wasn't sure what rank he was dealing with but decided discretion was the best approach. He roused the man lying on the bunk by gently shaking his shoulder and was rewarded with a sleepy yawn.

"What time is it?"

"Oh one fifty, sir."

"Jesus. Any coffee on the go?"

"Yes sir. How d'you take it?"

"Black, no sugar."

As the corporal went to get the coffee Walsh swung his legs over the side of the bunk, stood and walked over to the hangar doors. Pushing one of the doors open he looked out on the concrete apron. Silhouetted against the perimeter wall was his lift, a Westland Wessex. The helicopter was the only sign of life about the base; cockpit lights showed that the aircrew were carrying out their pre-flight checks and a member of the ground staff came into view as he walked from behind the Wessex surveying the surrounding area for obstructions or litter that could interfere with take-off. Even the signals shack, over to his left, showed no obvious signs of life but he knew that members of thirteen were inside monitoring traffic. He'd called with them earlier that day when he'd arrived from Belfast to see if there was any additional detail from Lynch and was rewarded with one flimsy confirming his lift, the schedule and the broadcast instructions. He had confirmed his transmission time with the "green" element and had drawn the necessary equipment giving it a basic check.

"Here's your coffee, sir. You'll have to be quick, sir. The flight's due off at oh two."

"Thanks. Anybody else coming along on this one?"

"There was meant to be a squad of Greenjackets going with you but they've been stood down, so it's just you as far as I know, sir."

He drank his coffee and looked at the sky. Ragged clouds drifted past illuminated by the moon. A light rain was falling and yesterday's snow was starting to melt. It looked as if he was going to have a damp time ahead of him. He walked back to the bunk and began his final kit check, not that there was much of it. Behind him he heard the Rolls-Royce turboshaft cough into life and the unmistakable whine of the main rotor beginning its cycle. He lifted his backpack and returned to the hangar door. The member of ground staff he had seen earlier signalled to the hangar that it was time to go. He drained the last of his coffee and handed the mug to the corporal.

"Thanks for the coffee."

"Don't mention it, sir."

"Well, I'd better be off."

Swinging his pack onto his shoulder he ran over to the Wessex and climbed on board through the starboard loading gate. An Army Air Corps sergeant pointed to the bench seat and signalled that he should put his safety harness on. Once he had strapped himself in, he reached into his smock and retrieved a pair of ear plugs. Once they were in place the noise level from the Coupled Gnome turboshaft dropped to the tolerable. He settled onto the bench seat as the Wessex lifted off. To the right the small town of Crossmaglen showed itself under the incandescent glare of its street lights. The pilot took a northerly course, never leaving them more than two miles from the border with the Irish Republic. Five minutes after take off the Wessex had reached about 1,000 feet; staying below the cloud cover, and was flying at 110mph. When they reached Newtownhamilton the pilot altered course so that the Wessex took a north-westerly direction and they continued, still hugging the border.

The flight to the drop-off point was scheduled at less than thirty minutes but the passage of time was hard to assess because it was a night flight and the loading gate was shut which effectively cut all links with the outside world. Walsh was surprised when the sergeant tapped his leg and held up his hand with thumb and fingers spread – five minutes to drop. The Wessex started to lose altitude as the pilot began his approach to Spur Hill.

He hunched over the backpack at his feet and gave the contents a final, somewhat futile, once-over; he'd checked the kit in Belfast, in Crossmaglen, and here he was, a creature of habit, checking it again. The last check he made was to the Browning High Power 9mm pistol that he carried in a belt holster in the cavalry cross-draw position on his left-hand side. He drew the pistol from the well used

Len Dixon vertical scabbard with his right hand and pushed the magazine release with his right thumb, gripping the ejected magazine between the middle and third finger of his left hand. Next he took off the safety catch and placing the thumb of his left hand on the cocked hammer and the top joint of his left index finger on the rear sight, he gently eased back the slide by pulling on the rear sight and scrutinised the ejection port for the tell-tale glint of brass that indicated a live round in the chamber. Once he was satisfied that the weapon was loaded he reapplied the safety catch and replaced the magazine. Thirteen rounds in the magazine and one chambered plus a spare magazine of another thirteen; and he hoped to God that he wouldn't need any of them. He re-holstered his pistol and looked up at the sergeant who now held up a single finger. The Wessex slowed in the air and the lurch in his stomach told him that the landing wasn't far off. The sergeant pulled back the loading gate and the chill of the night rushed into the cabin space. The helicopter stopped altogether and made the briefest of landings, the sergeant pointed to the gate and gave him a thumbs up sign, with a nod of his head he lifted his pack and dropped to the ground. As he sought cover the Wessex lifted back into the night sky and was off. The whole drop had lasted less than twenty seconds.

He lay in the bracken and took out his ear plugs, now able to listen to the Wessex as it continued on its north-westerly course. He scanned his immediate surroundings – the pilot had set him down on the eastern side of Spur Hill away from the farmhouses which lay to the west. The fact that the drop had taken place on the reverse slope hopefully meant that the locals hadn't been alerted to its possibility; the bulk of the hill should have lessened the noise of the helicopter. Be that as it may he wasn't going to start wandering around the hillside just yet.

He slowly crawled into a more comfortable position which allowed him a better view of the slope leading up to the crest of the hill. He pulled the left sleeve of his smock back and looked at his watch; the tritium numerals and hands gave off a faint glow, telling him that it was oh two thirty five. He was scheduled to be in place at oh three but the schedule would just have to be flexible – it was going to take him the best part of an hour to find the hide and get into position.

He waited another fifteen minutes before moving off keeping his profile hunched and as low to the ground as was possible without actually going on all fours or crawling. The light rain that had fallen at Crossmaglen continued to fall here making the ground soft so he had to be careful with his foot placement as he didn't want to leave size ten tracks all over the place. It took a laborious forty minutes to cover the half mile from the drop site to the hide with frequent stops to look and listen for anything that didn't fit with the location. At one of his stops, once he was satisfied that all was well, he took the opportunity to empty his bladder – the coffee he had drunk at Crossmaglen would only cause problems in the cramped conditions of the hide – no sense in making the job more unpleasant than it already was. Even though this was his third time at the Spur Hill hide it took him nearly ten minutes to locate the entrance. The hide was built into an old dry stone wall that was now overgrown with bracken and briar. He carefully felt around the entrance for any sign of interference – if the hide had been discovered a booby-trap was a distinct possibility. Nothing untoward met his search and he wriggled his way into the confined space feeling the walls, floor and ceiling as he went, in case a device had been placed inside. By the time he had crawled into position the exertion and the concentration he had given to the task was beginning to tell – he lay full length breathing slowly and deeply still listening for any sound that seemed out of place. Nothing upset his quiet solitude, so after another five minutes he set to work. Turning on his right hand side he pulled the pack level with his chest and removed the 30X spotting scope. He placed it to the front of the hide near the small gap in the old wall which was to allow his only view of the outside world for the next day. He rolled onto his stomach and taking the scope in his hands surveyed the moonlit farmhouse that lay below him to the north-west at a distance of some 900 yards. There was no apparent activity and his view was quickly obscured as the moon retreated behind the clouds.

He took another look at his watch – oh three forty-five – he shouldn't be expecting any movement for at least another two and a half hours, but he'd keep his eyes open nonetheless.

The Wessex had flown on to Enniskillen, from where the pilot had contacted thirteen at Crossmaglen. The "green" signaller in turn dialled the number he'd been given earlier. Lynch answered the call on the fifth ring.

"Yes?"

"This is green thirteen – the recorded delivery has been accepted."

"Thanks."

He stood and took off his jacket hanging it on the hook on the back of his office door. Four o'clock in the morning – he'd nearly dozed off a couple of times sitting at his desk waiting for the call, his back was playing up and he only had the camp bed to look forward to. The only consolation he had was the fact that he would at least be getting some sleep – Walsh would be stuck in that bloody hide for a day without any. He unfolded the bed and sat down to set the alarm on his desk clock for eight fifteen. His last thought before he fell asleep was to send one of the staff out to pick up some fresh clothes from his flat; another day in these clothes and he'd smell as bad as Walsh undoubtedly would by tomorrow night.

Lower Hill Farm started to come alive around 6.00am when Padraig Mullan walked out the back door with two empty buckets to collect coal for the range in the kitchen. His uncle Joe was inside making tea and would begin breakfast as soon as Padraig returned. Uncle Seamus was still in bed. Padraig filled the buckets in the coal shed and walked back to the house with little effort; years of work on the family farm had left their mark, he was a strong nineteen year old, not that tall but powerfully built. He put one bucket down so he could press the latch for the door that led in to the scullery.

"Hurry up for Christ's sake. The bloody range'll be out if you don't get a move on."

Padraig pushed the door into the kitchen open, bringing one of the buckets with him, he walked over to the old blackleaded range and lifted the lid to the fire.

"Joe it's fine. I'll soon have it goin', don't worry."

"Is that kettle boiled yet?"

"It is."

"Well you can wet the tea when you've finished stokin' the range. I'll go and wake that lazy brother of mine."

Joe climbed the two steps that led into the hall and then walked to the foot of the stairs. Resting his hands on the bannister he called upstairs.

"Seamus, stir yourself! There'll be tea out so hurry down!"

A muffled reply came from behind the bedroom door at the head of the stairs and Joe returned to the kitchen satisfied that his brother was awake.

Up on the hill Walsh had made a note of the activity down at the farmhouse and lifted his scope to scrutinise young Padraig's movements. The view afforded by the scope allowed for a positive identification. Once Padraig was back in the house he knew from previous experience that any interior views were out of the question until dusk at the earliest when the lights would be turned on inside. He'd have to make do with the exterior and be sure to keep a head count of all the bodies that showed themselves outside.

Joe and Padraig had finished their fries by the time Seamus put in an appearance. He hadn't washed or shaved and his unruly dark hair was even more of a tangled mess than usual.

"I didn't hear you come in this mornin'. Were you out with Sinead again?"

"And what if I was?"

"Oh, nothin'. Well, yes, when are you pair goin' to get married?"

"What you mean is how soon do we get a housekeeper."

"Never said same. I mean it's about time you got hitched. Jesus, you've been goin' out long enough."

"I'll ask her when I'm good and ready. Now's not the time and you know it, Joe. Later this year, maybe."

"Have you told her that you're plannin' to extend the house?"

"No that's a surprise for the weddin', and don't you go tellin' her."

"Well God knows you've put in for plannin' permission long enough ago, you should just get on with it. Anyway, do you want to go and get Francie and Jonjo or shall we send Padraig?"

"Let the lad go, it's about time he earned his keep. You hear that, Padraig?"

"Yeah. They're at their uncle's place aren't they?"

"Aye. You be there before nine."

"No problem, but I'll have to take the Peugeot, Arthur's got the Transit. He said he'd bring it back today."

"Aye I remember him sayin'. Just be careful, none of your stunt drivin'."

At oh eight ten Walsh saw young Padraig leave the farmhouse and get into the metallic green Peugeot parked some eight to ten yards from the back door. After a minute or so the car drove off and he made another note on his small pad.

Hugo Robinson had been up for over an hour and had eaten, for him, a substantial breakfast. He stood at the kitchen sink washing the last of his dishes – a tall spare man in his early fifties, divorced with no children, living for his job. He had moved back to Dundrum some five years ago; partly because he wanted to and partly because his desk controller thought it was a good idea. He had lived on the garrison at Ballykinler during his school holidays – his father had been the adjutant – and he had enjoyed the freedom of the beaches and the bird sanctuary at Murlough Bay. It had been a good place for him to grow up and it would be a good one to enjoy his retirement.

He dried his plates and put them away, closing the cupboard door just as the phone rang for the first time. He listened for the familiar pattern of rings and answered as the third sequence identified his agent.

"It's Finn."

Robinson put his drying cloth on the kitchen table and before he could make a reply the voice broke in once more.

"Are you there? It's Finn."

"Yes, Finn, yes. I was just finishing drying my breakfast things."

"Some of us got no fuckin' breakfast. Some of us were up all night thinkin'."

"And did you reach any conclusions?"

"Aye, I did. I'm not goin'. I don't need to be there so I don't. You've got what you need, you can leave me out of it."

"Finn you told me yesterday that you're meant to be transporting others to this meeting. What's going to happen if you don't show?"

"I don't give a fuck."

"Well you should. Here's what will happen – someone will tell the Mullans that you didn't show – the Mullans will wonder why and send somebody to find you – you will have run, and when the Mullans are told that you're nowhere to be found they'll cancel the meeting. Now that's bad for me but it's worse for you and here's why – you'll be found – you'll be questioned somewhat vigorously – you'll tell them what they want to know, and then they'll shoot you and bury your body God knows where. Does that sound about right to you Finn?"

"It's not fuckin' fair."

"And who ever said life was fair for God's sake. Go to the meeting. I've taken care of everything; the men coming to the meeting have been briefed and you will be taken care of. On that you have my word."

"You better be right. I'm the one takin' all the risks."

"Maybe, but look at what you stand to gain."

The carrot was produced again, but this time the pause seemed to last longer than it had previously; Finn was taking his time reaching a decision. Robinson was beginning to get edgy when eventually he spoke.

"OK I'll go."

"Good. You won't change your mind again will you?"

"I said I'll go, fair enough?"

"Yes. Well, if there's nothing else I wish you luck."

Robinson hung up and sighed deeply. For one dreadful moment he had actually thought that Finn was going to run and that would have ruined everything. The possibility of what would happen if he was caught had been enough of a threat to keep him on track. Everything was still a go and that would keep Lynch happy.

The members of the team were enjoying their breakfasts at the various hotels where they were staying. With one exception they had all enjoyed a sound night's sleep; Colin Lauder had been up until just after four nursing his knee. The pain killer and the anti-inflammatory he had taken had made little impact on the swelling although the pain wasn't quite as bad as it had been. He could walk without a limp if he was careful but he wouldn't want to try running on it. If he was able to rest his knee then it should be OK for the job tonight. He wasn't even contemplating counting himself out.

Harry Lynch had spent an uncomfortable night on his camp bed and the diet of coffee and digestive biscuits was playing hell with his stomach. He had found a packet of milk of magnesia tablets and was chewing a mouthful in an effort to ease his stomach cramp. All in all he was in a foul mood when his desk phone rang.

"Lynch."

"Robinson, I've spoken with Finn and after some hesitation he has finally consented to go to his meeting and keep faith with the arrangement."

"Great. Have you anything else for me?"

"Only a reminder to honour the arrangement and make sure that my man is taken care of."

"Oh don't worry – he'll be taken care of."

"He had better be. I've got three years invested in Finn and I don't want to see you and yours destroy my hard work."

"You're not the only handler and Finn's not the only agent. It might pay you to develop a sense of perspective regarding field operations in your locale."

"Just play this one by your own rules Lynch. Otherwise I will take this as far as I can."

"I'm sure you will, but if there is nothing else I've got work to do."

Lynch took the distinctly schoolboy pleasure in hanging up before Robinson could say another word. As for work he had little to do, it was now a case of waiting for Walsh's contact and nothing would make the time go any faster. He contemplated his camp bed but decided against another attempt at sleep. Instead he shuffled down the corridor to the kitchen and made another cup of bad coffee which he drank hoping to remove the chalky taste of the tablets. God, but he needed some rest and in a proper bed with clean sheets, but first the job, always the job.

An old Mark 2 Ford Escort pulled into the farmyard at oh nine seventeen and three men got out. The back door opened and the Mullan brothers came out to greet them. There was much good humoured shaking of hands and slapping of backs. The actions of the Mullans and men from the car confirmed one thing to Walsh – his position was unknown – nobody would behave that openly if they suspected that they were under surveillance. Scanning the mens' faces, he could be sure of two of the three new arrivals identities and he made the necessary entries. He wrote a detailed description of the third man whom he would refer to as "player 1" if the need arose.

"It's good to see the lot of you, but Jesus, you're a bit early. No matter, come on in and we'll get some tea."

Joe Mullan led the way back into the house, but turned just before he was through the scullery door.

"Sean, before you come in, would you put your car in the barn. There's been a lot of fuckin' helicopters flyin' about. No need to give them somethin' to look at."

"No problem, Joe, I'll do it now."

Sean McNellis got back in his car, started it up and drove it under cover. When he came out of the barn he slid the big doors shut and joined the rest of the men in the kitchen.

"Do you want tea Sean?"

"No you're alright. I'm not long after one. Anyway Joe, who all's comin' tonight?"

"Everyone."

"Christ Joe, everyone?"

"Everyone Sean. There's a lot to cover. Did you see last month's Starry Plough?", McNellis shook his head, "Well it doesn't matter if you did or not. Those bastards seem to think that South Armagh belongs to them. We're makin' plans to change that."

"What sort of plans?"

"You'll hear later Sean, when everyone's here."

After breakfast they went up to their rooms to finish packing the last of their gear. Mathieson was the last man to make it downstairs with his bags and he could tell from the glare that Colquhoun gave him that he'd blotted his copybook again.

Maureen was on reception as usual and waited with their separate bills. Wallets were produced and the accounts settled.

"I hope you had an enjoyable stay. I'm just sorry that you have to leave early."

Colquhoun and Mathieson lifted the remaining bags and went out to the car.

"So are we, but duty calls. One thing we didn't settle which you said you'd look into – did you find out if there was a trophy maker locally?"

"Yes I did Mr. O'Brien. There's a man in Armagh who does that sort of thing."

"I was wondering, could someone from the hotel drop it off for me. I'll leave money for expenses and the cost of the work and so on."

"I don't see why not, but I'll need a forwarding address to give to the trophy man."

O'Brien wrote an address down for Maureen and gave it to her along with fifty pounds.

"That should cover it don't you think?"

"It's probably too much Mr. O'Brien. Wouldn't it be better if you were sent a bill rather than this?"

"It's OK. I move about a lot. This way the cost's covered."

"Whatever you think's best."

Colquhoun walked back into reception with a sour expression. "If you're quite finished Mike we've got a boat to catch."

"I was just arranging things for the trophy. Is Jim not coming back in."

"Jim's in the car. We're late so come on."

"Well 'bye Maureen and thanks for all your help."

"My pleasure. Have a safe trip home."

Colquhoun stormed out to the car followed by O'Brien who could tell that something was very wrong even though he couldn't guess what.

"Did you have to be so ignorant in front of the girl?"

Colquhoun started the car and drove off a little too fast leaving deep tracks in the gravel driveway.

"Just button it!"

"I don't know what this is about but…."

"No that's clear. Like I told Mathieson, I'm running this job, and as leader I expect immediate response."

"And you'll get it John."

"Really? Well you two haven't been a good advertisement for that so far this week. What with you more interested in your bloody fish, and the skirt chaser in the back, we'll be bloody lucky to remember what we're here for."

Mathieson who'd been staring at the carpet in the back of the car couldn't contain himself.

"For Christ's Sake! We had to pass the time somehow, and it's not as if we did any harm. What'd you expect? The pair of us to run after you like a pair of fucking squaddies?"

"It might have helped."

"Ah, fuck off John. This part of the job has been about creating an impression and I think we did quite well, which is more than can be said if we played by your rules."

"Don't tell me to fuck off. Just remember who you're talking to."

"How could I forget. But you're wrong about this. Look, we'll get the job done, and you can bawl us out afterwards if there're any mistakes."

"OK, the subject's closed for now, but Jim, any more lip from you and I swear you'll be in more trouble than you can handle. Understood?"

"Yes John, understood."

"Good. Now we can get some work done."

He checked the time – oh nine fifty-five. There had been no activity since the arrival of the blue Ford Escort. Feeling hungry he reached into his pack, took out a Mars Bar and began to eat, chewing each mouthful carefully. The sickly sweet Mars Bar was no substitute for a hot meal, but he knew that was an impossibility – hot food had an aroma that travelled on the air and there was no way that the chance of discovery could be risked. Anyway there was the danger that any heating medium posed in the confines of the hide, the danger of fire couldn't be overestimated. And there were other problems – basic bodily functions were either unpleasant or impossible unless he moved out of the hide, and then there were the physical difficulties to be faced during prolonged periods of inactivity – he couldn't stretch properly and the damp had already crept throughout his body leaving him cold and susceptible to cramp. Yet again, he found himself giving thanks for the fact that this was a short job. On the two previous visits he had been watching for three and five days respectively. The effort on those occasions had led to nothing, this time would be different, very different. At least, that was the plan, but it could still all come undone. He finished his Mars Bar, putting the wrapper back in his pack, and gave his full attention to his watch on the Mullan brothers' farm.

By ten o'clock all the members of the team had checked out of their hotels. Liam McFadden and his group had stayed at the Slieve Coolan to play another round of golf – the weather had improved with the combined rain and thaw and the course was now clear. Martin Bradley had insisted on a return match – America versus Ireland; he hoped to make up for yesterday's humiliation on the snooker table. Everyone else had moved to new locations – all with the same vain hope that the time would pass quickly between now and their scheduled rendezvous. Numerous newspapers and magazines were read, copious quantities of tea and coffee were drunk and the time ground slowly by. That was the nature of waiting.

Padraig Mullan arrived back at the farm at twenty past eleven. Francie MacTeer sat beside him and Francie's brother Jonjo occupied the back seat. None of them was in good form. Seamus came out of the house when he heard the car pull up. The three younger men got out of the car and walked towards the house. Seamus held up his left hand, glanced at his watch and then looked at Padraig.

"Where the fuck have you been to this time?"

"It's not the lad's fault Seamus. He picked us up on time – it was on the way back – just over the border – fuckin' Brit checkpoint. The fuckers kept us for over an hour."

"Any rough stuff?"

"No."

"Then why has Jonjo got that bloody great welt on his face?"

"That wasn't the Brits Seamus, I got that the other night down at Coughlin's."

"Were you drunk again Jonjo?"

"Aye, I'd had a few."

"Jesus will you ever learn. You'd nothin' in the car then?"

"We'd hardly be here if we had, now would we. No, the fuckers just took their time searchin' the car and askin' us a lot of fuckin' stupid questions."

"So where are you now?"

"As far as the Brits are concerned we're headin' up to Belfast."

"OK lads, get inside."

The Peugeot was back in the yard at eleven twenty. Young Padraig was driving and from what he could see of them when they got out of the car he had his cousins Francie and Jonjo McTeer with him. That brought the total to eight – Sean McNellis, Gerard O'Neill, the MacTeers, the Mullans and "player 1". He made additional notes on his pad and then tried to work the cramp from his shoulders. This day couldn't be over quick enough as far as he was concerned. The quality of the light changed as the men in the yard moved into the house. The sky had taken on a threatening look – there were few things he could be sure of today, but he was sure of this, it was going to rain. Right on cue the first fat drops began to fall. The hide afforded him some protection, but after about five minutes there might as well have been a river running through it. The next time he pulled one of these jobs he'd be sure to ask for a snorkel only he didn't think anyone would get the joke. He lifted his backpack to make sure that the radio was secure in its waterproof cover. All manner of things could go wrong, but losing the radio wasn't one of them. Thankfully it was dry, even if he wasn't.

By two o'clock Colquhoun, Mathieson and O'Brien were back in Glaslough. The car was once again parked near the parish church, but this time they had not gone down to the lake side. Colquhoun and O'Brien had changed their shoes for walking boots and gone to the disused railway cutting. They were both carrying small backpacks and to any casual observer they looked like a couple of walkers out for a day's trek. Mathieson had stayed with the car where he now sat reading a newspaper. The heavy rain that had fallen in the morning had stopped, the westerly wind had seen to that. The sky was relatively clear but there had been a couple of squally showers when heavy bands of cloud had blown in. Thankfully these bursts of rain had been short. Mathieson looked at the clock on the dashboard – almost two fifteen, Colquhoun and O'Brien wouldn't be back until after three. If the rest of the team was as bored as he was, God help them. He put down the paper and lifted a copy of Car magazine, but the change in reading material didn't improve his mood; the magazine was full of reports on cars he didn't want or couldn't afford. This whole week had been enough to try the patience of a saint and it wasn't over yet.

Back in the changing rooms at the clubhouse Bradley and Bennett basked in the glory of having won their match with McFadden and Gatland. The Irishmen had been off their game, their minds had been elsewhere; both of them knew that if their concentration wasn't total then their performance would suffer. They would need to be completely focused tonight – Liam McFadden hoped the Americans would be as disciplined when the time called for it, there was no place for enthusiasm in the absence of experience, not tonight anyway.

Lauder sat in a cafe opposite the tourist information office in Monaghan. His knee was still giving him cause for concern; even the short walk from the car had made it throb. He reached into his pocket and took out the painkillers Pearson had given him, then thought better of taking one and replaced them. He looked out the window just in time to see Roper and Pearson come out of the tourist office. Both men were dressed for a day in the hills. They looked as he did, like typical trekkers with their walking boots, waterproofs and small backpacks. Their appearance was a marked change from the professional look of the past couple of days – their suits were packed in carriers in the boot of the Vauxhall, and in truth they all felt more at ease dressed as they were now.

Roper and Pearson crossed the street and joined Lauder.
"How's your knee? Those Co-Codamol I gave you helping at all?"
"I'm not taking them unless I need them and right now I don't need them."
"It's your choice, but remember what Alex said, it's never too late to back out."
"No way. It'll be fine. You two had better go and get yourselves a coffee or something."
Pearson went up to the counter leaving Roper at the table.
"Colin, I saw you limping from the car so don't bullshit me. It's fucked isn't it?"
"It's better than it was Alex. I can make it OK."
"Your call, I just hope you're right."

Peter Osborne sat in a pew at the rear of the Anglican Cathedral of St. Patrick's. Alan Scott and David Armstrong had gone for a walk around Armagh and had even talked about going to the Planetarium. Osborne had declined saying he wanted to go to church. Scott and Armstrong knew better than to make a joke of his faith and let him go. He looked at the old regimental colours that hung from the nave and thought of the men who had served and what they believed in. There was a long history of Irishmen serving in the British Army and much of it seemed to be represented here. All the campaigns, all the losses, they'd been for just causes. He hoped that all the men who'd served believed that what they'd been doing was right. He wanted to be right tonight, he wanted them all to be right.

After drinking more tea and coffee than was good for them Davison had made the suggestion that they should return to the lake. The permits they had acquired were for the week so with nothing better to do Todd and Hart had agreed. They had set their pitch at the same place hoping to do a little better than they had the day before. Maybe it had something to do with the positive change in the weather or maybe they were just a bit luckier but whatever it was they were catching more fish. Davison reckoned that they would need to leave around seven at the latest which left them about four hours.

He'd been in the hide for nearly thirteen hours and it seemed more like fifty. The main problem was that the confines of the hide didn't allow him to dry off, so with each new rain shower he got increasingly wet, and the wetter he got the colder he got, and with the cold came cramp. The lack of space made it very difficult for him to work it off. Things might not have been so bad if this watch had given him plenty to do, but there had been very long periods of inactivity that had left him bored as well as everything else. He checked his watch – fifteen fifty-one – over five hours until he was scheduled to call in. The thought had only entered his head when movement down at the farm made him lift his scope once more. A red Ford Transit van entered the yard and the driver got out, walked to the back door and knocked. The door opened and Seamus Mullan beckoned the man inside. The watcher hadn't been able to make a positive identification; the driver had had his back to him as he entered the house.

After a couple of minutes the driver re-emerged with both Mullan brothers behind him. This time Walsh got a good look at him and smiled – Arthur McFaul – another face and name. McFaul went to the rear of the van and opened the double doors. Four men clambered out of the back and he was able to check three of them off from the photos he had gone over time and time again. He added the Jameson brothers, Desmond and Martin, and Arthur's cousin Patrick McFaul to the list. The fourth man was bearded with long brown hair – he could have been Garvan McNabb but he couldn't be sure. The most recent photo of McNabb had shown him clean shaven, but a beard could be grown in a matter of weeks. He put his name on the list with a question mark beside it. The men made their way into the house while Arthur McFaul walked over to the barn and slid the doors open. He then drove the van into the barn to join Sean McNellis' Escort. When he came out of the barn McFaul closed the doors and followed the rest of the men into the house. Things must be getting pretty crowded in there – he now totalled thirteen certainties and there could be more bodies inside that he hadn't seen.

"Padraig would you and Francie and Jonjo go and get more chairs from next door."

"What, the good chairs?"

"Does it matter, we need seats, go and get them." As the lads went into the next room to retrieve the chairs from around the dining table the rest of the group found seats where they could. Joe Mullan didn't think the kitchen had been as full since his father's wake – the atmosphere was surprisingly similar – the same hushed conversations and the haze of cigarette smoke.

"Gerard open that window behind you before we all choke to death."

O'Neill released the catch and slid the window sash up. The smoke drifted out to be replaced with cooler fresher air.

"Have you anythin' to drink?"

"There's tea brewed on the range or water in the tap so help yourselves."

"Have you anythin' stronger Joe, or have you and Seamus joined the Pioneers?"

"Even you can wait a bit Sean. You'll just have to be doin' with tea."

"Jesus this is like bein' at your granny's. We're sittin' here doin' fuck all. There's thirteen of us – why don't you just tell us what this is all about Joe."

"We wait 'til everyone's here."

"And just when'll that be?"

"When they get here Sean."

"Have it your own fuckin' way."

"Watch your lip Sean. I'll not have that."

"Alright, I'm sorry Joe, but have you a pack of cards or somethin', I'm fuckin' bored."

"There's a pack in the middle drawer of the dresser."

Colquhoun left O'Brien in the woods beside the railway cutting and went back to the car. As he came around the side of the church Mathieson opened the driver's door and got out.

"I'm glad your back John. I was very nearly going to come looking for you. Is Mike OK?"

"Yeah, I left him keeping an eye on things. Anything of interest here?"

"Nothing, unless you count a dog having a sniff round the church. Anyway, I thought you said you'd be back after three."

"So, it is after three."

"More like four."

"Yeah, well I had to have a talk with Mike about the job tonight. He doesn't feel too happy."

"That's good, that's just fucking wonderful. Is he getting cold feet or what?"

"Not cold feet, but he doesn't think he can do the entry."

"Fine, I'll do it. He can take my place outside."

"You're sure?"

"What's the alternative; a weak link in the chain?"

"You're right."

"One thing John, I go in, you forget about my big mouth, OK?"

"You perform and we'll call it quits."

"Fine. Would you mind staying with the car while I go and take a look at the ground?"

"Help yourself. Go to the end of the access track and it's about 100, maybe 120 yards north in the trees. You'll spot Mike and then he'll show you, and give him a break – he feels pretty bad about tonight."

"At least he had the guts to speak up. I'll not mention it unless he does."

Colquhoun got into the BMW and passed Mathieson his Barbour jacket before he walked off towards the cutting; the sky had cleared but the experience of the day so far had shown them that it could cloud over and rain very quickly so the waterproof was a sensible precaution.

It took Mathieson nearly a quarter of an hour to find O'Brien who was sitting in the cover of a rhododendron.

"You look comfortable, where's the site?"

There was no mistaking the troubled look on O'Brien's face as he pointed at the marked tree.

"Put your back to the loop and it's about seven yards to the hole."

Mathieson gave the site a quick once-over. O'Brien watched his back, trying very hard to keep his thoughts to himself, but ultimately he had to voice his worries.

"Look Jim, I'm sorry about backing out, but I don't think I can hack it."

"You'll be outside doing my job so never say you can't hack it. That said, you fuck up outside and I'll kick your arse, understood?"

At least that managed to provoke a smile.

"Understood. Did Colquhoun say anything?"

"Don't worry about him. He's got his own concerns – first big job and all that goes with it – he's wondering if he can hack it."

"Do you think it'll be OK?"

"If it all goes to plan, if everyone does what's expected of them, yes it'll be OK. For now stop thinking 'what if', it doesn't do any good. Focus on the present and do the necessary."

"Thanks Jim."

"Aye", and he shrugged, "Let's change the subject. Is there a flask in that pack of yours?"

"There is. Coffee all right?"

"As long as it's hot I don't mind."

O'Brien pulled the flask from the rucksack and poured a mug for Mathieson and one for himself. They sat in the cover of the rhododendron, drank their coffee and wished for the time to pass quickly.

"Joe is there any food in the house?"

"Aye, we got a load of stuff in – there's bacon and sausages and bread – it's all in the fridge in the scullery – you boys help yourselves."

"Padraig do us a favour and make us a bacon sandwich would you?"

Padraig stopped reading his magazine, put it down and moved towards the scullery.

"Sit yourself back down. Sean don't you be givin' the lad orders. Get off your arse and make it yourself."

"For fuck's sake Joe I only asked him to make us a sandwich."

"I'm the one who does the askin' round here Sean and don't forget it."

"Well you could've asked everyone to turn up at the same time – sittin' here like a bunch of old women."

There were nods of agreement around the kitchen and a few mutterings; it was clear that there was sympathy for McNellis' point if view. Joe Mullan reckoned that in this instance attack was the best form of defence.

"And wouldn't that have looked good, you lot arrivin' like a fuckin' convoy? If you're comin' one car at a time it doesn't catch the eye. Look, Declan said he'd be here before eight. Then we can get started."

"And what about Peter and Joe?"

"They're walkin' in from New Mills Bridge. We'll see them later. Anythin' else botherin' you Sean?"

"Aye, why's there no-one mindin' the gate?"

"'Cos they're not needed. If the Brits showed up what could they do us for, sittin' around playin' cards? That's why there's no-one on security and that's why I said no guns."

McNellis thought over what Mullan had said, then got up and walked into the scullery to get the bacon and bread.

"You're the boss Joe."

"Really? It sounded like you were wantin' to run things Sean."

"No way Joe. All I want's a bacon sandwich. What about the rest of you?"

At that very moment Walsh would have given anything for a bacon sandwich; the tin of cold bacon grill that he'd just finished lay in his stomach like lead and it had done nothing to dispel the cold that had spread throughout his body. Down at the farmhouse nothing was happening; all he had to report was numbers – cold, wet and miserable for a bloody head count. Once again he cursed the ponce who had voiced concerns about the weather – the only reason he was stuck in the hide was to offer reassurance to some boy scout who was frightened by a little snow, snow that was gone now anyway. All being well he'd get the chance to give this particular hero an earful. He looked at his watch – eighteen twenty-one; still a few hours before he made his call. Maybe when it was dark he'd be able to exit the hide and stretch some warmth back into his limbs.

John Davison checked the time.

"Jesus fellas, we'd better pack up and get moving; it's nearly six thirty."
The lines were reeled in, bait and hooks were removed, rods taken down and the catch net emptied. All told it took nearly twenty minutes to clear their stand. With all the gear packed in the Landrover it was time to go. Stephen Todd took the wheel with Davison navigating and Graeme Hart taking his usual position in the rear. Todd drove back into Castleblayney and followed the N2 for Monaghan. They weren't the only ones on the road.

Colin Lauder's knee had eased considerably during the afternoon; he now sat in the front passenger seat of the Cavalier as Alex Roper drove towards Emyvale. From there they would take the road to Glennan and then Glaslough. Marcus Pearson rummaged through his rucksack in the back seat.

"D'you need any more anti-inflammatories?"

"I haven't taken all the ones you gave me yesterday."

"I only gave you six – you should've finished them by now."

"No, I've still got three left. I only took them when I thought I needed them. It's really improved a lot Marcus, don't worry about me."

"Well I want to take another look before we set off tonight, just to be sure, OK?"

"If it makes you happy, OK."

Chris Gatland drove the Granada estate out of the service station fore-court on the N54 on the north-east side of Clones. They were running a little early and McFadden decided to call a halt in Monaghan. They pulled into the car park at the cathedral about 20 minutes later with the time approaching seven thirty. When Gatland parked the car Bradley and Bennett got out to stretch their legs.

"How long do you reckon we'll have to wait Liam?"

"I think about an hour or so should do."

"If that's the case I think I'll join the Americans."

"Yeah, why not."

They both got out of the car and Gatland locked the doors before they followed Bennett and Bradley to the cathedral.

After a couple of hours reflection in St. Patrick's, Peter Osborne had gone for a walk around Armagh. The afternoon was marked by brief but heavy rain showers; the last of which he'd escaped by going into a cafe. He sat alone drinking a rather bland cup of coffee listening to the other customers' conversations. Their mundane, inconsequential nature came as no surprise. What, Osborne wondered, would be the tone and content if the people knew what he knew. What would it be if they knew what was to happen in a matter of hours? He concluded, as he had before, that some things were better left unknown. Any more introspection and he would have to back out of the job. He had paid for his coffee and gone to see if Scott and Armstrong had finished at the Planetarium.

They had already been waiting for nearly half an hour when he had eventually shown up. David Armstrong made a wisecrack about absolution in advance only for Osborne to inform him of the differences between Anglicanism and Catholicism; it looked as if the time for humour was long gone. Alan Scott had started the Cortina and set off on their roundabout route that would take them to Enniskillen and Monaghan. The drive had been all business with Armstrong and Osborne carrying out a final kit check. By eight o'clock they drove through Monaghan town and began their final approach to Glaslough.

Walsh had maintained his cramped vigil into the evening with little to attract his attention and thus alleviate his boredom. The highlight of the watch so far this evening had been young Padraig going to the coal-house to fetch more fuel for the range. Walsh had about fifty minutes to transmission time and there had not been any increase in numbers down at the farm. He gave the house and the surrounding outbuildings a detailed inspection; nothing had changed. Lynch had led him to believe that there would be nineteen, maybe twenty bodies at Lower Hill Farm; it could hardly be regarded as his fault if the number fell short of the expected total.

At twenty oh eight the screech of a loose fan belt refocused Walsh's scrutiny. He lifted the scope just in time to see a battered red Datsun Sunny enter the yard. On this occasion all four men got out and walked to the kitchen door. Seamus Mullan appeared in the doorway and beckoned the men inside. Walsh didn't have much time to check the identities of the four new faces. He was sure of two – the McHugh brothers, Michael and Enda. The driver could have been Paul Anderson; he made a note of the name with a question mark beside it. The fourth man he didn't know, so he was listed as "player 2". The total now stood at seventeen that he knew for certain – it was possible that there had been other bodies at the house before he began the watch – maybe Lynch was right.

Within a minute the man who could have been Paul Anderson – no – there was no doubt, it was, came out of the house and drove his car inside the barn along with the Escort and the Transit van. Walsh scored out the question mark beside Anderson's name while he manoeuvred the car into the barn. Anderson came out of the barn closed the doors and went back into the farmhouse. Walsh checked his watch again, twenty twelve. Time enough to rehearse the broadcast to thirteen at twenty-one hundred.

"We were beginnin' to think you boys weren't comin'."

"Ah come on, sure you know the best things are worth waitin' for Joe. Besides we had a little bother with the Brits."

"Checkpoint?"

"Aye, the fuckers got us just outside Killylea. All the usual hassles, but like you told us, we were clean, so they had to let us go."

"Now that you boys are here we can get down to business. Has everyone got a seat?"

There were nods and words of assent from around the room. Joe Mullan went to the dresser and lifted a copy of a newspaper from it. He turned to face the men sitting in the kitchen and held it up.

"How many of you have seen this?"

Mullan held the paper out and made sure that everyone got a good look at the front page. This time there were fewer comments from the group. The Starry Plough was the monthly journal of the Irish Republican Socialist Party, the political wing of the Irish National Liberation Army.

"Well it seems the INLA think they can call this turf their own – that we count for fuck all."

That did it – there were voices raised in anger making some colourful suggestions as to what should be done with the INLA's leadership. Sean McNellis stood up and spoke for everyone.

"I think a few boys should get their kneecaps done – just to give them the idea."

"Aye well, maybe so Sean, but we were thinkin' of somethin' a bit more permanent. The South Armagh Brigade will not have a bunch of hoods like the INLA dictatin' to us. They are gettin' too big for their boots, so we're goin' to get rid of them."

"Joe do you mean we're goin' to start killin' republicans? For fuck's sake that means we're no better than the Brits."

"That's not what I said Sean, but if they push us too hard that's their lookout."

"Joe this is all wrong. Jesus, Seamus tell your brother this isn't the way. Fellas come on. You know this is wrong."

No-one spoke in agreement with McNellis and it was clear to him that he had gone against the view of the brigade as a whole. The meeting was looking less like a strategy session and more like a witch-hunt by the minute. McNellis tried to smooth things over.

"Joe look it's just how I see things, I didn't mean nothin' by it."

"That's a good point Sean, just how do you see things?"

"How d'you mean?"

"Just whose side are you on Sean?"

"I still don't know what you mean Joe?"

The atmosphere in the room had changed – in the space of a couple of minutes it had gone from one of togetherness to that of persecution. McNellis was in trouble and he knew it.

"Maybe this'll help – how well do you know Dominic McGlinchey?"

He almost laughed with relief, this he could explain.

"He used to go out with Maura's sister; so I met him a few times round at her house."

"And that's it?"

"Joe are you sayin' that because I've met McGlinchey once or twice that I'm goin' over to the INLA?"

"You were soundin' a wee bit soft Sean."

"Soft! I was sayin' we should knee-cap the bastards – since when was that soft?"

"OK Sean calm down."

"Calm down Joe? What were you goin' to do if I didn't pass your little test? So I've met McGlinchey, big fuckin' deal. Just remember, my old man was lifted by the RUC in the fifties when I was a kid. My family has always been committed to the struggle and it'll stay that way."

"You've made your point Sean, now sit down."

A very relieved Sean McNellis resumed his seat; for one awful minute he thought he had really been in trouble.

"Right fellas, we need to talk over our approach to the INLA and then we're goin' to look at our way forward. South Armagh Brigade has got to take the fight to the Brits and to do that we have made some contacts who'll help."

Enda McHugh raised his hand and voiced everyone's curiosity.

"Who might these contacts be Joe?"

"You'll all see when McGrillen and O'Donnell get here."

The first members of the team to arrive at Glaslough were John Davison's group. Davison drove straight to the cutting and three men waited in the Landrover until Mathieson came out of the woods. He gave them directions to O'Brien's location and then walked back to the BMW and Colquhoun.

Colquhoun was sitting in the driver's seat listening to the radio when Mathieson opened the passenger door and got in.

"Davison, Todd and Hart are here. One of them will stay with their vehicle and give directions to the rest of the team as they arrive. You need to be calling in soon, it's five to nine."

"The check-in time is nine-thirty, but yeah, I'll need to find a telephone to make my call from."

"There's a kiosk in the village. I gave it the once-over when you were in the post office the other day and it's working – leastways it was then."

"I'll use it then. Did you talk things over with O'Brien?"

"Aye, he's taking my place. He was feeling pretty low about it but we talked it over and I'd say he's OK. So what did you do to kill the time?"

"Listened to the radio, read the papers, about half six I went down to the lake and watched the ducks, and you know what?" Mathieson shrugged, "All I could bloody think of was this job. I'll tell you this Jim I'll be glad when it's all over."

"Running things has its low points."

"Yeah, like seeing that your right hand man is more interested in chasing skirt."

"Fair's fair John; you said that was history."

"Christ knows, maybe you're right – live each day as if it were your last and all that."

"John it's like I said to Mike – stop thinking so much and stop asking questions – there'll be no time for that come showtime – you'll be too busy, we'll all be too busy. We can think about it afterwards and even then it's better not to."

Walsh had been going over the details of his report – he'd decided not to include full names, the thought of having to spell some of them for the RO's benefit was too big a pain and a waste of time anyway, so it was just going to be the numbers. He rolled onto his right-hand side and pulled the pack level with his chest. He eased the small Clansman set out, slipped his earpiece over his head, put the throat mike around his neck and turned the set on. He looked at his watch to see that it was twenty-one oh two – he reckoned the green RO back at XMG was beginning to sweat – time to call in.

"Hello, golf tango, this is Vigilant, message, over."

The reply came straight away – somebody was wide awake.

"Golf tango, send, over."

"Vigilant, have seventeen, repeat, one seven definites on site. Fourteen, repeat, one four positive india delta, one probable and two unknowns, over."

"Golf tango, seventeen, one seven definites confirmed, over."

"Vigilant, target practical, advise go, I say again go, out."

Harry Lynch sat in his office doodling on the A4 pad lying on the desk in front of him; time was passing at a snail's pace – God but he hated waiting. He was going to check the desk clock once again when the phone rang, no pause this time, he snatched the handset from the cradle.

"Yes?"

"This is green thirteen for Vigilant, seventeen definites, target practical, go, go, go."

"Received."

That was that then, the job was on, all he needed now was Colquhoun to check in for confirmation, and when he got that call he'd contact his other team in Belfast to give the movement order. After that it would be back to waiting.

Mathieson swapped places with Colquhoun so he could drive. At nine twenty they left the church car-park and set off on the short journey into Glaslough village. The phone box was just across the street from the post office which was where Mathieson parked the car. They sat for a few minutes surveying the area; Colquhoun was conscious of the possibility of running into someone who had seen him on Tuesday and the potential difficulty such a meeting could create. He needn't have worried – there wasn't a person to be seen on the street. Just before nine thirty he turned to Mathieson, nodded and got out of the car. Happily the "Telefon" kiosk hadn't suffered from the misuse that he had encountered in the phone-box in Armagh. He took a handful of change from his trouser pocket, emptied it onto the shelf, and carefully began to dial the London number including the international code that was necessary when calling from the Republic of Ireland. He was in luck the call went through on the first attempt; it was answered on the third ring, and he began pushing change into the slot.

"Yes?"

"This is Colquhoun. What's the news?"

"The job is on. The watcher reports seventeen, repeat one seven definites. Any problems at your end?"

"None."

"Then you'd better get moving. Happy hunting."

Before he could reply the connection was broken. He scooped up his unused change and returned to the car.

"Well?"

"It's on. Let's go to the railway cutting and see who else has turned up."

When Mathieson brought the BMW to the end of the access track his first thought was that he'd taken the wrong turn – the open space was now occupied by four other vehicles – a Cortina, a Granada estate, a Cavalier and a Landrover – everyone had arrived in the interval. He eased the beemer alongside the Granada, turned off and then both men got out. Davison jogged over from the Landrover to join them.

"What's the news boss?"

"It's a go, so you'd better get up the track and close that gate. Have you got the padlock and chain?"

"Right here."

Davison tapped the right hand pocket of his waterproof jacket.

"Good. When you've done that join the rest of us at the site, OK?"

"Yes boss."

Davison made his way up the track to the gate while Colquhoun and Mathieson walked to the wood on the north side of the cutting. Thankfully there wasn't much cloud cover so even though the light was fading rapidly it was still bright for the end of March. Colquhoun hoped that all the preparatory work on the excavation site had been completed – the less work that had to be done by torchlight the better.

When they got to the site they spotted five of the team poised with shovels; the rest of the men were spread out through the surrounding trees. Colquhoun looked to the diggers.

"OK it's on. Get your gloves on and you can start digging. The rest of you gather round."

Walsh had re-packed the Clansman set and even though he had made his report he was maintaining his vigil. There had been no movement around the farmhouse since he had called in but one thing had changed – the lights had been switched on inside which allowed him a limited view of the interior. From what little he could see they were having their meeting in the kitchen. The only other interior light he'd seen had been upstairs in the room that the plans, that had been acquired last week, indicated as the upstairs toilet – all the tea they had undoubtedly been drinking was obviously taking it's toll. No sooner had he thought about the toilet than he realised that he could use one himself. He had limited his fluid intake throughout the day but he still needed to take a leak. He looked at his watch – twenty-one fifty-five – he could wait until it was completely dark and then crawl out of the hide.

By twenty-two fifteen it was dark enough but as he was about to exit the hide some movement in the farmyard caught his eye – Christ, surely the heroes couldn't have arrived that early? He took a hard look at the yard – no, there were only four bodies that he could see picked out by the light shining from the scullery window. One of them stepped up to the back door and knocked. A few seconds passed and it was opened so that the four figures could move inside. That now gave him a total of twenty-one definites. He marked the time and the number in his notebook; even if the figures were something of a mess on the page his memory was more than up to the task of giving an exhaustive report. He looked at the farmhouse for another five minutes and decided it was safe for him to leave the hide. He slowly backed out and once in the clear he moved to the left keeping the old wall between himself and the farmhouse. Once again, making sure that he was unobserved, he relieved himself. He was sure a headshrinker would have something to say about it but there was no denying the very real pleasure in taking a much needed piss.

All eyes were on the two men who had come with Joe McGrillen and Peter O'Donnell. Of the brigade already assembled only the Mullan brothers knew who they were. Joe Mullan shook hands with the men, then turned to face the group.

"I told you that we had made some new contacts who would help us against the Brits – well here they are – Gerhardt Hoss and Jochen Pfilzgauer."

Each man stepped forward as his name was mentioned and gave a somewhat exaggerated bow. Hoss was the taller of the two, of a lean build with sandy coloured hair cut very short. Pfilzgauer by comparison was thickset with dark brown hair also cut very short. They both had fixed expressions which removed any question of their possessing a sense of humour – both men were strictly business.

"Where in under God's name did you find them Joe?"

Before Mullan could answer Hoss stepped forward and fixed a contemptuous glare on Jonjo MacTeer.

"You will find that my English is more than up to the task of communicating with you, which is no doubt more than can be said of your German. As for where Joseph found us it was the other way around. We met in Libya two years ago when we were training various organisations under Qaddafi's patronage."

"God in Heaven! Would you ever listen to him! Alright, take it easy Fritzie, I didn't mean any fuckin' harm, it's just my way."

Jonjo obviously thought that his effort at humour would calm things; he had raised several smirks amongst his friends, but he hadn't bargained on the Germans.

"You are ill-disciplined with no respect for authority. You are also stupid – making fun of someone you have no experience of. You behave like a child...."

Jonjo was out of his seat and tried to push his way through the men in front of him to lay his hands on Hoss. When it was clear that his path was blocked he made do with a verbal assault.

"You hold on! Just who the fuck do you think you are? You come here and start talkin' down to us – well fuck you! We don't need no help from some smart-arse German bastard...."

"Jonjo shut up and sit down before that big mouth of yours gets you into more trouble than you can handle. Gerhardt please pay him no mind; my baby cousin isn't too bright, he'll do as he's told, won't you Jonjo?"

"Fuck it Joe, we don't need their help. We've done OK up to now."

Hoss shook his head with apparent sadness and turned to Mullan.

"Jochen and I over-estimated you Joseph; a mistake we won't make again. We will leave as soon as possible."

"Now hold on a minute Gerhardt. Jonjo, no word of a lie, if you don't shut up I'll do for you, you stupid wee fucker – you don't have a clue what our friends here can do for us. Francie keep a gag on that brother of yours, and the rest of you listen, these boys know what they're talkin' about. Gerhardt tell us what you can do to make us the best."

Pfilzgauer, who had said nothing, looked around the room and wondered how these men had lasted in their chosen field for so long. Professionals they were not – more like a bunch of schoolboys – but they could be if they started listening to experienced advice. Hoss leaned on the dresser and began his address.

"Gentlemen we are here to teach you and to advise you. You will learn new tactics and methods. You will receive training in the use of firearms, explosives and communications equipment. We will show you how to maximize the effects of your actions. The British will come to fear you like no other group in Ireland because you will be the most professional, the most ruthless, the most dedicated group in Ireland. Where you have been, to borrow a phrase from Mr. Jonjo, "OK up to now", you will become the best."

Ten minutes careful excavation uncovered the blue water butt which was lifted clear of the hole and stood on end beside a poncho that had been spread out to act as a groundsheet. Colquhoun reached into the inside pocket of his jacket and retrieved the Brian Sampson knife which he now used to cut the seal on the container. The first things he took from the water butt were small plastic wrapped packets which he placed on the poncho.

"You all know your numbers so help yourselves", each man stepped forward and took a numbered package, "Jim come here and give me a hand with these would you."

Mathieson stood beside Colquhoun who passed him the remainder of the kit which he then laid out on the poncho – six L34A1s with three magazines apiece – four model 61 Skorpions with four magazines apiece – ten weapons in all. There were also two boxes of spare rounds for the L34A1s and the Skorpions. L34A1 was the British Army designation for the Patchett/Sterling Mark 5 sub-machine gun manufactured at Dagenham; it differed from the standard L2A3 Sterling because of its integral suppressor. The suppressor added six inches to the overall length of the weapon but reduced the noise level very significantly – and it didn't need special 9mm ammunition to do it – making the L34A1 one of the best so-called silenced weapons in the business. One of the six Sterlings had a piece of polystyrene taped on top of the barrel. Martin Bradley drew his own knife, a SOG, and cut the tape. He lifted the protective cover off and inspected the modification, making sure that it was secure. Colquhoun picked up a Skorpion, slung it across his chest and tapped Bradley on the shoulder.

"You know you gave our armourer a real nightmare with that."

"Well it looks OK if you ask me. You should have seen the guy's face at Litton's when I picked it up. You'd have thought I was stealing it."

"You mean this isn't issued kit?"

"Hell no. We were down in Arizona checking out their latest toys when I saw this one. It's brand new. You might say this is the first field test. Care to try it?"

Colquhoun took the weapon from Bradley and un-clipped the shoulder stock that was folded under the suppressor. Once he had locked the stock open he switched on the image intensifier and shouldered the weapon bringing the rubber eyepiece to his right eye. The position of the night-sight on the mount that had been brazed to the suppressor was for a taller man with a longer reach but there was no denying the effectiveness of the sight. Night didn't quite become day but the men of the team were easily identifiable as they moved amongst the trees. Colquhoun turned the sight off and returned the weapon to Bradley.

"Nice piece of kit, but to be honest I hope you don't get to use it in anger – you lads are here as observers."

"I won't use it unless I have to. Tell me this though, are you guys seriously going inside with those toys?"

"These toys would give you a very nasty surprise believe me. Don't knock it 'til you've tried it."

The model 61 was a little more exotic coming from the Ceska Zbrojovka plant at Brno in Czechoslovakia. It was a lot smaller and lighter than the Sterling, even with the suppressor that screwed onto the specially threaded barrel. But it wasn't just the dimensions that differed – the Skorpion was also of a different calibre – .32ACP as opposed to 9mm. The lighter round made the model 61 easier to control for a weapon of its size – controllability and size that made it ideal for work in confined spaces.

"OK listen up, we're going to have a weapons check before we set out – so let's get this tub back in the hole."

Mathieson helped Colquhoun place the water butt back in the hole only this time they left it upright. Weapons were collected and magazines slotted in place. Each shooter stepped forward, cocked their weapon and then placing their Sterling or Skorpion in the container they fired a short burst; the butt acted as a catcher for the empty cases as they were ejected so there was no need to scrabble around in the dark looking for spent brass. Satisfied with the function of their weapons the men applied safety catches and removed magazines which they topped up with the spare rounds that were in the two boxes Mathieson had laid on the poncho.

"Right I want that barrel re-buried and the surface cammed up, nothing fancy, we haven't got time anyway. Everyone happy?"

"One problem boss."

"OK Marcus let's hear it."

"It's Col's knee. He knackered it the other day and I don't think it's up to the mark."

Lauder stepped forward showing no signs of a limp but plenty of anger.

"Marcus there's fuck all wrong with my knee. There was no need for you to bring it up. If I had a problem believe me I'd have mentioned it."

"Look Col I was only doing my job. If you reckon it's alright, fine, just let me give it a going over. I can strap it up if necessary."

"If Marcus wants a look go along with it Col, understood?"

"Yes boss."

"OK I want you to complete your personal kit checks and I want you to check over your allotted partners for the usual creaks and rattles, and make sure your face camo is adequate. It's twenty-two twenty-five, we go in ten."

The five men who had dug up the water butt made short work of recovering it. The camouflage on the surface was not important as this site wouldn't be used again, but they made a reasonable job of disguising the worst of the digging marks. A brief scrutiny by filtered torchlight showed their work to be adequate.

Pearson shrugged off his small rucksack, undid the straps and reached inside for his first aid kit, while Lauder dropped his trousers. Pearson ran his hands over both knees and gave special attention to the left, which he gently twisted from side to side. Lauder's sharp intake of breath told him all that he needed to know.

"Col it's causing you too much pain mate. You're not going."

"Marcus just strap it up and I'll be fine."

Pearson opened his kit and brought out a roll of crepe bandage which he began to wrap around Lauder's thigh, he then brought it down around the knee-cap and around the lower leg, pinning it when he had finished.

"Just remember that this was your call. I've given you the best advice I can and you've ignored it."

"Just pack your kit Marcus, it's time we were going."

The men assembled in their pre-assigned groups making ready to go; Colquhoun gave the area one last sweep and when he was satisfied he signalled the first stick of four men to move out. Alan Scott took the lead as they set off taking an easterly heading. The next group followed them two minutes later. Scott's group were scheduled to stop at twenty-two fifty; the next teams would rendezvous with his and then the movement would begin again at twenty-three hundred. The distance they had to cover was just under a mile and a quarter and it would take the best part of an hour and a half to cover it; speed was not of the essence, care and consideration were. The final stick of four men left the clearing right on time at twenty-two forty-one with Jim Mathieson being the last man out.

Walsh was back in the hide looking down at the Mullan farm where nothing was happening. Even his view into the kitchen had gone – someone had pulled the curtains. The estimated time for the heroes to show up was midnight to oh oh fifteen which gave him about an hour to kill. Not for the first time he vowed never again, no more watching, no more cramp, no more eating cold food that tasted bloody awful and no more pissing in bottles when the luxury of an excursion was unavailable. They could find somebody younger, somebody keen and most importantly somebody stupid enough to volunteer for the job. He thought of his dad's advice when he had learned of his son's chosen profession, "don't volunteer for anything". A lot of attention he'd paid to that particular gem of wisdom when he was younger – he knew better now – this was definitely the last time.

Ian Walsh may have been wishing for an end to his watcher duties, but for Karen Aiken this was the last field job she would undertake; she'd been marked for greater things and after this one she would take her promotion and the desk that went with it. In the meantime she waited by her phone for the call that she'd been expecting from Harry Lynch. The rest of her team were waiting in the ready room. Eddie Fairbairn and Stan Hogg had arrived with the tanker from RAF Aldergrove about an hour ago, bringing the compliment up to the full twelve including herself.

She'd known about her promotion for three weeks and was looking forward to the new responsibilities. She was also looking forward to the chance to show a somewhat more feminine side than her present job allowed; she'd let her blonde hair grow out of its practical but boring page-boy, she'd let her nails grow and spoil herself to a manicure and she'd start dressing the way she wanted to rather than the way field jobs dictated. With a bit of effort people would notice that under the hard-nosed facade was an attractive woman in her early thirties. The facade would have this one last outing, one last mess to clean up.

At quarter past eleven Harry Lynch dialled the number in Belfast. Not surprisingly it was answered on the first ring.

"Yes?"

"Calm yourself Karen, it's Lynch. It's a go. Get your team on the road and be ready to start work no sooner than oh one and no later than oh one thirty."

"Understood."

"Any problems?"

"None."

"Good. Just make sure that you and yours get the house spotless. I expect nothing but your usual best."

"And you'll get it."

Lynch hung up. A good girl that Aiken, a pity that they would be losing her talents in the field but her promotion had come through and there was little he could do to stop it.

Aiken walked from her office to the stairwell and made her way down to the ready room. As she came through the double doors Jenny Ellison, the team's number two, was just finishing the breakdown of duties.

"…So we're clear on the team make up – team one, Beatty, Fairbairn, Hogg and Priestly on vehicles. Team two, Ballard, Chambers, Gray and Ramsey on cleaning. Team three, Aiken, Laing, Rowan and me on search and collection. Ian Walsh should be joining us sometime, so pay attention to him as he may have actually seen something useful up on the hill. Any questions?"

Phil Priestly put his hand in the air and responded to Ellison's nod.

"What about the vehicles on site, who's driving what?"

"We'll deal with that on site. Walsh should have a list of vehicles so he'll probably be doing the allocations – we'll talk to him when we see him."

Aiken made her way to the front of the room and began to unpin the farmhouse floorplan from the board, it would go into her office safe before they left. When she had folded it and placed it under her arm she turned to face her team.

"OK girls and boys we're on – time to go time. Eddie, you and Stan are in the tanker as before", there were groans from the rest of the team, "Yeah I know, the rest of us are squeezed in the van."

The van was something of a standing joke – a 1973 Commer that had seen better days. Like Aiken this was to be its last outing, she had made sure that a new vehicle would be purchased for the team, a sort of farewell gift.

"We need to be on site at oh one thirty latest so get your Marigolds and let's go."

Alan Scott had just set out on the third leg of the insertion. The four groups had moved out of the woods, glad to be clear of the tangle of undergrowth. The cloud cover was broken and a westerly breeze was blowing at about 5 miles an hour. The half moon was periodically covered by passing clouds so what light it provided was not constant, causing no great visibility problems for the team. Best of all it was dry.

Scott was following an easterly route along the railway cutting which was relatively clear of thick undergrowth and planted with trees on both sides. The light breeze sighing through the branches was distracting him; making him hear things that may or may not have been real. He stopped the forward movement of his group again with a raised right hand and a clenched fist. The other three members came to a halt and slowly crouched in the bracken continuing to scan the surroundings for any signs that they were under surveillance. David Armstrong was the last man in the group and when he stopped he turned to face in the direction of the oncoming second group, he would pass on the signal to halt to their lead man, and so the whole team would be made aware of the halt. For the third time since they had set out Scott listened intently for any noise that seemed out of place. Nothing, not a thing, he'd listened for nearly two minutes and all there was to hear was the wind in the trees.

He set off once more, slowly picking his way through the bracken and long grass, being careful not to break any stems that might attract the wrong sort of attention in days to come. At twenty-three thirty-seven Scott stepped over the border from the Republic into Northern Ireland and was totally unaware that he had done so; the border wasn't marked with a fence or signs, it was just a line on the map.

"…Anti-personnel attacks such as the one in September of last year must be planned with great attention to detail. The reason that you lost a volunteer was the recklessness with which you prosecuted the attack. The location was not in your favour and the numerical superiority of the opposition does not even seem to have been considered. Songs may be written about your heroism but you will be dead, and that is not the point of your fight against the British."

Hoss had made his address without notes. He had spoken at great length on the training they would receive and on the lessons to be learned from past successes and failures. He had answered all the questions that had been put to him no matter how obscure. Jonjo MacTeer's outburst was forgotten – the German's professionalism had won over any possible dissenters, even MacTeer himself was impressed with the depth of knowledge Hoss possessed about the struggle.

Pfilzgauer had listened patiently hoping to improve his English but there had been times when he had got lost in the specifics of what Hoss was saying, and as for the standard of English spoken by the men in front of him, well it would take some time to get to grips with it. Right now he wanted a coffee.

"*Ich mochte eine tasse kaffee, bitte.*"

"In English, Jochen."

Pfilzgauer sighed deeply and composed his thoughts from German into English.

"I want a cup of coffee please. *Haben sie…entschuldigen sie bitte.* I am sorry my English is not… *sehr…* very… good. Joseph I am… also… hungry."

"You should have said. Gerhardt we'll take a break and get Jochen and you somethin' to eat. How does a bacon sandwich sound?"

"Sounds good. What do you think Jochen?"

"*Was ist* 'bacon'?"

"*Der Speck.*"

"Oh I understand. Yes, that is very good, thank you."

"Right then we'll get you fellas a sandwich and some coffee. Padraig give us a hand here would you."

The atmosphere in the kitchen lightened with the end of the German's lecture. Cigarettes were lit and Enda McHugh pulled a bottle of Bushmills from the hold-all he'd brought in from the car. Glasses were taken from the dresser and generous measures of whiskey were poured and handed to those as wanted them. The talk centred around the arrival of the Germans and the changes they would bring to the Brigade. Out in the scullery Padraig was busy frying bacon on the gas cooker while Joe was getting some advice from Gerhardt.

"It's just that in the last year or so these buggers from the INLA have been pushin' us pretty hard. We were thinkin' of teachin' them a lesson. What d'you reckon?"

"My experience of in-fighting tells me you must be totally ruthless. The INLA are threatening your power and that cannot be. My advice Joseph would be to remove the problem."

"You mean kill them don't you?"

"Not necessarily all Joseph. When faced with two options I feel many of them will choose to stop rather than die. From what I know of the INLA they make political statements but are in reality criminals, is this not so?"

"We know that they're into drugs that's for sure."

"There is your excuse – the protection of your community from drugs and the dealers."

"We'll have to see what the brigade thinks."

"You are the commander Joseph, give an order."

"That's not how we do things."

"Then you will not win. You must have strong leadership. You must not be afraid of your authority and you must not allow any challenges to it."

Padraig had finished making the sandwiches and was waiting for the kettle to boil so that he could make coffee. Hoss opened the back door and called to Pfilzgauer who had been outside having a smoke.

"*Komm hier,* Jochen."

"*Ja, ja.*"

He pinched out his cigarette, dropping the butt in one of the bins beside the two steps that led up to the door; then he went inside gratefully accepting the bacon sandwich that Padraig offered him.

Walsh made another entry in his notebook at twenty-three fifty. A lone figure had come outside and lit a cigarette. Not much excitement in that, but the casual nature of the action betrayed the fact that the men inside felt secure. The loner paced about the yard while he smoked his cigarette – Walsh was glad to see that time was passing slowly for someone else. The back door opened revealing a tall man with blonde hair who called to the smoker, who pinched out his cigarette, throwing the butt in the bin before going inside. Why didn't he just throw the butt away or grind it under foot? That struck Walsh as odd so he made a note of it, the act probably meant nothing but he knew the importance of recording every detail. He checked his watch so he could note the time the man went back inside – twenty-three fifty-four – the heroes would be here soon, so he moved his area of scrutiny away from the farmhouse to the outbuildings and the immediate fields.

Alan Scott had begun the fourth and final leg of the walk in at twenty-three fifty. The team had moved away from the railway cutting and was now skirting around the edge of an open field. This was potentially the most risky section of their insertion – the last 450 yards brought them close to the only neighbouring property to the Mullan farm. Fortunately the team was able to stay in the shadow cast by the hedgerow so their visibility was not a great concern. Smell was, however, a possible danger as the breeze which was still blowing from the west could carry their scent and alert any dog or dogs there might be on the farm.

Scott looked closely at the farmhouse to his right and noted that there were no lights obvious on the ground floor with only one showing dimly upstairs. As his stick passed by the house there was no alerting bark from any dog so all was well. He moved on coming to a gate in the corner of the field which opened out onto the access track to the Mullan farm. Again he brought his stick to a halt while he surveyed the stretch of the track he could see. Colquhoun had been given no indication as to any sentries when he had called in, but that didn't rule out the possibility. Scott allowed two minutes to pass without any sign of opposition before climbing the gate. His group waited until he signalled all clear and moved across the track to the gate on the far side. This one was open but rather than accept the invitation to walk through it he crouched beside the gate post and ran his left hand up and down the gap to see if there was any sort of a line attached to a booby-trap. Finding nothing he ran his hand along its underside to make sure there was no tripping device attached here. Again he found nothing, leaving him with just one more check to make – the hinged side of the gate. It too was clear so he gently eased it open just far enough to allow him passage. Before he went through the gate he signalled to the next man to follow. The ground led gently uphill to the cluster of farm buildings which were partially obscured by a small stand of trees. Scott moved along the line of the hedge with the rest of the team strung out behind him. As he led them up the slope to Lower Hill Farm midnight came and went – it was Saturday 24th March.

* * *

By oh oh oh seven Scott was in place beside the barn that was on the north-western side of the farmhouse. He could see movement inside what the plans had referred to as the scullery. The rest of the team joined him over the next five minutes. Backpacks were opened and the plastic bags that each man had recovered when the water butt had been excavated were unsealed and the dark grey overalls removed. Making sure that the location was secure, the team put them on. Marcus Pearson distributed latex surgeons gloves, two pairs to a man, which they donned making sure that the cuffs of the overalls were covered. Tape was passed around so that the gloves could be fixed in place. The last thing the team members did was to pull their balaclavas into place, giving them a sinister anonymity. The backpacks that each man had carried in from Glaslough were piled up against the barn wall – they would be collected later. Colquhoun looked about the team to satisfy himself that they were all ready. As he did so, he noticed Mathieson fiddling with something around his neck, and his curiosity got the better of him.

"What the hell are you doing Jim?"

"I've twisted the frigging lanyard."

"Lanyard on what?"

"My stopwatch, I want to get a time on this."

"Take it off if it's a problem; there are more important things to worry about after all."

"There are?"

"You're too casual for your own good, you know that?"

"I'll survive. You worry too much John."

At oh oh seventeen he dispersed the team to their pre-assigned locations with the final instruction that the entry team would be going in at oh oh forty latest; nonetheless everyone was to be ready for the original schedule. Those men covering the south and west walls of the farmhouse quickly moved through the outbuildings giving them a cursory search. Colquhoun would have liked more time but he just didn't have it. Unless a nasty surprise was found in the barn or the livestock houses they would all be in position in five to ten minutes. If something unprepared for did crop up those involved would have to wing it and do their best. There was no way to plan for the X factor and he hated that fact. Maybe Mathieson was right – better not to waste time stressing yourself out about matters over which you had no control.

As Walsh looked down on the farm he had to admit that the heroes were damn good. He had been looking intently from midnight onwards and with the time now just after twenty past he had only seen three men as they went about the task of securing the outbuildings. Try as he might he couldn't spot the rest of the team as they took station around the farmhouse. Walsh was only a spectator but the tension he felt at that moment was nearly intolerable – God alone knew what it was like for the men around the farmhouse down below. Showtime was scheduled for oh oh thirty, it was now just a matter of hurry up and wait, but that was easier said than done.

Colquhoun had joined Scott along with Mathieson and Hart behind the cover of the wall that ran from the barn down to the slurry storage pit. The four men were now only fourteen or fifteen yards from the farmhouse's back door. They had been in position for five minutes yet the time was passing so slowly they all felt as if they had been there for an hour. The entry that had been planned was standard but lacked one element in Colquhoun's mind – surprise. The difficulty was how to develop that element without upsetting the plans of the rest of the team securing the perimeter. Time was not on their side, come twenty to they would go with the original plan, it had worked before and it would work this time. Scott maintained the watch on the door while the other three checked their weapons in preparation for the entry. Mathieson leaned in close to Colquhoun and Hart and beckoned them to come closer still so he could whisper to them.

"You know there was a battle near here once."

Neither of the men were aware of it, Hart shrugged and Colquhoun voiced his lack of interest.

"I couldn't care less – if a bunch of Micks wanted to slaughter themselves so what."

"That's just the point John, it wasn't a bunch of Micks, well it was actually, but they hammered a Scots army."

"And when was this?"

"June 5th 1646, the battle of Benburb, during the Great Irish Rebellion."

"Three hundred and thirty years ago! What possible relevance has that to us for God's sake?"

"We're all Scots – the entry team – it seems like payback, that's what I was thinking anyway. There were three thousand dead Scots on the field and the Irish killed a lot more afterwards as they attempted to withdraw."

"So this is going to be revenge for you is it Jim?"

It was Mathieson's turn to shrug.

"Why not John, I can think of worse reasons."

Hoss and Pfilzgauer had finished their sandwiches and were back in the kitchen leaning against the dresser, listening to Joe Mullan as he told the Brigade members of his decision regarding the INLA.

"It's simple boys, we're goin' to put the INLA out of business and no-one will point the finger at us for doin' it. And here's why – drugs. We put it about that they're dealin' drugs and I tell you we might as well be given permission to do it."

Sean McNellis shifted in his seat but a look from Mullan kept his mouth shut.

"I know some of you might not like goin' after these fellas but they're makin' a play for South Armagh and that can't happen. So what I want is reports on the likes of McGlinchey, O'Hara and Gorman. You know who they are and where they live so you'll be able to get good hard info about them. This will be our first job, then we'll take them out. This won't involve everyone so what I'm plannin' is that those of you not targetin' the INLA members will be workin' with Gerhardt and Jochen over the border. Once the INLA have gone then we can go after the Brits like never before. You boys know who's best amongst you for the INLA work so sort it out between yourselves."

Mullan turned from the Brigade to see Hoss nod at him in appreciation of his new found resolve. The conversation amongst the men of the Brigade was centring on the responsibility for surveillance and would keep them busy for some time.

"Padraig if you're not doin' anythin' would you go out and get some slack in for the range and then stoke it up for the night."

Padraig got up from his chair reluctantly and went out to the scullery to discover that he would need to go to the coal house for fuel as the buckets were nearly empty. As he opened the back door he wondered if he wouldn't be better off back at his ma's but dismissed the thought almost as soon as it had entered his head – his ma was a dreadful nag and besides he liked the farm even if Joe and Seamus could be real pains in the arse at times.

The latch on the back door made a loud snapping noise as Padraig opened it. The entry team behind the wall fell silent immediately. Scott maintained his surveillance through the gap in the wall as Padraig crossed the yard to the outbuildings. Once he had entered the coal house Scott turned to Colquhoun for guidance.

"We take him – he's our key. We'll need a gag. Now let's move."

The four men came out from behind the wall covering the back door to the farmhouse as they went. From inside the coal house came the noise of a shovel scraping into a pile of slack. Padraig had not bothered to turn the light on, so used was he to the task, meaning there would be no awkward shadows to hinder their entry. Colquhoun took the briefest of looks through the doorway; Padraig had his back to the door and was focused on the task of filling his buckets. When they moved, they moved deliberately not at a blinding pace.

Padraig had finished filling the second bucket and had just pushed the shovel into the pile of slack when the gloved hand fixed across his mouth. His first thought was that someone was messing about, but the pressure of the index finger under his nose was far from funny. If that was bad the words that were whispered in his right ear made sure that this was no joke.

"Behave yourself or you're dead."

As the words were spoken a cold hard object was pressed into the side of his neck slightly below and behind his right ear. The figure of a man appeared in front of him and the voice behind him whispered once more.

"My friend is going to tape your mouth. Call for help and you're dead; do as I say and you'll continue to live."

The hand relaxed slightly as the other man stepped forward to apply the tape to his mouth. Once the gag was complete the hand moved to the nape of his neck where it reapplied the pressure. They need not have worried about his calling for help – he'd never been so scared in all his life. His hands, which had been hanging useless by his sides, were pulled behind him and tied; once that was done any chance of escape was gone. The only decision that he was capable of making was to follow the whispering man's orders to the letter, if he did that maybe he'd be OK.

So far so good. The youngster had followed instructions and offered no resistance. Colquhoun tightened his grip on Padraig's neck, pressed the Skorpion that little bit harder and whispered once more.

"We're all going for a walk back to the house. It's not you we want, so once we're inside you'll be pushed out of the way. Stay down and don't move. If you move you know what'll happen."

Hart slung his Skorpion across his chest and lifted the two buckets of slack. Scott looked from the doorway to the house; there were no signs of life in the scullery, no tell-tale movement of shadow in the light pattern that lay on the ground below the window; it was clear for them to go. Scott went first followed by Hart, next came Colquhoun and Padraig with Mathieson bringing up the rear. When they got to the steps Hart put the buckets down and lifted the latch.

Joe Mullan heard the latch of the back door and the scrape of the buckets as Padraig lifted them from the step. Next he heard them being put down as Padraig turned to close the door. Again the scrape as a galvanized bucket was lifted from the floor in the scullery. He'd heard it all a hundred times before so he turned his attention to the Brigade members in front of him.

"OK boys, you must've reached a decision on who's doin' what."

Gerard O'Neill was about to tell Mullan what had been decided when the kitchen door opened.

The entry team accessed the scullery as quickly and as quietly as they could, taking their positions behind the door that led into the kitchen. Hart put down his buckets of slack and closed the back door. To maintain the illusion of normality he lifted one of them making sure that the effort would be clearly audible to the men in the kitchen. Colquhoun positioned Padraig in front of the door leaving enough room for him to reach around from behind to get at the doorknob. Weapons were made ready, Colquhoun looked at each member of the team and nodded once, they nodded in reply and then he opened the door.

The noises of buckets scraping on the floor had alerted no-one; the deliberations over the up-coming surveillance jobs had held the Brigade's attention. The opening kitchen door in no way seemed out of place so no-one looked. As young Mullan went through the door Mathieson started his stopwatch. As Colquhoun got his first glimpse of the room he couldn't believe the total lack of concern from the men in the kitchen as he pushed Padraig forward. Somebody looked toward the door and saw that all was not well – the tape on Padraig's face and the figure coming behind him – no, figures coming behind him – it was very wrong, and then all Hell broke loose. It was twelve thirty-nine.

If Padraig expected to live through the assault on the Mullan farmhouse he was wrong; Colquhoun wasn't prepared to risk an adrenaline surge from the youngster with the ensuing explosion of violence in an attempt at self-preservation, so the first three rounds fired went into the back of the young man's head. The lifeless body dropped to the floor and still nobody in the kitchen moved; this was the stuff of nightmare – instant paralysis of limbs, of vocal chords – nothing worked. Scott took station beside Colquhoun to the right of the door with Mathieson and Hart moving to the left; when they were in position they began to open fire at the men closest to them.

Hoss and Pfilzgauer, for all their training, only managed to move from their place at the dresser a matter of five or six feet before they took hits in the upper chest, neck and face. The only true professionals in the room, the only possible opposition to the hooded men and they were amongst the first to die. Joe Mullan stood by the dresser and watched as Hoss and Pfilzgauer fell in front of him; understanding replaced his disbelief and he too moved toward the hooded men. He tried to roar his defiance but the best he could manage was a strangulated scream which was cut short by a three round burst from Scott. Mullan's body fell on top of Pfilzgauer's. They had at least tried to fight – it was clear to all the members of the team that the momentary loss of function was wearing off; men were now trying to make a break for the door leading to the hall – trying to make a break not trying to overwhelm their attackers.

Mathieson and Hart were methodically working their way through the left hand side of the kitchen. They had developed a rhythm with one man firing as the other selected a target – when one man was reloading the other continued to shoot. Mathieson was the first to empty his magazine – he pushed the release button in front of the trigger guard with his left thumb while grasping the magazine with his fingers. He pulled the magazine sharply down and out, the momentum of the action carried his left hand to the spare magazines that he carried on his belt, dropping the empty he pulled a fresh one from the pouch and with the Skorpion turned on its side he pushed it into the well making sure that it locked in place. His left hand now moved to the cocking lever which he drew back making the weapon ready once more.

In the time it took Mathieson to reload Hart had fired two bursts – the bodies of his targets fell to the side of the kitchen table making the passage of those still capable of flight difficult; there were overturned chairs and bodies in the way. Mathieson moved forward as Hart now reloaded; he came level with the range and found that one man had attempted to take cover behind it – his whimpering was silenced with another controlled three round burst. Hart started firing again and between them they turned their section of the kitchen into a charnel-house obstacle course.

Colquhoun and Scott attempted to establish a rhythm of their own, but at one point both men were reloading simultaneously. The men on the right hand side of the kitchen now made an effort to reach the relative safety of the hall. Enda McHugh's body lay slumped over the two steps that led up to the hall way, he had been the first to run for the hall and had been shot by Colquhoun, taking hits to the neck and head. The first man to reach the hall door made no effort to sidestep McHugh's body, instead he planted his right foot firmly on Enda's back. The resulting downward pressure pushed the ribcage against the step's edge and it gave way – the cracking noise adding to the awful effects which filled the room – the phut of the suppressed gunfire, the clacks of the Skorpions' bolt mechanisms, the various whimpers and wails of the dying, the keening of those attempting escape. Yet, strangely, despite the appalling nature of what was happening in the kitchen the worst thing was the silence of the entry team.

Colquhoun and Scott completed their reloads in time to see two figures reach the hall way. A third man was in the process of clambering over McHugh's corpse as both men opened fire. Six rounds took him in the upper back and the side of the head and he slumped to the floor beside McHugh effectively blocking the doorway. Colquhoun and Scott moved forward drawing level with the hall door; a quick glance showed them that the lights were on and that the two men had left through the front door on the north side of the house. They let them run, they wouldn't get far. Satisfied that there was no threat to be faced from the hall they slowly moved toward the far right hand corner of the kitchen firing as they came. The last members of the Brigade had forced themselves into the corner – there was no way to escape, they could only hope for mercy, but the hooded men had their orders – no prisoners. Mathieson and Hart joined Colquhoun and Scott as they deliberately fired at the huddle of men in the corner. There was no resistance only the mute appeal of terror. The entry team marked their targets and continued to fire their controlled bursts.

Outside the perimeter teams had been in position for nearly a quarter of an hour when the farmhouse was entered. On the north side two teams covered the front door – Martin Bradley with Liam McFadden and Mike O'Brien with Marcus Pearson. The four men were alerted to the opening of the kitchen door by the illumination of the hall way which they saw through the frosted glass surrounding the front door. There was a chance of some company as shadows began to move toward them. Bradley and O'Brien, separated by thirty feet or so, tightened their grips on their Sterlings. Bradley had been surveying the front of the house with his image intensifier which was still turned on; one of the shadows coming down the hall switched on all the lights including the spotlight above the front door. The

Litton scope did its job all too well magnifying the available light and in so doing momentarily blinded Bradley who dropped his weapon and clutched at his right eye in an effort to dispel the pain. There was no point in McFadden taking the Sterling as the scope obscured the standard sights; Bradley's love of gizmos had rendered the weapon useless.

O'Brien, although he didn't know it, was the only shooter on the north side when the front door was flung open with such force that the hinges nearly buckled. Two figures ran into the light, the first bearded with long hair, the second clean shaven, in the spotlight both men looked to have black hair. O'Brien covered the first man with his foresight and fired with no apparent result; he'd jerked the first three rounds high and left. He fired again and this time the target went down. He readjusted his aim to the second figure, expecting the man to continue his run but he didn't, instead he dropped to his knees, outstretched his hands and began to scream.

"Don't shoot! For fuck's sake don't shoot! It's Finn! It's Finn! Oh Jesus, please don't shoot!"

O'Brien barely heard a word as he fired. The screaming stopped as the second man fell back and to his left. O'Brien maintained his watch on the front door but no other figures showed themselves. He'd barely had time to think once the door had opened, but now he lay prone staring at the two unmoving bodies that lay maybe twelve yards in front of him. The question had been asked – his training had taken control and answered it, but his training hadn't prepared him for the aftermath. With every passing second his understanding of his action grew, as did the sick feeling in his stomach.

"...OK?"

"What?"

"I asked are you OK?"

"Yeah I'm f-f-fine Marcus, honest I'm f-fine."

"Well you could've fooled me mate – you're shaking."

"The c-cold must be g-g-getting to me."

"Yeah right. Give me the Sterling before you have an accident. It'll be OK."

Walsh had left the hide as soon as he saw the entry team cross the yard and access the back door. He had little over half a mile to cover but he wasn't going to rush down to join the men of the assault team; the action may have made them a little jumpy and he didn't want to take a round from a pumped up hero. He was expected but discretion was the better part of valour; there was no sense in making this his last watcher job for the wrong reasons.

Colquhoun held up his left hand signalling a ceasefire, and Mathieson reached for his timer and pushed the stop button. A pall of cigarette and gun smoke hung in the air mingled with the smell of fresh blood. All four men looked at the results with differing emotions – Colquhoun scanned the bodies looking for any hostile movement which would have been rewarded with his opening fire once more, strictly an all work and no play response – Mathieson shook his head in disbelief at the ease with which they had swept the room and also at the time indicated on his stopwatch – Scott felt a sense of triumph, of exaltation, a vitality that he'd never experienced before – Hart looked at what he'd been a part of and try as he might he couldn't escape it and the shame that went with it. When it was obvious that there was no fight left in the room Colquhoun turned to the others.

"We need to clear the rest of the house – Jim, you and Graeme look to that, Alan and I will take care of the stragglers here."

Mathieson continued to shake his head.

"Have you got a problem with that Jim?"

"No, no. It's just this stopwatch – bloody thing must be broken."

"Why do you say that?"

"Well it's stopped on forty-nine seconds. I started it as you went through the door behind the youngster; we couldn't have been that fast."

"Under a minute? Christ, it seemed longer than that. Well we're not done yet, once we've finished in here I'm going to call in the rest of the team, so no firing for God's sake. OK let's get on with it."

Hart didn't move so Mathieson grabbed his arm and pulled him toward the hall door. They stepped over the bodies that lay on the step and took up the ready position outside the dining room.

"OK Graeme we're clearing the rest of the house starting here, so make sure that Skorpion's loaded in case we meet any strangers."

"Jesus Jim what did we do?"

"We did what we were sent to do and we did it well."

"But that was plain bloody murder."

"We don't murder the enemy; if they choose not to defend themselves that's their look-out. We're alive, they're dead – fuck them."

"But…"

Before he could say anything more Mathieson grabbed Hart by the front of his overalls and pushed him against the wall.

"Look, if we don't clear the house now some of our mates outside could get killed, you could get killed and most important I could get killed. Get a fucking grip. If you want to feel sick do it later."

Hart closed his eyes and took several deep breaths. His focus returned and with a nod he signalled to Mathieson that he was ready to begin the house clearance. Mathieson turned the doorknob and pushed the door open. They took in as much detail as possible and moved into the room dividing it into segments to be cleared before moving on to the next. Mathieson didn't expect any strangers and the dining room held no surprises; with the room clear they went on to what was described as a sitting room. It too was clear which left the first floor and the multitude of hiding places that the bedrooms afforded.

Back in the kitchen Colquhoun and Scott walked from body to body administering a *coup de grace*. Depending on the position of the head the shot went to the nape of the neck, the ear, or if the man lay face up, below the nose angled up slightly. The effect was the same – the destruction of the *medulla oblongata* and the extinguishing of life.

Colquhoun had been working his way through the fallen and was about to make sure of another when the man's eyes opened as he tried to breath in. His lungs didn't work properly, he'd taken three rounds in the chest, and bright pink foam bubbled at the side of his mouth. His eyes fixed on the hooded man leaning over him and he tried to say something. Colquhoun looked at the man, whom he recognised as Seamus Mullan, and saw his mouth trying to form words. After a considerable effort he managed to speak or rather sigh just once.

"Whoooooo?"

Colquhoun said nothing, but reached up with his left hand and grasped his balaclava. In one smooth motion he pulled it from his head and showed Mullan his face. Seamus looked up at Colquhoun and studied him – he saw nothing – no expression – no emotion – nothing. He made another effort to speak, even though the pain was beginning, even though his breathing was so hard.

"S-s-say s-some… thin'."

The only reply he got was a shake of the head. Colquhoun placed the suppressor under Mullan's nose and never taking his eyes from the dying man's he fired once and felt what Mullan had seen – nothing.

Mathieson and Hart had gone upstairs and cleared the bedrooms, the bathroom and even the toilet. They had been quick but thorough, checking in wardrobes and under beds with no reward. Mathieson had never thought for one moment that there was any opposition upstairs but it was a case of better safe than sorry. The two men stood on the landing and pulled off their balaclavas, both of them glad of the coolness that came with their removal.

"OK Graeme, get yourself downstairs and tell Colquhoun that the house is clear", the look on Hart's face was troubled so Mathieson stopped him before he could leave, "How are you feeling?"

"I don't know – tired I think – I just don't know Jim. I'll sleep on it and you can ask me then."

"Fair enough. Anyway, you better get down there and let the boss know we're clear."

Scott's euphoria had worn off. The slow deliberate dispatches were not the same as the initial action. It was hard to reconcile this with anything that he understood – the rules said that enemy injured were to be afforded every possible medical assistance, but not here, not now. Two of the men he had just killed might have survived with prompt attention; their injuries from the assault were bad, but they could have made it. He sat down on the floor, leaned against the range and closed his eyes. Dizziness overwhelmed him immediately and he had to open his eyes before he was sick. He looked across the kitchen at Colquhoun and noticed that he had taken his balaclava off. He supposed it didn't really matter, after all who was going to make his identity? Colquhoun turned to face him and frowned.

"Do I have to do everything myself?"

"No boss."

"Then get off your arse and get on with it."

Scott pulled himself to his feet using the range for support and moved to the far left hand corner where one of Mathieson's targets lay; he put the Skorpion to the man's right ear, closed his eyes and squeezed the trigger. This wasn't in the job description.

As Hart approached the kitchen door he heard the phut and the clack of the bolt block; he knew what was happening in there but he didn't have to look.

"Boss? It's Hart – house is clear. Do you want me to assemble the team?"

"Yeah."

"Do you want them inside?"

"Yeah, but send Armstrong and Davison to secure the access road – they can shepherd the cleaners when they get here."

"Understood."

Hart walked back down the hall way and called out to the teams on the north side.

"House is clear, you can come in."

Four men came out of the trees that acted as a windbreak and came toward the house. As the second pair drew level with the two bodies illuminated by the spotlight one of them placed the muzzle of his Sterling to the head of the nearest body and fired with his left hand covering the ejection port to stop the empty case disappearing into the dark. He bent over and lifted the empty before he repeated his action with the second body and then walked into the house. Hart saw it all and marvelled at the nonchalance – he never wanted to be that casual. Marcus Pearson stopped beside him and made the Sterling safe.

"I'm going to turn that spotlight off so make sure you've got your torch with you."

Hart fumbled in his overall pockets and brought out his signalling strobe which he turned on. The brief bright flash of light clearly identified him as one of the team – own goals would not be tolerated. He exited the front door as Pearson switched off the spotlight and moved to the west side of the house with his strobe flashing as he came. The team members responded to his calls and moved inside. Both Davison and Armstrong had been on the east perimeter of the farm and both of them were glad of the reception committee detail down on the road; neither of them was particularly interested in seeing the aftermath of the assault.

Hart had finished bringing the team in and was about to go back into the house when a voice called out from the direction of the slurry pit.

"You're not going to win a merit badge blundering around like that."

Hart turned toward the voice and levelled his Skorpion, flicking the change lever off safe.

"Easy, easy, I don't want to get shot and neither do you. I'm the watcher and I've been up on that bloody hill since yesterday."

"Come out where I can see you."

Walsh walked up to the gap in the wall and came forward into the light with his hands by his sides.

"Get your hands up! Up now!"

"Don't be so fucking melodramatic", but Walsh put his hands up anyway, "OK take me to your leader."

Walsh walked toward the house with Hart following; by oh oh fifty-two everyone who was meant to be was inside.

About three miles west of Killylea Eddie Fairbairn turned left onto the B210; with just over two miles to go the cleaners were going to be on site for oh one. The drive from Belfast had gone without incident although there had been occasions when the van had lost visual contact with the tanker because of traffic signals as they drove through Craigavon. Dave Beatty had put his foot down to catch up and looking in his rear view mirror Fairbairn could see the headlights of the van making the turn behind him. He reached to his left and shook Stan Hogg's arm.

"Wake up Stan we're almost there."

Hogg roused himself and reaching under the bench seat he brought out the holdall that contained the two High Powers that they had as insurance. The plan was that they would be met by two members of the assault team who would ride with them up to the farmhouse. The reception committee would be standing in the road with weapons slung and their hands raised – any break from the arrangement would result in an attempted hit and run.

Three quarters of a mile down the B210 Fairbairn made a right turn onto the road that led to Lower Hill Farm. Hogg press-checked both Brownings and when he was sure both were loaded he passed one, cocked and locked, to Fairbairn who placed it between his legs. After a couple of minutes the tanker made the final turn onto the access track to the farm. The van followed up the track and both drivers turned their headlights off, relying on their side lamps.

Davison and Armstrong heard the tanker approaching and stepped into the middle of the road with weapons slung and their hands up. The big Bedford came to a halt just in front of them and Armstrong moved to the driver's side so he could talk to Fairbairn.

"Bang on time. No problems finding this place?"

"Oh no, we can read maps and everything. Do us a favour though and take those bloody things off your heads."

"Sorry mate, forgot all about them. Hey John, take your headgear off, we're upsetting people."

"OK, step up and we'll get moving."

Both vehicles pulled into the yard outside the back door and the cleaning team assembled beside the tanker. Aiken watched as Dave Beatty and Mark Ramsey pulled the two sets of step ladders from the back of the Commer. Davison and Armstrong stood watching as gloves and plastic booties were distributed. Davison couldn't resist making light of their preparations.

"They'll be bringing out their buckets and spades next."

Unfortunately for him Aiken heard the wisecrack.

"And what's your name?"

"Davison ma'am."

"Well, Davison ma'am, smart arsed remarks like that may be funny in the playground but not here. Where's your boss?"

"Inside ma'am."

"Go and get him, I need a word before we begin."

"So we've you to thank for the green light?"

"Yeah, I'm Walsh, no doubt Lynch mentioned me."

"Not by name but we knew you were there."

"Is that "we" plural or the Royal prerogative, because one of yours didn't seem to know anything about me?"

"Did Hart give you a rough time?"

"Not really, but I might have given him one", Walsh smiled, "Enough of this charming banter, I'm going upstairs to use the toilet and then I'm going to start searching the bedrooms. Tell Aiken where I am if you would please?"

He picked up his rucksack and went through to the kitchen from the scullery. He stopped and surveyed the scene, then turned back to face Colquhoun.

"You have my congratulations – what a lovely fucking mess."

"I'm glad you approve."

Walsh nodded, smiled again and stepped over the bodies on the step as he made his way through to the hall way. Mathieson had listened to the exchange as he leaned against the cooker in the scullery. He liked Walsh's style and found it difficult to suppress a smirk. Mathieson's mood was not lost on Colquhoun.

"There you go Jim, someone even more irritating than you."

"And I thought I was in a league of my own."

Davison had come into the scullery during Colquhoun and Walsh's exchange and had waited patiently for an opportunity to speak which he now took.

"Boss, the cleaners are here and their leader wants a word."

"I'll be right with her. Jim get me a total on the number of rounds fired – here's my Skorpion and my unused mags – and I want any mags that may have been dropped collected. OK?"

"Sure. Davison get Roper, Lauder, Osborne and Armstrong to give you a hand collecting the packs and bring them to the back door."

"You must be Colquhoun. I'm Aiken, let's hear the result."

"Twenty-one – nil."

"Jesus Christ", she took a deep breath, "Are they all inside?"

"No, we've two out front. The other nineteen are all in the kitchen. They've all been made sure."

"How many vehicles have we to dispose of?"

"There's a van and three cars, I think, parked in the barn. Does that present any difficulties?"

"No we can manage that. Have we got a total yet on the rounds fired?"

"Not yet, but I'll have one for you in a couple of minutes. Your man Walsh is already here and he said he would be starting upstairs. Anything else I can do for you?"

"Yes. It would be a big help if I can use your warm bodies to move the "commodities" out and into the tanker."

"Once we've cleared ourselves we'll lend a hand."

"Thanks."

Colquhoun went back inside leaving Aiken with her team.

"OK everyone, this is going to be unpleasant. We have twenty-one corpses to shift so we'll be tackling this job together – usual team duties will not be started until we've cleared the house and loaded the tanker. I want everyone inside bagging bodies and collecting empty cases."

The team walked into the farmhouse and began the first phase of the clean up.

The backpacks had been recovered from behind the barn and the members of assault team who hadn't fired a round were stripping off their latex gloves and their overalls. Those who had were now standing in the scullery checking on the number of live rounds they had left. O'Brien and Pearson had fired eleven rounds between them and all the empty cases had been recovered so that only left the .32ACPs of the entry team to be accounted for. A total of one hundred and sixty-nine rounds had been fired in the kitchen and thankfully nowhere else – a fact that would make life easier for the cleaners.

"Have we got a total yet?"

"Yeah we have boss, one six nine fired."

"Right Jim, you give that to Aiken. Mike, time for you to make the call to XMG. I want our lift here for oh two latest."

O'Brien picked up his backpack and went out into the yard. He opened it and took out the radio set that had been selected specifically for this job; it was a multi-band CB unit the same as those used by the new converts to the latest craze to come from America. The signal was traceable but the broadcast should attract no attention, besides his call was pre-arranged and totally innocent – with such equipment available there was no point compromising a military net or risking the documentation of a telephone line. He switched the set on and extended the antenna before lifting the microphone. "Breaker breaker, this is "The Bear" comin' to you from his sick ride outside the homestead. If "The Birdman" has his ears on I could do with a pick-up, comeback."

O'Brien released the transmit switch and waited. After maybe twenty seconds the reply came through.

"Hello "Bear". "The Birdman" hears your plea. He'll be swoopin' by the homestead soon."

"That's a big ten four."

The crew at the "black hangar" would be with them on schedule. He packed up the set and went back inside to give Colquhoun the news.

Karen Aiken had set her team to work as soon as they entered the house. The men of the cleaner team were in the kitchen laying out the corpses in preparation for their removal. The women had begun collecting empty cases taking particular care to scrutinise the bodies to make sure that none had lodged in the clothing – they couldn't afford to leave one behind. Mathieson walked into the kitchen and nearly tripped over the bodies of Joe and Padraig Mullan.

"I'm sorry fellas, I didn't see you lying there. Not much chat out of you is there. Anyway, enough of that, I've a message for Aiken."

She looked up from the tangle of limbs and overturned chairs beside the kitchen table and raised her right hand.

"Over here, and we can do without the graveyard humour – this job's sick as it is. You got us a total yet?"

"Indeed. It's one six nine. Sorry we couldn't have been a bit more economical, but you know how it is."

"Yeah I do. Boys and their toys."

"Aye, well if there's nothing else I'll get out of your way."

"Just one thing before you go, we'll need all the keys for the vehicles back at Glaslough."

"Right, I'll round those up now, and I'll leave them out on the table in the scullery."

"That'll do fine."

As Mathieson left the kitchen, Karen Aiken spoke to all of her team.

"We've got five vehicles to collect at Glaslough and four to dispose of here so you have keys to retrieve. If you turn up anything interesting keep a note of who and what. Let's get this lot bagged up."

Phil Priestly and Mark Ramsey went out to the van and brought in the heavy-duty PVC body bags which they distributed amongst the team. The bodies were to be bagged, then carried out to the tanker, lifted up onto the roof, and then dropped inside through one of the top hatches. It was going to be more labour intensive than putting them in the back of a van, but the tanker would be a whole lot harder to search if they got stopped at a checkpoint on the return to Aldergrove.

Sharon Chambers was going over Jochen Pfilzgauer when she found something interesting – his wrist watch.

"Karen you better come here, I've got something."

Aiken crouched beside her as Chambers held up her find.

"You see the script on the dial – it's Cyrillic isn't it?"

"Yeah it is. OK, I want you to go over his clothing and check any labels."

"You don't think we've got Russians here do you?"

"Just check his labels. In fact, listen up everyone, Sharon's found something strange so I want you to look at clothing labels before you bag this lot."

By oh one twenty-five the cleaners had inspected all the bodies, taking any keys they found and any other items of interest, which didn't amount to much, a few wallets and drivers licenses. Aiken inspected the finds after telling the men on the team to put the corpses in the body bags, and get ready to take them out to the tanker. Only two had caught the team's attention – Pfilzgauer and Hoss, both of whom carried no ID, and who had no labels on their clothes either. Stan Hogg went out to the tanker and came back with a roll of red tape; he tore several strips from the roll and stuck them on the body bags containing the two mystery men. The easily identifiable bags would be separated from the rest and the contents would be given a very thorough inspection when they got to their final destination.

Several members of the assault team were pressed into service to help with the loading of the bags onto the back of the tanker. Davison and Armstrong had been sent back down the road to secure the area, but that still meant there were more than enough pairs of hands to lend assistance. Ian Walsh had been called downstairs by Aiken and had gone from bag to bag putting name tags with the corpses that he could positively identify. The last bags containing the bodies of the two men who had been shot outside were carried through the house to the kitchen. Walsh asked for both bags to be put down and unzipped. He bent over the first body and made a long study.

"I couldn't tell for sure from the hill, but there's no doubt that is or rather was Garvan McNabb. The beard doesn't make much of a difference, not close up anyway", he moved on to the last bag and looked at the occupant. "So that just leaves, yeah, I thought so, Sean McNellis."

Marcus Pearson who had opened the bag looked at Walsh and shook his head.

"I think your wrong with this one mate. He shouted his name as he came out the door. He definitely said it was Finn, I'm sure of that."

"No this is Sean McNellis alright. Finn – Sean they sound alike if you ask me. Besides, I don't think he's really going to object now is he?"

"I suppose not."

"Right then, zip him up and take him away."

Outside the body bags were lifted onto the tanker. Dave Beatty and George Rowan, being the smallest male members of Aiken's team, were volunteered to climb inside the tank to pile the bags; nobody was prepared to offer to do the job so Aiken had used a bit of gentle persuasion. Men really were suckers for the "little girl lost" act and Karen carried her role off with considerable skill.

The tanker had been "borrowed" from RAF Aldergrove, from where it made its usual supply runs to the bases throughout Northern Ireland that had helicopter pads. Civilian contractors had been used in the past, but threats from the paramilitaries, that had resulted in attacks, meant that nobody thought the job was worth the risk. The simplest answer had been to buy a tanker and paint it to look like "an innocent civilian". Thus the bases had been kept supplied with fuel, and once in a while certain tasks could be completed with a degree less risk.

It was just as well that both of the hatches on the roof had been opened; the smell of aviation fuel was damn near overpowering. A battery powered lantern had been rigged so that the men could see what they were doing. There was enough room to stack the bags lengthwise across the width of the tank; so starting at the end nearest the cab Beatty and Rowan had made a pile three bags high which extended to beyond the middle of the tank once all twenty-one bags had been packed. Ten minutes hard labour saw the cargo loaded.

Colquhoun assembled his team once all the bags had been brought out of the farmhouse. Eight of them were back in civvies having removed their overalls, gloves and headgear. The entry team along with O'Brien and Pearson hadn't changed; the six of them made a very marked contrast to the others standing in the yard. The unfired Sterlings had been distributed amongst these six, giving them at total of eight weapons in all.

"Before we go, any problems?"

Colin Lauder put his hand in the air, the grimace showed Colquhoun that the left leg was really starting to hurt.

"Let's hear it Col."

"It's my knee boss. I gave it a few twists on the walk in and it held up OK, but when I lifted one of the Micks out to the tanker I really fucked it up."

"Can you make the pick-up or do you want to go out with the cleaners?"

"I better go with them boss, if they'll take me."

"Oh don't worry they'll take you. Marcus I want you to take a look at it before we go, understood?"

"Yes boss."

Pearson helped Lauder into the house to get a look at his knee in the light of the scullery.

"Anything else?"

It was Martin Bradley's turn to indicate that all was not well.

"It's my right eye John – I can't see a damn thing."

"From what I hear – your fault. If the left one's working you'll be fine."

Bradley let the matter drop; Colquhoun obviously wasn't the sympathetic type.
"Right, I'm going to square things up with Aiken and then we move."

With the tanker packed Aiken's team had split into the three separate teams outlined at the briefing in Belfast. Colquhoun walked into the kitchen and saw Mark Ramsey up a step ladder digging a stray round from the wall. Two of the women were still searching for empty cases; the initial search of the room had yielded one hundred and fifty-three, the last sixteen were going to prove awkward. Sue Ballard was also up a ladder but rather than digging for strays she was scrutinising the pelmet that covered the top of the curtain rail – at first glance an unlikely hiding place but it wouldn't be the first time it had been used.

"Is Aiken about?"

"She's with her team and Walsh giving the bedrooms a final check."

Colquhoun made his way upstairs and found Aiken leafing through two Allied Irish Bank savings books. She held one of them up for Colquhoun's attention.

"Does that look like the savings of a poor border farmer with less than sixty acres?"

He saw a figure of nearly one hundred thousand pounds and shook his head.

"I shouldn't think so."

"Neither did we", she looked up from the bank books, "Is there something I can do for you?"

"I just came to let you know we're out of here – our pick-up is due at oh two. Also I'm afraid one of mine has knackered his leg and will have to go out with your lot, if that's OK?"

"We'll squeeze him in somewhere."

"Thanks. Then I'll be off."

"See you next week at the post-mortem."

Aiken returned to the scrutiny of the figures in the two books she held. Colquhoun was given the distinct impression that she was oblivious to his presence and that any attempts to save face would be ignored; he tried anyway.

"Yeah, I'll see you then."

He felt he'd have had more success talking to the wall. He retraced his steps to the scullery to find Pearson packing away his medic kit. Lauder looked much more relaxed than he had out in the yard and the hypodermic syringe that Pearson was stowing away told him why.

"Are you qualified to use that, it's diamorphine, isn't it?"

"The stupid bugger was in that much pain I felt it was justified. He's going to need looked at when they get him back to Musgrave. That knee's a bloody mess."

"OK, you can join the rest of the lads. Col we're going now, but Aiken says you'll get transport back to Belfast."

It was all Lauder could do to reply with the morphine running through his system. He managed to look up at Colquhoun and just about held his head steady while he tried very hard to focus his eyes.

"Thanks boss."
Back out in the yard the rest of the team were ready to move.
"Time check, somebody?"
"Oh one forty-two boss."
"Jesus, we're late. OK fellas let's go."

Walsh and Rowan had moved on to Sean's room where they had found little of any real importance until Walsh pulled open the third drawer of the chest that stood on the left hand side of the bed.

"Hey Karen, I've found their passports."

Aiken was still in Joe Mullan's bedroom with Jenny Ellison going through the remnants of the paperwork that she'd found in a shoe box pushed to the back of his wardrobe.

"Pocket those. Anything else?"

"Not really, oh hang on, yeah, there's a couple of copies of Penthouse."

"I meant anything of interest."

"Maybe not to you, but I'm sure Sharon would go a bundle on Miss October."

"Stop being a pig and leave Chambers alone."

Walsh came back into Joe's room brandishing the issue of Penthouse that he'd been talking about.

"Come off it Karen, that's just the sort of chest complaint that she likes – too bloody big."

"Drop it Ian. We've got work to do and time's not in our favour. I mean it, joke's over."

"OK. Well we've finished our rooms and by the looks of it you're more or less finished in here so maybe we should get back to the kitchen and see how the ladies are getting on."

"Now you're being condescending."

"And I thought I was being charming."

"You wouldn't know how, but you're right, time to go and check on things downstairs. You can go and see how the boys are doing in the barn, and take Rowan with you."

Ten minutes had taken the assault team down the access track to the junction with the public road. The men had followed a mostly downhill route until they came within seventy yards of the "T" junction where the track took an upward path. The junction occupied a small bare hill top; the hedges having been cleared away to be replaced with fences. There were no overhead power or telephone lines which made it perfect for the team's purpose.

Armstrong and Davison had taken station on either side of the junction and it was Armstrong, being the closer, who made the report to Colquhoun, as the rest of the team moved into the field to the left and took up an all-round defensive position. He let Colquhoun come to him and lie up close as he whispered his brief.

"There's been no movement down here at all boss. Quiet as the grave."
"Glad to hear it. Any noise from up at the house?"
"Not a thing, and I've been giving myself ear-ache to pick something up."
"OK now we wait."

More bloody waiting, but, not for the first time, the team thanked their lucky stars that it was dry. The cloud had been blown eastward leaving a clear sky with the result that it was now beginning to feel cold, but better cold than wet. Conversation was impossible so minds turned to the job. Some men wondered about the characters of those who had died – had they been evil men, had they deserved their fate, would they have acted in a similar way if roles had been reversed? The conclusions were all pretty much the same – it didn't matter – the important thing was to walk away – physically, maybe even mentally.

The shooters had slightly different concerns – they weren't too worried about the men who had died – their pre-occupation was with their own characters and what the assault had taught them of themselves. None of them had cause for comfort, but some of them chose to ignore the reality.

One thing all of them would have agreed on was the need for sleep. They had been up for at least eighteen hours, which was nothing in itself, the physical exertions had been limited, it wasn't that kind of tired, it was rather the mental activity and more specifically the type of mental activity that had drained them. The job at the farmhouse may have been done, the pick-up was due any minute, but they all knew the penalties for complacency. Every noise seemed amplified, every movement appeared threatening, they were extremely edgy, but no matter how hard they willed it, time passed no quicker.

They all heard it before they saw it – the whump, whump, whump of the rotor blade as the pilot slowed the helicopter in the air as he searched the ground for the arranged signal.

Colquhoun reached into the outside right pocket of his Barbour and produced a strobe light the same as Hart's. He switched it on and the brief pulses of bright light acted as a beacon.

From fifteen hundred feet up the border landscape appeared almost black and virtually featureless. The only sights that broke the monotony were the single lights that picked out a farmyard here and there or the glow that came from the streetlights of the villages nearby – Glaslough to the west, Caledon to the north and Killylea to the north-east. The flight time and the bearing told the young flight-lieutenant that he had brought his Puma to the approximate area; all he needed now was the beacon to bring him into the right landing point. Night flying was not his, not any pilot's favourite pastime, but as long as you kept a close watch on the instruments and an even closer watch on your surroundings everything should be OK. His co-pilot, an Air Corps sergeant, had already moved aft to the cabin space in preparation for loading, so the whole landing sequence would be down to him.

He saw a flash to his left and turned his full gaze on it – yes – definitely a flash, almost due west at what seemed almost a mile. He turned toward the beacon and began his descent. As he approached the strobe he looked for any lights on the road; a vehicle travelling late at night would mean his having to circle until the junction was clear, happily there were no headlights at any point on the road that he could see. The closer he came to the ground the more definition he got of the surroundings – the road became clear, the fields, the hedges, the fences. The flashing strobe guided him to the junction; as he made his final approach he looked for any overhead obstructions, an alternate landing site had been selected in one of the fields just in case the pilot couldn't make the primary, but there were no obstructions. The twin back wheels touched the road surface momentarily before the nose wheel came down, the pilot kept the two Turbomeca turbo shafts cycling for take-off as the Air Corps sergeant opened the port loading gate.

The noise from the engines was deafening as the Puma came in to land. The helicopter was flying without navigation lights so for the team members the first view they had of it was not so much the Puma itself as a black hole in the sky. As it closed toward them the faint glow from the instrument lights showed through the cockpit canopy. As it flared for landing the team began to move. The first men to the port side of the Puma were unarmed – it had been agreed that the shooters would give cover and that they would be the last men on board. Alex Roper was the first man to reach the gate and once he was in he turned to help the sergeant pull the rest of the team on board.

The interiors of most military helicopters weren't built for comfort and this new SA 330L was no exception – the seating was rudimentary benches with stowage space underneath. The first group were safely on board so Colquhoun signalled the shooters to make their move. They ran to the helicopter in pairs and handed their weapons on board first – these were made safe and stowed as they clambered through the loading gate. Davison ran from the far side of the road around the front of the Puma and joined Colquhoun as they became the last men to step up to the cabin space. All fifteen men were now on board and strapping themselves in with the safety harnesses. Colquhoun squeezed through the companionway that led to the flight deck. The pilot had turned in his seat to face aft and saw him coming forward. Colquhoun gave him the thumbs-up and then pointed his index finger skywards. The lieutenant nodded and took the Puma up. The whole extraction had taken less than ninety seconds.

Colquhoun nearly lost his footing as the helicopter lifted and he felt the familiar lurch in his stomach indicating the radical change in motion. He reached to the co-pilot's chair and lifted the headset that was hooked over the head restraint. Once he had put it on and adjusted the mouthpiece he was able to talk to the pilot.

"Nice of you to show up on time."

"No problem. You know, we keep a tighter schedule than most airlines."

"Glad to hear it. So what's our ETA for Hereford?"

"It's oh two oh seven now – we'll have you home by oh four latest. In the meantime sit back and enjoy the flight."

"Sure. Well, I'll leave you to it."

He replaced the headset and went aft to see how things looked there. Some of the team had produced sets of ear defenders and were settling onto their benches. A bottle of Glenfiddich had been produced from somewhere and was doing the rounds – a nip wouldn't do anybody any harm. When it came to his turn Colquhoun took a good pull from the bottle. The nearest available seat was beside Mathieson and as he sat down Colquhoun realised just how tired he was. He looked at Mathieson, gave him the briefest of smiles and leaned his head back against the bulkhead; he was asleep in under three minutes.

Up at the barn the men of the cleaner team were finishing the search of the cars before moving on to the Transit van. Boots, the engine compartments, the exteriors, including wheel arches and hub caps, and the interiors were the main areas for scrutiny; not having the luxury of either an inspection pit, or for that matter the time, the undersides and the exhaust systems were left untouched. The Peugeot and the Ford had yielded nothing but there was something interesting in the red Datsun Sunny; under the battery which had been disconnected and removed Phil Priestly had found two sheets of A4 paper wrapped in a plastic bag. The pages were covered in a child-like script, though it wasn't the style but the content that was of interest. Both pages formed a surveillance report on a chief-inspector of the RUC – it was clear that this man was to be a target and soon. Happily for him the South Armagh Brigade wouldn't be targeting anybody in the near future, but the find was important and would no doubt lead to his re-location and a re-assessment of his personal security arrangements.

"How much longer do you think you'll be with the vehicles?"

"You can tell Karen that we'll be clear in about fifteen."

"OK Phil, I'm going back inside to check on the girls and then I'm going to allocate the car keys. Oh by the way Dave, if you're driving the Commer back to Belfast you've got a passenger."

"Who?"

"One of the heroes has done for his knee. He's shot full of morphine so you won't get much sense out of him."

"You get sod all sense out of them at the best of times, can't see that it'll make much difference."

"Just get him to Musgrave – they can take care of him at the military wing."

"Where is he? You know I'd hate to leave him behind."

"Last I saw of him he was asleep in the front seat of the van and I don't think he's in the mood to wander off. Right, if you need me you know where to find me."

Walsh left through the sliding door closing it behind him. He had got about halfway across the yard when the sound of the helicopter carried up the slope from the road. He stopped and listened as it made its approach. This was, to his mind, potentially the most dangerous section of the operation; the noise, the blocking of the road, the dependence on the plan unfolding flawlessly, there was no room to deal with unforeseen difficulties and that worried him.

The back door opened and Karen Aiken came out into the yard to stand beside him.

"Noisy bloody things aren't they. I mean why couldn't they have just gone back the way they came?"

"Not dramatic enough for them Karen. Besides I think they were beginning to miss the comforts of home and wanted back in a hurry."

Right on cue the Puma's twin engines became even louder as it lifted off. The extraction was complete and the assault team were on their way. Walsh and Aiken heard the engine and rotor noise fade into the distance as the helicopter flew east.

"Comfortable cages for our very own scary monsters."

"That's a bit harsh. Every job has its tool and on this occasion they were it. Talking of jobs, how's it coming along inside?"

"Another hour should see it clear. We've got all the cases, so the floor is getting a thorough wash down at the minute. Some of the furniture will have to go in the back of the van."

"Why?"

"One of the armchairs has got blood on it and a couple of the kitchen chairs have taken hits which would be hard to explain. So, the easiest way to avoid a problem is to take them with us. How are the fellas coming on with the vehicles?"

"They'll be finished in a quarter of an hour or less – there's just the Transit to do. I'm going to share the car keys out and then it'll be a case of waiting for you."

"There's no need for you to wait on me."

"I thought we could take the BMW that's parked at Glaslough and take our time getting back to Belfast."

"If you're making a pass your timing is lousy."

"God forbid. I just meant that it's not every day you get to drive a beemer on somebody else's time. Anyway, you're not my type and you outrank me so it would be doomed to failure from the start."

"Well then, that being the case I accept your offer of the lift but only because I like BMWs."

"OK. Let's go inside and I'll sort out who's driving what and then I can give you ladies some help with the furniture."

The appearance of the kitchen was a marked improvement on what it had been an hour ago – the floor was clean – the bad smell, a mixture of burnt powder, cigarette smoke, blood, urine and excrement, had been replaced, in part anyway, by the heavy chemical smell of bleach. Stray rounds, and there were only seven of them, had been dug from the walls; a job made easier because of the old lime plaster that covered the brickwork. The range had even been stoked so there was a warming fire in the grate to counter the draft that came from the open doors and windows.

Walsh stood in the scullery doorway and marvelled at the willingness of the girls to undertake such unpleasant work. He had never heard a complaint from one of them and there was plenty of reason for them to complain; having to search a body not long dead, that had lost control of bladder and bowels, in his view it just wasn't fitting for a woman to do it. Yet, here they were, their feet covered with plastic booties, their hair netted and their hands covered by the obligatory gloves, and there was no denying it, they were bloody good at it. They had an attention for detail that men didn't have. He turned to the table in the scullery and lifted the nine sets of keys that had been left there. The keys of the cars that the assault team had used were all marked so that meant he only had to match four keys with the four vehicles out in the barn.

"OK girls, bar the furniture removal I think we're done. Jenny you stay with me, the rest of you take a break."

Jenny Ellison would be taking over from Aiken when she went to her desk so this would be Jenny's last job as a subordinate. The two women began their sweep of the kitchen at the far end of the room and worked back to the scullery door. As she drew level with the range Ellison lifted the rug that had been moved while the floor was washed and replaced it. Nothing appeared to be out of place except them.

"What do you think?"

"I didn't see anything that we need to go over again. If we get those chairs moved I think that's all really."

"OK Jenny, you go and get Walsh and Fairbairn. Tell them I said we needed their brawn to shift some furniture, and make sure they put some booties on to cover their mucky boots."

Ellison left the farmhouse and went across the yard to the barn. Before she could lay a hand on the door it slid open and Ian Walsh stepped out.

"Karen wants you and Eddie inside now to shift some chairs."

"I was just on my way, but I'll get Eddie", and he turned back to face the interior of the barn, "Hey Eddie, I need you to lend a hand moving some chairs."

"And she said that you're to put some booties on to cover your boots. We've got spares in the van so help yourselves."

Once the two men were kitted out with covers for their feet they made short work of moving the dining chairs out of the kitchen. Not so easy was the moving of the armchair out to the van; it was old with a heavy timber-frame and stuffed with horsehair, and even when they turned it on its side it proved awkward to manoeuvre through the two doors. After much effort and no small amount of swearing they managed to lift the chair into the back of the van. Aiken and Ellison followed them out with the two remaining kitchen chairs which they stacked alongside the armchair.

"You two could take that on the stage if you wanted; you were almost as funny as Eric Sykes."

"When I want your opinion Jenny I'll ask for it."

"And so like a comedian – touchy – can't stand jokes at his own expense."

"Try this for funny, you get the pleasure of driving the Datsun and it really is a beauty so you'll be well matched."

"Personal insults aren't funny Ian."

Walsh had regretted the comment as soon as he'd made it. Now he'd have to apologise and he'd better sound sincere, after all Ellison was going to be his new boss within the fortnight – they may have matched each other in rank now but that was all going to change.

"No they aren't. I suppose I'm a little on edge – although that's no excuse. I'm sorry Jenny, it won't happen again."

"Apology accepted."

She sounded as if she meant it, but he knew he'd have to watch his step in the future. He looked at his watch – oh two forty-one – if everything was OK with Aiken they could start moving out. She must have been thinking the same thing because she called the whole team together by the back door.

"OK listen up. The house is more or less finished, Jenny and I are going too give it a final sweep top to bottom. While we're doing that Ian is going to allocate vehicles and those who are driving anything here can go. Eddie you're expected back at Aldergrove for oh five thirty latest and there'll be a team there to meet you. The cargo is going out in a Chinook from our hangar, but keep it low key anyway. Any questions? No. then let's get on with it."

Walsh looked at the list he had made and called out the names.

"Jane, Sue, George and Stan; I only need you four at the moment. Dave, Eddie you're in the Commer and the tanker, you pair can go any time you like. Oh and Dave don't forget your passenger whatever you do."

"How could I forget. I'll have the bugger snoring in my ear from here to Belfast."

"Just get on with it."

The step ladders were brought out from the farmhouse and stowed in the Commer beside the chairs. Next, hairnets, gloves and booties were stripped off and put in a "Hospital Waste" bag which was thrown into the back of the Commer alongside the chairs. Everything would go into the hospital incinerator at Musgrave. Walsh picked up his backpack and took out the spotting scope and the Clansman.

"Dave do me a favour and take these back to our stores would you?"

"Why didn't you give them to the heroes before they flew out?"

"'Cos it's our kit and they'd never have given it back."

"Aye well OK. Give them here.

"Thanks Dave. You know it's easier for you to take them back. If you get stopped you can explain it."

"You owe me one Ian."

"Goes without saying."

The last job before the van and the tanker were driven away was the removal of three small rucksacks from the cab of the Commer. These contained changes of clothing for the cleaners driving the assault team vehicles away from Glaslough. As Walsh and Beatty pulled them past Lauder, he woke up, albeit briefly.

"We home yet boss?"

"Not yet, go back to sleep."

The snoring resumed straight away and Beatty looked daggers at Walsh, little winged ones.

With nothing left to do the two drivers got in their cabs and started up. The van was going first this time with both vehicles following a different route – they would drive north to Caledon and then on to Dungannon where they would join the M1. The van would go as far as the A55 turn off and take it, leaving Beatty and Lauder less than a mile from Musgrave. Fairbairn would take the turn for the airport at junction 9 along the A26 and drive straight through to the RAF base. Their respective drives should take them less than two hours leaving them both well within the schedule.

Stan Hogg was taking the Transit van, Sue Ballard the Escort and George Rowan would drive the Mullan brothers' Peugeot. They were to take different routes into Belfast and dump the vehicles around the city, leaving them unlocked without the keys; these would find their way into the sewer system like so many before. At oh two fifty Hogg set off in the van, followed by Ballard and then Rowan.

The remainder of the team waited for Karen and Jenny to return, but there was none of the usual banter – when the clean-up had been under way it had required their full attention allowing little time for reflection – now that it was finished the reality of what they had been a part of began to occupy their thoughts. Talk of the job would come later, but for the moment nobody felt like it, they just wanted to go.

Aiken and Ellison had started upstairs and systematically worked their way through the bedrooms, bathroom and toilet. The first floor was clear so they came back downstairs to give the ground floor a final check. Jenny made sure that the front door was locked and rejoined Karen as she looked into the dining room to survey the re-arranged dining chairs. Everything looked normal which was exactly what they wanted.

They came down the two steps into the kitchen and made the final sweep. After nearly five minutes scrutiny they had finished; the only things out of place were the holes in the plaster work where the stray rounds had lodged.

"I think that covers it Jenny. Time to set the fire."

Aiken opened the latticed door to the grate and lifted the coal shovel that stood beside the range. She thrust the shovel into the burning coals which she then emptied onto the rug which began to smoulder and then burn. Once she had closed the grate door and replaced the shovel both women walked to the scullery door and watched the fire take hold.

The linoleum that covered the floor had made washing it down easy; the hard smooth surface hadn't allowed any fluids – blood or otherwise – to seep into the wooden floor below. It now made the fire spread easily – the high linseed oil content in the material supported and encouraged combustion. With the doors and windows left open the draft created by the gentle breeze outside quickly fanned the flames. Aiken and Ellison watched as the flames spread across the floor to the second armchair which began to smoulder.

"Watching it isn't going to speed things up. It's nearly oh three – time we were leaving."

"Do you think this'll do?"

"The rest of the house is clear. Even if we only lose this room it'll be enough. Anyway, there won't be a mad rush to this house to put out any fire. By the time the brigade gets in there hopefully won't be anything left."

The cover on the armchair ignited and the atmosphere in the kitchen turned acrid.

"Come on Jenny, let's get out of here before we choke."

Aiken stopped to close the back door on her way out leaving it unlocked. It was her hope that everything would look as natural as possible by the time the fire investigation people from the police and the fire brigade started picking over the remains. She came down the steps from the back door and gave her final instructions to her team.

"I'm sorry the others aren't here for this but I'll say the same to them later – you've all done a bloody good job and you've done it quickly with the minimum of fuss. I'm glad to say I was your team leader and I hope you think I was a good one. We've still got a little work ahead of us so let's get it done. Jenny, you and Doris take the Datsun, the rest of us have a little walk to Glaslough, so let's go."

The Datsun's fan belt screamed as Ellison turned on; the car was in a pretty miserable state with a gear box that needed treatment. She had difficulties getting it into reverse, but eventually managed to back out of the barn. Walsh looked on, tempted to make a smart remark, but bit his lip – nothing he could say would be regarded as funny. The Datsun drove out of the yard and down the access road leaving the last members of the team to watch the flickering light from the spreading fire as it played on the walls and ceiling of the scullery.

"It's oh three so we should pair off and get going. Ian have you passed out the keys yet?"

"No. I didn't know whether to leave it until we got to the pick-up point or do it here."

"We'll do it here so that we don't get bunched up. Have you got the padlock key?"

"Yeah, it's on with the Landrover keys, those are yours Phil, so you'll be opening the gate. Sharon you get the Cavalier, Lizzie you're in the Cortina and Mark you'll be taking the Granada. Bear in mind it's not ours, so don't break it."

"I'll look after it as if it were my own."

"Try looking after it as if it were mine or Karen's OK? Less chance of you coming to grief."

"OK you've got your keys so you can pair off – boy/girl, boy/girl, boy/girl. Don't forget your change of clothes – we don't want anyone covered in mud stopped with a new car, understood?"

There were nods of assent from everyone, so Aiken continued.

"Take the walk out slowly, no-one's looking for us but that doesn't mean we can thrash about either, so be careful. See you all back in the canteen for coffee later. Phil and Sharon you two first."

The last six team members made their way behind the barn and set off down the field toward the gate. Aiken and Walsh were the last pair to leave and as they walked along the hedgerow they periodically looked back to the farmhouse. It wasn't until they had made the road crossing and had drawn level with the neighbouring farm that they saw a faint flicker above the trees; the fire had undoubtedly taken hold of the house. There was no way of telling how bad the damage would be, they would find that out subsequently, for now getting home was the most important thing.

Part Two

Dermot Gormley rolled over and looked at the luminous dial of his "Big Ben" alarm clock which sat on the bedside cabinet – it was just after twenty-five to six, time to get up. He pulled back the covers and swung his legs out of bed. The rug did little to take the edge off the cold as his feet touched the floor. He had never been fond of a warm bedroom but there were times when he wished for heat, particularly first thing in the morning. He had been getting up around this time for his whole life; even now that the farm had diminished to little more than a small holding that helped to pass the time, which seemed to pass very slowly now that he had reached his sixty-seventh year.

He stood and walked to the bedroom window to take a look at the day. He gently pulled back the curtain, careful not to make too much noise that might wake his wife Brid, and looked out on a day full of promise – clear sky and no wind to speak of. He looked up the hill towards the Mullan boys' place and his thoughts of a pleasant spring day disappeared – a pall of smoke rose from the direction of the farm – either the farm house itself or the outbuildings were on fire, he couldn't tell which.

"Brid, wake up! The Mullan place is burnin'!"

Brid struggled out of bed and joined her husband at the window. She crossed herself as she took note of the smoke rising in the windless air above the curtain of trees.

"Mother of God. Dermot get you downstairs and telephone the fire brigade, and call Joe to see if he and Seamus are alright, and don't be forgettin' young Padraig either."

Brid's decisiveness gave Dermot a sense of purpose and he left their bedroom to make the calls. Brid said a prayer for the Mullans as she looked toward the farm – she'd never had much time for them but this sort of misfortune cleared a lot of ill-will – that was maybe putting it too strongly, but they were headstrong boys, in her eyes, who didn't think too much about what they said before they said it. She remembered the way the two brothers had talked down to Dermot in the past and the memory of their lack of respect still rankled with her. Padraig was different – he had always been obliging and pleasant any time she'd had dealings with him – a shame his uncles couldn't be more like him. She walked over to the bedroom door and taking her housecoat from the hook she made her way downstairs to the kitchen.

Dermot stood by the dresser with the telephone receiver in his right hand; he looked to Brid as she came into the room and cupped his left hand over the mouthpiece.

"They're connectin' me with the fire brigade."

Before he could say anything else the control room at Fire Service Headquarters in Lisburn came on line.

"…You wish to report a fire?"

"Aye, the Mullan boys' place is alight. We need an engine out here quick."

"That's fine sir, but I need some details. Where are you calling from?"

"I'm callin' from home, just across from the Mullan place."

"I'd gathered that sir, but where is that exactly?"

"It's off the Coolkill Road, before you turn for Tynan. We're not far from Glaslough."

"And do you know the name of the town land?"

"I think it's Lemnagore."

"Right sir, we're getting this on the map. You're being a great help; now could we have the address please?"

"The Mullan place is Lower Hill Farm, Hill Road, Tynan."

"Do you know if anyone is in residence at the farm sir?"

"Well, there's Joe and Seamus and young Padraig but I don't know if they're in, not for certain anyway."

"So that's three people. One last thing sir, could we have your name and telephone number?"

"The name's Gormley, Dermot Gormley and the number's 0861 -----, but if your boys have trouble findin' the place I'll go up to the road and show them the turn-off."

"That's very good of you Mr. Gormley; it would do no harm, thank you."

"Right you be. I'll get up to the road now."

"OK Mr. Gormley, the engines are on their way."

Dermot put the receiver down and reached for his coat.

"And where do you think you're goin'?"

"Brid I told the man that I would go up to the road and I'm goin'."

"In your pyjamas?"

Sure enough, Dermot stood in his bare feet still dressed for bed.

"You go and get dressed and I'll call Joe to see if everythin's alright."

All the details supplied by Dermot Gormley had been passed on to the Fire Station in Armagh; Phil Carson the Station Officer was busy contacting the police as his volunteer crew prepared to take the two engines to Lower Hill Farm. It was standard practice for the Fire Service to pass on details to the police of any fire but on this occasion Carson was transferred to Special Branch which told him this was no ordinary fire site.

"Is that you Phil?"

"It is."

"It's John Harbinson here. I heard you've got a fire out at the Mullan farm."

"Yeah, so what of it?"

"Oh come on Phil, you mean to tell me that you don't know who's running the Provisionals in South Armagh?"

"I'm a fireman not a policeman. That's your job John. I just put out fires."

"Well, I would approach this scene with extreme caution; you know what I'm saying?"

"Understood John; I'll pass it on to the crews, and I'll be going out there myself."

"I'll see you there then. There's going to be plenty of activity from my end. I've got calls to make, so thanks for the info and just make sure your lads are careful."

"Thanks John, I'll see you later."

Carson replaced the handset and got up from behind his desk in time to see the second of Armagh station's two engines pull out into the street with lights and sirens flashing and blaring. He walked through to the station's control room and saw Stephen McCoubrey manning the radio.

"Stevie get on to Jim in the lead wagon and tell him that the site is the home of a suspected terrorist and that Special Branch have advised extreme caution. You can also tell him that I'm on my way to take charge of the scene, OK?"

"Yeah, I've got that."

McCoubrey was lifting the radio's handset as Carson returned to his office to collect his white helmet and water-proofs. He walked to his white Vauxhall Cavalier and threw his gear onto the front passenger seat before getting in and starting up. The sight and sound of his light and siren allowed him to clear the town in a couple of minutes – then it was out into the countryside as he followed the A28 toward Killylea.

It was the best day that March had had to offer yet, with a clear sky and a gentle westerly breeze. Carson passed through the village of Killylea and took the turn for the B210 before he reached Caledon. This was where he had to be careful of the route as he wasn't too familiar with the location. The road narrowed to little more than a single track with the hedges on either side in need of cutting. As he drove along he could see branches lying on the road, ripped out by the passing fire engines – it must have been like driving through a green tunnel in places. His route sloped upwards, and, as he came to the crest of the hill the dense hedges were replaced by fences on either side of the road. He was so distracted by the change in the surroundings that he almost passed the old man signalling from the lane on his left-hand side; even though he brought the car to an abrupt halt he had to reverse to draw level with the turn. The old man came around to the driver's side of the Cavalier and waited as Carson wound down the window.

"If you're here for the fire it's at the end of the lane."

"And you'll be?"

"Dermot Gormley, I called you boys out. Saw the smoke from my bedroom this mornin'."

"Right you be Mr. Gormley. If you get in I can drop you off but you'll have to stay away from the scene while we get the fire out."

"That's decent of you son, thanks."

Carson drove down the lane and stopped at the fork in the track for Dermot; who got out with the words that he would be over to the Mullan farmhouse before the firemen left. Carson continued along the lane and came up the hill to the yard. The two appliances were parked in front of what remained of the house. The calm movements of the crew showed Carson that there was little to do in the way of fire-fighting – thin wisps of smoke were rising from the shell of the old farmhouse – the roof had collapsed and those windows that hadn't broken in the fire were blackened with wood smoke – the fire had burnt itself out.

The telephone on his desk started ringing, but this time it didn't wake him – Lynch hadn't slept since the previous night – he'd been sitting in his office running every possible outcome of the job through his mind, and the whole futile process had drained him. He lifted the handset from its cradle with some effort and spoke.

"Yes?"

"It's Aiken. Everything is clean – house, vehicles, the lot."

"And the final score?"

"Twenty-one nil."

"Sweet Jesus! That's beyond expectation; have you got positive ID on all of them?"

"No, there're two unknowns and they could be foreign nationals. The bags have been marked with tape so the pick-up crews will be able to sort them out and the flight crew have been briefed about their importance so there won't be any mix-ups."

"Right, then I'll get on to the forensics chaps at the college and have a team ready to give them the treatment. Oh I nearly forgot – everyone's back OK?"

"I can only speak for my people, but they're all here; except Eddie Fairbairn – he's still up at Aldergrove dropping off the tanker, but he's called in to say that the transfer has gone OK but there could be a bit of a problem with clearance."

"How so?"

"The flight's not scheduled."

"Shit, there's always something; you get back to Fairbairn and tell him that the flight is to wait until they get a green light. There's no sense getting anybody annoyed."

"Is there anything else you need to know?"

"No, I just need to hear from Colquhoun that his team got home safely."

"Well, their lift arrived on time and they were away from the site at oh two oh five, so they should be just about ready to get their heads down."

"OK Karen, thanks for checking in. You get some rest and I'll see you bright and early on Monday."

Lynch hung up and considered leaving – he'd been at the office in Leinster Gardens for nearly a week and wanted to get back to his flat for a long hot bath and a decent sleep in a real bed. As he looked around the room for the umpteenth time he noted the wallpaper that was beginning to peel above the radiator – it wasn't that long since the whole building had been refurbished in a Regency style – and he made yet another mental note to have the decorators called so they could fix it. Then again, they could just strip the bloody lot and put up something a bit quieter; the Regency stripe had been giving him headaches all week or at least that was the way it seemed. As if in agreement with his thoughts on the interior decoration a pain was beginning to develop at the back of his head but much as he would have liked to call it a day and go home he knew he had at least three calls to deal with before he left. He rubbed his eyes and took a deep breath before settling into his chair – more bloody waiting…

…it was ringing again; Lynch slowly stirred himself and reached across the desk to answer the telephone, fumbling the receiver, letting it fall on the leather desktop – God but he was tired.

"Yes?"

"It's Colquhoun…"

"And about bloody time too!"

"Sorry sir, but I had things to do with the team, and it has been a long night."

"Enough excuses. Tell me, have you any news of import?"

"The whole team came through, performed well and scored successfully."

"And no losses?"

"We have one man down with a bad knee, but he's being taken to the military wing at Musgrave by your cleaners. Other than him not really – oh yes, one of the Americans did for his eye but it's nothing serious."

"Well that's not my problem – I didn't want to turn this into a hands across the ocean job – bad enough having the two chaps from the Republic."

"They had their uses sir, and they'll be going home as soon as they get their civilian kit from you people; the Irish lads and the Americans."

"Good. Before I go, I better offer you my congratulations on a job well done. It was the result we wanted. You can pass that along. Lastly I'll see you on Monday for the de-brief."

Lynch had heard and said enough and so brought the conversation to a close by hanging up. Another item of business to deal with; he reached for his personal directory and found the number he wanted – a brief conversation set the wheels in motion for the impromptu medical examinations that would be carried out that weekend.

One last call to make and then he would go home. The problem was he didn't relish the prospect – the call would be too early if he made it now – better to set his alarm and call later.

Phil Carson picked his way through the smouldering debris of the Mullan farmhouse. The two crews that had arrived at the scene before him had damped down the remains of the house – the roof timbers had caught fire and collapsed with the subsequent fall tearing through the first floor leaving a tangle of tiles and joists at ground level. None of the possible occupants had been on the scene and judging from the evidence thus far no-one had been home. He looked at his watch – seven oh five – and decided to give Special Branch a call. He walked out of the wreckage and back to his car to put the call through to the Fire Station in Armagh.

Stephen McCoubrey took a note of Carson's instructions and put the call through to the RUC barracks in the town.

"Armagh RUC, can I help you?"

"This is Fire Officer McCoubrey, I need to talk to Inspector Harbinson in Special Branch if he's there."

"I think he's about somewhere, I'll just connect you to his office."

McCoubrey waited as his call was transferred and the extension on Harbinson's desk rang – after maybe a dozen rings it was lifted and an agitated voice answered.

"Yes?"

"This is the Fire Service; Station Officer Carson told me to call Inspector Harbinson…"

"This is Harbinson."

"…it's about the fire at the Mullan farm. There're no apparent casualties, but the house is a complete loss. He said that your people would want to take a look at the scene as soon as possible."

"Right. You tell him to keep the scene as closed as he can. I've got calls to make and then I'll be with him in about an hour – tell him that. No casualties, you say?"

"None apparent yet sir, but they haven't been through the house properly, so they could turn something up."

"Aye, well we'll see. Thanks for the call."

Since the first contact from Phil Carson that morning John Harbinson had been busy making a series of calls to set up certain mechanisms – now that the full extent of the damage to the Mullan house was known he could activate those mechanisms.

"Make sure those roof timbers are secure before you go poking under them, d'you hear me Maurice?"

"Yes sir, I'm being careful."

"Has anybody turned up anything?"

Denis Sloan straightened up from the area he'd been surveying and called to Carson.

"We think we've got the ignition site sir. It's over here."

Carson and one of his teams were now searching through the debris of the farmhouse – the other team had been stood down and had returned to Armagh – better to have one appliance on standby just in case. He made his way through the burnt out wreckage to look at the remains of a cast-iron range that was partly covered with charred floor boards that had fallen from the upper storey. The area in front of the range was severely burned with the floor timbers completely burnt away – the floor appeared to have been covered with linoleum, and this too, was badly burnt. It was Carson's experience that, once it was alight, linoleum was the very devil to extinguish.

"You see the way that the floor timbers have burnt all the way through?"

"Yes."

"Well, we haven't come across any damage to that depth – so far this looks like the best bet."

"It certainly looks that way, well done Denis."

The fire investigation team would have their work cut out, but in all likelihood this was just another domestic fire that could be put down to sheer bloody carelessness. As he took another look around the site one thing still troubled Carson, where the hell were the owners? No doubt they'd turn up, but if John Harbinson was right about who they were then he didn't expect a hero's welcome.

The reconnaissance flight lifted off from the landing pad at Bessbrook and flew in a north-westerly direction to photograph the burnt out shell of the Mullan farmhouse. Another of the contingencies put in motion by Harbinson was placed on standby at Gough barracks in Armagh – the Bomb Squad of Ammunitions Technical Officers would be making a slow deliberate search of the Mullan house, outhouses and surrounding property, but not before the aerial pictures were developed and compared to those already held on record. The most important guideline was not to rush into a situation not of their making – if the opposition controlled the turf casualties were a definite possibility – they would take all the time necessary to secure the area and with a bit of luck no-one would get hurt.

His desk clock alarm rang at ten, and Lynch almost fell out of his chair as he scrambled to turn it off – God but he would be happy to sleep in his own bed tonight, and most of tomorrow too if truth be told. He decided a cup of something was in order so he walked down the hall-way to the kitchen and made another mug of what passed itself off as coffee. When the kettle had boiled and he'd poured water into the mug he lifted a spoon that was sitting on the formica work-top only to discover a ring of coffee staining the surface. God! if there was one thing he hated it was slovenliness – untidiness he could live with but making a mess for the sake of it annoyed him. He expected better from the staff at the Gardens; he would be sure to make everyone aware that such behaviour would not be tolerated.

A couple of minutes later a far from happy Lynch was back at his desk leafing through his list of telephone numbers; when he came to the one he wanted he lifted the receiver and dialled the ten digits – the analogue exchange whirred and clicked as the connection was made and on the second ring the rich toned voice answered.

"That had better be you Lynch."

"It is sir, and may I apologise for calling you so early on the weekend."

"Damn it man, I've been awake since before six. Stop kissing my arse and give me the news."

"Very well sir. The job has been completed with no losses to us, but the opposition has been totally wiped out…"

"What's the total?"

"Twenty-one sir."

"Good God Almighty! Twenty-one you say, good…. good. When are you holding the de-brief?"

"Well sir, my people won't be back until tomorrow and the others are going to drive down first thing on Monday, so it was left for Monday lunchtime."

"Right. Well I suggest that you give me your preliminary report later that day, at…. let's say the Carlton. I'll be there from five and you'll find me in the reading room."

"Understood sir."

"Right, well you can run along Lynch."

Before he could make any reply Sir Alex Johnson hung up. Lynch sat with the receiver in his left hand thinking about his ultimate superior – Old Etonian – First from Oxford – brief tour in the Grenadiers – final career move into the family business of power in the Civil Service – leading to the exalted position of Permanent Under Secretary to the Home Office – all in all one of the most ruthless men one could ever care to meet. He wasn't looking forward to the meeting on Monday and he reminded himself to avoid the obsequious approach; Sir Alex quite clearly saw through that.

Those concerns would just have to wait until Monday however; the promises of a hot shower, a double malt and a warm bed couldn't wait any longer. He put the handset down on its cradle, got up, reached for his jacket and left his office. Without a word to the security staff he lifted a set of keys for one of the "Department's" cars and walked out onto Leinster Gardens. It was the first time he had been outside in a week and even the polluted air of central London smelled sweet by comparison to his office. He got into the Ford Cortina, and added to the smog as he drove home.

Johnson sat in his study considering the possible results of the action against the Provisionals on the South Armagh border; if everyone involved kept their mouth shut the result would be quite remarkable – a lot of people would be spending every waking hour wondering just what the hell had happened and who was responsible, but if the truth should somehow be divulged then heads would roll. He wasn't prepared to consider the negative; only time would tell if the operation had been a complete success, but the fact that one of the most active so-called "brigades" had been wiped out was most definitely a cause for celebration. The potential for gathering new intelligence from amongst the leftovers and the new recruits would leave South Armagh a valuable source for years to come. The new "brigade" would take months, years even, to establish itself and in that time it would be penetrated to the point where no attacks could be launched without prior knowledge. Johnson was more than happy with the immediate outcome and the future looked decidedly rosy. If the operation satisfied all considerations there would, of course, be more to follow, and the longer such covert works yielded positive results the better the chance of actually winning this dirtiest of dirty little wars.

By 1230 the aerial reconnaissance was complete and the film that had been shot of the Mullan farm was being sent post-haste for processing in the lab at Gough Barracks. When the new pictures were available the analysts gathered for a comparison with existing intelligence photographs. After a painstaking hour during which nothing of any moment had been noted the ATOs from the bomb disposal team were called in. They in turn gave the pictures a lengthy scrutiny but could come up with nothing; any useful data in the form of vehicle tracks had been obliterated by the two fire appliances as they had driven along the lane, footprints, if any in fact remained, were obscured by the shadows cast by the hedgerows, and finally, the helicopter had touched down on the road so no imprints from the undercarriage had been left. Not that any such details were being speculated upon by the analysts or the ATOs – they were all looking to see if the fire was a set-up to draw the security forces into a trap. The final assessment was that if it was a trap it was a rather desperate one – really, who would go to the length of burning down their own house as a means of drawing the army or police into a trap? Not even the PIRA would go to such extremes, but that said, caution would be exercised in the approach to the farmhouse and the search of the remains and the farm buildings.

By the time John Harbinson had made all the arrangements for the surveillance and search and then driven from Armagh to the Mullan farm the Fire Service had reached the conclusion that there were no casualties involved in the fire. At a little after one o'clock Harbinson pulled up behind Carson's Cavalier and got out. He watched as one of the fire men walked over to Carson and pointed to him, in the meantime he leaned against his car, lit a cigarette and waited for the senior Fire Officer to join him.

Phil Carson walked over to Harbinson taking his gloves and helmet off as he came; he was covered in grime from the fire and had worked up quite a sweat in the course of the search.

Harbinson grinned and shook his head as Carson came to a halt in front of him.

"Looks as if you've been busy Phil."

"Aye, and bugger all to show for it so far. The forensics boys'll have to get to work on this one if it's anyway dodgy because all we've come up with is an accidental fire most likely started by a coal sparking from the range in the kitchen."

"And no sign of the occupants?"

"Not a thing, and we'd have found them if they were here. It looks as if your boys were out when this happened."

"Lucky them! Still they'll be more than a little pissed off with their house burning down. But I suppose we should have known that this one wasn't going to be neat and tidy."

"What makes you say that?"

"All the cars have gone, there should be at least two and there's a Transit van as well, and not one's on site. It looks as if the Mullans have gone away for the weekend. Oh well, at least we've got all the registration details; I'd better get on the blower and have them looked out for."

"Aye, I guess we've both got calls to make."

Harbinson crushed out his cigarette and got into his car, reflecting, as he reached for the radio handset, that it was just as well that he had made all his contingency calls that morning – soon the Mullan farm and surroundings was going to be swarming with all manner of experts – ATOs, forensic staff, fire investigators and God alone knew who else.

At 1431 a Boeing Chinook landed at RAF Lyneham to be met by a variety of vans all bearing civilian markings. The crews of the vehicles had been waiting patiently for the big twin rotor helicopter since midday but final flight authorization had taken longer to acquire for the unscheduled trip than anyone had expected and in the interests of playing down its significance a patient approach had proved the best – better that than ruffling feathers and drawing unwanted attention by making an issue of the flight's importance. In less than ten minutes the cargo of black polyurethane bags had been unloaded and the vans left the base via the several access gates that bypassed the main security entrance. Two of the bags, specifically marked with red tape, lay in the back of a Commer van that was being driven south to the Royal Military College of Science at Shrivenham.

The ATO and his team arrived from Gough Barracks in their distinctive armoured Ford Transits – two units had been sent, giving the Bomb Squad eight men to work with. Two cars had already come from Armagh bearing five Special Branch officers; two of whom were now guarding the entrance to the lane. The lead Transit came to a halt beside Constable Derek Patterson and the passenger door opened. Without leaving his seat the team leader, a young captain, gestured to Patterson.

"We've got the right place then?"

"That you have sir. You know we were expecting you and your lads about half an hour ago. Did you get lost or something?"

"Every bloody road looks the same, give me a break."

"Well, you know what they say about officers – can't read a map to save their lives."

"Not you lot as well! Christ, it's bad enough that I have to put up with that from my own, but comedians in the RUC I can live without."

"Ah well, you're here now sir, and that's the main thing. I just need to log you and your team in. It'd probably be the easiest if I give you the clipboard and you fill in the names. Oh and could you mark the arrival time as well please, it's ten to three."

Patterson stood back from the Transit as the captain wrote the team's names down and put a call through on his Motorola to Harbinson, who was organising the rest of the Special Branch team up at the farmhouse. By the time he had informed his superior of the ATOs arrival the roll was complete. He took the clipboard and pointed up the lane.

"Just keep heading along the lane – it takes a sweep to the left and then up to the yard. My boss, Inspector Harbinson, has set up a temporary command post in the yard. No doubt you'll be wanting to coordinate with him."

"We won't be going to the farmhouse just yet. I want a slow approach on foot first just to be sure that there aren't any nasty surprises along the track."

"Are you sure that's really necessary sir? After all the fire brigade have been in and out with two big engines and we've been up and down that lane a couple of times, and…"

"And you're not qualified to say whether an area is secure from devices. We'll do it our way."

Patterson raised his hands in mock surrender and stepped away from the lead vehicle. As the camouflage clad members of the Bomb Squad clambered out of the Transits Patterson walked back to his partner Dave Larmour who was leaning up against their Ford Cortina with a Sterling sub-machine gun casually balanced in the crook of his left arm. Patterson shook his head and took a couple of deep breaths.

"Is it just me or is it a waste of frigging time doing a full sweep of the route in? Look how many people have been up and down that bloody lane so far today and nothing's gone bang!"

"Aye, well, I know what you mean Derek, but he's just being careful. Anyway by the looks of that young fella he hasn't been on the job too long, so he's probably trying to make the right impression."

"I take your point, but they could still save some time starting at the junction with Gormley place. Let's face it even the Provos aren't going to risk friendly civilian casualties with a bomb along that shared section of lane."

"Do you want me to tell him?"

"If you would; I don't think laughing boy's too impressed with me."

While Larmour trotted over to the ATO's Transit, Patterson radioed Harbinson again to say that the ATO and his team were coming in on foot – the news was greeted with a philosophical "Jesus Christ" – Special Branch were in for a long day.

Hugo Robinson stood in front of the large bay window in his living room, the mug of coffee in his right hand forgotten and growing cold. He looked out at the water of Dundrum Bay and the sea beyond, but the view made no impact on him at all. He should have heard from Finn by now; the details of last night's meeting and the result of Lynch's interruption should all be ready for his next report, but nothing, not a word. He'd deliberately got up early but such an expedient had proved unnecessary. He had been second guessing the possibilities all day, but no matter how hard he tried he couldn't escape the fact that he just didn't trust Lynch. Lynch was the fly in the ointment, the little man who would never understand the finer points of agent-handling, but sadly the one with all the power and the patronage to aid its use.

Another thing had been nagging Robinson and that was the fact that he had passed on the information that had made last night's operation possible. His devotion to the job and the rules of, as Kipling had called it, "the great game", had undoubtedly endangered Finn – one of the most valuable intelligence assets that anyone had secured in Northern Ireland. It was so difficult to be sure that one was doing the right thing, and at times it was very hard to live with the consequences.

Robinson closed his eyes and tried to picture himself as a child running along Ballykinler strand – this was his escape mechanism; a means of relieving the pressure, but it didn't work this time. He opened his eyes and looked out at the bay; hoping that paying attention would distract him. The tide was running fairly low and there was a near windless calm. He'd take Hervey for a walk and try to clear his mind.

He walked into the kitchen and lifted his coat down from the peg on the back door. As he shrugged on his weather beaten wax-proof he lifted a pair of binoculars from the dresser – maybe there would be some bird life of interest on the sand bars exposed by the low tide. Thus prepared he looked over to the sleeping form of Hervey his black labrador who was curled up on his bed next to the kitchen radiator.

"Come on old boy, time for your walk."

Hervey got up and stretched; then, seeing his master ready for the off, he padded over to the back door which Robinson now held open. Before going outside Robinson switched on his answering machine in the hope that Finn would make contact while he was out.

The exchange with the old man had been surprisingly cordial. The captain had expected some venomous "Brits Out" rhetoric; at least that was what he had been led to expect from just about any local in this part of South Armagh. But no, Dermot Gormley had merely asked their business and had even offered to "keep an eye" on the two Transits that were now parked in the junction of the two lanes. The ATO had expressed his gratitude but told the old man that he couldn't accept as the area was not safe as yet. Seemingly satisfied Dermot walked back to his house telling the soldiers to be careful as he left.

The team were now slowly moving along the lane – one man on either side of the track with an opposite number on the field side. The only tools being used were eyes and hands – any electronic equipment may have speeded things up but it could also trigger any device that they came across. There was no substitute for vigilance so everyone was giving the hedgerow the utmost scrutiny, looking for anything that seemed out of place, but no wires, no disturbed earth, no broken branches, nothing to break the monotony, and in all honesty that was the way the ATO liked it, even if it did lend sympathy to Patterson's point of view.

Their progress had been slow but they were now only a hundred or so yards from the farmhouse; up ahead the ATO could see the Special Branch men grouped around one of the parked cars. Even with their destination in sight there was no notion of the team hurrying – the search would be carried out by the book with no deviation. Every man on the team knew that it was better to be slow and arrive in one piece than to rush things and not arrive at all.

John Harbinson looked down the lane at the slowly advancing Bomb Squad and at the same time cursed and forgave their caution. His men had been sitting on their hands for over half an hour – the time, however, had not been completely wasted – search areas had been designated and a discussion had covered the reservations that some of the men had about working their way through the partially burned out farmhouse. In truth none of the team had worked on a fire site and they didn't want to miss anything.

A crash followed by a stream of bad language came from the remains of the house – Phil Carson had stayed on the site waiting for the fire investigation team to come from headquarters in Lisburn, and rather than waste his time he had continued his search on his own now that the second fire engine had returned to Armagh. Harbinson was more than glad that Carson's men had left before the ATO and his team had arrived; he could just imagine the exchange that would have taken place if the second engine had been held up while the Bomb Squad carried out their search of the hedgerow. The problem with this particular job was no-one really knew who had ultimate authority; each service probably thought they had, but the ATO was only there because he'd been invited, Special Branch were there because it was the Mullan farm, so maybe Carson was right, until the fire had been fully investigated the whole area was under Fire Authority control.

Harbinson looked at his watch and another problem became apparent – it was just after four o'clock, so it would be getting dark around six. If the search was to continue all day they were going to need some form of lighting. He would ask the ATO if there were any arc-lights and generators at Gough – Special Branch didn't have any kit along those lines that was for sure.

A very dirty Phil Carson walked out of the wreckage and came over to the huddle congregated around Harbinson's car. He took his helmet off and slowly shook his head.

"I called Lisburn bloody hours ago – where the hell are those lazy sods – well there's bugger all I can do on my own. Any sign of 'Felix'?"

"Yeah, they're playing it safe down the track. Take a look for yourself."

Harbinson pointed down the lane to the oncoming figures of the Bomb Squad and Carson turned to take in the view; turning back he let the Branch men know his opinion.

"Jesus Christ! The world and his wife have been up and down that bloody lane, what the hell is their boss playing at?"

"Give him a break Phil, he's just being careful. Anyway, as you said, nobody's showed from Lisburn, so we've got time to kill. I don't know about the rest of you but I could do with a brew; so who brought the flasks?"

At 1826 the Commer van made a left turn into the Shrivenham estate, stopping briefly at the main security gates for the driver to ID himself and state his business. "Bikini Alert" status was "Black" so no effort was made to search the contents of the van which suited the men inside just fine. The Ministry of Defence policeman waved them on and the van carried on up the gently sloping road toward its final destination.

One of the great things about MOD establishments was the fact that it was assumed that nearly everyone had no idea where they were going – the sign posting was superb. The particular red-brick block that the driver wanted was somewhat detached from rest of the College buildings with a strip of trees providing additional privacy. The driver steered the van down a ramp that led to a basement entrance, sounded his horn once and waited.

Less than a minute had passed when the rolling shutter door to the left of the van opened; three men emerged from the gloomy interior, two of them pushing hospital trolleys. The driver stayed behind the wheel as his passenger got out to lend a hand. No words were exchanged as the two bodies were lifted from the back of the van; for that matter little or no attention was paid by the delivery men to the reception crew or vice versa – if asked later what the physical appearance of both sets of men had been the best anybody could have said was "average".

With the transfer complete the passenger returned to his seat in the van and the trolleys were pushed back into basement corridor. The driver executed a three point turn and drove the van back up the ramp following the road down to the main entrance. When the van came to the junction with the main road the driver glanced at his watch – 1837 – if he kept his foot down they'd be in Gosport in time to get a nightcap.

The fire investigation team had been hard at work since they'd arrived, collecting samples for analysis back at their laboratory. Sections of the linoleum that had escaped relatively unscathed were cut from the floor – they would be of particular interest as the high concentration of linseed oil meant that it burned with great intensity. If the range was the ignition site the floor covering would have helped the fire to spread. Every square foot of the house had been photographed as Carson had led them through the wreckage, pointing out the details he and his men had noticed on the first inspection. Lab tests would finalise the judgement particularly when the gas chromatography results were taken into account. The samples would be tested for evidence of accelerants which would be obvious to gas chromatography analysis – if such evidence were found then the apparent accident would become arson. The general view of the investigators was not in favour of arson however; years of experience didn't detect anything suspicious – it just didn't look or smell like a deliberate fire.

The remains of the front and back doors were assessed and no signs of a forced entry were apparent. It was difficult to tell if any of the windows had been forced, but there were no obvious signs on the team's inspection. With the almost complete loss of the house and contents it was impossible to tell if a robbery had been disguised by arson, but that was really a matter for the police anyway. The only thing that stood out during the search was the lack of personal documents – even in a total loss situation something would have survived if only in part but in this case there was nothing. During the search of the farm buildings no evidence such as cans of inflammable liquids had been uncovered other than what would be expected on a farm, and the quantities were not out of the ordinary. If this was a case of arson it just might show up under laboratory scrutiny, but for the moment it looked very much like an accident.

The accident assessment was giving John Harbinson some trouble. It wasn't that he didn't believe the experts from the Fire Service; it was just that he didn't believe in accidents where the Mullan brothers were concerned. When people were as careful as these two had been over the years he found it hard to accept that they would be stupid enough to leave a stoked range unattended. It maybe didn't smell like arson, but for Harbinson the possibility of carelessness was too good to be true. Another thing that didn't add up was the fact that, as one of the fire investigators had told him, no document remains had been found, not a driving license, bank book, even a passport, nothing. With all the vehicles gone added to a lack of any papers it certainly looked as if the Mullans were gone, but why leave the range fully stoked? They must be up to something and something very big by the look of it.

Another thought crossed his mind so he took his Motorola from his pocket and called Patterson.

"Derek has anybody made a stop to ask any questions or a pass that has caught your eye?"

"Nothing sir. It's been quiet as the grave down here."

"OK, keep your eyes peeled and let me know if anything crops up."

"Just one question sir. Are we here for the night?"

"I shouldn't think so, but I'll keep you posted."

Harbinson broke contact and looked around the yard for the ATO – he wanted to know if anything had come to light during the Bomb Squad's sweep of the area. He couldn't see any of the ATO's team around the yard or at the Transits, so he went over to the large barn and looked inside.

Four members of the team were working their way through the various items of farm machinery and the storage bins that were lined against the interior walls. The lighting in the barn was inadequate to the search requirements so the beams of four torches flitted over the areas under scrutiny, giving the illusion of motion. Harbinson found the moving lights disorienting and was glad of the chance to lean against the work-bench which was just inside the door. One of the soldiers, a sergeant, finished his search of a large galvanized feed bin and came over to the main door.

"Anything I can do for you sir?"

"I was just curious to see if you'd turned anything up?"

"Not a bloody thing sir. The Mullan brothers are too bloody smart to leave any kit lying around for us to find. Now, if you were to spend a week going over the farm land, well, that might tell a different story, but these buggers usually have all their gear salted away somewhere over the border."

"So you're looking on this as a waste of time sergeant?"

"Not at all sir. This is all good training. Besides we've got a new boss and he needs the practice."

"Give me a shout if you do find something, OK?"

"No problem sir, but I doubt if we will."

The smell of disinfectant, the dull green tiles on the walls, and the sound of dripping water, none of these things helped the pervasive negative quality of the mortuary. Major Denis Sopel looked at the two new arrivals and thought that neither of them would be enthused by their present surroundings, nor their condition either for that matter.

Sopel had received the call around lunchtime, telling him that "two parcels" would be arriving in the late afternoon, and that his services would be required for "unwrapping" – where did these people get their euphemisms from? – did they think they were being clever? – God only knew. The other order he'd been given was that he should recover any "tags" that were left in the "parcels". Sopel would have to work quickly – he had to perform two autopsies and then produce a concise report for delivery on Monday morning – without any mishap it could be done, but he was only to have the services of one assistant. Cause of death was not a concern – what was of interest was any clue that would aid identification. He'd done this sort of work before – trying to put a name to a body that couldn't be identified before or after some servant of the Crown had shot it full of holes or worse.

He looked at the two bodies that had been removed from the heavy duty polyurethane bags; nothing he saw gave him any clue as to who or what these men had been, their clothing was non-descript, apart from the small marks under the nose their facial characteristics were unremarkable. His mortuary technician, Sam Harper, came in from the scrub room checking his surgical gloves for a close fit. Sopel reached for a pair of shears – first things first the clothing had to be removed and sent for analysis, maybe there would be some clues there, but that wasn't his concern.

"You get the boots Sam and then give me a hand with his clothing."

Harper removed the laces completely and loosened the boots as much as possible before pulling them off.

"Don't forget to keep each individual's gear separate. We've got bags for each man's kit and somebody's coming round to collect them later tonight."

Both men worked in silence as the clothes were initially cut, then removed and finally neatly folded for packing in the bags provided. Even allowing for their previous experience both men found the task difficult – dead weight in this case meant just that – both bodies were mature, well nourished males, the lightest of whom still tipped the scales at over 180 pounds.

"OK Sam, I need X-rays. We'll start with the thick-set chap first. It'll just be the head and chest so it won't take too long."

They manoeuvred the trolley across the corridor, the rubber wheels squeaking in resistance to the white tiled floor, and into the X-ray room before transferring the body onto the bench. Harper placed an X-ray transparency under the head and retreated behind the shield that screened both himself and Sopel from any harmful radiation as the exposure was made. The procedure was repeated for the chest region and then it was the turn of the taller man. When they had finished taking the X-rays they returned both men to the dissection room. Harper took the transparencies away for developing leaving Sopel alone with the two corpses.

He checked that a fresh tape was ready in the recording system that had been recently installed; technology had finally come to the RMCS and it made the troublesome requirement of a note taker, or worse the need to stop periodically to take notes oneself, a thing of the past. With the system ready Sopel began his external examinations, again beginning with the thick-set man.

He began with a general physical description; specific measurements such as height and weight would be taken later when Harper returned. Once he had completed his brief description he then turned his attention to distinguishing marks such as birthmarks, physical abnormalities and scar tissue. It was with the last category that Sopel found something to record – there was the puckered scar of an entry wound just below the left clavicle. With some effort he turned the body over so it was lying face down; on the left-hand side there was an exit wound, about half an inch above the superior border of the scapula, and five inches across, which was clearly marked by a star-shaped pattern of shiny scar tissue. The wound had not been closed with any degree of skill leading Sopel to the conclusion that it had been suffered in the field where there was no immediate access to medical facilities. The size of the entry and exit wounds favoured a rifle round rather than a pistol, but a large calibre handgun firing high velocity ammunition could possibly have done the damage. One thing was certain; the victim was no stranger to armed conflict.

In addition to the entry and exit wounds there were ligature scars around both wrists as well as numerous scars on the forearms and hands with two deep ones on the face – Sopel's initial conclusion that this man was a career soldier or even terrorist seemed to be backed up by his analysis.

Next, he took a series of swabs from both hands and then scrapings from beneath the fingernails. Both sets of samples were labelled and he placed them alongside the bag of clothing belonging to "subject one".

He was in the process of inspecting "subject two" when Harper returned with the developed X-rays. Sopel pointed at the microphone suspended above the examination tables and drew his hand across his throat indicating that Harper should keep quiet before the machine was turned off. Sopel finished his analysis before pausing the tape and walking over to the X-ray viewing screen which he turned on.

"Anything interesting?"

"Just what you'd expect sir. Both men have three rounds lodged in the thoracic cavity and one in the head. None of the rounds have fractured although there is some deformation. Should be fairly straightforward to extract them."

"Well let's have a look."

Harper fixed the first transparency on the screen, allowing both men a frontal view of a skull which had an entry wound below the nose and the clear image of slightly misshapen bullet lying perhaps an inch below the roof of the parietal bone at the rear of the skull. These were precisely the details that Sopel was hoping for, but something else showed up on the X-ray, something unexpected.

"Which one of the two does this shot belong to?"

"It's the shorter bloke sir."

Sopel went back over to the table and opened the corpse's mouth, turning the head from side to side as he examined the teeth.

"Come here and have a look at this Sam. I think we've got a foreigner."

Harper joined Sopel and looked into the mouth; the upper left lateral incisor, and behind it the cuspid and the bicuspid were covered by a metal crown and the surrounding gum showed evidence of infection.

"That is most definitely not local work. I'm going to have to call Peter Jefferson and hear his opinion, but I'll have to get clearance first. Before I start sounding off is there anything odd in the other chap's head X-ray?"

"No sir, nothing like this anyway."

"OK, you get him ready for a full examination and I'll make my phone calls."

The 4-tonner Bedford had arrived with the lighting equipment and generators just after eight o'clock and after half an hour of fumbling in the dark, bright halogen spots lit up the farmhouse and the yard. The fire investigation team from Lisburn had collected all the evidence they wanted and had departed; the ATO and his team were still picking over the site, still empty-handed, and Harbinson's men were by now somewhat pissed off that their efforts were ineffective. The site was clean – that was the only conclusion to be drawn from the fruitless search – maybe the forensic tests in the lab would throw up some evidence of foul-play, but Harbinson wasn't so sure. He leaned against his car smoking his umpteenth cigarette weighing up the immediate possibilities and concluded that no purpose was being served by continued efforts at the farmhouse. To carry on with the search was to waste time that could be better used listening to the local gossip – if the Mullan brothers had made a move someone would know and Special Branch would pin the information down one way or the other.

He looked around for his men, seeing that they were dispersed throughout the remains of the house. He walked over to the nearest man, Sergeant Bill Kirkpatrick.

"That's it Bill. We're achieving bugger all here – time to go. Get the rest of the lads together and I'll call Patterson and Larmour to tell them we're on our way out."

"Who's going to look after the site when we've gone?"

"The ATO and his boys can keep an eye on things; he seems keen enough."

"Are you sure that's the right way to deal with it sir?"

"You know something Bill; I get nervous when you call me sir. Maybe you're right; I'll call the boss and see what he has to say."

"No offence sir. It's just that that young Rupert seems a bit of a tit. Leaving things in his hands could lead to a real balls up."

The reference to the ATO brought a smile to Harbinson's face. Kirkpatrick had fifteen years experience and an opinion that was worth listening to.

"Yeah you're right Bill. I'll call McCleary and ask for a decision. As a matter of interest have you found anything?"

"Bugger all. The fire seems to have got everything."

Hugo Robinson had eaten a dinner that he hadn't really wanted, his appetite virtually non-existent. His walk on the beach had thrown up more questions than answers and the distance covered had not brought the hoped for fatigue that could have silenced them with sleep. The only positive effect of the exercise was a content, exhausted labrador – Hervey was curled up by his radiator in the kitchen.

No messages on the machine and no contact from Finn subsequently. Something was badly wrong and Robinson was now certain what it was – there would be no call tonight, not tomorrow, not ever – damn Lynch and all his kind – all that time and effort for what? Robinson wasn't conceited enough to think that his was the only agent/handler operation in the North, but he did feel that it was one of if not the most important. Finn was shaping up to be a valuable source and Lynch and his hooligans had ignored his potential and acted like the thugs they were. He'd have something to say to Lynch as soon has he could contact him. If that didn't work then there was another avenue open to Robinson.

Peter Jefferson had answered the call despite his wife Pamela's protests; when Sopel had passed on the details he immediately wished that he hadn't. The dinner party invite was two months old and he was backing out at the last minute – he took a deep breath and told Pamela.

"An emergency? For Christ's sake Peter you're a bloody dentist! What can be so important that you have to drop everything and go into work tonight of all nights?"

"Come on Pammy, I've got to go…"

"Don't call me Pammy, you're not getting out of this so easily. I'm going and that's all there is to it."

"And what are you going to tell Sarah and Jonathan?"

"That you had an emergency that couldn't wait – that'll give everyone a laugh – emergency root canal or something. You are such a weakling at times Peter!"

She had slammed the front door on her way out leaving him no opportunity to reply. When it came to having the last word Pamela was an expert. He had breathed out through his nose, closed his eyes and tried to calm down. Shit, shit, shit, shit, shit. Saturday night and when he should have been accompanying his wife to a party where was he going? To look at some foreign dental work belonging to a very dead foreigner – bloody marvellous.

Two hours later all thoughts of his wife, dinner parties and arguments were forgotten. Sopel had been right to bring him in on this one; there could be no doubting the foreign origins of "subject one". The large crown on the upper left teeth was not the only sign of overseas dental work – on the lower jaw, both left and right, there were two other crowns, smaller admittedly, but also of stainless steel. In the west, for cosmetic reasons crowns tended to be made from material that could at least simulate the colour of teeth, such as porcelain. Such factors were of little concern in the cash strapped and hence more practical Eastern Bloc. Swaged stainless steel crowns were a cheap way of dealing with decay and poor oral hygiene; the fact that this man had possessed a smile capable of scaring small children wasn't important – anyway most people with bad teeth would be similarly afflicted. Judging from his dental work Peter concluded that this man had come from behind the Iron Curtain, and had been of a lowly enough position not to benefit from expensive dentistry.

Sopel had already pointed out the extensive scar tissue that this man had accumulated over the years – that and the state of his teeth led them to the joint conclusion that he was part of a training cadre from a Warsaw Pact military or paramilitary unit. Jefferson straightened up and looked over to Sopel who was carrying out the autopsy on "subject two". Sopel looked up from the chest cavity, which was clamped open, with a quizzical expression on his face. Jefferson pointed to himself and then the office, indicating his intention to take a break. Sopel nodded, looked back at the corpse and then held up his right hand with his fingers spread – "see you in five minutes".

Leaving Sopel to whatever butchery he had to complete, Jefferson went into the office, sat down and began to go over the brief notes that he'd made during his examination. There was no doubt in his mind that he was dealing with a foreign national, but what really intrigued him was the background to this man's arrival at Shrivenham. The hypotheses that worked their way through his mind ran from the mundane to the bizarre and outlandish. Writing his report wouldn't be half as interesting as speculating on "subject one's" reason for being here – who was he, who did he work for, why was his death regarded as necessary, where had he been killed and by whom? The half glazed door rattled as Sopel came into the office drying his hands on a paper towel.

"Well Denis, how are you coming along with your friend?"

"There's maybe another hour's cutting and then I can sew him up. Bugger it! I'm going to be here all bloody night, what with writing reports and so on."

Sopel walked over to his desk and sat down heavily as was his habit. He leaned back in his chair and put his feet up on the well-worn Moroccan leather panel on the desk top before tossing his paper towel in the bin and rubbing his hands over his face. It was obvious to Jefferson that he was tired and that it would be a long stretch through to the morning.

"Well if you need an assistant I'll lend a hand."

"Thanks for the offer but Sam's enough help. Anyway I thought you'd want to get back to Pamela ASAP."

"Not tonight. We were just about to go out when you called and I'm not exactly in her good books."

"You should've said."

"Denis you said it was an emergency – besides I've never done one of these before."

"Yeah I wanted to talk to you about that."

"Why is there a problem?"

"Not really, but this never happened."

"What cloak and dagger and all that?"

"I'm serious Peter. You write up your report and then you forget everything."

"Oh come off it…"

"Listen, this whole business doesn't exist. Those two outside don't exist, the operation that led to their being here never happened and the report you file is for one man only. After he's read it, it won't exist either. Is that clear enough Peter?"

"Just who are we working for?"

"Oh for Christ's sake! Don't answer a question with a bloody question. I had to get clearance for you for this job; which was given because I said your discretion could be relied upon – don't prove me wrong."

Jefferson opened his mouth to speak but the look on Sopel's face made him think better of it. He returned to his notes and tried to put all of his curiosity behind him. Sopel opened the centre drawer of his desk and withdrew several sheets of red paper. He leaned across the desk and held them out to Jefferson.

"How's your handwriting?"

"Legible."

"Good. Then you can write your report. Sign and date each sheet when you've finished it. Right I'll leave you to it, I'm going back to finish number two. You might want to take a look at him when I've finished just in case there's anything of interest in the dental field."

"OK Denis, and I'm sorry I didn't take you at your word. As soon as I'm finished this'll be forgotten."

"Believe me, it's the best way to deal with this sort of thing."

As Sopel returned to the scrub room for a clean gown and gloves, Jefferson turned his attention to his report reflecting on the strange world he had become a part of and the need for complete discretion.

John Harbinson sat across the desk from his CO flipping through his notebook finding the relevant details to answer Alex McCleary's questions. The wall clock made a series of clicks and whirs before it chimed the third quarter – 10.45pm and Harbinson was beginning to feel the need of sleep.

"…nothing that you can see as an indicator?"

Harbinson's concentration had slipped and he knew that McCleary wouldn't put up with anything less than his best.

"I'm sorry sir; I didn't catch all of that."

"Tired aren't you?"

"Yes sir. The whole bloody day spent out at the Mullans' and not a bloody thing to show for it."

"Aye, well if that's the case it's down to forensics to prove if it was foul-play and all we can do is wait and see if the brothers turn up. You've run a good investigation so far John but you need to be on top form to keep running. Go home and get some sleep."

"What about you sir?"

"I'm just going to give Kirkpatrick a call and then I'll be off home myself."

"Right you be sir, I'll see you out at the farm in the morning."

Harbinson took his coat from the chair back and left the office, carefully closing the door behind him. McCleary looked at the notes he'd made during the discussion of the circumstances to date – the Mullan house totally destroyed by fire – no sign of the occupants – no remains of documents belonging to the Mullans discovered in the wreckage – no obvious evidence to suggest arson – no incriminating physical evidence found in the wreckage or in the outbuildings – no vehicles on site – all told nothing. McCleary hated unresolved cases and this one wasn't starting well. He got up from his desk and left his office; maybe Kirkpatrick would have some news. He walked along the first floor corridor to the stairs and went down to the communications control room. He took an empty chair and put the call through himself; there was no need for formality Kirkpatrick had been under McCleary's command for over ten years.

"Hello Bill, this is Alex. Just want to check the situation, over."

"Your voice procedure is as ropy as ever sir. Other than that I got nothing to report."

"Is Patterson OK?"

"He's out having a last look about the place before he gets his head down."

"Have you got somewhere to sleep sorted out?"

"Yes sir. We've taken some floor space in the hay loft. The lads from the Bomb Squad are still here and they're going to secure the area; leastways that's what the Rupert says."

"John said he was a bit keen."

"That's a word for it."

"Just remember that you have to work with him."

"I'll bear that in mind. Are you coming out here tomorrow?"

"Aye, I'll be out with John in the morning."

"It's hardly worth the trip."

"Well if it wasn't the Mullans I doubt if I'd be coming. As a matter of interest what's your view of this thing?"

"Looks like an accident and proving anything else is going to be a real bastard."

"That's what John said."

"And he'd be right. I honestly don't know what we've got here but I don't think we're going to get any easy answers."

"What makes you say that Bill?"

"Just a feeling – this whole thing looks too neat."

"We'll see. Anyway Bill I'll let you go and I'll see you in the morning."

"Thanks for the call sir."

McCleary returned the handset to the cradle, but rather than leaving for home he sat and mulled over Kirkpatrick's words – no easy answers – nothing of substance to build an investigation on; it seemed to lead to no resolution, a very unsatisfactory state of affairs, one that McCleary resented.

Sopel had finished work on "subject two" with a series of stitches that closed the thoracic cavity. The "tags" had been recovered and bagged; if they were going for forensic evaluation they wouldn't have far to travel – the RMCS had a forensic ballistic lab that put must civilian facilities to shame. Both Sopel and Harper had gone to the scrub room for a wash and fresh gloves before they began work on the second autopsy.

Just as Sopel was about to make his initial incisions on "subject one" Jefferson came out of the office with several red sheets in his hand.

"I've finished Denis. Where do you want me to leave it?"

"There's an out tray on my desk – put it there."

"If that's all then I think I'll go home."

"Sorry Peter, remember I want you to take a look at the other chap before you go."

"Right, I'll be with you in a minute."

Jefferson left his report on Sopel's desk and then went into the scrub room for a pair of gloves. He came back into the dissection room to find Harper standing at the end of the examination table supporting "subject one's" head as he held the jaw open. Jefferson took a pen light from his trouser pocket and looked into the open mouth. There was nothing instantly remarkable about the dental work; all the fillings were competently executed in amalgam, but there was one crown on the lower left first and second molars.

"Sam could you tilt the head back about a couple of inches?", Harper made the adjustment and Jefferson took a closer look, "Yeah, it looks as if you've got two eastern Europeans, this one's got a stainless steel crown as well."

"OK Peter; put that in your report and then you can call it a night, oh and if you need more paper it's in the middle drawer."

Harper rejoined Sopel with "subject one".

"You up for this sir? We could always come back tomorrow and finish this off."

"We could, but we're not going to. Make sure there's fresh tape in that machine and I'll start."

Sopel took a clean dissection knife from the trolley to his right and began the standard "Y" shaped incision beginning at the right shoulder just below the join with the clavicle. The cut ran down to the centre of the abdomen ending at the underside of the sternum. He repeated the cut, this time from the left shoulder, effectively drawing a "V" on the corpse's chest. The last major incision he made ran from the sternum down to the symphysis pubis, the join at the centre of the pelvis. This completed, he began to cut along the ribs at the costal cartilage severing the sternum from the rib cage. When he finished the necessary cuts he removed the sternum, placing it on the trolley to his left. Having removed the sternum he next attached a set of retractors to both the left and right sets of ribs; the way was now open for him to begin his examination of the upper thorax and the retrieval of the three rounds that were lodged there.

Sopel had concluded from the X-ray of "subject one's" chest that the rounds were spread in a pattern running from right to left. The first had entered between the first and second ribs impacting on the top edge of the second rib causing a slight deflection towards the sternum; the round penetrated the right lung and came to rest in the right pleural cavity. The injury caused by the round had been extensive, with the lung deflating and the pleural cavity being filled with aerated blood, such a wound would not have been immediately life threatening but the victim would have been severely incapacitated. Sopel applied suction to remove some of the fluid from the cavity that was obscuring his view of the lung. He then palpated the superior lobe and was rewarded with the feel of a hard object that didn't belong in the delicate tissue of the lung. Rather than waste time with a careful removal, Sopel excised the whole section of lung that held the spent round and placed it beside the sternum.

The second round had impacted the clavicle near the sternum causing it to radically change direction, and instead of penetrating the muscle around the shoulder and neck, it had moved across the chest following the line of the right clavicle over the sternum with it finally lodging on the underside of the left clavicle. Sopel could actually feel the round when he applied some pressure with his fingertips; so he was able to quickly remove it after making a small incision allowing access for a pair of forceps.

As the second round joined the portion of lung and sternum on the trolley the doors swung in from the corridor, and a motorcyclist walked to the first rank of examination tables. Sopel turned to face the newcomer as Harper again paused the tape.

"Are you here for the clothing and physical samples."

"Yeah."

"Fine, but let's get a few things clear. Number one – you're late – you were meant to be here before eight – it's now nearly midnight, and this job is time critical. Number two – you don't saunter in here with a casual attitude. Number three – you call me sir."

"Sorry sir, it won't happen again."

"Glad to hear it. Now, the bags you want are sitting on the bench to your right, take them and go."

The dispatch rider collected the samples and sealed bags of clothing, putting them in the large hold-all slung across his chest. When he'd finished he stood unsure of his next move. Sopel looked at his obvious discomfort with amusement before dismissing him. The rider nodded and acknowledged the order with a suitably chastened "Yes sir, thank you sir", before leaving.

"Jesus Sam, where do they get them?"

Before Harper could answer the glass in the office door rattled once more as Jefferson came out into the dissection room.

"Finished Peter?"

"Yeah, it's all in the tray. Now, if you don't mind I'm going home to see if I can patch things up with Pamela."

"Best of luck, and thanks for coming in at such short notice."

"Forget it Denis – besides it was interesting."

Jefferson pulled on his coat and walked out; leaving Sopel and Harper to complete the examination of "subject one".

The third round was, in Sopel's opinion, the one that had killed the man. It had entered the neck at the larynx, causing significant damage to the cartilage before impacting on the fifth cervical vertebrae. From here it had changed direction moving upwards along the oesophagus in the direction of the jaw before lodging against the hyoid bone. The destruction of the larynx would have made breathing virtually impossible, and married to the damage to the right lung this pointed to asphyxiation as being the most likely cause of death – leastways it would have been if somebody hadn't made absolutely sure by putting one in the brain.

These discoveries were entirely academic, but Sopel's curiosity needed satisfaction even if he was merely retrieving the rounds. He looked at the incisions and the damaged tissue and considered his role; years of training and a desire for service, and where had it led him – to a basement dissection room carving up some unfortunate like a butcher. To hell with the department; he'd put it all in his report anyway, showing them that he was just as professional as they were.

He quickly cut down to and around the hyoid bone this time locating the round with the tip of his right index finger before removing it with forceps. With a clatter it joined the others on the trolley – three down and just the one in the head to go. Harper looked at the wall-clock and yawned.

"Feeling tired Sam?"

"Yes sir, and I was thinking that this chap's going to be just as dead in the morning, so maybe we could call it quits tonight. What d'you reckon sir?"

"Yeah you're right. I'm starting to feel a bit jaded myself. Tell you what, we'll get these two locked up and then you can go."

"Right sir."

It took them a quarter of an hour to clear the dissection room and scrub up, so it was nearly ten to one in the morning when Harper left. Sopel went back into his office and fell onto the couch, hoping for a few hours sleep before he started writing his report.

* * *

Sopel woke at seven feeling stiff and sore; it was the first time he had slept on the couch, and he hoped it wasn't going to become a frequent occurrence. He got up and stretched, feeling the knots in his shoulders – God, but he wasn't going to repeat this in a hurry. His first thoughts were of the report he had to write, but he quickly discounted that in favour of coffee. Fortunately he had a filter machine in his office and it was soon bubbling away. He walked out into the dissection room and looked at the comparative mess that Harper and he had left after their fastest of rushed jobs attempting a clean-up. One thing that Sopel had always prided himself in was running a pristine operation; as he looked at the dirty examination tables and the unemptied steriliser he realised that the department's order for an immediate report had taken away his authority, his control.

He went back into his office, poured himself some coffee, and sat on the edge of his desk considering his position. Ever since he had taken command of the forensic pathology group at Shrivenham he had been under the illusion that he was his own boss; one phone call from the department and his compliance with its demand had shattered that illusion. He had no option but to obey the order, but the insult to his professionalism cut deeper than one of his scalpels. Damn it all! He was expected to behave like a butcher – do some cutting and retrieve the evidence of somebody else's dirty work, and the worst thing was that he had willingly accepted the task. Arguing with himself wasn't going to achieve anything, except maybe remove the last vestiges of self-respect that he possessed. He finished his coffee and decided to clean up the dissection room – one thing the department couldn't do was take away his basic standards when it came to cleanliness.

He began by starting a new cycle on the steriliser just to make sure that his instruments were clean before washing down the examination tables and the floor. He hadn't had to tackle the menial task of cleaning like this since his student days and it surprised him that he could take pride in such a mundane job. He looked at the surface of the second table and thought a little darkly that it was more than clean enough to eat from, not that anyone would. He closed his eyes briefly and shook his head, admonishing himself for his unfortunate observation. With the tables and floor finished he returned to the steriliser after he had secured a new pair of gloves from the scrub room.

So intent was he on taking the clean instruments from the steriliser that he didn't hear Harper come in at eight thirty.

"Morning sir. I didn't realise that you'd swapped jobs."

Sopel put a retractor down on the instrument tray and turned to face his assistant with no hint of a smile on his face.

"We left everything in such a mess last night that I felt a tidy up was necessary, that's all."

Harper looked at his CO and realised that he was in no mood for lame attempts at humour so he settled on a more businesslike approach.

"Is there anything else needs doing sir or would you prefer it if I prepare "subject one" for the cranial examination?"

"I'm just about finished here Sam, you get him ready and while you're at it lay out the instruments as well."

"Yes sir."

As Sopel finished arranging the instruments on the tray Harper removed "subject one" from the cold storage and lifted him from the trolley onto the examination table. Next he selected the additional instruments that Sopel would need for the procedure, being careful to check the function of the small circular saw. Sopel went into the scrub room once again to don fresh gloves and a gown, and on his return he asked Harper to put a new tape in the recording machine before he began.

Luckily "subject one" had very closely cropped hair which removed the necessity of a shave; Sopel marked a guideline around the skull with a chinagraph pencil, giving him a clear indication of where to cut. He put the X-ray back on the viewer for one final check of the round's location – as he remembered, about an inch below the parietal bone towards the rear of the skull. He lifted a scalpel and began cutting along the line, the tissue of the scalp put up a brief resistance to his blade but was ultimately no match. Once he had made his incision all the way around the head he started to cut with the surgical saw. The high pitched whine of the saw's motor deepened as it met the obstacle of the frontal bone. The unmistakeable odour of bone burned by the friction of the cutting edge spread throughout the dissection room; no matter how many times Sopel performed this procedure he couldn't ever get used to the smell. Four minutes of careful cutting were rewarded with a neat incision all around the skull; only in a couple of places had the saw cut through the protective sheath of the dura mater resulting in leaks of cerebrospinal fluid. Sopel now made a cut all around the interior of the cranial cavity, aiming to separate as much of the dura mater from the actual brain as possible. This accomplished, he gripped the dissected section and gave it a couple of sharp twists – left and right – until it came away form the head altogether. The surface of the brain was now exposed allowing Sopel to recover the fourth round from "subject one". If he had been spending a reasonable amount of time the round would have been extracted with care, but that was not the case. On this occasion Sopel made two major incisions on the left-hand side of the brain towards the rear – one running left to right along the central sulcus to the longitudinal fissure, and the other a horizontal section running through the parietal and occipital lobes – when completed he lifted a section weighing about eight ounces out of the cavity and placed it on the tray to his left. The round was in this section of the brain according to the X-ray and now that it was excised Sopel would have no trouble in finding it.

He stepped away from the body overcome with a desire to go outside to breathe some clean air; Harper could take care of things for a while.

"I'm just outside for a minute or two Sam. When I get back we'll bag these two up, and then I'll phone for a pick-up."

"Whatever you say sir. I'll start putting things in order."

Sopel walked along the corridor and up the steps to the ground floor and then out through the double doors that marked the main entrance to the medical centre. There were some clouds in the sky, but it was a fine sunny day and a world away from the dissection room. It was only when he stood outside that Sopel realised that he was still wearing his surgical gloves and gown; if somebody should see him – so what? He was tired, his self-belief was in tatters and when he came right down to it he just didn't care.

Lynch woke about ten-thirty – he had promised himself a bath, some decent food and a drink – his head told him that the generous measures of malt last might had been a little more than he should have drunk. He pulled himself into a sitting position and then got out of bed, lifting his dressing gown off the chair beside the wardrobe. He padded through to the living room, his slippered feet barely making a sound as he walked across the various rugs that covered the parquet floor. The untidy clutter of the room, with its eclectic collection of artefacts from around the world, showed the absence of a feminine touch. Lynch had had a housekeeper once, but her ideas on cleanliness and order were somewhat at odds with his so they'd parted company; as for a wife, such an idea was totally alien to him. There was no doubt in his mind that women had their place, but it wasn't telling him how to keep house or being married to him for that matter. He sat down in a wing-backed armchair before lifting his telephone off the Turkish carpet that he'd bought all those years ago in Cyprus; a bit threadbare but worth having in his estimation. He made a call to his secretary at Leinster Gardens which was answered on the third ring.

"This is Lynch, any messages?"

"I'll just check the log Mr. Lynch; bear with me for a minute."

Liz was a good secretary; discreet and always willing to work weekends, the extra pay didn't hurt, but Lynch liked to think that she was one of the few dedicated to their job.

"Nothing on your personal list and nothing in the general office log."

"Good. As a matter of interest what time do you finish today Liz?"

"Four o'clock Mr. Lynch."

"Fine. Well, I'll check in about quarter to."

"I'll be here."

"I'm sure you will be. I'll speak to you later."

Lynch hung up and reached for the A4 pad sitting on the coffee table; he'd make some preliminary notes as he had breakfast. With luck there would be no distractions and he could spend the bulk of his time preparing for his meeting with Johnson tomorrow.

"And you've found nothing that identifies the Mullans as the PIRA?"

"Not a bloody thing sir. We were at it all day yesterday as you know. The ATO and his lads had a really good look over the place and they had no joy. As far as evidence linking the Mullans with any group is concerned I'm fairly confident that there's nothing to find. As for proving that this was malicious the only hope we have is if the forensics people from Lisburn find something."

"There's still the slurry pit to be drained. The ATO said he'd be back with a tanker to pump it out, you never know what they might find."

"I got the feeling he thought this whole job had been a waste of time."

"You could be right John. There's another thing though; did you get the registration numbers of the Mullan vehicles circulated?"

"I did aye, but if you're thinking about feedback you can forget it sir – it's too early yet."

"Too much to ask for I suppose. They'll turn up somewhere, the cars or the Mullans."

McCleary and Harbinson had been looking around the wreck of the farmhouse and the outbuildings since their arrival over an hour ago; both were dirty and the lack of success did nothing to improve their humour. McCleary had seen enough and walked back to Harbinson's car. There was no doubting the older man's bad temper and Harbinson knew from experience that this sort of unproductive investigation drove his boss around the bend, so he too returned to the car.

"Right, here's what we do. Kirkpatrick's wasted keeping an eye open down at the entrance so he's coming back. Patterson can stay and run things here once I've got some uniforms sent out to keep him company. We get the team together back at Armagh and then we start listening out for any news that may be doing the rounds. If we get nothing from that we can start on people who'll talk to us. How does that sound John?"

"It's better than poking around here getting nowhere."

"Fine, then we'll go."

Harbinson got into the driver's seat and started up. With McCleary occupying the front passenger's seat they drove back down the heavily rutted lane that had seen so much traffic over the last two days. When they reached the junction Harbinson pulled over; at first glance there was no sign of the two men from Special Branch, then two figures appeared from the hedgerow, both carrying Sterling sub-machine guns. McCleary took note of the care both men had taken with their cover – all too often men would have taken the easy way out and sat in the car – he was glad that the men on his team were professionals – then again he would have expected no less from Bill Kirkpatrick.

McCleary got out of the car leaving Harbinson to make the necessary call to Armagh.

"Well that was an informative visit."

"Like I said last night sir, bugger all worth seeing."

"Yes Bill, I have to say you're right. Anyway I've decided to get some uniforms out here. How do you feel about looking after them Derek?"

"Definitely sir."

"Good, because I'm leaving you in charge of the site. Bill, you're to come back in once they arrive. Then we can start seeing what noises are being made, if any."

"Could take time sir. We'll have to check on the other local faces and see what they're up to."

"I'm aware of that Bill. Look, we'll have a meeting when you get back."

"Yes sir."

McCleary got back in the car, leaving Kirkpatrick and Patterson to continue their seemingly pointless vigil.

"You got a bit close there, if you don't mind me saying so, I mean, telling the Super his job."

"I've known Alex McCleary a long time sonny boy, and I wasn't telling him his job; so shut up and get back in your bush."

"You don't have to take it out on me, sergeant."

"Well that's where you and I would differ; you see I'm the sergeant, you're the constable, this investigation is offering us nothing to work with and best of all it's going to rain."

Sure enough, the clouds had been rolling in from the northwest all morning and there had been a few drops of rain earlier on. Before both men got back under cover they took waterproofs out of the car – miserable was bad, but wet and miserable was just a little too much.

By the time Sopel got back to the mortuary Harper had nearly finished clearing the debris. Both subjects one and two had been bagged up again ready for collection, the examination table was clean and the steriliser was going through yet another cycle. He'd even put the two large tissue samples over on the dissection bench so that Sopel would have easy access to magnifying optics if needed.

"Christ Sam you've been busy."

"Not really sir, you've been gone nearly an hour."

"As long as that?", Sopel rubbed his temples and breathed deeply, "OK, let's get this business finished."

He went into the scrub room for one last set of gloves and then returned to the samples. He sat on a stool and began with the section of lung. The soft tissue gave no obvious signs of the path taken by the round – the pulpy material seemed to have closed up as the bullet had penetrated – so Sopel relied on touch. He gently palpated the sample and feeling a definite resistance towards the apex he picked up a scalpel and cut into the tissue to be rewarded with a scrape of metal on metal. He put done the scalpel, lifting a pair of forceps to finish the extraction of the round. Once he had secured the round in the forceps it was simply a matter of gentle teasing to bring the round clear of the lung. He dropped it with a clatter into the enamel kidney dish that Harper had left on the tray.

The brain section proved somewhat easier to work on. The make up of the tissue meant that closure was not as complete as with the lung. When he looked at the underside of the sample the damage caused by the passage of the round was apparent. Gently he cut away at the site of the damage determining the path of the round. He continued to cut along the path until he met resistance again. Forceps aided the removal of the round and it too clinked into the kidney dish to join the one taken from the lung. Sopel got off his stool and lifted the kidney dish.

"Sam, would you clear this stuff up while I clean these."

After a couple of minutes cleaning and drying, Sopel was able to put the two rounds in the small plastic envelope with the other two he'd removed from "subject one" yesterday. His gloves went into the waste bin for burning and his gown joined the others for the laundry before he washed his hands. He looked in the mirror and a haggard, unshaven figure looked back – he was more than thankful about his upcoming leave – ten days of thoughtlessness were exactly what he needed. A phone call and a report stood between him and a comfortable bed – best to get them out of the way – time was still a factor.

Sopel removed a sheaf of red paper from his desk drawer as Harper began the final clean up. He leaned over his old desk, momentarily forgetting the task in hand, thinking of the optimism which his father had shown in buying the desk – "When you're in general practice a solid piece like this will give the patients a sense of security" – if the old man could see him now, what a joke! He shook his head to dispel such thoughts, picked up his fountain pen and marked the first sheet – Observations on Autopsy "Subject One". He checked that the relevant cassette was in his tape recorder and pushed "play" to hear his own voice give the details of the basic physical description. Once he'd heard enough he pressed "pause" and began putting the details down on paper. Sopel wrote for two hours without a break, during which time Harper had tried to tempt him with coffee twice, but had only received a snarl for his trouble. By one-fifteen he'd finished writing and then began reading through his script making any necessary corrections as he went. When he'd completed proofing his report he called Harper into the office.

"Right Sam, I want the rounds for ballistics, and any other material connected with subjects one and two is to go for incineration. I don't want you to miss anything, understood?"

"Yes sir. Would that include the X-rays as well?"

"Christ! I'd completely forgotten about them. No they've got to go with the report, bring them in here now. Thanks Sam, that could've been a real disaster."

"No problem sir."

Sopel wondered how he'd been able to forget something as important as the transparencies – they were the last thing he wanted lying around. Harper brought them into the office before he made a final sweep of the dissection room. While Harper was checking for any errant material Sopel put his report, the X-rays and the tapes he'd recorded during the two autopsies in a red pouch. Once he had checked that everything was accounted for, including Jefferson's orthodontics, he sat back down and made the telephone call that would hopefully end his involvement in this business. Somebody must have been waiting by the phone because the connection had barely been made before it was answered.

"Yes?"

"This is Sopel at Shrivenham. My report's ready for collection and there're six cassettes and eight X-rays as well."

"And they're the only copies?"

"The report's handwritten and the only copies of the tapes and the X-rays are the originals. You're getting the lot."

"That's good."

"Look I'm not stupid, the orders were clear on that score."

"I take it that the "parcels" have been re-wrapped?"

"If you mean the two corpses I've just butchered, then yes, they're bagged up and ready to go to whatever hole in the ground you've got lined up for them."

"Take it easy Sopel."

"I don't even know who the hell you are, so don't tell me to take it easy. I've done my bit, just hurry up and clear your mess away."

"We're all on the same side Sopel, try and remember that."

"Just get somebody over here."

"They'll be with you in fifteen latest."

The line went dead and Sopel leaned back in his chair closing his eyes as he did so – it would all be over soon – until the next one anyway. He contemplated the exchange that he'd just had and realised that his little outburst would, no doubt, be noted and passed along the chain of command within the department. It was just the sort of thing that would stand against him with the grey men; well, too bloody bad, at least it would show them that he couldn't be taken for granted. No sooner had he comforted himself with this thought than another crossed his mind that shattered the illusion – the department owned him, not just now, but in the future too. He may think that his independent spirit would somehow keep him detached, but the truth was that he couldn't make a move without their knowledge – they might not be keeping him under scrutiny all the time, but he would never know when. This wasn't what he'd signed up for – another depressing thought was about to take root when Harper came into the office.

"How about that coffee now sir?"

"Thanks Sam. I think I'm ready for it now, and I'm sorry for biting your head off earlier."

"That's OK sir. I know this job's been a bit of a strain, then again they always are."

"So you've done work for the department before?"

"That's not for me to say sir."

"Soul of discretion, is that it?"

"Let's just say I know what's good for me sir."

"You're very right Sam. OK, when everything's been cleared up I think we'll call it a day, I'll make sure that the extra duty is logged, unless you want to put in for an extended leave?"

"That's alright sir, but the extra money won't go amiss."

Is that all that really counted – the extra money? God, if only it was that simple. Harper poured the coffee and they sat in the office drinking until they were interrupted by the arrival of four men from the department. The group leader came across the dissection room to the office, leaving the other three at the door. The earlier encounter with the courier had obviously filtered back to the department as this man was courtesy itself.

"Good afternoon sir. We're here to make the collection. I believe you have a pouch for delivery – I can take that from you now. So unless there are any special details the lads and I will be out of your way as quickly as possible."

"Carry on… I don't know what rank you are."

"That's alright sir, let's just say you've got seniority. We'll be out of here in no time, and my boss says sorry for any inconvenience."

Sopel was about to let the man know what he thought of the second-hand apology when the possibility that this was exactly what was wanted stopped him; he bit his tongue and then made a saccharin reply.

"It's been no trouble at all, just doing my job."

The somewhat puzzled look on the man's face told Sopel that he had perhaps overdone things; then again, maybe he'd been led to expect an outburst as confirmation of Sopel's unsuitability and the apparent good humour had thrown him. Either way he left the office with the pouch and went about his business. Good to his word the body bags were removed on trolleys in short order – a couple of minutes and the dissection room returned to normal – a tidy facility ready for the next session. Harper shook his head a couple of times and turned to his CO.

"I'm glad those bastards have gone, they make me bloody nervous."

"And why should that be?"

"I can never figure out whose side they're on."

"Probably their own Sam. Well they've gone now and I suggest that we follow suit."

"Right sir. I'll see you tomorrow at the usual time."

Harper lifted his jacket down from the row of hooks in the office and then walked out into the corridor. Sopel remained seated behind his desk. He spent most of the afternoon thinking about his present position – the only meaningful conclusion he reached was that he should stay in the forces even with the department's control, there just didn't seem to be any practical alternative; the private practice his father had wished for looked like an impossible pipe-dream. He went home before six with very few of his old certainties intact.

Lynch had called his secretary at Leinster Gardens at a quarter to four to learn that there had been no calls; he reiterated that he wanted no subsequent contact, so it was with some surprise that he answered his department line just after six.

"I'm sorry to bother you sir. I know you left instructions, but something's come up."

"Well for Christ's sake spit it out!"

"Yes sir. I've got a Mr. Robinson on hold for you and he won't take no for an answer. I've told him that…"

"Put him through."

The line went dead momentarily as Lynch was put on hold and then Robinson's irate voice came through as the connection was made.

"Is that you Lynch?"

"Yes."

"Well congratulations you bastard."

"For what?"

"Don't play innocent with me. You know damn well what this is about."

"If it's about your playmate Finn you know more than I do."

"Your department was paying a visit because I told you about the Brigade meeting. I've been sitting by my phone waiting for him to contact me and not a word. There's only one conclusion to be drawn – your bloody heroes took him out."

"As I said Robinson, you know more than I do."

"Don't give me that Lynch. I'll just say this, if Finn has been removed, I'm not without influence, and your department will have to face the consequences."

"Right I've been patient and reasonable, but you're pushing a little too hard. If he did get in the way, too bad, I've got better things to worry about than some South Armagh Mick."

"I had time and effort invested in that South Armagh Mick as you call him…"

"Robinson I don't give a damn…"

"Well I think you will."

Lynch slammed the handset into the cradle, angry that Robinson had succeeded, yet again, in making him lose his temper. Arrogant bastard – he seemed to think that the whole intelligence operation in Northern Ireland stood or fell because of him. Now he was issuing threats for God's sake! Annoying as that was, the reality was even worse; Robinson was connected and his access to "the old boy network" could create major problems. Lynch tried to comfort himself with the fact that he had friends in high places too, but somehow it wasn't enough. When these people closed ranks they tended to look after their own. Lynch only had two possible courses of action, one was to call Robinson's bluff and do nothing, the other was to call Sir Alistair and let him deal with the fall out. Neither option appealed to him, but inactivity was inexcusable and Johnson would crucify him for doing nothing so he lifted the handset and dialled the number from memory. He knew immediately that the call was answered that this was not going to be easy; the butler, footman, whatever took the call and asked him to wait while Sir Alistair was found and brought to the phone. Oh shit, he'd bothered the man at home on the weekend when he was obviously busy and that would have repercussions. Getting on Johnson's wrong side was more trouble than Lynch wished to deal with. He was thinking of the possibilities when Johnson, clearly annoyed, snarled at him down the phone. Even though he was expecting it, the venom in Sir Alistair's tone surprised him.

"This had better be bloody important Lynch. I've got guests and I don't appreciate you interrupting."

"Well I think it could be sir. It has to do…"

"Oh for God's sake get on with it!"

"Yes sir. I've just had a call from Five's man in Ulster, Hugo Robinson, you may have heard of him."

"I know the name. Continue."

"He's been running a turncoat who was taken out on Friday night, and to say the least he's pissed off."

"Is he now? And what relevance does this have to me?"

"He's issued a threat – says he's got connections and is prepared to use them. He isn't happy that I've rode rough shod all over his little patch of the turf."

"I understand your worry, but don't, I can take care of Mr. Robinson and his connections."

"Thank you sir."

"Well if there's nothing else I'll see you tomorrow as arranged."

Lynch put the phone down – it could have been worse, a lot worse. Now that Johnson was aware of Robinson's threat the problem was neutralised. Oh to be a fly on the wall when Johnson tore strips off that overgrown schoolboy, now there would be an exchange worth hearing! The internal damage that such divisions might cause could not be overestimated – the lack of inter-agency cooperation alone could result in entire operations being lost – forward planning counting for nought – personnel put at risk or worse. All these things could stem from the vanity of one man; if Robinson started making a nuisance of himself who knew where it might end. The worst case scenario was for him to go public, but no self-respecting operator would do that, no, Robinson would take a dressing down and retreat to some corner to lick his wounds for a while. The very idea of him going public was inconceivable, and Lynch dismissed it almost as quickly as it had entered his head.

Lynch returned to his notes for the de-brief tomorrow; the interruption from Robinson had taken some of the shine from what looked like the best of text-book operations, but now that Johnson was looking into the matter he could return to his self-congratulation. He had picked the teams, he had planned the logistics, he had developed the legends, he had solved the problems anticipated before, during and after the job, one man controlling the complex movements of over fifty people, and there hadn't been one slip, well nothing of any consequence. No matter what way he looked at it the conclusion was the same – he was very good. It just remained to be seen if everyone lived up to his standards. He'd start finding that out tomorrow, beginning with the de-brief.

Throughout the course of Sunday evening there was great activity at Shrivenham. The bodies of subjects one and two had been taken to the forensics laboratory, where fingerprints and more samples were taken. Fingerprinting "subject two" proved to be something of a trial as both hands had contracted in death leaving the lab technician with no easy access to the fingertips. There was no alternative and time was against him, so he took the unfortunate step of breaking the subject's fingers; as he saw it the man was dead and the added injuries were post-mortem, anyway he had a job to do. Breaking the fingers took a surprising amount of effort, but once they were straight the application of ink and the gentle rolling of the fingertips onto the sample sheet was complete in a matter of minutes. The dermal nitrate tests were carried out to determine if any powder or primer residues were present on the hands of the two men – unlikely as it seemed contact with or the use of firearms could just possibly aid in their identification. Swabs were taken from both subjects' hands with particular emphasis to the backs of the hands and the palms; the problem was that the tests were not foolproof, contact with other materials such as fertilizer, tobacco and even urine could produce the same blue colour after diphenylamine was added to the sample. The big problem was that both sets of results came up negative.

The clothing and such personal effects as there were had also undergone a series of tests. Nothing conclusive had been found – the clothing was of reasonably good quality, but nothing distinctive picked it out – the lack of manufacturing labels made identification almost impossible. The frustration at finding nothing was beginning to tell on the forensic team. The only excitement had been caused by one of the wrist watches; there was no doubting its origin; it was Soviet, military issue, and mechanical with a 17 jewel movement. The green dial bore a Soviet red star above a parachute and two stylised aircraft; on the back of the case was a serial number and the engraved image of a sunrise. Its very existence had led to some wild speculation, but the favoured theory was that it had been acquired during a foreign training session, most likely in Libya. Much was made of the watch, but in reality it was the only tangible result of the laboratory investigations, not much to show for over five hours work, but there was still the possibility that something might turn up when the samples had been fully examined.

All the additional information joined Sopel and Jefferson's reports in the pouch and by twenty-one hundred it was placed in the hands of the courier who would be driving it to Leinster Gardens. He was in luck tonight as the usual motorcycle run was deemed inappropriate – the contents of the pouch were too valuable to risk on a dispatch rider's questionable interpretation of speed limits and the wrong sort of attention that could bring. Traffic police interference notwithstanding he hadn't been overwhelmed at the prospect of riding to London on a crisp March night – the car would at least be warm and the radio would be something of a diversion. He set off on his uneventful drive mindful of the fact that he should stay well within the bounds of speed restrictions – the delivery was important but not time critical – as long as it was in the safe at Leinster Gardens for the morning meeting that was all that mattered.

* * *

"Morning Mr. Lynch. Have a good weekend off sir?"

"Yes George. I have to say my own bed was a very welcome improvement on that torture trap of a camp bed."

"Yes sir. You'd think that when you reach our time of life the need to sleep in those things would've passed."

"That's where you're wrong George – slave to duty and all that. Anyway it's done now. Is there anything in the safe for me?"

"I was just going to mention it sir, a package was brought in late last night from Shrivenham."

"Good. Right, well I'd better take a look at it before the hordes arrive."

"Expecting someone sir?"

"Yes. I should have five bodies this morning from about ten-thirty onwards. Just send them up to Liz; she'll look after them if I'm not ready."

"Very good sir."

Lynch made his way to the office at the rear of the ground floor that held the strong room. Leinster Gardens was equipped with a walk-in vault that held two additional safes for documents of a particularly sensitive nature; it was to one of these that Lynch directed himself. He used the key that unlocked the combination and then made the series of left and right turns to the dial that opened the safe door. A large red pouch had been deposited in the safe and it was this that

Lynch removed before closing the door, spinning the dial and removing his key. He retraced his steps to the hall and then made his way upstairs, stopping at his secretary's desk. Liz hadn't checked in for work yet so he propped the pouch against the desk before bending over to leave her a note – SHOULD BE 5 BODIES HERE FOR A MEETING BY TEN-THIRTY. GET THEM COFFEE AND I'LL CALL YOU WHEN I WANT THEM. With his housekeeping taken care of he lifted the pouch and walked to his office to begin reading the reports.

First out of the pouch were Sopel's observations on the two bodies that he had examined. Of the various distinguishing marks that Sopel had noted the entry and exit wounds were the only truly interesting finds. They clearly showed a connection between the subject and conflict and given the anomalies displayed by both subjects one and two it seemed a fair deduction that they were both combat experienced. Be that as it may Lynch was no closer to knowing just who these two men had been.

Jefferson's report came next; Lynch had never expected that forensic orthodontics would ever have any impact on his job but he was prepared to consider any expert opinion. The record of the general dental health of the two men had no real interest for Lynch, but when he came to the descriptions of the swaged stainless steel crowns present in both men he gave the report his undivided attention. Foreign nationals had not been expected and having this confirmation of Iron Curtain involvement was something that had only been dreamed of in the past. Yet here it was in black and white – these men were definitely not Western Europeans. Previous speculation concerning Eastern Bloc involvement in republican activities had only been concerned with the training camps in Libya and the procurement of weapons. Now he could place foreign personnel in South Armagh; the ramifications for future operations against the PIRA could be far reaching. Lynch was allowing fancy to fly him to a land of unrestrained anti-terrorist operations – such a policy decision would be for Johnson not for him – better to calm down and finish the paper work.

The general forensics report on the clothing and personal effects offered nothing other than the confirmation of the professionalism of the two men – no clothing labels – no documents – the Soviet issue wrist-watch was a bit of a slip-up, but other than that no identifying marks. The preliminary tests such as the dermal nitrate showed up negative and the fingerprints would take forever and in Lynch's opinion yield nothing. All told pretty thin, which was much as Lynch wanted it – too much information always meant difficulties – too many people would know small details which if assembled might just produce an incriminating whole.

The final report in the pouch made no reference to the two men brought in from RAF Lyneham; it did however make uncomfortable reading for Lynch as it cast some doubt on the discretion of Sopel. The opinion that was offered by the department's man at Shrivenham was that Sopel should be watched but did not as yet offer a definite security risk. If the only fallout from this job was a disaffected doctor at Shrivenham then Lynch could live with that – besides, who would believe Sopel – it was a fantastic story and the man's previous involvement in department work meant that he was compromised. No, it was merely a minor irritation. The difficulty with Robinson, now that was potentially disastrous but out of his hands, Johnson would fix that, and then it would be simply a case of moving on to the next job.

He looked at his desk clock and was surprised to see that he had spent over an hour reading the reports. It wasn't ten-thirty yet but he thought he'd better have a look and see if there were any arrivals.

Colquhoun and Mathieson had been up since before six, they'd eaten a quick breakfast and had then caught the dawn train from Hereford to Paddington. It was a short taxi ride from the station to Leinster Gardens which cut out the need for a crushed trip, albeit a short one, on the Underground. They now sat like a couple of schoolboys waiting for an interview with their headmaster – neither of them was overly comfortable with the surroundings or the fact that this was a department facility; doing the department's bidding was one thing but answering to it was another. Colquhoun in particular resented the deference he had to offer the likes of Lynch, and rank had nothing to do with it.

This was a new experience for Mathieson and he was nervous – he'd never been 2IC on one of these jobs before and in all honesty he preferred to be a team player rather than a decision maker. His usual attitude of the joker Jack-the-lad wasn't going to work here; he felt distinctly out of his depth and decided to let Colquhoun handle the de-brief, he was only going to speak if spoken to. He had just reached this decision when the noise of footsteps coming from the stairwell diverted his attention away from the cup of awful coffee that he had been given by Lynch's secretary on their arrival. Two women and a man came into view and it took a moment for him to realise that he was looking at the cleaner team leader, her 2IC and the watcher – their working clothes were a world away from the smart appearance they had now adopted – all three looked professional – bankers, solicitors, something of that sort. He put down his cup and got to his feet, followed by Colquhoun and they had just started to exchange greetings when a small figure came down the corridor.

"I'm glad to see everyone here early. Well, if you'll follow me we can get started. I'm sure none of you want to take a whole day over this so the sooner we begin the better."

The uncertain look on Mathieson's face produced another comment.

"Not much to look at Mr. Mathieson, but I'm in command here so just follow me would you."

"You're Lynch?"

"That's right Mr. Mathieson. You obviously didn't score too highly in the intelligence tests."

"I'm sorry sir. It's just that you're not what I expected."

"I never am. All joking aside, let's get on with it."

They followed Lynch back down the corridor and entered the large conference room opposite his office. The wallpaper was identical to the Regency stripe that Lynch had, but something about the scale of the room gave the burgundy and cream design a subtlety that it could never have in his much smaller office. The room was brightly lit by a series of brass mounted ceiling lights as the panelled shutters had been closed depriving the occupants of any natural light which also gave the room a certain timeless quality. An antique mahogany dining table surrounded by chairs occupied the centre of the floor; Lynch walked to the far end of the room and settled himself into the carver at the head of the table beneath a large blackboard that covered the back wall. The two groups, the representatives of the cleaners and the assault team took their places on either side of the table, arranging their notes and other documents before sitting.

"OK, ladies and gentlemen, I want to hear your reports in chronological order. Keep the anecdotal information to a minimum and I want no note taking – everything that you've brought with you stays with me as per instructions, understood?"

There were nods of assent from around the table.

"Very well, then we'll start with Mr. Colquhoun."

From his seat, to Lynch's left, Colquhoun began with the methods of entry of the various members of the team and their several journeys to the accommodations that had been secured for them – all of which passed without incident. He gave a brief description of his group's activities in surveying the weapons' burial site. Details such as the two encounters with the security forces – the RUC checkpoint and the border crossing manned by the Army were covered. Even his group's encounters with the American tourists did not avoid mention. It was a thorough and thankfully concise report. Colquhoun was about to begin detailing the congregation at Glaslough when Lynch raised his hand, obviously calling for a halt in proceedings.

"First class so far, but I want to hear from Miss Aiken. Karen if you'd be so kind."

"There's not much to tell sir. The preparations for the clean-up were as per your orders – I didn't deviate from them and as you know I waited for your call giving the final order to go. Walsh's stint in the hide may be of more interest."

"Is that true Walsh – see anything of any importance?"

"Not really sir. Lying in that bloody hide for a day wouldn't be anybody's idea of fun."

"I wasn't asking if you enjoyed yourself – I take it that you didn't – what I want to know is did you see anything noteworthy?"

"Well there was one thing sir. One of the unidentifieds came outside for a smoke which seemed odd."

"How so?"

"It just seemed strange that a man would come outside for a cigarette when all his mates were inside. Let's face it sir, they'd been in there all bloody day and I know for a fact that they weren't all non-smokers. What I mean is why go outside, unless you were a stranger to the men inside. There was also something about the way he smoked."

"Explain."

"He cupped the lit end of his cigarette so that the glow didn't show and when he put it out he nipped the end of the cigarette and put the butt in one of the bins at the back door."

"And what did that indicate to you?"

"Well, soldiers smoke like that sir. So taking it that he was unknown to the men inside and the way he smoked, if I had to hazard a guess, I'd say he was a professional."

"You're basing an awful lot on one form of behaviour, but you can't be sure."

"Maybe not sir, but I'm paid to make observations, and I think this is a fair one. Besides there was other evidence to support my theory which was turned up by the cleaners – a foreign watch and a lack of clothing labels."

"We're getting beyond ourselves here. Let's get back to your team Colquhoun, carry on with your report."

Colquhoun now took the department's players through the wood at Glaslough, the weapons retrieval and the walk across the border to the Mullan farm. There were no extraneous details and the matter of fact delivery lessened the impact of the assault when Colquhoun began the description of the entry team's snatch of young Mullan and the method of access to the house. He could have been talking about a trip to the supermarket to buy groceries for all the effect he had on his audience. Lynch had met some cool types in his time but when Colquhoun described putting three rounds into the back of Padraig Mullan's head he realised that this man was ice cold; he exhibited no feelings whatsoever. As the description continued Lynch ignored what was said but kept his eyes fixed on Colquhoun. By the time the house had been secured Lynch concluded that, firstly, Colquhoun was a very dangerous man, and secondly, he didn't like him. He returned his attention to the substance of the report just as Colquhoun afforded him the opportunity to move to Aiken's description of the clean-up.

"…team arrived and we lent assistance."

"I think I can stop you there and move along to the rest of the cleaners' report. If you would be so kind, Karen."

Aiken looked at her notes and began reading. Her delivery was every bit as cold as Colquhoun's but Lynch knew that it was purely a businesslike approach – he knew that Aiken had been affected by what she had seen – he couldn't say the same for Colquhoun.

"…and the drive from Belfast was routine although we had a couple of separations between the tanker and the van – nothing of any consequence. On arrival at the site we noted that perimeter security had been fixed at the road/lane junction and were informed that the site was cleared. When we got to the yard we began work immediately as per the briefing held earlier on Friday. The interior mess had been kept to the kitchen alone, with two additional casualties at the front of the house. Each body was checked and it was during this element of the clean-up that the watch and the lack of clothing labels that Walsh mentioned became apparent. The two individuals concerned were bagged and marked differently so that they could be taken for analysis. I then took charge of the search for any documents that may prove of interest and that's when I found these."

She removed the two bank books from her portfolio and passed them to Lynch. He opened them at the pages listing the entries and read the two balance figures, emitting a low whistle when he had added the two numbers.

"One hundred and nine thousand, four hundred and fifty-eight pounds. There's obviously a lot of money in border farming. Do we know where this all came from?"

"No sir. In the time we had we couldn't come up with more than these and their passports. Best guess, a mixture of Provo money and what the Mullans made from smuggling."

"Well it's our money now. I'll pass this along to someone with the necessary handwriting skills and we'll get it transferred."

"I'm not sure I understand."

"You are not meant to, Colquhoun. This is a department operation and as the saying goes "to the victor, the spoils". If you must know we operate on a very small budget and this will make life considerably easier."

"I just don't see it as an appropriate action…"

"Oh that's rich, coming from the boy-scout who led a team that killed twenty-one", Walsh had listened with growing disbelief and could contain himself no longer, "Have you ever got a screwed up sense of morals. You and your heroes…"

Colquhoun slammed both hands down on the table and sprang to his feet almost overturning his chair. He raised his right hand and pointed deliberately at Walsh.

"I wasn't going to mention your insubordination, but now I have. I've had enough from you, you've got a smart mouth and it's just talked you into more trouble than you can deal with."

Now it was Lynch's turn to voice his displeasure.

"Is that so Mr. Colquhoun?' Walsh here may overstep the mark once in a while but in this instance he has a point. Furthermore if discipline is called for I'm his CO and I'll administer it. You are not the only one who can raise issues of insubordination and I'm sure your commander would be fascinated with a report about your little outburst."

Colquhoun calmed down immediately and resumed his seat.

"I'm sorry sir. It's just that the irregular nature of your department takes some getting used to. The question of the money was beyond the normal scope of operations, that's all."

"What happens to that money is none of your concern", Lynch could see from Colquhoun's expression, however, that he was going to have to offer an explanation, "but if you must know it will give us the greatest satisfaction that the Provos are funding our work against them. Now let's finish what we've started and let's remember that we're all on the same side. Understood Walsh?"

"Yes sir."

Walsh looked at Lynch and knew from the narrow eyed glare that he would have some explaining to do later. It was yet another instance of his big mouth landing him in trouble, yet another explanation of his continued status as an NCO.

Aiken continued her report, detailing the removal of the Provo vehicles, the routes taken and their subsequent disposal. Her team had followed the same practice as Crawford, leaving the cars and the van in areas of Belfast where they would prove too big a temptation to thieves. The assault team's vehicles had also been collected from Glaslough and driven back across the border. Knowing that Colquhoun would ask, Aiken pre-empted him by saying that all the personal kit belonging to the team members was en route to Hereford and should be available for collection later that afternoon. She finished by giving the latest news on Lauder from the military wing at Musgrave Park Hospital – he was resting after exploratory surgery had shown severe ligament damage in his left knee. He was going to be out of action for some time but if he was the only serious casualty the operation had gone extremely well.

Lynch allowed the group a moment's reflection on the details before asking if there were any questions. When none were forthcoming he looked to his notes and then made his own contribution.

"I have little to add to what's been said other than to fill in one of the blanks that will have doubtless been preying on your minds – the two unidentifieds. I've received an interim report from forensics and although it is not conclusive the best guess is that we have two Eastern Europeans."

Lynch paused and scanned the faces around the table; the expressions ranged from eyebrows raised in surprise to the smug knowing look etched on Walsh. Leaving him aside an impact had been made, and having achieved his aim Lynch resumed.

"Now, there may be some fallout from these gentlemens' untimely demise but I don't think so. At best these were two mid-grade training officers and it is unlikely that they'll be missed. The effect that it will have, however, is the intensification of operations against the PIRA; the government will not look too kindly on our friends in the East becoming directly involved in our domestic troubles."

"So we can expect more of this kind of work?"

"Mr. Mathieson, I was beginning to think that you'd left us."

"Not at all sir. I just didn't have anything to say."

"Well, in answer to your question I can't say for certain, but it would seem likely. Does that satisfy?"

"To be honest, no sir. It has always seemed to me that we should have been doing this sort of job all along – from the start if you will. I never needed the excuse of some Ivans showing an interest to get tough on the bastards in Ulster."

"I take your point, but regardless of the apparent change in thinking at the top it now looks as if we're going to take the fight to those selfsame bastards. Does that satisfy?"

"It'll do sir."

"Fine. Are there any further questions?"

"Just one thing sir."

"What is it Walsh?"

"Well, I was wondering if there had been any noises on the ground locally?"

"Not that we've heard so far, and I should say that we don't expect to hear anything. You all did the job with consummate skill and if there had been any problems they would have become apparent by now. Anybody else?"

Again Lynch looked around the group to see if anyone needed clarification on any point – a few furrowed brows, but overall he sensed a quiet resignation.

"Right then, it just remains for me to say that any documentation relating to this job must be left in my custody and that to all intents and purposes this whole episode never took place. Mr. Colquhoun, Mr. Mathieson thank you both for your attendance. We know where to find you if we need you, but in the meantime it just remains for me to bid you good day."

Both men stood and as Mathieson left the room Colquhoun pushed the sheaf of papers together and placed them in front of Lynch. He nodded once, said "Sir", in a tone that could have been judged dismissive and walked out. The remaining department group sat in silence for nearly a minute before Lynch breathed out theatrically and shook his head.

"I want you all to give thanks that a man like that only comes to this department once in a while, even you Walsh. And just let me say that your behaviour was nothing short of bloody stupid. I honestly credited you with more wit – I won't make the same mistake again."

Walsh considered Lynch's words and realised that if that was all that was coming he had got off lightly; then again Lynch had a memory like the proverbial elephant so any notions he might have had about moving into the officer classes may just as well die now. Then again, what was the attraction of being an officer; take Aiken as an example – she was going to be commanding a desk in a week's time. For Walsh, watcher duties notwithstanding, there was no substitute for work in the field, and it looked as if he was going to be getting plenty of additional experience.

"Now that the heroes have gone, has anybody any points to make or questions they wish to raise?"

Jenny Ellison, who had contributed nothing throughout the course of the debrief, spoke up.

"It's been plaguing me all weekend sir, but what I want to know is am I taking over from Karen, and if so does that mean I'll be running clean-ups like this one in the future?"

"In answer to the first part of your question – yes, Karen's desk is yours. As for the second part, I have a question of my own – don't you feel up to leading a team?"

"I don't know sir. I don't think anyone could be sure, not until they actually have the job to do."

"That's honest. I suppose we just have to wait until the situation arises. Have you anything to add Karen?"

"Speaking for myself, I would say that I didn't know that I was up for Saturday morning until I had to do it, and to be honest I wouldn't want to do it again."

"I sympathise, but remember this, all of you; jobs like this one crop up now and again and there will always be a need for people to clean up the aftermath. You all knew the special requirements of the department when you were approached in the first place. Your continued discretion is vital – our operations are not open for discussion; so if you need a confessor you have to keep it within the unit and the bad news is that I'm the best you can hope for."

"I don't think either of the ladies was throwing in the towel sir. It's just that Saturday morning was extreme. None of us who were there are going to wipe out the memory – that kitchen was like something out of your worst nightmare."

"Right, well if it helps any of you I had similar experiences in Cyprus against EOKA; so I know what it's like. All I can say is that it gets better. Anyway, this isn't getting the job done, so let me have all your paperwork and you can go. You've all got some time off – put it to good use."

Aiken looked at Lynch as she passed over the papers, his small figure hunched over the various sheets of orders, schedules and scribbled notes.

"What about you sir, have you any time off?"

"Not me Karen, no. I've much too much to do – you know the saying – no rest for the wicked – fits me rather well."

Aiken followed the others out of the conference room reflecting on Lynch's words – no rest for the wicked – now there was food for thought.

Phil Carson sat at his desk in the Fire Station and tried to relax; he and the watch crew had been called out to a domestic fire just before five that morning, the house was a total loss but the young couple and their baby daughter had been rescued and that was the only thing that counted. It was at times like this that the job was at its most satisfying – a positive result with the knowledge that people had been given a second chance. Then again, there were the strange situations that he encountered once in a while, like the fire at the Mullan house on Saturday morning. There were no apparent casualties, no obvious evidence of arson, nothing, in fact, that answered any of the questions that he had.

Tired as he was, he couldn't take his mind off the details of the burnt out house. John Harbinson from Special Branch would be calling with him later that afternoon, doubtless looking for some clues, and he had nothing to give him. The preliminary report from headquarters wouldn't be ready for at least a week and anything he had to say would be groundless speculation without it. He went over the details of the scene but nothing stood out, no detail that would magically allow him to pull an explanation from the hat and leave Harbinson speechless. His sense of achievement from that morning's rescue was diminishing and he couldn't even manage to shut his frustrations out with sleep – his mind was too alert to the problems cast up by the Mullan fire.

He leaned forward in his chair and pushed himself upright on the edge of his desk. He needed a distraction and walked through to the kitchen to see if there were any members of the new duty watch having lunch only to find Stephen McCoubrey nursing a cup of tea as he leafed through The Sun.

"Stevie don't you have a home to go to?"

"I was off yesterday sir, and today I'm only on the phones, it's not as if I've got a load to do."

"It's just been a long couple of days. Is there any tea in that pot?"

"Aye there is sir, and not long brewed so it should be OK."

Carson poured himself a mug full and added his two customary sugars. The sweet black tea revived him somewhat but it didn't take his mind off the farmhouse fire so he sat down to talk with McCoubrey.

"Anything of interest in the paper?"

"It's all politics; Callaghan's getting the usual abuse, The Sun's calling for a general election, looks as if there's going to be a vote of no confidence, so that could happen."

"And what do you think?"

"Sure it makes no odds to us – we'll have the same lot over here anyway, and either way it'll be a useless shower that they get in London. You'll have Callaghan on one side and Thatcher on the other, and a lot of bloody difference they'll make; all they'll do is move seats. Nothing changes – sure they're only interested in money, bloody politicians."

"As long as they leave us alone to do our job."

"Aye sir, but they might not even do that."

"We should be alright, never you worry Stevie. There'll always be fires to put out."

Ellison and Walsh had gone for an early lunch but Aiken had declined saying that she might as well familiarise herself with her new office at the Gardens. The room she'd been allocated was somewhat on the small side, with a desk, three chairs and two filing cabinets accounting for most of the floor space, but being amongst the most junior members of department staff she supposed that it would have to do. She took her seat at the desk and looked around her new domain – the Regency motif was continued with yet another stripe design on the walls, although here it was a more subdued magnolia and pale green combination. The colour scheme didn't bother her that much, she'd be able to cover it up with some appropriate pictures; after all it was her office and she couldn't see any reason that would stop her from personalising it. The reproduction walnut veneered desk was a definite improvement on the strictly utilitarian metal obscenity that she was leaving behind in Belfast; she opened and closed every drawer, noting that the previous occupant had taken care to totally clear the contents. She'd seen enough; the office would do, so she made her way down the corridor to check out the kitchen.

She was looking through the formica panelled cupboards for something else to drink other than Maxwell House instant coffee when she became aware of a figure in the doorway. When she turned to face the newcomer she was surprised to see Eddie Fairbairn.

"What are you doing here Eddie? I thought you'd be staying in Belfast for a while."

"No such luck Karen. Dropped the tanker and cargo off at Aldergrove, got a call on my return to Belfast, straight back to Aldergrove and here I am."

"Looking awfully smart."

"Oh thank you. You like this?"

Fairbairn made a somewhat theatrical turn and bowed, showing off his light-weight slacks, polo shirt and linen jacket.

"Very continental, but if you don't mind me saying a bit on the skimpy side for London in March."

"Observant as ever, but not too skimpy for Cyprus, even this time of year."

"So you're off to Cyprus?"

"Did I say that? Never mind where I'm off to, tell me this though, have you seen Lynch?"

"Finished the de-brief about half an hour ago, so he's either in his office or the conference room."

"Thank you. Well, I'll be seeing you."

The tall spare figure of Fairbairn left Aiken to her search and thoughts about the mixed bag of personnel that the department drew from on occasion.

"…and you see him this afternoon?"

"Yes sir."

"Well I hope that the lads in the Fire Service have something for us. I'll tell you one thing John, I know it's early days, but to have heard nothing is bloody strange."

"I know sir, and it's not even a case of people being unwilling to talk to us, there's just bugger all for them to say. The only thing is as you say it's early days, so maybe somebody will come up with an explanation that sounds plausible."

"Have any of the lads heard anything since Saturday?"

"Nothing of any substance. All we know for definite is that the Mullan brothers and young Padraig have disappeared. No sign, nothing, and that's it."

"Well, all we can do is keep at it. What time do you see Carson?"

"Half-three."

"Right. Well I'll be here if anything turns up, so you let me know if there's any news from the Fire Service when you get back."

"Will do sir. The lads are scheduled to be back around five so I told them that we'd be having a meeting, so I'll see you then."

Harbinson left his boss's office and returned to his own. He opened the file on the Mullan fire and checked through the bald facts that they had on record. Nothing looked out of the ordinary and he moved on to the two statements that had been taken from the Gormleys; they'd seen nothing, heard nothing, leastways if they had they weren't telling and to be honest Harbinson didn't get the impression that they were hiding anything. This case was shaping up to be a real pain in the arse – lots of physical evidence and no detail.

"I sympathise Hugo, but really, just because this chap of yours hasn't been in touch constitutes no evidence of foul play. Give it a few days. He's probably holed up with some tart somewhere."

"Stephen it's not as simple as that and you bloody well know it. He gave me the time, the place and the names of a meeting, a meeting that was targeted by us, which he attended and I've had no communication from him since."

"I still don't see what your concern is."

"For Christ's sake! I've invested a lot of time in this source, he was just becoming useful, and then along comes Harry Lynch and his department with a *carte blanche* from Sir Alistair Johnson and all my work gets blown to hell. This sort of action just keeps us involved in a dirty mess that we'd be better off out of."

"I take your point, but what do you want from me?"

"I want you to put that bastard Lynch in his place, and I want you to put a rein on Alistair Johnson – he's behaving like a hooligan."

"I don't think that he'll be too amenable. You've got to remember his position and more importantly your own."

"I see, he's Permanent Under Secretary whereas I'm just some prole, he's a god-like creature and I should remember my place. Not good enough Stephen, the man's a liability and playing at soldiers isn't going to solve matters over here."

"Alright, I'll see what I can do. I'm seeing him for drinks later at the Carlton so I'll test the waters then, but I'm making no promises."

"I understand, but you do realise what's at stake here?"

"Yes, yes. Call me tomorrow and we'll see where we stand."

"Thank you Stephen."

Robinson replaced the handset, putting his right hand on Hervey's head as the labrador sat patiently at his master's side. He gently rubbed the dog's head as he thought about the consequences of his conversation with Sir Stephen Phillips; Lynch wasn't the only one with friends in high places – although friends was putting it a bit strongly – they'd attended school together and their relationship was at best cordial. The one thing to Robinson's advantage was also unfortunately a potential weakness, and that was the fact that Stephen Phillips was, for all his power and prestige, an insecure man; he'd relied on the protection of others at school and nothing that Robinson saw now showed any fundamental change in the man. He could only hope that Phillips would follow his counsel and stand up to Alistair Johnson. But to sit and go over the possibilities would drive him to distraction so he got up and switched his answering machine "On", just in case. He then lifted his coat off the peg behind the door and picked up Hervey's lead from the kitchen table.

"In the meantime old boy it's time for your walk."

Fairbairn's appearance at Leinster Gardens had been something of a distraction – not particularly welcome – but a distraction nonetheless. Such business as needed to be addressed was covered in one sentence – "Our mutual friend at "Gloom Hall" would like a call". Lynch told Fairbairn that he would contact the "friend" after he'd spoken to Johnson, which was accepted and with that Fairbairn had gone. Lynch didn't like borrowing personnel from other bodies, less still colluding with them, but needs must when the Devil drives. Anyway, that was a matter for tomorrow.

He spent the next two hours going through the papers that had been left after the de-brief, and was glad to see that his instructions had been followed to the letter with nothing missing from the papers he had asked for. He shuffled all the papers together into one pile, lifted them and made for the stairs, stopping at Liz's desk on the way. She was busy updating Lynch's files, but made a welcome stop as her boss obviously wanted to have a word.

"Yes sir?"

"Liz, could you do me a favour and get a personnel file from the central records people in Whitehall."

"And the name of the subject?"

"Mathieson, James, no middle initial. His file will be classified because of his present regimental status, but I want it."

"Anything specific that I should be asking for?"

"Well…not really, but if there are detailed psychological tests on him I'd like to see those."

"Coming to work for you is he?"

"He already has, but I think he has potential away from the band of heroes he's mixed up with. He's got a brain and I think he should be given the chance to use it."

"Well, I should have it in a couple of days at the most, but you know what the clerks are like at the MOD."

"There's no mad rush necessary. The end of the week will be fine."

Lynch then made his way down stairs to the basement with its paper shredder and incinerator. He carefully fed the various sheets of orders, reports, communication flimsies, even the surveyor's report on the Mullan house that had been taken from the planning office in Armagh, all went into the shredder. Sopel and Jefferson's reports were next for destruction, and even the notes that Colquhoun, Aiken and Walsh had made, which would have made no sense to anyone outside the operation, all these found their way into the Burroughs machine. When all the documents had been chopped into ticker tape Lynch carried the bin over to the incinerator and burned the lot. He fed in all the shredded paperwork and with that complete he added the X-rays and tapes that had come from Shrivenham – in a matter of minutes all physical evidence of the department's involvement in the Mullan raid ceased to exist. The only details that remained were the memories of events that were carried in the heads of the team, and Lynch was fairly confident that that was where they would remain.

Back in his office Lynch went through the notes that he had made in preparation for his meeting with Johnson. He had to bear in mind that even these would eventually find their way into the shredder in the basement before the operation could be regarded as truly deniable. He rehearsed his delivery of the report for Johnson over and over again until he was satisfied that he had included no extraneous detail – he knew well enough by now that Sir Alistair would not stand for any time-wasting. Finally he put his notes into the wall safe in his office and called the front desk to make sure that a car and driver would be available to take him to the Carlton for five-twenty – the meeting was scheduled for five-thirty but he knew that it was best to build in a safety margin; anyway Johnson might just appreciate his being early.

"Sorry John, I know you came here expecting some answers but I've heard nothing from Lisburn and I don't expect anything for maybe a week."

"Forget the forensics Phil, just give me an opinion on what you saw."

"Same thing as you – a burnt out house and bugger all else."

"Jesus Christ, don't give me that crap Phil, you can do better than that. I've got to go back to McCleary and give him something."

"I'm not here to do your job John. You lads in Special Branch are meant to have all the bloody answers and if you're having problems don't come crying to me."

"OK understood. Look it's just that we're hitting a blank wall on this one. Nobody's saying anything and in all likelihood there's bugger all to be said – we've got nothing at the scene and you know damn well that the longer this sort of thing goes on the less chance there is of us turning anything up."

"John I'd love to help, I really would, but I've got nothing for you, not yet anyway."

"Well if that's all there is then I'll leave it, but as soon as you get anything from Lisburn pass it on."

"Sure, as soon as I get it you'll be next in line."

A quarter of an hour later Harbinson was back in McCleary's office passing on the bad news. It was a sign of McCleary's frustration that he nearly bit Harbinson's head off, but John knew that if that was all he had to put up with he wasn't doing too badly; his boss was well known for his explosive temper and this was just another example of it. The only good thing to come from the exchange was a renewed determination to push the investigation along – at the group meeting McCleary and Harbinson were going to pressurise their team to go out and extract information by any means necessary.

The entrance to the Carlton Club gave little indication of the power that the institute had enjoyed through its membership; the facade had no palatial pretensions just a solidity that mirrored the establishment figures who had formed the backbone of the membership over the years. Prime ministers, cabinet ministers, industrial kingpins and, of course, the aristocracy, all these sections of the establishment of the realm had enjoyed the relative calm of the club's surroundings.

Calmness could not have been further from Lynch's mind as he walked through the front door into the hall. A uniformed member of staff made an approach, alerted, no doubt, by Lynch's somewhat lost expression. Once he had stated his business and with whom he was shown up to the reading room. He had a quick glance at his watch and noted with satisfaction that he was five minutes early. He then took in his surroundings, the high backed club chairs, the well aged bookshelves, the deep piled carpet – all gave an impression of comfort. The gentle rustle of news papers, the chink of glasses on table tops and the miasma of cigar smoke that hung in the air gave another – power.

He absorbed the atmosphere and realised that he really didn't belong here; the best he could hope for was to be an outsider given the opportunity to look through the portal once in a while for as long as he was useful to one of the powerful. Another thought struck him as he looked about the reading room – he didn't want to belong here – the mentality of the Alistair Johnsons of this world was something alien to him. He walked further into the room and passed several ranks of bookshelves before he came to the solitary seated figure of Alistair Johnson, Permanent Under Secretary to the Home Office and Knight of the Realm. Lynch announced his presence with a discreet cough, and Sir Alistair who had been reading the Daily Telegraph lowered the paper and gestured to the chair opposite. Lynch sat and waited as whatever article in the paper was finished. Eventually the paper was lowered again and folded.

"Right Lynch, let me hear what you've got and then I'll tell you what has happened regarding your friend Robinson."

"Yes sir. Well, as you already know the final score was twenty-one nil; from a purely operational point of view it was a complete success. The entry team only suffered the one casualty and that is being dealt with by the hospital authorities."

"Is there any possibility of details leaking from this source?"

"None whatsoever sir. The injury is being covered as a training accident, and besides the man is from the Regiment so no-one will ask any questions."

"Good. Continue."

"My people cleaned the house from top to bottom and recovered certain documents that show a very healthy financial situation with the South Armagh Brigade."

"How healthy?"

"One hundred and nine thousand, four hundred and fifty-eight pounds."

"Good God!"

"I know sir. It appears to be a mixture of Provo money and the proceeds of a smuggling enterprise."

"And what of it?"

"I was hoping, with your permission sir, to recover it for departmental funds."

"By all means. Carry on."

"There were two unidentified bodies at the scene and they were sent for forensic evaluation at Shrivenham. I read the reports this morning and it would appear that we are dealing with two foreign nationals – specifically Eastern Europeans. I don't need to tell you of the possible ramifications of Warsaw Pact involvement sir, but you can appreciate that it puts a different complexion on operations in Northern Ireland."

"So they couldn't help but get directly involved could they?"

"It certainly looks that way sir."

"Well such a circumstance only lends weight to Kitson's views on terrorism. We've got to put an end to this nonsense in Ulster, and I think that you've given us the start that we needed. You have my congratulations and I should tell you that they are not offered lightly."

"Thank you sir. You mentioned earlier that there was some additional information on the Robinson situation."

"Indeed I did. A colleague of mine, you don't need to know who, contacted me this afternoon. He is one of our dovelike brethren, and has now got a flea in his ear courtesy of Robinson, who has a long standing connection with him. As you said to me Robinson claimed to have friends in high places, and it seems he wasn't bluffing."

"So what is the potential for real problems? After all, I've got a large number of people committed to this operation sir, and a bleeding heart with a guilty conscience could be disastrous."

"No need to worry. I've got the measure of this particular bleeding heart, and Robinson knows that to take matters further would be a grave misjudgment. You won't hear any more of this matter."

"I hope you're right sir. I have responsibilities…"

"Lynch, if I tell you that the issue is dealt with why do you doubt me. Never cast doubt on my word, is that understood?"

"Yes sir."

"Right. You can forget about Robinson; he's not going to create any additional problems. With regard to an ongoing operation in Ulster take it as read if you should get details of similar impending activities by our Mick friends, set the wheels in motion and take them out; we want more successes like this one."

"I can offer no guarantees sir, we can only do our best, but you have to appreciate the operational difficulties."

"They don't concern me Lynch. Your department considers itself the best in this field, don't make me regret my choice."

"But you have to understand the number of people involved and the level of trust I have to place in them – without that the whole operation would become common knowledge…"

"Are you saying that there's a problem?"

"No sir. What I am saying is that the longer such a task is in the departments hands the greater the chance of carelessness – familiarity breeds contempt."

"Don't talk to me about carelessness. I won't stand for it, is that understood?"

"Yes sir, but as I said I'm dealing with people and the circumstances are somewhat unusual. Neither of us wants an error, the consequences don't bear thinking about."

"There will be no talk of fallibility."

"But sir…"

"Lynch for the last time – keep your house in order, or by God I'll hand things over to someone who can. Has that finally penetrated?"

"Yes sir."

Arguing was obviously going to be of no use. Johnson was clearly convinced that he was right and the threat of outside involvement was the final straw; Lynch had a pretty low opinion of the shadow warriors – all too often in the past their high self-esteem had not only jeopardised a job but ended in a whole team being compromised – and he didn't want them making a hash of his work. There was only one thing for it and that was to offer Johnson whatever assurances he could – God preserve him from politicians playing at soldiers!

Johnson by contrast seemed satisfied with the seemingly humble figure seated opposite; it never occurred to him that Lynch held him in contempt – he was used to people being overawed by his status. He had all the details he required so he could see no point in prolonging the interview.

"Well that just about covers everything so you can go Lynch."

Johnson picked up his newspaper and before Lynch could say his farewells he was immersed in whatever report that had taken his interest. Lynch made his way out of the Carlton Club glad to be free of Johnson and the kind of individual eligible to wear the club tie. He stood by the kerb and hailed a taxi; ordinarily he'd have expected a wait of several minutes but such was the powerful draw of the Carlton that a cab appeared in seconds – rank hath its privileges – or something like that. Lynch opened the rear door and settled onto the broad bench seat. The cabbie set the meter and called from the front seat.

"Where to guv?"

"Leinster Gardens."

He had originally planned on returning to his flat but after the meeting with Johnson he decided to go back to the office and destroy the last paper evidence of the job at the Mullan farm. He'd show Sir Alistair bloody Johnson how to run a deniable operation, and if there was no paper evidence of its existence there was nothing tangible to create difficulties. That only left the human factor and Lynch reckoned he knew his team members and could trust them.

He had just put the key in the lock when the telephone began to ring; opening the door and placing his sports bag and purchases on the hallway rug he walked unhurriedly to answer it. He looked at his watch as he held the handset to his ear – ten to seven.

"Crawford."

"Gerry, it's Dave – Dave Beatty."

"Oh, hello Dave. I thought you were across the water; I take it you're not, hence the phone call."

"Sharp as usual. You know you should get a job where you put your intelligence to good use."

"Ha bloody ha. Anyway Dave what can I do for you?"

"Two weeks leave and sod all to do. I thought you might be up for a drink."

"Always am. You just give me a when and where."

"If we keep it local one of us can crash at the other's place, and…"

"I know the pit you call home Dave, so you can kip at mine, and that means we'll be starting at "The Rodney". Fair enough?"

"It'll do for a start, but we haven't arranged a time yet."

"Today's Monday – how about Wednesday?"

"Do the best. So I'll see you in "The Rodney" about eight."

"No problem, I'll see you then."

"Looking forward to it, and I've got some news you'll find interesting."

Crawford knew the sort of game Beatty was playing and decided he was having none of it.

"Bollocks to that Dave, tell me now."

"Not on the phone Gerry, you know the score. You'll just have to wait 'til Wednesday."

Before he was able to press Beatty further the line went dead; leaving Crawford wondering what the information was, and giving Beatty the satisfaction of getting one over on the old man. Crawford hated being in the dark but there was no sense in wasting time and effort thinking about the possibilities of Beatty's disclosures so he lifted the bags bearing the fruit of his shopping trip up west and walked into the kitchen. He retrieved a pair of scissors from the cutlery drawer so he could remove the annoying labels that were tagged on the two pairs of trousers he had bought at Cordings.

So far, all he had done in the course of his time off was to spend a frankly stupid amount of money on clothes and, as a means of expiating his guilt, working out to the point of collapse in the gym at Chelsea Barracks. Everything he had done thus far had been of a solitary nature – the forthcoming drink with Beatty would be a welcome distraction from the dark thoughts that were beginning to take hold of him. He was plagued with doubts about his place within the "Department" and for that matter he was starting to question the existence of the organisation itself.

He put his new trousers down and taking a glass from the drainer he poured himself a large Hennessy – no matter what way he looked at it the brandy wasn't going to make the problem disappear or even dull the sharp edges of his questions, but what the hell! He went back into the living room, taking the bottle with him, stopping at the hi-fi to put on Previn's recording of Rachmaninov's second symphony. The strings of the first movement began to swell as Crawford took his seat on the couch opposite the shelves that held the speakers along with the few personal possessions that marked the flat as his – photographs of the family he didn't see and mementoes of the foreign postings he wished to remember. He refilled his glass with brandy as the first movement built to its climax, taking with it some of the bitterness he felt.

Lynch had systematically cleared his office working through the contents of his desk and his personal safe – virtually the only papers he had recovered had been his own notes. The last thing he collected before going to the basement was the desk-top scribble pad which bore a couple of references which, in themselves meant nothing but if connected properly, could be potentially embarrassing. He made one last stop in the duty office before taking the stairs down to the shredder and incinerator. Satisfied that the office safe contained nothing of relevance he took his own small collection of paperwork to the basement for destruction.

He stood watching the bag of shreds ignite and burn away to nothing – Johnson could posture all he wanted concerning the integrity of this operation, but when it came to evidence Lynch was now certain that any leaks wouldn't be coming from his department. In a couple of minutes the last written evidence of Friday night/Saturday morning's operation was no more and Lynch returned to his office. He slumped into his chair and contemplated the events of the day, concluding that any further scrutiny of the job would serve no purpose – he'd done all he could and it was time to go home and have a drink. He opened his desk and retrieved the bottle of Scapa single malt that he had promised himself on a successful outcome; after today he felt that he more than deserved a couple of drams.

Any thoughts about a job well done couldn't have been further from John Harbinson's mind. He sat in his office reflecting on the progress of the investigation to date; every enquiry that had been made by Special Branch had been met with the same response – total ignorance – nobody knew anything, at least not of any consequence. His team had been asking questions for two days and had nothing to show for the effort. There wasn't even unsubstantiated gossip. The facts remained that the Mullan farmhouse had burned down and that the Mullans couldn't be found; after two days of questions and observations the team was no closer to a solution than they had been when the initial call came through from Phil Carson.

Harbinson leafed through the file that the team had been building since Saturday – a lot of verbiage detailing every move that the various team members had made and not even a sniff of some hard fact – no wonder that McCleary was doing his nut. The only shred of comfort that he could draw from the investigation to date was the certainty that something would break, the longer the Mullans went undetected the more likely it was that some piece of information would leak out. It stood to reason that in a small community, no matter how tight lipped, somebody would know something and that it would eventually become common knowledge.

It was hard to explain the frustrations that this particular investigation was creating; not only did Harbinson feel, to say the least, irritated by the lack of progress but there was also the known activities of the Mullans to consider. Men like them didn't just vanish and he was worried by their potential activities – they had to be up to something. He looked at his watch and was surprised to see that it was just after nine. He realised that he was only going through the motions and that nothing worthwhile would come from his continued presence in the Armagh station. The team had a meeting scheduled for ten in the morning, maybe something would break between now and then. He closed the file, locked it in his desk and left the office. As he walked out to his car he realised just how bone tired he was; the thought of a good night's sleep was unbelievably welcome, the Mullans could keep until tomorrow.

* * *

Phil Carson had spent the early morning out at the Mullan farm. Sometimes it was possible to return to a fire scene after several days and pick up a detail that had been overlooked on the first inspection. It did happen – but not this time. He'd picked his way through the debris and nothing he saw said anything other than ACCIDENT. He wasn't sure what he had expected to find but whatever his hopes there simply was nothing there.

When he got back to the Fire Station it was nearly midday – time enough to give the fire investigators in Lisburn a call; not that he really expected any news from them but at least he could tell John Harbinson that he had made the effort. He went into the kitchen and retrieved a mug of coffee before making his call. Once he was back at his desk he put the call through to headquarters. After about ten minutes of being placed on hold and subsequently being connected to the wrong department he was eventually put through to the boffins in the lab only to hear what he expected – no conclusive evidence to offer you at the minute – give us a few more days and we might have something for you. So that was that – Harbinson would be pleased.

About the only interesting point raised in the course of the team meeting that morning had been a casual remark passed by the most junior member of the group.

The catalogue of futile actions was nearly complete when Derek Patterson stated what should have been obvious.

"Suppose they're dead."

It was that simple and yet it had been ignored as a possibility. The Provos were forever cleaning house – why shouldn't the Mullans become a target for a little in-house feud? Then again there had been no indication of any local difficulties within the PIRA; the only noises were being made by the INLA which as usual was dissatisfied with playing second fiddle to the much bigger and better financed Provisionals. The Starry Plough had featured a couple of articles in recent months that implied an attempt to shift the power in south Armagh to the INLA. But the INLA didn't have the skill or imagination to target the Mullans in this way – the INLA would be more likely to leave the brothers and their nephew in a bloody heap in Armagh town centre – no – Patterson had raised an interesting possibility but nothing more than that.

The unfortunate thing was that as Harbinson sat at his desk he found himself wishing for a neat solution to this investigation and if that meant the Mullans turning up dead then that was just too bad. If he was being completely honest with himself he would have to say that such thoughts went against his character – Harbinson was a church-goer and despite the common view of a strict Protestant upbringing he was no bigot; even more at odds with general perceptions was the fact that he didn't hate his opponents in militant republicanism. His feelings were more akin to pity for the dead-end that these people had brought themselves to, and that was why he found his present mood hard to reconcile.

The lack of progress was really beginning to annoy, he wanted to be doing something no matter how inconsequential. To that end he lifted his jacket and walked out into the main office area. Patterson was sitting at his desk writing up yet another report sheet when Harbinson tapped him on the shoulder.

"Derek follow me, we're going on a little drive."

"Where to sir?"

"Out to Gormley's farm."

"You mean he's come up with some new information sir?"

"No it's just to get out of the office, sitting around here is starting to wear me down."

Crawford had woken just after four that morning to find that he had drunk half a bottle of Hennessy and had passed out on the couch. He remembered seeing the overturned glass and the stain the brandy had made on the rug. He had dragged himself into his bedroom and had barely managed to strip off before rolling into bed. His last thought had been to make sure and clean the rug in the morning. He woke for the second time, although regaining consciousness was probably a more apt description, just before midday with a beauty of a hangover. He very quickly realised that seeking solace in a bottle was no answer – the department was still there and running away from it wasn't going to change anything. He remembered his comment to Sean Kavanagh the week before "I'm bloody good at what I do", and gave it serious consideration. If he really was that good then he should stay where he was and make sure that people like Kavanagh became just as expert. He was starting to come to terms with his nature and the stupidity of attempting to go against it but the understanding of who and what he was offered little comfort.

Such thoughts on top of a hangover were no way to start a day – food, now there was something that wouldn't take up too much effort. He walked into the kitchen and started preparations for an omelette; the eggs and the coffee he was going to filter would go some way to settling his stomach. In an effort to dispel the silence that hung heavily throughout the flat he switched the radio on and tuned it to Radio 3 being lucky to catch the first movement of a good recording of Mozart's clarinet concerto. The music had a calming effect that made the mood of five minutes ago seem unimportant, and the omelette when it was ready showed Crawford that the simple things very often were the best.

When he was finished he stood at the sink washing his breakfast dishes and he realised that too much time alone could create problems of its own. He knew he had to get out amongst people and actually do something – to continue his solitary pursuits was going to push him all out of shape. He showered and changed before leaving his flat on Hoskins Street; the weather wasn't exactly helping his cause but surprisingly he found walking in the late March rain had no impact on his feelings.

He had come down Romney Road and turned towards the Thames – the masts of the Cutty Sark stood out against the grey rain clouds – Crawford made his way towards the ship and the throng of tourists that surrounded it. Even in March the tea clipper was a draw for coach loads of foreign tourists, the weather making no appreciable difference to their number. There were Japanese, Germans, French and Americans. It was to them that he tagged himself on, for language reasons if nothing else, as they were told about the tea races of the nineteenth century; the sense of belonging and participating gave him a focus, a sense of community that he hadn't felt in a long time.

When the two Special Branch men had arrived at Dermot Gormley's the old man had been out checking on both his small holding and the Mullan farm. His wife Brid had asked both men to come in and get a cup of tea while they waited. As Harbinson and Patterson sat at the kitchen table the senior detective took the opportunity to run some questions on the Mullan brothers. Surprisingly Mrs. Gormley proved more than forthcoming, and by the time Dermot came in and took off his boots they had a clear picture of the nature of neighbourly relations. The old man had been somewhat guarded, but one fact that he did let slip was the conversation he had overheard on his weekly trip to Coughlin's bar – it seemed that the Mullan brothers' disappearance had been noted and that they weren't the only ones. Harbinson didn't want to outstay his welcome so he offered his thanks for the tea, as did Patterson, and both men left. It was obvious that the exchanges at

Gormley's had got Harbinson thinking but the only comment that the young officer could draw from his superior on their return to Armagh was "Interesting".

"Giles, it's Lynch."
"Glad you could call; I take it you got my message from Fairbairn?"
"Yes, he was here yesterday. Look, I've got rather a full diary at the moment, so what can I do for you?"
"Not a lot, it was just to see if you needed any further assistance from the chaps in the "Big House" in Dublin?"
"For the moment no, but possibly in the future."
"I understand. Well, keep in touch."
"I will, and thanks. Do me a favour and pass it along."
"No trouble at all."

And that was that, another potential loose end that had been tied off. Lynch knew that the operatives of the SIS could be relied on for their discretion and much as he didn't like moving in non-departmental circles, he had to admit that they were good operatives. Furthermore, there were definite advantages in keeping in their good books.

The telephone call to Giles Redfern at "Gloom Hall" had been his first act on his arrival at Leinster Gardens; now he was able to turn his scrutiny on the reports that had come in from the various teams that had been at RAF Lyneham on Saturday. They had all checked in with the briefest of comments; the task complete details ranged from "delivery successful" to "cargo unloaded", all of them innocuous but all of them confirming the disposal of the results of the raid. Foundation piles, new stretches of motorway and in one case the concrete bedding for a new swimming pool had all received certain additions.

All the reports added up to more paperwork that had to be shredded and burned. Not for the first time Lynch considered installing a shredder in his office but discounted the notion almost as quickly as he thought of it – the ease of use could breed complacency and that would lead to mistakes which he couldn't afford – besides, the walk down to the basement was about the only exercise he got these days. He'd dispose of the various notes later but a quick glance at his desk clock showed him that it was time he placed a call to Curzon Street, Hugo Robinson's administrative home. It wasn't that he enjoyed the prospect of speaking with his opposite numbers at MI5 but they had something he wanted. The phone rang four times before a young man answered – Lynch asked for his contact by name whilst failing to identify himself – after about a minute the handset was lifted again.

"Jones?"
"Jonesy it's Harry Lynch."
There was obvious pleasure in the reply.
"Mr. Lynch, now what can I do for you, as if I didn't know, something sneaky?"
"Jonesy I have need of your peculiar talents and I need them quick."
"What's the job?"

"I would prefer to tell you face to face if you don't mind. How soon can you be at "The Garden"?"

"Give me half an hour."

"Fine I'll see you then."

Lynch hung up and turned to his personal safe to recover the two bank books and the passports that Aiken had taken from the Mullans. Daffyd Jones would need the documents to work on if the department was to successfully transfer the funds from the AIB in Dundalk to its own account. Jones was a specialist who flitted from one organisation to the next whilst owing little loyalty to any one in particular. Lynch had first met him years ago when Jones had served in the Intelligence Corps. At that time he had taken a little too much interest in the financial affairs of the Adjutant, and not being as adept as he was now he'd paid the penalty finding himself in the glasshouse. His potential had been noted and on his release he had been brought into the fold with specific training in document alterations. It was this skill that Lynch wanted to use; knowing full well that he would have to negotiate a price as Jones would be doing this strictly as a homer.

The half hour went quickly and true to his word Jones arrived on time. He was shown into Lynch's office by Liz a little after three o'clock. He took a seat and pointedly looked at his watch just to let Lynch know that time was money.

"OK Jonesy, no pleasantries. I need a letter closing two deposit accounts and requesting that the funds be transferred to an account in England."

"Right sir, questions."

"Go ahead."

"What examples of handwriting have you got?"

"Just a signature."

"Brilliant! OK, what's the educational standard of the account holder?"

"Left school at 15 to run the family farm."

"Would the use of a typewriter look out of the ordinary?"

"Hard to say, but I see what you're driving at."

"Yeah, is the bank manager going to be immediately suspicious of a typed letter. He just might be but it's the best I can do without a full example of the hand. But we're getting ahead of ourselves – do you have an account already opened in this man's name?"

"Not as yet, no."

"Then I'm going to have to open one."

"So you'll have to get the signatue right of course."

"Absolutely. Fraud, theft, misappropriation, whatever you want to call it, is never easy. I'll open the account and close it with a transfer to one of your choice. My fee will naturally be larger to cover my expenses."

"Rest assured you'll be well paid. There's just one additional problem Jonesy. The chap the money belongs to is an Ulsterman – can you do an accent?"

Jones dropped his native Cardiff tones and adopted a believable if rather flat Belfast accent.

"Is this what you're lookin' for?"

"A man of many talents Jonesy, it'll do."

"Well if that's all Mr. Lynch you can give me the details and I'll have a result for you within a fortnight."

Lynch passed over Joe Mullan's passport and the two bank books – Jones took hold of them but Lynch didn't release them immediately; instead he fixed Jones with a meaningful stare.

"Jonesy you'll see that there's rather a large sum involved; just don't go getting any selfish ideas, OK?"

"I understand. Have no fear, I'm not as stupid or as greedy as I used to be."

"Glad to hear it. Then I'll see you within a fortnight."

With a nod, Jones pocketed the documents and left.

Lynch stayed at his desk thinking about Jonesy, the money, the possibility of recovering it, the rounding-off of the operation; the epilogue was how he would have described it. If the last pieces fell into place with the ease that the rest of the job had done he would be more than satisfied. He lifted the "safe placement" reports and went down to the basement.

Crawford had spent the day like a tourist; he'd gone on board the Cutty Sark, something he hadn't done since his schooldays, learning a lot about the tea trade from the extensive exhibitions that were arrayed throughout the cargo decks. When he'd finished there he walked back to Greenwich Park and the Royal Observatory. The rain had stopped, and although it was still overcast it wasn't a bad afternoon. Certainly the gangs of coach parties and other tourists didn't appear to mind; then again nobody came to London at the end of March expecting good weather.

As he trooped around the exhibition at the Observatory Crawford realised the importance of developing interests outside the department. Even the tourist sites of Greenwich showed him that there was more to life than the job. He'd seen enough during his time to make most men cynics but he'd been lucky to be possessed of a level of detachment that allowed him to escape most influences, but even that capacity was diminished and he was starting to buckle under the pressure. He would definitely be talking to Beatty about his dilemma tomorrow night.

* * *

Jones sat hunched over his drawing board looking at the results he had achieved in duplicating Mullan's signature. The last four efforts on his pad were just about passable. One thing he had learned over the years as a "copyist", forger had such grubby associations, was that the less education a person had the more deliberate the signature. Joe Mullan had a distinctly childish hand and getting it just right was surprisingly difficult. Mullan had obviously held the pen as if it were some wild creature; to have a light grip was to give it the opportunity of escape, he had overcome this by nearly strangling the pen. The signature in the passport was so heavy as to have nearly cut through the paper. This in itself caused Jones problems as he had to select a grade of paper for his typed letter that would not rip apart under the heavy pressure of the ball-point pen that he was going to use; and a heavy grade of paper had a quality that might seem alien coming from a farmer in South Armagh. Then again, how many Mick farmers had over a hundred thousand in change lying about?

Lynch hadn't needed to tell Jones where the money was coming from; the bank details, the name and the colour of the passport had been enough. The only thing that worried him was getting the letter and the account details from the new bank just right. He leaned over the pad once more and ran off half a dozen quick signatures all on the same line. He lifted a blank sheet of paper and covered the top half of the signatures and compared them to the signature in the passport that had been similarly divided. The similarities were undeniable so he reversed the cover and looked at the top half of the signatures. They too were good matches; these last efforts were the best yet, he doubted if they could be identified as copies by anybody but the most expert. Not that there was ever going to be any question of suspicion – the signature was going to match perfectly – Jones wasn't going to close the account, rather, he was going to leave a few hundred pounds in it – the money was being transferred to another bank not taken out in cash. All told the method and commission would be flawless. Some might say that there were easier ways to achieve the same result, but Jones didn't have much sympathy for easy – after all it was that sort of a cavalier approach that had cost him nearly a year in prison.

Now that he was satisfied with the signature he could start work on the letter. He selected the oldest, least serviced typewriter from amongst his considerable collection, an old Imperial, and fed the sheet of heavy grade paper into the roller. Bearing in mind Joe Mullan's limited education he typed a letter that was grammatically incorrect as well as being salted with several spelling mistakes. With that finished he looked over his handiwork. The wording and spelling looked about right but on reflection Jones decided to tone it down a bit – he didn't want to make Mullan appear a thick "Paddy", he did have over a hundred grand to his name after all and this wouldn't be the finished article, he hadn't opened the new account and thus obtained the necessary bank details to include with this letter to the Allied Irish Bank in Dundalk. He'd give the wording some more thought before he made his final draft.

He looked at his watch and saw that he had sat the morning through and that it was now passed midday. It never ceased to surprise the way in which his work with documents consumed his time – something to do with concentration perhaps. He decided to call one of the typists from Curzon Street, whom he'd had some success with in the dating stakes and see if she fancied a late lunch. He had planned to open the account that afternoon in a branch of the NatWest on the Edgware Road but it could wait until tomorrow, anyway he had to get into character and that would take some preparation. He made his call to the typing pool and was pleased to find that he had a date, subject to him paying of course. He agreed to meet her at a little Italian place that he knew on Vigo Street not too far from the centre at Curzon. It was twelve twenty-five which gave him nearly an hour to catch the Tube at Finchley Road and make his way on foot from Bond Street station to Bellini's.

The vote of no confidence and the possibility of a General Election had been weighing heavily on Sir Alistair's time. His position as Permanent Under Secretary was not in question, but he did face the prospect of a change of administration and that meant an unsettling period of transition. There didn't seem to be any doubt that the Conservatives would win and that meant the new Prime Minister would be a woman. Johnson didn't see himself as a male chauvinist but he had very definite views on the suitability of women in politics. He was sitting at his desk, mulling over the benefits of having the Tories back in power with the fact that his ultimate superior would be a woman; he could see that his own department at the Home Office stood to gain with a new batch of ministers and junior ministers who at least spoke the same language, but he wasn't so sure if there would be the same freedom of action that he had enjoyed, particularly of late. Thoughts of action reminded him that he had a call to make, so lifting the receiver of his secure line he dialled the extension number that would put him through to his opposite number at the Cabinet Office. The telephone was answered on the second ring by an obviously flustered Stephen Phillips.

"Phillips."

"Stephen, it's Alistair. I was wondering if you'd had any more time to think over what I said on Monday?"

"If you're worried about Robinson, I spoke to him yesterday."

"And?"

"And he's not pleased, but I think he can be relied upon to keep his mouth shut."

"I don't give a damn if he's pleased or not. He has no option but to keep his mouth shut. What evidence does he have? His source fails to make contact, it wouldn't be the first time that some Mick ran for the hills. Nobody has told him anything that proves or disproves this wild theory he has developed."

"But we know that he's right Alistair.

"And we will keep it amongst ourselves, won't we Stephen?"

"But..."

"Oh for Christ's sake, we're not back in the bloody quad. Get a grip man. We were all agreed that action needed to be taken and by God it has been."

"I just think that there are aspects of this action that require additional consideration."

"Do you now?"

"Yes, I do. I want a meeting of the group to clarify matters."

"That's your prerogative Stephen, but we were all agreed. It's a bit bloody late in the day to be having second thoughts you know."

"You don't need to tell me that. It's just that I think we have other options to consider. Just looking at my diary…. Saturday would suit and I'll contact the other members – shall we say the Carlton?"

"Fine. I won't forget this Stephen, you can be sure of that."

The line went dead; the arrogant little bastard had had the nerve to hang up on him! Doubtless he'd be contacting the others to put his point across; well two could play at that game, Johnson started making calls.

Robinson strode along the strand at Murlough with Hervey off chasing imaginary rabbits amongst the dunes. The rain was falling heavily with a north-westerly wind driving it cold into the sand. Robinson was unconcerned by the weather, his mind was on other things. The conversation he'd had with Phillips yesterday had offered no solutions. No matter what way he looked at it there was no hope for retribution. Finn was dead, of that he had no doubt, so there was nothing he could do for him, but he had hoped to make life difficult for Johnson and his pet thug Lynch. Such an outcome looked distinctly unlikely, with the best that Phillips could offer being a meeting of the group. Robinson knew the score – the group would close ranks and any dissenters would be dealt with severely – Johnson would prevail and the whole bloody mess that was Ulster would carry on indefinitely.

The sense of frustration that he felt was becoming intolerable. Robinson had a self-righteous streak which he was aware of; he had considered the possibility that he was over-estimating the importance of his position, but discounted this with the fact that, as he saw it, he wouldn't have been given the job in the first place if his opinion didn't count for something. Fundamentally that was what dismayed him the most – why give him this responsibility and then ignore his counsel?

He was allowing himself the luxury of feeling hard done by, not the most intelligent thing, but worse than that he was losing his sense of perspective. The longer he walked the greater the injustice visited upon him became. Various courses of action crossed his mind; thoughts of press involvement to simple physical revenge against Lynch – all were considered and all rejected as being reckless and fanciful. The only notion worthy of consideration was that of resignation. It was, after all, the gentleman's way out. He would not be forgotten for the principled stand he was going to take.

He called Hervey to him and the soaking labrador came bounding out of the dunes scattering a flock of seagulls that were standing huddled against the rain. The angry cries of the gulls mirrored his sense of outrage, but if he had really given it thought he would have realised that their desolate calls better defined his position – that of aloneness.

After Crawford had taken in the Greenwich exhibition, he had walked back to the Thames following the riverside path towards Westminster and then having crossed at Battersea Bridge he had walked back along the opposite bank. He hadn't been following any distinct plan, just walking through the rain showers that came and went with the westerly wind. By the time he'd got home it was after ten and dark. He'd switched on the television to catch the ITN bulletin and had poured himself a nightcap. The events of the day had passed before his unfocussed gaze – he was dog-tired. He had sipped at his brandy, realising that if he wasn't careful he'd fall asleep on the couch again so he had finished his drink and had gone to bed.

He slept for ten hours straight, the longest spell of uninterrupted sleep he'd had since his return from Belfast. He showered, dressed and walked to the cafe around the corner from his flat and enjoyed a leisurely breakfast. While he tackled his "full English" he compiled a mental list of the groceries he needed and planned his route through Greenwich and the various shops he would need to visit. By eleven thirty he was back in the flat, busy with all the domestic duties that he had frankly let slip – it wasn't that his flat was a mess, it never was, but a general tidy up and clean was more than necessary. It would have been easy to bag up his dirty clothes and take them to the cleaners on Trafalgar but Crawford preferred to do his own laundry; two of the first luxuries that he had bought when he'd moved into the flat had been a washing machine and a tumble dryer. He was just finishing off the last of his shirts when the phone rang. He set the iron down carefully on the board and picked up the phone just as the answering machine began to click in; after a couple of seconds confusion with Beatty's voice sporadically coming through over various electronic beeps, whines and whistles, Crawford managed to switch the machine off.

"Sorry about that Dave, bloody machines."

"More like the careless forgetful sods using them. Do you know what time it is Gerry?"

"No, I've been ironing."

"That figures. Christ, only you could spend leave doing your bloody washing."

"I was just finishing off what I'm wearing this evening."

"Well it's eight fifteen, so get changed and get your arse round to "The Rodney"."

"Sorry Dave. I must have lost track…"

"Never mind that, you're buying the first round when you get here. Get a move on, I'll see you in ten."

After the quickest of quick changes and a run to the pub, Crawford came through the corner double doors just before half past. Being a Wednesday night the pub was far from full, the regulars occupied the stools around the bar and a few of the booths were occupied by drinkers engaged in earnest conversations. He looked around the bar and picked Beatty out at the far corner booth facing the doors. Beatty lifted his pint glass, which was nearly empty, and signalled to Crawford to get him another. He stopped at the bar and placed his order. With the drinks purchased he walked over to the booth and slid onto the bench seat facing Beatty.

"I hope you're still drinking "Director's Bitter"."

"Why change a good thing? And you're still on the brandy."

"Yeah. Thought I'd get a double seeing as you're a drink up. Anyway, here's cheers."

"Cheers", both men raised their glasses in a half-hearted toast and drank, "God but that's good. So what have you been up to other than ironing?"

"Oh not much. A couple of trips up west and that's it really."

"You need to get out more Gerry. You'll turn into a real hermit if you aren't careful."

"And what have you got going that's so bloody marvellous?"

"If you must know I'm seeing a real cracker of a nurse at the weekend. She's got some time off so we're heading down to the coast for a couple of nights."

"Lucky you."

"Yeah, well that's what you need."

"Wouldn't work. I'm just not in the frame of mind for that sort of thing."

"Let me guess – job getting to you?"

"Yeah, something like that. I've been doing a lot of thinking and I'm not sure if I can carry on with this."

"Don't talk wet. If you'd been in on the job I've just pulled off then maybe you'd have something to moan about."

"Oh yeah. This would be the big secret that you couldn't talk about on the phone."

"Indeed. We were tasked with the cleaning job."

The mention of cleaning got Crawford's full attention.

"Where was the job Dave?"

"Armagh, down on the border…"

"Near Glaslough."

"Yeah, how'd you know?"

"Because Kavanagh and I were down there last week dropping off some kit."

"Did you know who or what for?"

"Wasn't in the brief so I didn't ask."

"Well then I can fill in the blanks. As you know the Mullan brothers ran the South Armagh Brigade…"

"You say ran, past tense."

"Exactly – that was the job. A team from Hereford swept the house and we went in to clear up. Jesus, what a mess they left! You should have seen it."

"So the Mullans are no more. Can't say that they'll be missed."

"Wasn't just them Gerry, it was the whole bloody Brigade."

"What?"

"You can take that sick look off your face. I'm never going to believe that you feel sorry for those bastards. But yeah, it was the whole lot."

"Christ Almighty. How many?"

"Twenty-one."

"You're not winding me up are you Dave?"

"Now why would I do a thing like that?"

"I don't know, you've got a pretty sick sense of humour."

"Not that sick. Look, it happened, believe me."

"OK. But a firefight like that must have attracted some attention – I mean there's been nothing in the press."

"Who ever said there was a firefight? This was a simple take-down. No witnesses, nothing to report."

"You mean the team just went in and slotted everyone?"

"More or less."

"Jesus, that's cold."

"Maybe so, but do you really think those bastards would have treated us any differently if the shoe had been on the other foot?"

"No, they probably wouldn't."

"Absolutely. Don't go all sentimental over a shower like that Gerry, they're not worth it."

"I wasn't, but it does make you think though."

"There you go thinking again. What's the problem. We've been waiting for years for some prat in Whitehall to grow a backbone and let us do the needful in Ulster. Now it looks as if the wait's over. All I'll say is it took too bloody long."

"Yeah you're right. It's been a long time coming. Just a shock, that's all."

Beatty looked mournfully at his empty glass and then nodded in the direction of Crawford's which was empty too.

"All this talk has obviously given us a thirst. Same again?"

"I wouldn't say no."

While Beatty was at the bar, Crawford tried to put what he'd heard into context with the thoughts he'd been mulling over for the past week. Could he continue working for an organisation capable of overseeing an action like that? Proficiency in the job was one thing, but how could he take pride in a job that left twenty-one people dead. Then again, he hadn't actually killed anybody, he'd only opened fire the once, outside Carrickmore, and that was old news. Dave was right, you put the uniform on and you do what you're ordered to do, if you gave it too much thought you'd go mad, "Ours not to reason why", and all that. He'd just reached this conclusion when Beatty returned with the drinks.

"Dave I want to ask you a question and then I'll drop the subject."

"OK, let's hear it."

"How do you deal with the outcome of a job like the other night?"

"Simple; they got what they deserved and better them than us. I'm not going to lose any sleep for them."

"I wish it was that easy for me."

Beatty who had been raising his glass put it back on the table and leaned towards Crawford.

"Oh for fuck's sake Gerry, do you for one moment think it's easy? Let me tell you it's not, but what's the alternative? Worrying yourself sick over a bunch of scum who'd put you in the ground as quick as look at you? Not me old son and not you either. Get a grip. Fuck it, I wish I hadn't told you."

Crawford sat back in his chair and raised his open hands.

"Dave it's not just this job, I've been having doubts for months."

"Does this go back to the business in Carrickmore?"

"I suppose it does. You know I lost it."

"Not from what I heard. The way I heard it you were the only one who didn't."

"I ran Dave…"

"So would anyone given the chance under those circumstances. Look, would Lynch keep you on the team if you weren't up to it? Don't kid yourself, the old bastard's not that generous."

"I don't know if I can keep it up or not. Maybe I should go and see Lynch, tell him what's on my mind."

"I wouldn't do that if I were you. Like I said he's not that generous; it's more likely that he'll hang you out to dry and then where would you be? Certainly no better off than you are at the moment; at least you've got mates who'll look out for you."

"You really think he'd drop me?"

"No doubt about it. Believe me Gerry, you're better off where you are. Anyway, this subject's getting us both down. We're on leave, with no responsibilities and nowhere to be in the morning. What say you to moving on somewhere else with a bit of life about it?"

* * *

At nine-thirty Jones had walked into the National Westminster Bank at the southern end of the Edgware Road to open the account that would eventually receive the funds from the Allied Irish Bank in Dundalk. By ten-fifteen the account was opened with a balance of £310.00. The whole process couldn't have been easier – the only detail that the bank had required from him was a specimen signature. His only concern had been the maintenance of his faux accent – he needn't have worried, the only experience of Ulster accents the bank-teller had was what she had heard on television. Any suspicion she may have had was set aside as soon as it was clear that he was putting money into the bank and not asking to take any out. She had been quite disappointed that "Mr. Mullan" wasn't really interested in availing himself of any of the banks numerous services, but it was still going to be a feather in her cap that such a large account would be coming to the branch.

Once he had returned to his flat on Nutley Terrace he telephoned Lynch to give him the good news concerning the new account. He was slightly deflated when he was told that Mr. Lynch was out, but he left a message that he should call Jones, at home, on his return. He now had all the information to complete the letter to the manager of the AIB in Dundalk, but rather than rush into the task he made himself a coffee and took some time over reading the morning paper.

Lynch had spent a frustrating morning at the Ministry of Defence clearing some paperwork that could have been dealt with over the telephone but for the officious little shit who jealously guarded his position of limited authority. Even after two hours of wrangling there had been no successful resolution of the budgetary difficulties that had been thrown up over the nature of the department's expenditure. Lynch's efforts to explain the special status of the department within the realms of the Army had fallen on deaf ears. With no immediate prospects of victory he had left the apparatchik to count his balance sheets or whatever it was that he did.

On his return to Leinster Gardens he was given Jonesy's message by Liz and put a call through from his office.

"Jonesy, it's Lynch. What news?"

"The account's open. I have a nice new NatWest pass book for a Mr. Joe Mullan and this afternoon I'll get the letter completed and away to Dundalk."

"Glad to hear it. I'll speak to you when you've got a result from the Allied Irish."

"I'll be in touch."

With Jonesy's letter and the new account to cover the transfer things should go smoothly. This piece of good news went some way to dulling the pain from his meeting this morning; a private fund would offset the financial constraints that the department could face if that arsehole in Whitehall got his way. Then again, he wouldn't have his way for long – the group of five would make sure that the MOD would do as it was told concerning future department expenditure. Lynch couldn't see any long-term difficulties for the department with any covert work of the type just completed, not now, that it had full support where it mattered.

Phil Carson replaced the handset, resigned to the call that he would now have to make but not liking the prospect any more for that; Lisburn had just passed on their preliminary results from the tests that they had been conducting. Not surprisingly the lab had uncovered no evidence of foul play. Carson knew how much Harbinson had been hoping for just that kind of evidence and here was confirmation, albeit preliminary, that it didn't exist. The sooner he made the call the sooner he could get on with some real work so he lifted the receiver and dialled Harbinson's direct line. He must have been waiting at his desk for any sort of news because the telephone had hardly completed its first ring when it was answered.

"Harbinson."

"John it's Phil Carson. I've just had the investigators from Lisburn on the phone and I thought you'd want the news right away."

"And I can tell by your tone that the news isn't good. Am I right?"

"It's still early days…"

"Bollocks to that Phil. Just tell me what they said."

"Well the preliminary tests have shown no evidence of the use of any accelerant or other inflammable. The linoleum floor covering seems to have supported and spread the combustion from the coals which fell from the range, the flames in turn spread throughout the house leading to a total loss of the property. Putting it most simply – an accident."

"Pretty much what you said on Saturday. Any chance that something interesting might turn up in the additional tests?"

"To be honest I don't think so. Lisburn knows its job and I don't remember them ever having made a mistake."

"That's what I thought. Thanks for the call Phil."

"Tell me this, are you fellas any closer to an answer regarding the whereabouts of the owners?"

"No and this one seems to be getting more complicated as time goes on. But that's not your concern Phil. Look, I've got things to do – not least to pass this good news on to McCleary – so thanks for your help and you know where to find me if anything new shows up at the lab."

Carson did not envy Harbinson – the task of passing on bad news to a superior was never much fun and from what he had heard McCleary was not the easiest of men to work for. One thing he had to say in his own favour was that there was no way in which the RUC could come back and criticise the Fire Service – he and the forensics people in Lisburn had done their utmost to help. It was too bad that the lab didn't appear to offer a simple solution to Special Branch's problem; it now looked as if it was going to be a slow hard slog, everything he supposed police-work was meant to be, and something he was grateful to have no part in.

"Nothing?"

"That's what he said."

"Shit! Jesus, you'd think they'd have turned something up."

"I'm sure they would have if there'd been anything. It just means that we have to go back through the files and see if there's something we've missed."

"We haven't missed anything John, and you bloody well know it. This one stinks but we can't get anyone to talk about it. All we've got is a list of missing Provos that's getting longer and bugger all else."

"Maybe they've all found their way into a bog. It wouldn't be the first time."

"Now you're sounding like Patterson – wishful thinking isn't going to solve this one. There're too many people involved for that; how many have we got now – near a dozen prominent members go missing all at once? No, the bastards are up to something, and that means we've got to keep on our toes."

"It just strikes me as odd sir that all these fellas go missing at once."

"Just because old man Gormley tells you that the talk of Coughlin's bar is the disappearance of the Mullan brothers and some of their playmates doesn't make it so. He could be leading you up the garden path, did you ever think of that?"

"I gave it some thought, and that's why I talked to his wife."

"You never told me that John, and it isn't in your report. Anyway what did she have to say?"

"Just that there's no love lost between the Mullans and her husband. Which leads me to the conclusion that he isn't the most obvious man to do them any favours."

"So you think they're all dead?"

"Well it makes as much sense as them all being off planning some big job along the border. They've never done this before to the best of our knowledge so why would they start now? Besides the sacrifice of the farm seems a bit extreme."

"Alright then. Let's for one moment go along with the possibility that somebody did the world a favour and wiped out most of the South Armagh Brigade. My question to you John is who?"

"I don't have a clue sir, I wish I did."

"Well until you find me a corpse we keep the investigation as it is."

"But the present line of enquiry isn't getting us anywhere sir."

"So we stick with it until it does or we exhaust it. Is that understood?"

"Yes sir."

Crawford woke a little after one and was amazed to find that he felt little the worse for wear; Beatty had called a mini-cab at "The Rodney" and they had gone to sample the pleasures of the west-end. A couple of night-clubs and several more brandies had released a lot of his tension; he was actually surprised to find that he had enjoyed himself. By the time he had parted company with Beatty it must have been nearly three in the morning and about half past when he had fallen into bed. He had passed out almost immediately and enjoyed an uninterrupted night's sleep

He sat up in bed and looked over at his clothes that were lying in a heap where he'd dropped them and decided that a useful start to his day would be to tidy them up. As he went through his trouser pockets to remove loose change and his wallet he discovered a piece of paper, ripped from a diary, bearing a telephone number and the name 'Christine' – wonders would never cease! Obviously he had managed to strike up a conversation and had maintained her interest long enough to get a contact number – too bad that he had had to fortify himself with brandy to achieve it. That was hopefully the least of his worries; the problem now was to remember just what 'Christine' looked like and to then make the call which was hopefully expected. Beatty was right – he needed to get out more and stop being so introspective.

He thought about giving the girl a call, looked at his watch and realised that, at two-twenty, she'd probably be at work, it was Thursday after all. Thursday....that meant he had five days before he was due back at work. He'd have to call Lynch tomorrow to find out just where he was wanted – hopefully he wasn't going back to "the Big House" in Dublin; he'd had enough action in the meantime, a soft job back at the depot would suit him fine.

Robinson had driven to Newcastle to catch the last post at four-forty-five. He had been working on his letter of resignation all day and as his anger had increased so too did the bitter tone of the letter; by completion it was pure vitriol. He had made three copies of the letter – one for his section chief, another for the Director and the final version, which had undergone a re-write, for Alistair Johnson. He knew only too well that contacting the man personally was of little consequence, but it made him feel better to know that Johnson would be vilified by certain sections of the community once the reasons for his resignation became common knowledge.

As he dropped the envelopes into the postbox he felt a sense of release; the years of subterfuge were now at an end. The duplicitous nature of his operations over the years had undoubtedly taken their toll but he was finished with that. He walked back to his car, safe in the knowledge that, as far as he was concerned, he had struck a blow against an establishment that was capable of destroying a valuable asset like Finn and of wrecking his efforts to aid the quest for a solution to the "Irish Problem". He drove back to Murlough and for the first time in months he was able to take Hervey for a walk on the beach with a clear mind.

* * *

Now that the job at the Mullan farm was finished and the de-brief was dealt with, Lynch felt somewhat at a loose end. He only had the funding battle with the MOD to worry about and, once he had informed Johnson, even that would be of little concern. There was nothing for him to get his teeth into – Aiken still had another week's leave before she took up her desk job – there was nothing in the pipeline operationally -Jones was taking care of the banking business – all in all he was thankful that it was Friday and he had a weekend's inactivity to look forward to. But that didn't solve the immediate problem of what to do.

He left his office and walked down the corridor to the kitchen to get himself a cup of coffee. He experimented with the instant granules; first to see if making the coffee stronger improved the taste, and when this didn't work he weakened the brew but only succeeded in making it insipid and undrinkable. That did it! He emptied his mug into the sink and went looking for Liz, who was sitting in her usual place, typing reports.

"Liz I want you to get on to the caterers and tell them that I want a decent coffee maker for the department, and make bloody sure that they don't fob you off – I'm fed up making do with the crap that they call coffee."

"Filter, percolator – what kind of machine do you want sir?"

"I don't give a damn as long as the end result is drinkable. You can tell them that they don't even need to worry about the coffee, I'll bring my own."

"Absolutely sir. I'll call them right away."

Feeling better for actually having achieved something he went back to his office. He rested his elbows on the desk and sighed heavily; solving the minor problem of the department's shitty coffee had brought him up to eleven-thirty, leaving him the whole bloody afternoon to struggle through. He turned around and opened the nearest filing cabinet in an attempt to invent some work. Whoever had said that you could always find some task to fill up the time was an idiot. He was just about to slam the drawer shut when he was saved by the telephone ringing, his direct line which meant it was potentially something interesting.

"This is Lynch."

"Mr. Lynch, it's Gerry Crawford."

Not so interesting, but a distraction nonetheless.

"And what can I do for you Crawford?"

"Well sir my leave's up next Tuesday and I was wondering what posting you had in mind for me?"

"Well I hadn't actually given it much thought. Where would you like to go?"

"Not operational sir, if it's all the same to you. What about the depot sir?"

"No, there's nothing for you there; they have a full training staff at the moment. How about "The Fort"? I'm sending young Kavanagh down there. You could accompany him."

"That'd only be short-term sir, and I…"

"Well it'll give me time to think of what to do with you won't it. So Gosport it is. Be there on Monday night."

"Yes sir."

He replaced the handset – "The Fort" – he supposed it could be worse. Then again the thought of having to spend – what – probably a fortnight with the oh so cocksure Sean Kavanagh did not fill him full of enthusiasm. The idea of having to put up with a lot of civilians wasn't too appealing either, but the facility at Gosport catered for a mixed bag of trainees so he'd have to make the best of it. As Lynch had said it was only until another permanent posting came up. God Alone knew what that might be but better not to waste any time thinking about the possibilities. As Beatty had said the other night he spent too much time worrying about things over which he had no control.

Jones had come home at lunchtime from Curzon Street to find that the second post of the day had been delivered. He took the envelopes from his mailbox on the ground floor and noted that one of the letters bore an Eire postage stamp. It was addressed to a Mr. Mullan, but the house and flat number were the only details of concern to the Royal Mail. Jones wasn't particularly worried about using his own address – the signature on the request letter had been perfect and the money was being transferred to another bank, so there really shouldn't be any problems.

Once inside his flat he opened the letter to see that it was indeed from the manager of the Allied Irish Bank in Dundalk. He said that a bank draft was being forwarded to the NatWest on Edgware Road and that it should be with the bank by Monday. He finished the letter by expressing his sorrow at losing the bulk of Mullan's account and by wishing him every success in his business endeavours in

London. If only the rest of the world was as accommodating as the bank manager in Dundalk – it would make life so much easier for Jones. All he had to do now was let the draft clear into the new Mullan account and then transfer the funds to the department account, the details of which Lynch would supply when they were needed. After that, all he had to do was think of a reasonable fee – five hundred quid seemed about right – and then think of a way to spend it!

Johnson sat at his desk leafing through a report on the imminent change of administration which would come with the General Election. The Conservatives were more in tune with the senior civil servants and the direction that they wished their departments to move in – so it appeared that the Permanent Under Secretaries would be able to manipulate their respective Ministers to a more successful degree than they had under Labour. The report had brief biographies of prospective Government Ministers and Johnson noted with satisfaction the number of old boys who could be relied upon to do what they were told. Johnson looked forward to having the Home Office more or less to himself; not that it hadn't been, but with the Conservatives he at least wouldn't have to hide details of certain operations. Labour had had a typically proletarian attitude about openness and with it had come an unhealthy fixation with disclosure. Labour's big problem had been a wish to lay the mechanisms of government bare. Happily the Conservatives weren't afflicted with a similar complaint.

He set the report on his desk and gave the meeting of the group tomorrow some thought. No matter what way he looked at it the group was going to endorse his position. Stephen Phillips could make as much noise as he liked at Robinson's behest, but the best he could hope for was a three to two vote against him. He reached across his desk and pressed the intercom button that linked him with his secretary.

"Yes Sir Alistair."

"Janet could you bring me some coffee and some shortbread through when you've got a minute."

"Straight away Sir Alistair."

He leaned back in his chair just as the muffled bang shook the windows in his office. His secretary burst into the office without knocking, her concern obvious from her expression.

"Are you alright Sir Alistair?"

"Yes Janet. Be a dear and find out just what that was."

It was the worst single breach of security at the Palace of Westminster. An under vehicle booby-trap had exploded as a car drove up the exit ramp from the underground car-park. The driver of the car had been singled out and targeted because of his outspoken views on the security question in Northern Ireland. Airey Neave's views were well known; his utter contempt for terrorists was a matter of record and with a Conservative win at the General Election he would have moved from shadow spokesman to Secretary of State for Northern Ireland. The completion of an electrical circuit by the mercury tilt switch and the subsequent detonation destroyed his life, his future and robbed many individuals of a trusted friend. All such thoughts, recriminations, and the numerous sage pronouncements, would come later – in the meantime such security measures as were appropriate were put into effect.

All the emergency services were on the scene in less than three minutes. A very quick appraisal of the bomb site and the condition of the victim showed that their rapid response was to no avail – Airey Neave was dead at the scene. Because of the use of explosives the emergency services were joined by Ammunition Technical Officers in case of secondary devices. Within a quarter of an hour there were so many organisations on the scene that coordination of efforts became a problem – a definite case of too many chiefs and not enough indians. The final straw was broken with traffic being brought to a standstill as a cordon was thrown up around Westminster. Tempers frayed as those who should have been on site found themselves on the wrong side of the barriers.

The big problem for the police was that various individuals were assuming authority and were somewhat obstructive when it came to identifying themselves. All too often the word "security" entered their explanations and the police were left none the wiser. Beneath this layer of confusion was a sense of disbelief and anger that, not only had there been an attack against Parliament, but also the fact that Airey Neave had been the victim.

Lynch was in the process of clearing his desk when his direct line rang; he quickly stuffed the files into his safe and lifted the handset.

"Lynch, this is Johnson. There's been a bombing here, at Westminster. I need you working on this immediately."

The unexpected nature of the news took a couple of seconds to sink in. Finally Lynch was able to reply.

"I understand sir. I have two questions – one, are there any casualties, two, has there been a claim?"

"There is one dead so far as I know. It's Airey Neave."

"Jesus Christ!"

"I know. I want heads for this one."

"And you'll get them sir."

"To your second question – no, there's been no authenticated claim as yet, but you can lay very short odds on our Irish brethren."

"Do you want me down there sir?"

"No, I think you're better off at Leinster Gardens. You'll have space there to work, which I couldn't guarantee here."

"Right sir. Well I'll get some extra bodies in here right away and then go to work on the Republican haunts."

"I want reports every twelve hours. If you find somebody likely I want to know and then I want action."

"When do you want my first report sir?"

"Ten tomorrow morning; I don't expect you to have anything for me before then. You'll be able to reach me via this line, but you are to leave no messages – you speak to me and me alone – is that understood?"

"Yes sir."

"Well we both have work to do, I suggest we get on with it."

The line went dead and Lynch was left holding the receiver as a torrent of questions washed through his mind. The monotonous buzz of the disconnected line brought him back to the present and he replaced the handset. There were set protocols and procedures for dealing with the aftermath of such an event, but it was such a long time since they had been put into practice that they needed dusting off. Lynch began by making a list of available manpower and the telephone numbers at which they could be contacted. One thing was certain – all leave would be cancelled for any personnel living in and around Greater London.

Once the orders went out all the ports of exit from Great Britain were put under intense scrutiny. Of particular interest were the ferry terminals, particularly those servicing the Republic of Ireland. Vehicles were stopped and searched as were foot passengers, sailings were delayed and numerous people detained. The airports yielded several suspects, some flying to Dublin, some to Shannon and even two young men flying to Spain who missed their flight and lost their tempers, but despite all the effort nobody connected with the Neave murder was found on the initial sweep.

The Chief Constables and the heads of the security services involved were not surprised at the lack of success; all too often in the past such measures had been for little more than show – the public had to see that something was being done. The reality was that if the guilty were to be caught it was going to take a long investigation; a combination of persistence and, to some degree, luck. And even if a result was obtained the sad truth was that the courts were ill-equipped to deal with terrorists – a civil sentence was the worst they could look forward to and they would be entitled to the normal rates of remission.

The news of the bombing was broadcast on radio and television bulletins – the initial shock and subsequent outrage was felt right across the country. County Constabularies with no initial responsibility were put on standby, the alert status for all MOD bases was raised, the effects of increased vigilance spread from the capital like the ripples on a pond's surface when a pebble is thrown to the centre.

Crawford heard the report late – he'd been out. He was about to call Leinster Gardens when he noticed the flashing light on his answering machine indicating messages. He pressed "play" and listened to an increasingly irate Lynch demand immediate contact. He dialled Lynch's direct line and braced himself. The phone barely had a chance to ring when Lynch snatched the receiver from the cradle.

"It's Crawford sir."

"Where the hell have you been? No – never mind. Get yourself in here straight away."

"I'll be with you as soon as possible sir."

There was nothing more to say so Crawford hung up. He lifted the grip that he always kept packed and left his flat in search of a cab.

* * *

The post didn't arrive until about nine-thirty, a little later than usual for a Saturday. The Associated Press offices had been busier than usual – the Neave murder had developed considerable interest and those heavyweight foreign newspapers without correspondents in London relied heavily on either the AP or Reuters for column inches.

One of the envelopes drew no more initial attention than any other – the contents, however, sparked a flurry of activity.

"STATEMENT FROM ARMY COUNCIL, THE INLA 31 MARCH 1979.

THE IRISH NATIONAL LIBERATION ARMY re-iterate that one of it's active service units was responsible for the execution of Airey Neave, British Shadow Government Spokesman on Northern Ireland.

The INLA successfully breached intense security at the House of Commons to plant the device, consisting of one kilo of explosive. After taking stringent precautions to ensure that no civilians would be injured the ASU returned safely to base.

Airey Neave was specially selected for assassination. He was well known for his rabid militarist calls for more repression against the Irish people and for the strengthening of the SAS murder gang, a group which has no qualms about murdering Irish people.

The INLA took this action in pursuance of it's aim to get the British occupying forces out of Ireland. We recognise that this task is not going to be achieved in a short period of time. We are armed, trained militarily and politically, and able to sustain what is going to be a long struggle.

We are not associated with any other group as reported in sections of the mass media; neither are we a cover group for the Irish Republican Army (Provisional). The Irish National Liberation Army is an independent military organisation whose primary aim is to secure a British military, political and economic withdrawal from Ireland and establish the right of Irish people to determine their own destiny.

As a republican socialist organisation we recognise that the cause of Ireland and the cause of Labour are linked and, in the words of James Connolly, we cannot envisage a free Ireland without a free working class. British imperialism is responsible for the sec-

tarian divisions within the Irish working class and we pledge ourselves to rid Ireland of imperialism and all it's manifestations.

Signed: Seamus Clancy.

A call was immediately put through to the anti-terrorist branch at Scotland Yard. Within ten minutes a team arrived to take possession of the document. Fortunately only one member of the AP staff had handled the letter and once their fingerprints had been taken for elimination purposes the team left with their prize.

When the anti-terrorist officers returned to Scotland Yard the letter and the envelope was handed over to the lab technicians who would carry out the preliminary investigation. The most important detail to ascertain was the authenticity of the claim. It was a sad reflection on human nature that there would always be bogus claims for a high profile attack like the Neave murder.

The postage time was recorded on the envelope and it hadn't been posted until after the attack had been carried out so it couldn't be discounted that quickly. There was really no point checking the prints on the envelope given the number of people who had handled it but the tests were carried out anyway. The letter itself was of much more interest, but when the prints obtained were compared the only matches came from the staffer at the AP – "Seamus Clancy" had clearly worn gloves.

The next tests carried out were much more subjective, in that the wording of the statement was compared to all the claims that had been received by radio stations and newspapers. One verbal statement from the INLA had been made using a recognised code word – the wording of the written claim was almost identical. One detail stood out in the written statement that had not been repeated anywhere else, and that was the weight of the device – one kilo – so by midday the feeling was that the statement was genuine, which left the anti-terrorist branch with a real problem – the INLA was a relatively unknown quantity on the mainland and the intelligence held on it was at best patchy. With a serious lack of hard intelligence at their disposal planning any operations against known republicans resident in London looked to be of little value. The involvement of other security services would have to be considered and the inevitable clash of personalities overcome.

By lunchtime the Commissioner of the London Metropolitan Police was given the preliminary report from the forensic lab, he'd already seen the wording, and armed with this information he made the decision that no statement was going to be released confirming one organisation as being that responsible. The media would continue to be fed a line that militant republicans were under suspicion and that enquiries were being pursued in that direction. Once he had reached this decision he placed a call through to the Home Office and said that a rider would be across directly with confirmation of responsibility for the Neave murder.

Sir Alistair Johnson sat at his desk in the Palace of Westminster and read the paper sent from Scotland Yard. He read it twice, taking in the meaning and the bad grammar, and realised very quickly that the claim should be forwarded to Lynch immediately. The first mention of the INLA showed him that he was out of his depth; certainly he'd heard of the INLA but as to who or what they were he was none the wiser. This was information best dealt with at Leinster Gardens.

He read the document through for a third time and marvelled at the ability of, in his view, the worst of scum to rationalise the most sordid of actions in the name of a cause. Airey Neave's death had been pure bloody murder, there was no other way of looking at it. He knew that he would make use of the present security situation come four o'clock at the group meeting at the Carlton. If ever there was a powerful argument for ongoing covert operations in Northern Ireland the Neave murder seemed to be it.

The document sent from Scotland Yard had occupied all his time since he had come into his office at Westminster after lunchtime, but there were two other letters that needed his attention. He picked up the first and noticed that it was postmarked "Newcastle, Co. Down". It didn't need the greatest powers of deduction to figure out the identity of the sender. He read through Robinson's letter and if Hugo had been there to witness the expression on Johnson's face he would have been disappointed. The disclosure of his resignation came as a mild surprise but Johnson had to congratulate Robinson on the inventive use of language. His insults were so much more original than the standard Anglo-Saxon expletives – "an insatiable blood-lust" and "the vicarious fulfilment of puerile fantasies" in particular caught his eye. At no time did his colour rise or his temper approach breaking point; truthfully, Johnson would have appreciated opposition of Robinson's calibre on a more regular basis.

Robinson's resignation could possibly present some short-term difficulties, particularly with Phillips taking his side. Johnson knew he would be confronted with yet more vitriol and specific accusations at the meeting later that afternoon, but Robinson had made a grave error of judgement by supplying all the details necessary for him to defend the charges.

John Harbinson was working his way through the new sheaf of reports that had piled up on his desk over the past couple of days. Each member of the team had been diligent in the pursuit of information on the Mullan farm fire and each member of the team had found precisely the same thing – nothing. Even Bill Kirkpatrick had received no information of substance – just a repetition of the rumours that were doing the rounds of the local bars; that something terrible had happened at the farm and that the Mullans weren't the only ones to have disappeared. The more Harbinson thought about the rumours, the more he tended to agree with McCleary, even more so with the news from London yesterday. McCleary had said he thought that the South Armagh Brigade were up to something – Airey Neave's murder could be just that something.

Harbinson took his suspicions to McCleary's office only to have them written off.

"So we're to put the Mullan investigation on the back burner?"

"That's what I've been told. The press have been given nothing concrete but the working assumption at the moment is that the INLA claim is genuine."

"But the Mullans surely look likely for the Neave murder?"

"Maybe, maybe not. The timescale doesn't look right for a job like this. We're talking weeks of planning here and they've only been missing for a matter of days. The orders are to keep our eyes open for McGlinchey and his playmates and listen out for any local gossip."

"And what about the Mullans?"

"They'll turn up, probably when we least want them to, but they'll turn up."

Lynch had been up all night, he hadn't even had a chance to pull out his camp bed to get some sleep, and the strain was beginning to tell. He hadn't been the only insomniac at Leinster Gardens – Aiken, Ellison, Walsh, Crawford, Kavanagh and Beatty had all answered the call that meant an end to their leave. By the end of the day they'd be joined by twenty additional bodies coming over from Kent and Hampstead; he'd asked for the full twenty from the depot but not surprisingly it was sending manpower to the Channel ports so he'd had to get in touch with his old friend Fulton over at Hampstead. The part-timer had been only too happy to lend a hand and had been able to give Lynch a full team to add to the twelve bodies he was getting from Ashford. He didn't want any teams out and about London because, in his view, any sources they might come across would be expecting attention, better to leave it for a couple of days. That was not to say that their time would be wasted – the amount of background reading and forward planning for any field excursions would give them more than enough to occupy their time for the next couple of days.

Every last detail on the INLA had been dug out of the files; every known player, every known associate, known sympathizers, possible sympathizers, people in the republican community in London who might offer assistance, and so it went on. They had made pages of notes which would be typed up and distributed along with copies of the few photographs that the department had. And the truth was that, despite their best efforts, the hand-out that had taken a whole night's work to assemble didn't amount to very much. The INLA had always been the poor relation of the Provisionals and had never achieved consistent results that had brought it to the ongoing attention of the security forces, that was, until now.

Lynch made his way to the kitchen in search of coffee, knowing that the new machine had yet to arrive. He had just put the kettle on to boil when he was joined by Crawford, who was also in search of coffee.

"Afternoon sir."

"Hello Crawford. Have you and Kavanagh finished the list of suspects for London?"

"For all the good it's going to do us, yes. Nobody's going to be dumb enough to hang around after this one. This is one big exercise in futility, and all it's going to achieve is a lot of pissed off rebels in London."

"You should be more careful in your choice of words – this could, after all, be my exercise in futility."

"Well, to be perfectly frank sir, I can't see you being that bloody stupid."

"So it's as well for you that this is someone else's bright idea. You're quite right, it's a stupid waste. We'd be much better off hitting the bastards on their home territory."

"We'd never get away with it sir."

"Oh I think we would on this occasion. Maybe now is the time to take the gloves off."

The kettle boiled and Lynch made coffee for both of them. Crawford took a sip, adopted a pained expression and set his mug down.

"Well, I don't know about that sir, but if you're right you could start by making them drink this."

"I know what you mean Crawford, but what an inhuman way to dispatch them. Anyway, I'm going into the conference room to allocate areas for the teams next week. If you would get the rest of the bodies stirred and in there for half an hour's time I think that'll finish us for the day once I've settled who's doing what."

"Right sir."

Sir Alistair Johnson's driver sat behind the wheel of the government issue Jaguar and waited for his principal to walk from one of the numerous minor entrances to the Palace of Westminster. A door opened but the first man to exit was one of Sir Alistair's two Special Branch officers; all government ministers and some of the most senior civil servants had protective officers and in the wake of the Neave murder security had been tightened. The Special Branch man carefully checked the immediate surroundings and when he was satisfied that the area was secure he brought Sir Alistair and the second officer out of the door and they covered the short distance to the car. The destination today was the Carlton, not a great distance but the need for vigilance was not lost on the driver or the two officers – where Johnson was relaxed, they were tense, giving every passer-by the most intense scrutiny. The lead man from Special Branch stepped to the car and took the rear passenger door handle in his "weak" left hand, before opening the door. His partner moved to Johnson's right and took station as Sir Alistair installed himself in the rear seat. The lead man then got into the front passenger seat and his partner made his way around the rear of the Jaguar and got into the car from that side. The doors had barely closed before the driver moved off, accessing traffic quickly thanks to the uniformed officer on points duty. Less than fifteen minutes saw them pulling up outside the Carlton and the protection team went through the whole process in reverse to see Johnson safely through the doors of the club. Once inside he walked swiftly through the lobby and made his way to one of the committee rooms which had been secured as the group's meeting place. He was early and took the opportunity to inspect the room before the others arrived; he wouldn't have put it passed Stephen Phillips to attempt some amateurish effort at recording proceedings. Not being an expert himself presented some difficulties in checking through the room; a professional would have been lost for choice in locating a bug, but Johnson managed, at least, to search the furnishings. He checked under the mahogany table that filled the centre of the room and then scrutinised the undersides of the sixteen chairs that surrounded it. The ornate silver hunting scene that formed a centrepiece to the table offered numerous hiding places amongst its nooks and crannies but Johnson found nothing. He looked at his watch to see that he had a few minutes to spare before the group was due to assemble so he quickly looked about the drapes and the blinds that covered the windows running along one wall, again nothing came to light. Once he had done that he was able to sit down and await the others.

At five to four the door opened and Robert Acheson came in, followed immediately by Oliver Scott. Greetings were exchanged and seats taken. Right on the stroke of four James Urquhart arrived which left Phillips, the man who called the meeting in the first place, to bring the complement to five, and he was late. The other four men sat quietly; nobody wanted to break the silence until Phillips put in an appearance. Johnson looked from one man to the next – Acheson, another former Grenadier Guardsman, hard and impassive, nothing to read in his expression, Scott, an academic and new to his post, distinctly nervous and unable to maintain eye-contact, and finally Urquhart, the banker who always looked at matters in terms of debit and credit, again nothing showing on his face. Johnson quickly realised that he couldn't tell which way the meeting would go and he didn't like the uncertainty.

By ten past four the annoyance amongst the four men, while unvoiced, was palpable. Acheson could eventually take no more waiting and got up to leave just as the door opened and an apparently unfazed Stephen Phillips took his seat at the head of the table.

"Sorry to keep you waiting gentlemen. I've just had a meeting with the chairman of the JIC which I just couldn't leave."

Acheson returned to his seat but couldn't let the opportunity of criticising Phillips pass; the animosity between the two men was long standing.

"This meeting – I hope it has changed your damn fool view of affairs in Ulster."

"Actually it hasn't Robert. If anything it has reinforced my position."

"Airey Neave is lying dead at the hands of these scum and you feel that we should show them some respect? For Christ's sake, how can you think like that?"

"Simply. The reality is that we could kill terrorists from now to doomsday and there'd always be more to take their place. I was opposed to the action last week and now we have a serious breach of security at Westminster. The whole Ulster problem is just too expensive, and before you fly off the handle Robert, think for one moment just what your own feelings are towards the Province."

"This is not a personal question Stephen, it is greater than that. Do you really expect us to believe that Neave was killed in revenge for what happened last week? There is no way that such an operation could have been mounted that quickly. For you it's just a matter of convenience – what you're talking about is capitulation and I for one will not tolerate that."

"I never said that Neave's death was an act of revenge, but it did clearly show the cost of keeping up this sordid little war. I'm talking common sense; our continued presence is costing us too much in terms of capital and material. It's time to look for another way."

Johnson had listened to the exchange with a growing sense of indignation. Phillips' last remark was more than he could bear.

"Stephen if you really think that way then you should resign. Another way? You arrogant little prig! A man whose boots you aren't fit to wipe died yesterday, and you ask us to make peace with those responsible. To hell with that and to hell with you for daring to think that way."

Both Urquhart and Scott came alive at Johnson's intervention, and as soon as they had had their say Johnson knew he and Acheson were in the minority. It was Urquhart who first raised his voice in opposition.

"Now steady on Alistair."

"Oh Jesus, not you as well James? I thought we were agreed in the action we took. Surely you don't think we should be making conciliatory noises?"

"Well a lot of what Stephen has said is true…"

"Oh for Christ's sake!"

"Let me finish Alistair. A lot of what he has said is true. The action in South Armagh may have been counter-productive…"

"There is no way of knowing how that is being viewed. It's too bloody early!"

"That's as maybe Alistair, but with all due respect…"

"Don't you dare patronise me James."

"I wouldn't dream of it. What I was going to say was that we should wait until a full evaluation of that particular job is at our disposal. A continuance of this new policy could be dangerous."

"Patronising or no, you're still talking about capitulation."

"Now you're being obstructive Alistair. I know that gut reactions can lead you in a certain direction, but you have to realise that a more measured response under these circumstances may be more appropriate."

"And you have to realise that that sort of soft soap crap may confuse the sorry morons we have to call "Minister", but it won't work with me. These bastards in Ulster have been dictating the course of our actions for far too bloody long, and now, when we've finally sent them a message that we've had enough you want to offer them an olive branch."

Scott now made his opinion on the matter known.

"Stephen has talked sense Alistair. Look at the potential fall-out from operations such as the one we endorsed last week."

"You're worried about that now Oliver? Damn it all, you were happy enough to see a body count last week. We were agreed, and now as soon as something negative crops up people are running for their bleeding hearts. I thank God I'm not that spineless."

Phillips had been watching developments; if he hadn't been sure of the support for his position before the meeting, he was now, and it was with that certainty that he now spoke in an attempt to calm the atmosphere.

"Losing your temper isn't going to advance your argument Alistair and neither is resorting to insult. The group appears to have changed it's emphasis and I suggest that we discuss that change in a civilized manner."

Johnson and Acheson were fuming but neither man offered Phillips the opportunity for any additional attack. What had been a four to one decision in favour of the assault on the South Armagh Brigade had shifted in a matter of a week to a three to two division in apparent favour of seeking some sort of negotiated settlement. Phillips had clearly been sounding out Scott and Urquhart to see which way they would jump if the group were to re-appraise its stance on Ulster; clearly the Neave murder had shaken them up. Their weakness was something that Johnson had not foreseen and he quickly realised that he should have taken notice of it. Phillips obviously had and was exploiting it for his own ends; he had seen a vanity, a self-importance, a misplaced sense of self-preservation in both men that made them pliable. Johnson did not see himself as some kind of altruist fighting the good fight, he knew himself to be selfish but it did not extend as far as the timorous response of Scott and Urquhart. The truth as he saw it was that the fight should be conducted with the utmost vigour – Friday's bombing only reinforced his opinion.

"…and furthermore I feel we must accept that the abilities to respond to the terrorist threat are over-rated."

Acheson could contain himself no longer and stood up, pointing an accusing finger at Phillips.

"Over-rated? What the hell do you think last week's action was? A perfect operation with the opposition wiped out – I call that a success. You are asking us to capitulate to the threat of a handful of scum."

"I am asking you to look at the realities."

"Your realities are all about balance sheets and have nothing to do with honour and integrity, commodities of which you possess absolutely none."

"I resent that, but I'm prepared to let it pass. I feel that we should make a decision regarding the future policy of the group in Northern Ireland."

Acheson had made no move to resume his seat and now made his way to the door.

"I am not going to dignify this farce by voting on what is obviously a foregone conclusion."

He slammed the door as he left and Phillips turned to face the remainder of the group, his smug expression undisguised. Johnson knew by the knowing smiles which Scott and Urquhart shared with Phillips that Acheson had been right to leave – nothing he could say now would make the slightest bit of difference to the outcome of any vote.

"It's clear that the group has had a change of heart; one which I feel it will have cause to regret. I will not be changing my position and I wish to make it a matter of record. Now as there is nothing more for me to add, I bid you good day."

Johnson walked out of the committee room and left the new group to finalise its position regarding the new policy dispensation for Northern Ireland. The Neave murder had supplied them with the easy out that allowed them to ignore the weakness of their own expediency. Johnson knew that his lack of judgement about Scott and Urquhart had meant an end to the covert activities of the department, for now anyway, but he was certain that his personal position could not be called into question. The proper administration of power was the best indication of a man's abilities, and Scott and Urquhart had shown themselves to be sadly lacking.

Johnson passed out of the main entrance of the Carlton to be met by his two bodyguards from Special Branch. Once again he went through the security charade and made his way back to the car waiting at the kerbside. As he settled back into the leather upholstery of the Jaguar's rear seat he reflected on his own position within the group; he had the remainder of the weekend to reach a conclusion, one which would affect the future operations of the department and the overall direction of policy regarding terrorism. He felt a sense of righteous indignation at the failings of others, but nothing but a sense of congratulation for his own position.

If Johnson had been truly honest he would have recognised the relative security of his own position and the fact that it was always going to be someone else he put in harm's way, but his capacity for self-analysis stopped short of total honesty and so he missed the point.

* * *

Lynch had come back into Leinster Gardens to go over the team lists for the sweeps of known republican haunts in London. The more he looked at the names of pubs and the associations for which they were known, the more he felt that any intelligence gathering operations were a complete waste of time. If he had been involved in the Neave hit he would have made sure that he and the rest of his ASU were out of the country by the fastest method and that meant airports. Looking at the time elapsed between the explosion and the efforts to secure Gatwick and Heathrow, it looked more than possible for the terrorists to have caught a flight out of the country. Even with the undoubted sensitivity of the Westminster bombing some of the airlines were proving obstructive in supplying full flight manifests for Saturday. Lynch looked at the sheaf of print-outs that had been passed on to him from the police at the two main airports and decided that the painstaking work of going through them could wait – a day either way would make no difference, the INLA would always return to Ireland so they'd catch up with them eventually. Any results from the lists would only come about with the co-operation of overseas agencies and with it being a Sunday he wasn't going to achieve anything in the first place. Just another aspect of the investigation that Johnson had dropped in his lap that wasn't going to amount to anything.

The various aspects of the investigation added up to a real problem for Lynch – too many tasks and not enough staff to undertake them. It was going to test all his skills of man management to divide his limited resources with the utmost effect. He looked at the flight manifests again and decided that he was only going to waste two people on them. The checks on sympathetic premises were going to cost him most in manpower, but there was no substitute for human intelligence in these circumstances. Lynch really wanted to contact Johnson and tell him that the whole exercise was and would be a waste of time and effort. He would have further added that the best way of finding the gang responsible for the Neave murder was to wait and run an operation similar to the Mullan farm job; it might not be publicly accountable but due process and doing what was right were very often mutually exclusive in Lynch's view.

He had lifted the receiver of his personal line and had even started to dial Johnson's home number when he hung up; he knew that direct contact with Johnson would only lead to an acrimonious exchange that he would ultimately lose even if he was right. The past week had been a roller-coaster of peaks and troughs for Lynch – the success of the Mullan job, tempered by the fact that he could tell no-one on the outside and then the disaster at Westminster with the death of Airey Neave, something for which he had no responsibility, but as part of the security community everyone was tarred with the same brush. There were times when he truly hated the secretive nature of his job and the lack of understanding that others had for it. It was an imperfect world and the more Lynch considered the opposition and the controllers the more he wondered if he made any difference. For once he would like to be running things.

After the all-night stint at Leinster Gardens Crawford had returned to his flat on Hoskins Street and allowed himself the luxury of a long lie-in on Sunday morning. It was nearly midday when he finally got up, and after debating a solitary lunch at home versus a solitary lunch in one of the Greenwich cafes he decided on someone else doing the catering. He called at the newsagents next door to his flat and bought all the heavyweight Sunday papers – the Times, the Telegraph and the Observer. Weighed down with newsprint he made his way to Vinci's, an Italian cafe that served a good lunch. He pushed open the front door and was assaulted by the aromas of any good Italian establishment – freshly grated parmesan and strong coffee. As with Bellini's he was known by the proprietor and after saying his hellos he made his way to his usual seat at the rear of the cafe facing the front door.

Once he was installed in the booth he discarded all the unnecessary supplements to the papers and concentrated on the main news sections. All three papers had covered the facts of the Westminster bombing accurately, but then again they were all relying on the same press releases from the police and the Palace of

Westminster authorities. The coverage differed when it came to speculation on the perpetrators and also for the biographical details on Airey Neave.

He read through the various reports as he ate his lunch, only once coming on a report that mentioned the INLA, and even then it was as a splinter group of the Provisionals, a lunatic fringe group that was totally undisciplined. Crawford shook his head at the notion that terrorists could be disciplined – they could give themselves all the airs and graces that they liked, he'd read Clancy's statement and thought it disgusting, as far as he was concerned they were all murdering bastards.

The biographical details on Neave were a little lacking in depth. The Old Etonian's escape from Colditz Castle was the best known detail of his life, and his status as a British hero was played to the limit. The *sang-froid* with which he walked out of Colditz dressed as a German officer on January 5th 1942 was well covered, but his subsequent war record of working within M.I.9. was either ignored or unknown as was his membership of P15. The fact that Neave had helped write the book on escape and evasion was missed, his importance to the security and intelligence communities and the esteem in which he was held, also missed. Crawford wasn't surprised, the discretion with which the "Establishment" operated, even in these seemingly public moments, was well-known. The one thing that none of the papers missed out on was the anger felt across the nation at this appalling murder – Neave was a hero, a man who had escaped from the seemingly escape-proof Colditz, a man of undoubted courage, a man who had served his country with unswerving devotion, and he'd been murdered by that most cowardly of methods, the car-bomb.

Crawford looked at the reports again as he drank his coffee and knew that the nation's anger would only grow when the INLA statement was released. The cry would go out for a tough response and the new government, which looked an increasingly likely prospect, would be given a cast-iron excuse for delivering it. After what Beatty had told him about the Mullan farmhouse assault, he could only speculate on the fate of the men responsible for Airey Neave's murder, and he realised that he would work tirelessly for that fate to overtake them.

Bill Kirkpatrick had spent an uncomfortable night watching the back of Maura O'Driscoll's house. The house was just another anonymous little box that formed part of the Housing Executive estate on the outskirts of Newtownhamilton that backed on to some farmland. The cattle shed that had been his base for the watcher job had a secure roof but the lack of rain had unfortunately been wedded to a clear sky that had made for a cold night. His coffee had run out hours since, as had the meagre rations he'd allowed himself, and he was fed up. Old intelligence said that Maura's sister Finoula had gone out with Dominic McGlinchey, and as the apparent leader of the INLA it was possible that he was using the O'Driscoll house. The order had come down from on high that all known associates of the INLA members were to be put under surveillance, and after all the choice sites had been allocated to the senior members of the team, it fell to Kirkpatrick to keep an eye on the back of Maura's and the fields that connected to the patch of unmown grass that passed for a garden at the rear of the house.

A whole night's watching had revealed nothing. If the geniuses at headquarters ever read situation reports they would know that Maura was currently engaged to Sean McNellis, a member of Joe Mullan's South Armagh Brigade of the PIRA, and therefore an unlikely supplier of a bolt-hole to McGlinchey; what with the INLA at daggers drawn with the PIRA. The only point of interest was the fact that not only had there been no sign of Dominic but also that Sean was not in evidence. Reports had said that McNellis had been missing since the fire at the Mullan farm. His apparent absence could confirm any of the theories that had been flown in the past week, and Kirkpatrick being a methodical man wanted to clear up the first investigation before moving on to the unlikely possibility that "Mad Dog" McGlinchey would show up at an old girlfriend's house.

He looked at his watch and was annoyed to see that it would be another two and a half futile hours before he could call it a day at seven o'clock. The only good news was that the weather looked as if it would stay fine which meant that his walk back to the car would be dry. He picked up his binoculars and gave the rear of the O'Driscoll house another look. The interior showed no change since his last inspection; that would be the tenor of his report reinforced with his view that this particular surveillance had been a waste of time.

Alastair Johnson sat in his study, a glass of Macallan, barely touched, rested on his desk; his elbows were supported by the arms of his chair, his hands pressed together, palm to palm, and he rubbed the bridge of his nose with the index fingers, as he was want to do when giving a matter serious contemplation. He'd been replaying yesterday's meeting since he'd left his wife and daughter at the dining table following Sunday dinner.

Try as he might he could find no way of circumventing Phillips. The fact remained that the operation in South Armagh had been carried out without official sanction – the group of five had acted independently, making their own rules as they had always done. The Neave murder had come at the worst possible time – just when the first large-scale success had been achieved against the PIRA the weaker links in the chain had been scared off by the spectre of personal risk that the Westminster bomb had created and all thoughts of prosecuting a robust action against terrorism had vanished.

To attempt a continuation of covert activities was a possibility, but a risky one. There was no telling what Phillips would do under the circumstances. Better to go along with the wishes of the majority and pay close attention to events as they unfolded. An opportunity would present itself, particularly with a new government and the changes the Conservatives would bring, so, irritating as it was, it would be best to wait until something happened that would allow him the chance to resurrect the operations of the department. With that decision reached he picked up his glass and sipped appreciatively at the single malt. The only thing he had to do now was phone Lynch and tell him the bad news and that the dogs would have to be called off.

Robinson had followed the bombing story in the press and, thinking that he would be able to offer some assistance, had almost succumbed to the temptation to call his section chief. He had actually lifted the telephone on Friday and begun dialling the number – the realisation that his resignation had either arrived or was in transit had stopped him. There was nothing that he could offer and if London felt the need of his services they knew where to find him. The one rash action of letting his ego get in the way of common sense had made him an outsider; his situation was made worse because he knew where his action had taken him – a stupid man could have blamed others for his predicament and become self-righteous, but Robinson wasn't that stupid.

He stood at the large window in the living room looking out towards the calm grey waters of Murlough Bay, not that there was much to see in the overcast darkness. He knew that his future was in the hands of others, specifically Stephen Phillips, and it gave him no sense of comfort at all. All he could do now was wait. If he heard nothing from Phillips in the next week or so he realised that he wasn't going to hear anything. A future of long walks on the strand and bird-watching at the reserve beckoned – not the most productive of endeavours, but then again, at least it would be free of the subterfuge of his past.

* * *

By nine-thirty the whole team had been assembled at Leinster Gardens; the London locals had arrived first, to be followed by the individuals who had travelled up from the depot in Kent. All told Lynch had twenty-five bodies to control for the sweep of the known republican haunts; just enough to make an effort that would keep the bosses happy. He brought them together in the conference room just down the corridor from his office. Seating was limited so some of the team had to stand, those more sure of Lynch and their position within the department leaned casually against the bookcase that ran the length of one wall, normal discipline just didn't apply, not as they saw it anyway.

Lynch had been sitting at the head of the table as his personnel had congregated, now that they were all there he stood to address them.

"I'm glad to see you all here and that the "ring of steel" around London didn't stop any of you."

The irony of his opening wasn't lost on the group and a few amused chuckles could be heard in the room.

"Yes, well, enough of that. We've been tasked to carry out the surveillance on the locations where our less skilful friends would only make a hash of things. To that end I've split you into four field teams of four, with a further five staying here to act as a control group. The bad news for the five is that you will have additional responsibility to go through the flight manifests that we've been forwarded from Gatwick and Heathrow. Karen Aiken will be running the headquarters team so I'll let her take control now."

Aiken called out the names of the four members of her team and led them from the conference room to make a start on the lists. Lynch divided up the remaining personnel and gave them their areas of operation. By ten-twenty the conference room was empty except for Lynch. He had sent the various teams out to start trawling for any snippets of information with the knowledge that, unless the INLA were rank amateurs, there would be bugger all intelligence worth gathering. There was no doubt in his mind that he was overseeing a wasted effort, and with that positive thought in mind he picked up the team assignments and walked down the corridor to give them to Aiken.

Jones woke just after ten; thankfully he didn't have to be in Curzon Street until after lunch, so he'd taken advantage of the fact and when he'd knocked off on Friday he'd asked Claire from the typing pool to go away for the weekend. He was pleasantly surprised when she'd said yes, and they'd spent Saturday night in a small hotel he knew in Broadway – it had been a long drive, but the meal and the company had made it more than worth the trouble. They'd arrived back late last night and, after he'd dropped Claire off at her flat with a promise to take her out for dinner on Wednesday, he'd gone straight home to bed.

He rolled out of bed and walked into the kitchen in search of a cup of coffee and his first cigarette of the day. With a Dunhill in hand he went to his front door to be disappointed with the lack of post, not even junk mail that would at least have given him something to read as he drank his coffee. He switched on the transistor radio, but couldn't find a channel that didn't irritate so he turned it back off.

After he'd showered and dressed he sat down with the Yellow Pages and flipped through the banks section until he got the number of the Natwest on Edgware Road. A three minute phone call, with the confirmation of his new account number, told him all he wanted to hear – the account in Dundalk had been transferred to London – Lynch had his money and Jones would have his five hundred quid – the week couldn't have got off to a better start.

Johnson had travelled up from the country that morning and had used the time spent on the early morning drive to finalise his strategy in the light of the group's change of stance. He had concluded that opposition to Phillips would be counter-productive but that the activities of Lynch's department could continue in a intelligence gathering vein. Any information that was accrued could be stored and used when the opportunity presented itself – Phillips wouldn't always be in a position of control.

The government Jaguar pulled up at the Home Office on Queen Anne's Gate and the two Special Branch officers shepherded Johnson in through the front doors. He made his way to his office, saying perfunctory good mornings to those individuals he encountered along the way. He collected the several files proffered by his secretary and, telling her that he did not wish to be disturbed, made his way into his office. Once he was seated behind his desk he made the call to Leinster Gardens. The phone was answered on the second ring by an irate Lynch.

"This had better be important."

"I should say it is. This is Johnson."

Lynch hadn't expected to hear from Sir Alistair for a day or two, hence his somewhat terse response to the phone call. He changed tone for his superior.

"Sorry sir. What can I do for you?"

"There's been a change in thinking amongst the group, which I hasten to add is not my choice. The Neave business has put the cat amongst the pigeons – or doves I should say. Ultimately it means no more jobs like the other week. And furthermore anything your department comes up with in the course of investigations into the INLA activities in London is not to be acted upon."

"What?"

"I wasn't aware that you didn't understand English. I think the meaning of what I said was clear enough."

Any thoughts Lynch may have had regarding deference to Johnson evaporated with the news that he was to cease operations forthwith.

"So you mean to tell me that there's been a sea-change in policy and that the bleeding hearts are in control?"

"More or less, and I'd advise you to temper your tone."

"Would you sir? Well, with all due respect, fuck you! I've been sweating blood for the past month and a half over this job and the future application of this new policy, and now you tell me that because a few spineless bastards get cold feet I'm to call a halt to things? Jesus Christ! This isn't some bloody game – this is for keeps."

"I'll remind you once again just who you're talking to. I could make you and your whole department disappear, just remember that."

"Oh yes, you'd turn on me but your precious little group would allow a bunch of scum to get away with bloody murder."

Johnson saw that threats were of no consequence so he tried a different approach.

"I understand your annoyance at the change…"

"Annoyance! Is that what you think? Jesus! You really have no idea, none of you have a bloody clue, and don't think you can soft-soap me on this one. I've risked a hell of a lot more than my career on this job, and even with those risks it was the right thing to do."

"I know, I know, and it will be the right thing again, you'll just have to be patient."

"You just don't switch this sort of thing on and off. My people have been given their orders and it'll seem bloody strange for a reversal to come so quickly."

Lynch was proving to be a troublesome opponent, but there were means of dealing with him – Johnson decided to bring matters swiftly to a close by playing the personal card.

"I don't care how you do it, just get it done. The consequences otherwise would be unfortunate to say the least. You've got how long left with the department? Not forgetting your pension of course. Do I make myself clear?"

"Very clear… sir."

The disgust in Lynch's voice was obvious. Was it solely for Johnson or for himself at bowing to the implicit threat, or a combination of the two? It didn't really matter to Johnson; he'd achieved his aim, having made an enemy of Lynch was of no consequence – a little man like that counted for nothing in Johnson's sphere.

"Well I'm glad that's settled. You take care of things will you Lynch?"

"Yes sir."

"Good, good. Keep me informed if there is any information coming from your investigations, there's a good chap."

"Yes sir."

Johnson saw no need to prolong the conversation now that Lynch had been brought to heel so he hung up. He couldn't see any future difficulties with Lynch – he was more worried by the possibility of ongoing confrontations with Phillips – strange how a weak man could prove to be a dangerous adversary.

Lynch sat looking at the telephone receiver in disbelief. He'd heard some disgusting things in his time with the department but the exchange he'd just had with Johnson surpassed them all. The outline brief that had covered the planning and commission of the operation in South Armagh had been on his desk for five, maybe six years, the word had come down from on high that it could be put into effect, and now when the gloves should well and truly be off a group of spineless bastards decided that it had been a step too far. It didn't make any sense to him.

Chances had gone begging in the past, and after only one real success they would continue to be missed. The logic behind the change of heart defeated Lynch. Try as he might he couldn't figure out where the new plan would lead policy. Perhaps there was no plan – perhaps it was going to be a series of reactions to events. Could the Whitehall warriors not see that such a response could only lead to defeat? No, they probably couldn't – they were politicians after all, and they dealt with strategies based on expediency. The only conclusion he could reach was that there had been a collective loss of nerve; which didn't help him one bit – he still had to come to a decision about the present intelligence gathering operation, how to end it, and how to do so without raising suspicion as to the motives. He knew that if certain members of the team became aware of the new thinking they would be nearly impossible to control; so he wouldn't let them know. He'd let the operation continue – the reality was that a lot of man hours would be spent achieving very little – the INLA members might be considered to be on the lunatic fringe but they were smart enough to penetrate Westminster, and if they were that smart they weren't going to hang around London basking in the limelight.

Lynch was fairly sure that he could make the surveillance job a distraction and that by mixing his results or rather the lack of them with the investigations of the other security and police forces he would have a believable concoction to feed to his people no matter how unpalatable. It was important for morale, if nothing else, that his people should never become aware of the sea-change that had overtaken them. The same went for operations in Ulster; if there was no definite intelligence to work on then there couldn't be any planned assaults. As the department controller Lynch knew he could make Johnson's command fit and disguise the new reality from his team. The problem remained that he had to live with his own duplicity – damn the Johnsons of this world for putting him in that position, for it meant that he was a slave to the actions of others; others who were in fact the enemy. Johnson obviously had no idea what he had just done, but Lynch was only too well aware – if they couldn't fight terrorism on equal terms they would lose, and that was what hurt more than anything else.

Phil Carson had been up for most of the night dealing with a fire-bomb at a local draper's shop – it was so bloody easy – slip a device the size of a cigarette packet into a coat pocket and if it detonates you've got thousands of pounds worth of damage. Sadly for Mr. Sinclair who owned the shop that was exactly what had happened; a family business, three generations in the making, now a burnt out wreck, and yet Sinclair had shrugged his shoulders philosophically and said that he'd rebuild.

By the time he got back to the Fire Station it was close to midday and he was absolutely shattered. He parked the Cavalier and went up to his office to find a large manila envelope propped on his desk. He picked it up, sat down and ripped it open to find copies of the test results from the Mullan farmhouse fire. There was a covering letter which did little more than tell him what was in the envelope. He set it to one side and looked at the various documents from the lab in Lisburn. The most conclusive was the paper listing the results of the gas chromatography tests. He looked through the list of compounds encountered in the test and saw that there was no evidence of the use of accelerants that would point to arson. Taking everything into consideration the only reasonable conclusion was that the fire had been the result of an accident – specifically that coals had fallen from the kitchen range and that the linoleum on the kitchen floor had ignited spreading the flames throughout the kitchen and subsequently through the rest of the house. Harbinson was going to be disappointed, but at least he would know for certain that he was dealing with an accident.

"Thanks for letting me know. Tell you what, do me a favour and send over the report – I'll have it copied and returned."

"No problem John. I'm just sorry that we couldn't be of more help."

"Doesn't matter. To be honest we've got our plate full dealing with the local end of the Neave bombing."

"I hadn't heard that there was a local connection."

"Aye, well you will tomorrow. The papers will be full of it."

"So who are we talking about?"

"You'll see tomorrow. Look, I'd better take your news to the boss. Thanks for all your help and could you pass that on to Lisburn."

"OK, I'll do that."

John Harbinson sighed heavily as he put the phone down; it wasn't that he'd really expected some positive information from Lisburn but the fact that the Mullan investigation had yielded nothing annoyed him to say the least. He picked up the brief series of notes that Bill Kirkpatrick had made during his stint on watch at Maura O'Driscoll's and looked again at the comments on Sean McNellis and his association with the Mullans. This whole sorry mess was connected, of that he was sure, he just couldn't prove it. He sighed again as he pushed his chair back before getting up and leaving his office to walk down the corridor and share the good news with his boss, Alex McCleary.

Surprisingly the Superintendent's door was closed, so Harbinson knocked, and was rewarded with a muted "Come in". The reason was clear when he entered the room, McCleary was on the telephone, but managed a gesture to the seat in front of his desk which Harbinson took. McCleary managed a few grunted acknowledgements on the phone before hanging up and turning his full attention on his second in command.

"That was headquarters bending my ear about our friend McGlinchey. Have you any news for me John?"

"Nothing that's going to make your day."

"Well spit it out."

"Phil Carson has just been on with me and he gave me the great news that the forensic investigators up at Lisburn have drawn a total blank on the Mullan fire."

"That's bloody marvellous, but I suppose it means we can get on with the INLA enquiries with no distractions."

"You mean that we're to forget the Mullans?"

"I didn't say that, but we've got other things to worry about. No, the Mullans can just wait, if anything turns up we'll re-open the investigation. Fair enough?"

"Aye, whatever you say sir."

"Well it is what I say. So you can give your full attention to the discovery of the whereabouts of dear Dominic, OK?"

Harbinson got up and left McCleary's office feeling something of a failure because of the lack of a result with the Mullan fire. As he walked back down the corridor he consoled himself with the new challenge of bringing down the INLA leadership; at least, on this occasion, he had some tangible evidence to work with.

Jones looked at his watch and decided he had more than enough time to call Lynch before he walked to catch the train that would get him into Curzon Street before the end of the lunch hour. He dialled the number and waited for ten rings before an out of breath voice answered.

"This is Lynch."

"It's Jones sir."

"Well what is it."

Jones knew that Lynch could be short-tempered, but he detected more than that in his old boss's voice.

"You all right sir?"

"Thank you for your concern Jonesy, but there's nothing you can do. I was in the conference room when the phone rang and I had to run to answer it, that's all. Anyway, what's your news?"

"Well I called the NatWest this morning and the draft is through from Dundalk. The balance stands at £109,310."

"Thank God something's going right. How long do you reckon on holding it in the account?"

"It doesn't really matter sir. When do you want it?"

"Let me see….the account it goes into is already in place, so I can't see any obstacles. End of the week would be fine. Just one thing Jonesy – the last three digits aren't the same as those detailed in the bank book total, why is that?"

"I left £458 in the Allied Irish account and the £310 is my own. I reckoned there'd be less suspicion if I didn't close out the Dundalk account completely."

"I see. Then there only remains your fee to be settled. How does two thousand sound?"

Jones nearly dropped the handset – two thousand was a lot more than he had ever considered – in truth he had thought he would be pushing things to ask for five hundred, and here was Lynch offering him two grand.

"That's more than generous sir."

"I know it is Jonesy, but I'm buying more than services with it, I'm buying your silence. Just don't forget that."

Jones understood the implied threat, knowing only too well the stupidity of crossing a man like Lynch.

"You can rely on me sir. When this is put to bed it'll be as if it never happened."

"I thought you'd see it my way. I'll be in touch to let you know the where and the when."

The line went dead as Lynch hung up and Jones replaced his handset. Two grand! For a few hours work! It was the best bloody pay-day he'd ever had, and one that he'd never be able to brag about. Jones knew when to keep his mouth shut and, knowing Lynch as he did, this was definitely one of those times. He left his flat with thoughts of two thousand pounds and how to spend it – the beginning of the week had just got even better.

Alistair Johnson had spent an uncomfortable forty minutes with Robert Acheson. The Permanent Under Secretary to the Foreign Office had been in a foul mood. Johnson reflected on the colourful expressions Acheson had used in reference to the other members of the group and wondered if people would recognise the men from the descriptions. Two days since the Carlton meeting had in no way calmed his colleague and it was only with great effort that Johnson was able to convince him that they would give every appearance of resigned agreement but that they would in reality be playing a waiting game. Acheson had always been the chief advocate of direct action and the thought of seeing his policy discredited and discarded was more than he was prepared to bear; he had tried to persuade Johnson to join him in allowing a continuance of covert activities, and it was this potential stumbling block that had caused Johnson the greatest difficulty in removing. Thankfully he'd managed to show Acheson the possible dangers of such an action – the thoughts of public disgrace and ruination were even less palatable than the seemingly dishonourable course they were now following. A calmer Acheson had left his office, the anger was still there, not diminished, but for the moment contained. The day had not started well, what with the puerile explosion of bad temper from Lynch and the no less puerile outburst from Acheson, and it was now going to get worse – he had a lunch appointment with Phillips.

He left the Office at quarter to one with his entourage in attendance. The drive through central London was slow but uneventful and at five past the car pulled up outside White's. The men from Special Branch walked Johnson all the way into the dining room and up to his table. It was a mark of the discretion of the other diners that hardly a head was turned and that there was not so much as a lull in the conversation. There was no brinkmanship today – Phillips had arrived on time, but Johnson was damned if he was going to apologise for being five or six minutes late. The briefest of greetings were exchanged as Johnson took his seat and then both men got down to the serious business of deciding what to eat. Johnson reached a decision first and picked up the wine list; scanning its contents quickly he picked a reliable Chablis with no thoughts for Phillips and his taste. A waiter took their order when it was clear that both men had had enough time to make a selection and it was only then that Phillips spoke.

"I'm glad you could make it Alistair."

"And why shouldn't I pray tell?"

It was obvious that Johnson's rejoinder had caught him off guard and Phillips did his best to appear magnanimous.

"It was just the way things were left on Saturday. I thought that there may be some ongoing unpleasantness and that is not what I want."

"Not at all. I think my position is perfectly clear as is Robert's, but that won't interfere with our professionalism. The group has reached a majority decision and we can only go along with it."

"Well I'm very pleased to hear it. Which brings me swiftly to the other piece of business I wished to discuss."

"So I was right in thinking that this was more than just a bridge building exercise."

"In all honesty, yes. It's about Hugo Robinson."

"And what about him?"

"He's resigned."

"I know. He had the nerve to send me a letter explaining his reasons and in addition he used the opportunity to call my character into question."

"You have my apologies for that…"

"Oh let me guess Stephen, you want him back in the fold at Five?"

"Not exactly. I'd like to see him as a special adviser to the group."

"For God's sake he's a whistle blower."

"Yes, and as such it would be better to have him under control. Besides when it comes to Ulster he knows what he's talking about."

"Did he make overtures to you on this?"

"No."

"Right. Well you can have your lackey, but under no circumstances is he ever to be given the full details on what happened in South Armagh."

"Suppose he should find out? After all, he will have to be given full access."

"Just remember Stephen that you are a part of the group which gave its assent to this particular operation, and as such you stand to lose as much as the rest of us. Give him access to everything but this one; he can't learn details that aren't on file. The paper trail is non-existent and no-one will talk about this job, but let's just say if he should discover the details, he'll never get the opportunity to release them."

Before Phillips could say anything the first course arrived and both men observed a discreet silence as the waiter served them. Johnson's thinly veiled threat was not lost on Phillips and when they were once again alone he made his reply.

"It sounds as if you're saying that should Robinson make any disclosures he'll be taken care of."

"He'll never get the chance to make any disclosures. As I said you can have him, but the condition remains – any indiscretions and he is forfeit."

"I understand."

"I hope you do, for all our sakes."

With the business of the meeting concluded both men attempted to enjoy their lunch, but neither of them felt in a buoyant state of mind – Johnson had wrung a concession from Phillips regarding Robinson, but the balance of power in the group had shifted – Phillips was in control, but was still fearful of Johnson. Such thoughts preyed on the minds of both men and spoiled their appetites.

The statement from the INLA was eventually released to the press on Monday afternoon – too late for the daily newspapers, but the evening press and the television and radio news covered it at some length. A press release from the Metropolitan Police contained some information on the INLA, which was duplicated by the Palace of Westminster press office, but there was little substance to what the statements said. Archivists at the BBC and ITN searched through the research material available to them and to the general consternation of the news editors found that there was little hard copy on this "republican splinter group". Emotions were still running high and with that public sentiment in mind some of the less scrupulous newspapers ran uneducated and inflammatory pieces. "Paddy bashing" was condoned if not openly encouraged and more real or perceived grievances were stockpiled for the republican propaganda machine.

Robinson had risen early, his resignation wasn't cause for his adopting slothful habits, and had taken Hervey for a long walk. On his return to the house at Murlough he had assembled such paperwork as was in his possession. He was somewhat surprised that there had been no communication from London giving instructions for its disposal or detailing its collection. By lunchtime he had built a pile of various papers and dossiers that stood nearly a foot high. He sat with a mug of coffee and a sandwich reflecting on the substance of the work of several years – it didn't amount to very much. The recriminations and the self-doubt began to work on him and he spent several hours trying to answer the questions that assaulted him in waves.

By mid-afternoon the failures, real and perceived, had triumphed and Robinson felt the need of escape – sitting at home was serving no purpose – he could at least take Hervey out for another walk. He had just shrugged on his waterproof when the phone rang. He put down Hervey's lead and lifted the receiver.

"Hello."

"Hugo. I'm glad I got you, I've got some news that you may find interesting."

"Well I must say I wasn't expecting to hear from you Stephen. So what's this interesting news?"

"I was having lunch today with our old friend Johnson."

"Spare me the sarcasm Stephen, we both know he's a shit. Anyway, what possible interest could this have for me?"

"There's been a sea-change in policy. The Neave murder has convinced us that a vigorous approach to the Ulster problem is counter-productive."

"And?"

"And in essence you were right. Johnson has been put in his place and has retired to Queen Anne's Gate to lick his wounds as it were."

"I still don't see what this has to do with me."

"Well your resignation caused quite a stir, not least with Johnson, but it did impress several people as a matter of principle. Now I know that I can't get you back in the fold at Five, but I have gone one better, you are now special adviser to the group."

All thoughts of failure disappeared in an instant. What he had just heard surpassed any hopes he may have harboured for his future – special adviser – to the group! Working as Five's senior officer in residence in Ulster was as nothing by comparison – in effect he would answer to no-one. It seemed too good to be true.

"What does Johnson know about this?"

"Oh, he's accepted it. We discussed it over lunch. All you have to do is say yes, and that's it."

"That's all very well Stephen, but there are going to be problems. For instance how am I to source material from Five when it is unlikely that anybody there will even talk to me?"

"If there is any problem I'll access material personally and as far as any of the security services are concerned you'll be working directly for the Joint Intelligence Committee – they daren't ignore that."

"What sort of security coverage will I have here?"

"You're not far from Ballykinler, what about the army?"

"Absolutely not! You forget that I'm intimately acquainted with the army's methods and they are not suited to this sort of detail."

"What about your former colleagues at Five?"

"If they were needed I would be concerned about their response time. I could be left to my own devices for too long."

"So what do you suggest then Hugo?"

"Bring the Secret Intelligence Service into play in Ulster and give them the job."

"Five aren't going to like that."

"If you want me to give the group advice then let me make the choices that are going to affect my safety. I don't think that is too much too ask."

"Well if you think that that is the way to progress, who am I to argue."

"Then I suggest that you get on to Century and set things in motion. They'll be able to move bodies up from Dublin to cover me in the meantime."

"Right Hugo, I'll get it sorted today. One last thing before I go, I better tell you that we expect a strategy document next week, if it's not too much trouble."

"You'll have it Stephen, just remember that it will purely be an opinion piece; there's no way that I could produce anything based on hard facts in the time allowed."

"I understand Hugo, but be that as it may we would still like to see an outline paper from you."

"I'll get on it straight away Stephen, and thank you for taking care of things with Johnson and the rest."

"Never think of it, least I could do and all that."

One phone call and an old school tie had changed so many things – at the lowest level, Robinson was back in the fold having never really left – at the highest, security and intelligence policy in Northern Ireland would never be the same again.

By seven that evening Crawford and Ellison had been in three pubs in the Kilburn area of north London, all with republican connections and none of them with any useful intelligence to offer. The other teams had been deployed across the city and without exception they had achieved the same result. Crawford was sure that casual observation of the regulars in any establishment was going to reveal nothing – realistically no professional terrorist would be stupid enough to show their face so soon after a major event like the Westminster bombing, if they were indeed foolish enough to remain in London.

They had been sitting in "The National" for about an hour and Crawford was well into his second pint of Guinness. It was a bar that he had frequented over the years and his was an accepted "face" although here he was known as "Gerry Crossan". The clientele were a mixed bag; ex-pat Irish rubbed shoulders with locals, with a sprinkling of wannabe radicals from the LSE who travelled to the bar in the hope of meeting some genuine hard cases. Crawford had picked up a few low-grade tips in the past and he hoped that something might turn up, although he wasn't going to hold his breath. In addition to his feelings of futility regarding this job he was concerned about Jenny Ellison – for a department hand she was conducting herself like a beginner with too many direct looks around the bar and an apparent unwillingness to play the part of the girlfriend. They were sitting side by side at a table close to the bar and near the exit which afforded a good view of most of the customers. Crawford leaned over to her and for the rest of the drinkers it must have looked as if he was whispering sweet nothings to his girlfriend.

"Smile as I talk to you. Now I don't care if you outrank me or not, you're behaving like a bloody amateur. You know the drill, smile and laugh at my jokes and relax for God's sake."

She entered into the spirit of things and replied with a possibly over-enthusiastic smile which split her previously strained expression.

"I'm just bored and if you're honest so are you."

"Bored or not we've got at least another hour of this. Look, I've got to go to the toilet and I'll go to the bar on the way back – do you want another drink?"

"Yeah, you can get me another half of Guinness."

"Good girl, remember what I said and just relax, OK?"

"Sure, I'll be fine."

Crawford got up and made his way to the rear of the bar and the gents. There was a poster advertising an Irish folk group who would be playing in the pub on Friday night taped to the outside of the toilet door – he took a note of the time – with a bit of luck somebody would be making a collection for "the cause" – and with a bit more luck they might be known and of interest to the present investigation. On his return to the bar he ordered a pint and a half of Guinness, as the drinks were poured and settled he took the opportunity to scrutinise the various men sitting and standing at the bar. The snatches of conversation that he picked up were concerned with runners and riders at the races and the fortunes of Arsenal football club – nothing to spark his interest.

When he returned to their table with the drinks he re-took his place beside Ellison. The double doors to their left opened and a group of five men walked in, talking loudly. Judging from their accents they were Irish and by the way they were dressed they showed themselves to be labourers in the building trade – stained jeans and boots caked with cement dust. By way of enquiry Crawford quickly glanced at the new arrivals and raised his eyebrows, Ellison looked the men over and turned back to Crawford shaking her head. Neither of them recognised any of the men from the photo-montages that they had studied, not just today, but over many months.

For the next hour or so Crawford and Ellison maintained the pretence of a couple out for a quiet drink, while they were in fact taking in all the details of the drinkers in "The National". By nine o'clock they had both had enough and decided to leave the pub. Once outside they continued to act out their role until they reached their car, a department Ford Escort; Crawford unlocked the door on the driver's side, got in and opened the passenger's door from the inside. He started up and set off once Ellison was settled.

"Well that was a complete waste of time."

"I don't know so much Jenny – I got one useful pointer – there's a shindig at "The National" on Friday night – it'll be packed full of Micks and sympathizers – you never know we might get lucky."

"So where are we going now?"

"First off, I'm dropping you at your flat and then I'm going home to mine."

"But what about filing our reports?"

"God you're keen! If you want I'll take you to the Gardens, but it's after nine and even Lynch has got to sleep sometime. I don't think he'd be overjoyed if you handed him a report at this time of night. There'll be time enough for that tomorrow."

"Yeah, I suppose you're right. OK, home it is then."

Patterson looked at the luminous dial on his watch and noted with disgust that only ten minutes had passed since he'd checked it the last time. He'd been volunteered for the O'Driscoll surveillance at today's meeting; Harbinson had said he needed Kirkpatrick and that it would be good experience for a young officer like Patterson, so here he was, bone cold on a pointless job in a bloody cattle shed. On nights like this he could cheerfully say goodbye to the RUC but he knew such thoughts would be short-lived; he loved being a policeman.

All such notions disappeared as his attention was attracted by a light coming on at the rear of the house; he lifted his binoculars and looked in through Maura's kitchen window. As he watched, Maura came into the room, filled the kettle and switched it on, she opened a cupboard and retrieved two mugs which she set on the counter. Nothing strange in her making tea or coffee except that Maura was meant to be on her own. As he continued to watch a man came into view – medium height, stocky build, close cropped brown hair, clean-shaven. His 16X50 binoculars made the man appear to be about thirty feet away, close enough for a positive identification and Patterson was pretty sure he knew who he was looking at. He made a series of entries in his notebook covering every detail of what he saw. There was no way he wanted to make a fool of himself when he made his report tomorrow.

* * *

Crawford had collected Ellison at ten to eight at her flat and after negotiating the start of the rush-hour they had been the first to arrive at Leinster Gardens just after quarter past. They had gone up to the conference room and written the report for their activities of the previous day. There wasn't much to say and by half past they stood in the kitchen while the new Gaggia machine brewed some decent coffee.

"You've been with the department a long time Gerry, what's your view on the present job?"

"Window dressing."

"Oh come on; you've got to see a greater worth in what we're doing than that, otherwise you wouldn't do it."

"You really think we're going to walk into some north London pub and see the players responsible for Airey Neave's murder? Isn't going to happen – those lads are long gone – we're just closing the stable door."

"I never saw you as a cynic."

"Ha, that's funny. You know, Sean Kavanagh thinks of me as some kind of idealist. Anyway, that coffee's brewed and I'll have mine black."

"To suit your mood?"

"No, it's just the way I like it."

As Ellison poured him a mug of coffee they heard footsteps coming along the corridor just before Lynch came into the kitchen.

"And there was me thinking I was early. Be a dear Jenny and pour me some of that thank you. Well you two must have something for me to be in this early."

It was Ellison who answered him.

"Not really sir. We came in to get our report on yesterday squared away."

"I'm sure it'll be just as fascinating as the others I've read so far. Let's see it."

Crawford and Ellison stood in silence as Lynch went through the brief report. The way in which he breathed forcefully out through his nose punctuated every boring paragraph. They watched him raise his eyebrows when he approached the end and waited in anticipation when he'd finished.

"The *ceilidh* on Friday looks interesting. How many bodies do you think you'll need?"

Ellison hadn't really considered manpower, but fortunately Crawford had, so he answered and saved her any embarrassment.

"We talked it over sir, and what with me being known in "The National" we thought that it might be best to keep it to a minimum effort – just Jenny and me. A minimum approach, no additional cover, and we go in completely clean; otherwise there might be the danger of attracting the wrong sort of attention."

"Good point. Until then you pair are off the surveillance details. I don't want you spotted at any other pubs – let's keep this as natural looking as possible. So in the meantime you two can lend a hand here collating any stuff that turns up from the airline manifests, OK Jenny?"

"Yes sir, I'll get started right away."

Ellison left the two men in the kitchen and went in search of Karen Aiken. Lynch put down his mug and looked at Crawford.

"D'you think there's much point to all this?"

"To be honest sir? No I don't, but there's always a slim chance – you never know – something might turn up."

Patterson had made an early start; truth be told he'd hardly slept a wink when he'd managed to get away from the job at Maura O'Driscoll's, and he'd come into the station to check through whatever files there were connected to his sighting. There were a few photographs; some group shots from republican rallies, some long-range telephoto lens jobs that were a bit on the grainy side, but they all confirmed to Patterson's mind that he was right. He took the files into the canteen and had breakfast – a full fry and a mug of strong sweet tea. He flipped through the background details in one file as he ate. Try as he might he could make no connection between his man and Maura – maybe there was no history and he had merely been in the right place at the right time – then again, the boss always said that he didn't believe in coincidences – that everything happened for a reason. Whatever the reason Patterson was sure that he'd discovered something of interest and that further investigations were necessary.

The clock on the canteen wall showed quarter past nine – the boss would be in by now so Patterson decided to go and see him immediately. After the second unanswered knock on McCleary's door Patterson went in search of John Harbinson. He wasn't in his office either, but Patterson found him in the communications room hunched over a desk reading.

"Sorry to interrupt sir, but could I have a word?"

"Can't it wait until the team meeting Derek?"

"Well it could sir, but I'd rather have your view on this first, if you wouldn't mind."

"OK, let's hear it."

Patterson had barely finished recounting the details of his night's surveillance when Harbinson lifted the first available phone and located McCleary. When he'd finished a very brief conversation he turned to Patterson.

"OK Derek, you and I are going to have a word with the boss, follow me."

Instead of going to the Superintendent's office Harbinson took Derek to one of the interrogation cells explaining that there was no chance of being disturbed. McCleary was waiting for them as they entered and took their seats. Harbinson got things under way.

"Tell the boss what you told me."

Patterson set the files on the table along with his notebook and began with his arrival at the cattle shed. Fortunately for McCleary and Harbinson it wasn't long before the report reached the detail of specific interest.

"At ten twenty-one Maura O'Driscoll came into the kitchen and began preparing tea or coffee. She was followed after, maybe a minute or so by a man."

At this point in his narrative Patterson reached for the topmost file, opened it and took out an 8X10 black and white photograph. He turned the photograph around to face McCleary.

"I've no doubt that this is the man I saw sir."

"No doubts?"

"I was looking at him with 16X50s sir, no doubts."

McCleary took the photograph from Patterson and regarded the image of the man from East Tyrone; he put it on the desk and drummed his fingers on it a couple of times before addressing Harbinson.

"Well John, it looks like we've got two jobs on our plate, one, see what McGlinchey and his outfit are up to, and two, see why Dessie Grew is making house calls in Newtownhamilton." "It certainly looks that way sir."

"Doesn't it just. Well congratulations Derek, and for your good work I'm giving you the pleasure of learning all you can about Grew – the who, what, when, where and why – every detail. Is that understood?"

"Yes sir."

Hugo Robinson had spent the morning re-examining his files, separating the various suggested policy documents he'd written over the years from the actual operational papers. He read through those documents he had retrieved and by lunchtime he had the bare outline of his first consultation paper for the group drawn in his mind. He got an A4 pad and began making notes, concentrating on the ineffectual policies that the British government had implemented over the years in Northern Ireland and how a continued application of those same policies would lead to an extended and expensive stalemate. He then specified possible policy changes and applications- these ranged from an unthinkable unilateral withdrawal to an all-out military action to eradicate terrorism of all political hues. It was clear to him that such extremes measures would be distasteful to the new majority in the group, and with that in mind he began to lay the foundations for his solution.

It was after three o'clock when he put his pen down; truth be told he had more notes to make before he began drafting the report, but he'd missed lunch and was feeling hungry. He went into the kitchen to make himself a sandwich and a cup of tea. As he examined the contents of his fridge he realised that he would have to make a trip for provisions – that was one thing he had quickly come to miss on his return to Ulster – a good delicatessen – a decent grocery for that matter. He finished the last of his honey-roast ham, and cut a large wedge of the Wensleydale to accompany his sandwich. Hervey, ever the optimist, stood patiently by his master waiting for the titbit that invariably came his way.

Once he had finished his late lunch and washed up he returned to the draft.

He introduced the paper with an overview of the historical facts, beginning with Partition and the Government of Ireland Act, moving along to the outbreak of republican violence in the 1950s, then coming up to date with the growth of the civil rights movement and the oppression that the minority community felt itself to suffer at the hands of the unionist majority, and finally he detailed the outbreak of the so called "Troubles". The next section dealt with the cost, both human and material, that had been spent in the pursuit of a pro-Union policy. The figures spoke for themselves – they were huge, running to tens of millions of pounds.

Robinson set his pen down and rubbed the back of his neck – there was no doubt about it – he had the beginnings of a first-class headache. He looked out of the living room window at the bay – the sky was overcast but happily it wasn't raining – a walk would clear his head. The report could wait, besides he wouldn't be giving it his best efforts if he was distracted by a headache. He got up from his desk and walked out to the kitchen where he took his coat from the peg behind the door. Lifting Hervey's lead he opened the back door and called the black labrador to heel.

Patterson's time had been filled reading and re-reading the file material on Dessie Grew. He had paid particular attention to the photographs that showed that Grew had on occasion changed his appearance; even taking the alterations that had cropped up from time to time into consideration, Patterson was confident in his identification, and was sure that he would know the man again. He was going out on surveillance tonight and while he was pleased by McCleary's confidence in him he really wasn't looking forward to another night in the shed. It was, however, a necessary evil – an ongoing connection between Grew and somebody at O'Driscoll's, most likely Sean McNellis, had to be proved. Once that was done requests to headquarters for electronic surveillance and more manpower would be more favourably treated. With a bit of luck they would be able to discover why a big player from East Tyrone was taking an interest in South Armagh; maybe there was a link with the fire at the Mullans. If that could be proved it would tie up a lot of loose ends. Patterson reflected on the possibilities of promotion and gave thanks for his keen eyesight.

Crawford had spent a frustrating day working his way through the Aer Lingus flight manifests for the Friday evening and Saturday morning flights from Gatwick to Dublin and Heathrow to Brussels. In particular the names of British and Irish nationals had to be checked up on, so when he had compiled a full list of names he'd contacted the Irish embassy and the British Passport Office at Petit France with a request for full details of the named individuals to be forwarded to Curzon Street – it was a roundabout way of doing things, but it was easier to let the outsiders think that the security services were chasing the information rather than the department which they'd never heard of. Anyway, the very mention of "Five" got a certain result that couldn't be achieved with references to Leinster Gardens; let people think what they wanted as long as the information arrived.

In both instances he was promised the information first thing on Thursday, which meant that he could devote all of Wednesday to the coverage of the flight manifests of Pan-Am and Continental Airlines. Only two carriers, but it really was like searching for a needle in a haystack – a total of seven flights – over two and a half thousand names – maybe twenty nationalities. And at the end of all the hard graft there was no guarantee that the people he was looking for were on any of the flights that he was checking. He'd only been working on this for a day but the uncertain nature of this type of investigation was already beginning to wear his patience thin. At least he had Friday's job at "The National" to look forward to; it probably wouldn't yield any useful information, but anything was better than sitting in an office looking at lists of names.

He realised that sitting looking at the lists wasn't going to achieve anything – he didn't have a preternatural deductive gift – the names of the bombers weren't going to just light up on the page. If they were here amongst the lists it was going to be sheer hard graft that would identify them – as for catching them, well, that was another matter entirely. He got up from his desk and made his way to the stairs nearly bumping into Ellison as she came out of the kitchen, coffee in hand.

"You were almost wearing that you know."

"Well if some people weren't in such a flaming hurry maybe I wouldn't need to be so careful."

Crawford held up two hands and bowed his head by way of apology.

"I'm sorry, I've just had enough this day."

Ellison accepted what was probably going to be the best effort at an apology that Crawford was capable of, and nodded in agreement.

"I know what you mean, can't say that I'm far behind you, but I've got one more page of names to go through."

"Why don't you call it quits tonight? It's not as if you'll be able to forward them to anyone at this time. Besides I've still got the Escort and I can give you a lift home."

"No thanks, really, I have to clear this list, I'm behind as it is."

"Well, don't ever say I didn't ask. I'll see you tomorrow."

"I'll be here, and if we both have the time I want you to take me through your plans for our night out on Friday."

"No problem, there's not much to cover."

"Yes, well I want to get it right this time."

"Understood, 'til tomorrow then."

"Goodnight Gerry."

As he made his way down the stairs and out to the car Crawford reflected on Ellison's words – it was pleasing to have an officer admit, if not in so many words, that they could learn from and take the advice of an NCO – experience counted for something after all.

Patterson had managed to avoid the temptation of looking at his watch since he'd recorded the time that he began his surveillance of the O'Driscoll house. Three incident free hours had passed with nothing for him to report – no lights showed in Maura's house – she wasn't at home. This did not mean that it had exactly been a waste of time; Patterson had set his mind to making some sense of the facts as they stood, taking recent events and arranging them in chronological order and trying to make a connection. Some of the hypotheses were frankly absurd, but Patterson was sure that there was something joining the Mullans, McGlinchey, Grew, and even the Neave murder. One thing that he was sure of was that proving it would be difficult, but he knew that he wasn't going to prove it sitting around watching nothing. He could understand the reasons why this was a one man detail – surveillance of the front of Maura's house was well nigh impossible – there were no empty houses to set up in and it was a Republican estate. That said, sitting in a cattle shed wasn't going to secure the evidence that would give them the necessary phone tap; in his view they should tap the phone now and hope that something would turn up; if there was a positive result it would more than excuse any legal indiscretions.

* * *

Lynch was back at his desk early hoping that something of interest had come to light and that the progress reports would actually make interesting reading for once. The disappointment grew with each "will continue to carry out surveillance" or "attempting to make contact with a previously reliable source" that he read. In all honesty the field investigation was a waste of time and effort. The best hope for success lay with Aiken's team and their painstaking search of the flight manifests. With that in mind he lifted her report and read it with a mixture of admiration and irritation, admiration for the amount of work that she had cleared in only a couple of days and irritation that it had yielded no results as yet.

Lynch finished the reports and composed himself before lifting the receiver to place his daily call to Sir Alistair Johnson. He dialled the Home Office number and was rewarded with an answer on the forth ring.

"Yes."

"It's Lynch sir. Just checking in with my daily."

"Anything to report?"

"Nothing concrete; the surveillance jobs in the sympathetic pubs are still under way but nothing so far, and the flight manifest checks are nearing completion, but as you know sir we are relying on the good offices of other agencies."

"That's as maybe Lynch, I'm just interested in results."

"I know sir, but I can only deliver if my people turn something up and as yet they've uncovered nothing."

"Lynch may I remind you that there has been a policy change and for your department to prosper in the future it has to give me something tangible."

This was more than Lynch could take; he considered the alternatives – knuckling under or reminding Johnson of some present realities.

"We gave you something tangible in South Armagh and it wasn't bloody good enough. Now you want me to conjure something out of thin air to justify my department's existence. Well it doesn't work that way. The sooner you realise that my people aren't life size chess pieces to be moved around for your amusement..."

"Don't take that tone with me Lynch. I still want the previous standards to be applied in Ulster but I'm in the minority. Give me some ammunition to use against the doves and I assure you that your department is secure."

"Very well sir."

If there was any further comment from Johnson he wasn't aware of it as he returned the handset to the cradle. Lynch was only too well aware of his own shortcomings but he hoped that if someone were ever to categorise him as a bastard that it would be amongst better company than Sir Alistair Johnson. The man had no concept of loyalty and his views on what was best for Britain boiled down to what was best for him; all the posturing about positive action in Ulster was sanctimonious crap, Johnson was just like any other politician, and under present circumstances that made him particularly dangerous.

Speculating on the department's future was pointless – it had been around in one form or the other for a very long time and would still be there when present events had become ancient history. As controller Lynch was responsible for the department's continuity and with that in mind he opened his safe and withdrew the deposit book for an account in the name of a Mr. M. Cummings held in the Manx Depository, Douglas, Isle of Man. This was the account to which Daffyd Jones would transfer £107,000, possibly the only positive aspect of the whole South Armagh operation. He lifted the receiver again and placed a call to Curzon Street, but after several attempts to locate Jonesy without success he left a message that he should be contacted at work at the earliest opportunity. There was nothing for him to do now but wait, in that respect the job never changed.

By ten-thirty the whole team had assembled for the daily report and tasking session. Harbinson could tell from the general attitude of the men that there was no good news; at times like these the job was a trial that they could all do without. The main difficulty at present was not the fact that no-one was talking, it was that there simply wasn't anything to talk about. If Special Branch couldn't pick up on rumour and half-truths it made investigations well-nigh impossible, unless of course they had "smoking gun" forensic evidence which in the INLA case was irrelevant and as far as the Mullan fire was concerned didn't exist.

Harbinson had allowed the team to go through their reports one by one with nothing of any great significance being detailed; even the suggestions for possible actions in the hunt for information on McGlinchey and his friends lacked inspiration. It was going to be a long hard slog with no guarantees of success, but if they did get a result how much more satisfying. Harbinson knew that such thoughts were enough to sustain the team, just enough; but as he looked at the men sitting in front of him he realised that they needed some sort of affirmation, something to get their teeth into. The problem was rapidly becoming one of morale – the team obviously felt annoyed that there had been no closure or even progress on the Mullans and the INLA investigation was shaping up to be the same – if this continued heads would drop and if their enthusiasm left them then there would be little chance of that success.

The meeting broke up with Harbinson issuing orders for continued surveillance on known haunts and the pursuit of information from reliable sources. Patterson was about to leave the room with the rest of the team when Harbinson called him back.

"You kept very quiet Derek."

"Nothing to say sir. Last night was bloody boring, Maura wasn't even at home, and if you don't mind me saying sir one man isn't much use on his own."

"Well you must have a suggestion so let's hear it."

"Tap her phone now and put a team together to see where and what the South Armagh Brigade are and up to and see if any connection can be made with Grew."

"You've obviously put some thought into this Derek, but two things come immediately to mind – one, the INLA are the priority, and two, we don't have the manpower to spare. It's frustrating I know but that's the way things stand at the moment."

"If that's so sir we're not going to get a result."

"You don't have to tell me that, look, carry on with what you're doing, and we'll see what happens."

Patterson shrugged and left Harbinson to think over the hollowness of his words – carry on with what?

Robinson had risen early and had started work on his draft document for the group as soon as he was washed and dressed. The effort of committing his thoughts to paper had cost him a headache yesterday but a good night's sleep had cleared it and now he was rattling the words off with a speed that surprised him. The note making phase was over and he was actually getting down to the outline paper itself; perhaps it was the new found freedom of his position of adviser that sped things along, whatever it was, he was glad of it.

He had covered the historical background, the failures of the Stormont government, the failures of direct rule, the security policy that had led to an escalating level of violence – in essence he had painted a very black picture but now came the glimmer of hope in his suggested new direction. He had no doubts that it was a bold answer to a seemingly interminable problem, no doubts about the pain it would cause sections of the polity in Ulster, further afield even, but the prize was worth it, and the prize was peaceful resolution. He was sure that with the group's change of heart his ideas would be listened to, if not acted on, action may take a little more time but he was ready for that. All the passage of time had achieved in Ulster was death and destruction; those losses would continue but Robinson hoped that work on his plan, behind the scenes, would bring them to an end.

His idea of an inclusive negotiated settlement based on a commitment to democracy would have the likes of Johnson shaking their heads in disbelief, but if he had learned one thing as an agent handler it was that virtually all principles could have a price tag attached to them. As he saw it the whole problem could be solved if enough money was thrown in the right directions, and if the media was allowed controlled access there would be no going back – nobody wanted to look like an enemy of democracy. Fundamentally the whole plan stood or fell on the greed and vanity of the protagonists. Nothing that Robinson had seen over the years indicated that this was a false appraisal, and knowing the three men in the group who he had to persuade as he did he felt reasonably confident that they would agree.

The greatest difficulty he foresaw was the necessary effort to bring terrorists into negotiations, in particular republican terrorists, the loyalists were just gangsters fighting for their own little patches of turf, but the republicans had clear ideological goals. Talks had been attempted before – in 1972 the PIRA leaders had been flown to the mainland for talks with the then Home Secretary, William Whitelaw – if it had been done once it could be done again. The characters within government would, with one or two dissenters, agree to the process, and the military establishment would do as it was told – the greatest potential obstacle was the public. Robinson made the point that the maintenance of secrecy was of the utmost importance. If there was any prospect for success it was best, in his view, to keep it private until the public could be given a *fait accompli*, should negotiations fail then they should fail privately where damage could be limited. Such a careful approach would undoubtedly find favour with the vanities to be encountered at Westminster and in truth it would make it easier for Robinson and the necessary staff to make contacts away from the glare of the media spotlight.

The final section of the proposal dealt with the timescale he envisaged the process filling. He talked about the confidence building measures that would be part and parcel of the negotiations and how slow progress was desirable over the quick fix. He committed his overall opinion to print by saying that he could not see a successful outcome to the plan in less than 12 years, such were the obstacles that had to be overcome. When he counted the pages of the document on completion he was surprised to see that he had 17 sheets of closely typed script; inspiration had given his efforts a certain impetus.

He moved from the upright office chair at his desk and sat in a more comfortable Chesterfield as he read through the paper marking the few necessary corrections as he went. Working his way through the draft he became convinced that the proposals he was making would find approval. The incisive nature of the plan shone brightly and Robinson congratulated himself on seeing a way forward where previously there had only been stalemate. It was nearly seven o'clock when he finished proofing the document; satisfied that he had included every facet of his plan in the proposal he left it on the desk beside his typewriter – the final corrected draft could wait until tomorrow – he'd done enough today.

Crawford had spent most of the day going through the last of the flight mandates compiling lists of names that would be checked against records by clerks whose enthusiasm for the task ranked alongside his own in the disinterested stakes. With the examination of every sheet of names his conviction that he was wasting his time became more secure – the INLA team were either back in Ireland, north or south, or had gone to ground somewhere on the mainland, possibly in preparation for another job. All the speculation in the press was in total ignorance of reality, as were the pronouncements of various politicians. "These people cannot be allowed to win and will be hunted down with the full vigour of the law", was a particular favourite of Crawford's; it unwittingly reinforced everything he knew about terrorism and applied a more conventional societal view to the bombers as ordinary criminals. When were people going to wake up to the fact that these people weren't criminals and that they had already won by detonating the bomb that killed Airey Neave? He knew the depressing answer to his question – probably never – and if that was the case the terrorists would never be defeated, and every effort he made against them would be like his mandate checking – a waste of time.

He looked at the list of names sitting on the desk and shook his head; he never had been a gambler but he would have taken any odds on the innocence of everyone on the Pan Am mandate. He was fed up and was very close to walking into Lynch's office to say that he was taking up the Monckton post with immediate effect, but he knew that he still had the surveillance job in "The National" to look after. Thoughts of the republican haunt reminded him that he needed to talk with Ellison about Friday night, so with that in mind he left his desk to track her down. She wasn't at her desk but knowing how conscientious she was he reckoned that she wouldn't have left for the night at only twenty past seven. Sure enough he found her making herself a coffee in the kitchen.

"Could you get me one of those?"

"What do you say?"

"Sorry, could you get me one of those, ma'am."

"I give up! You were meant to say please!"

"Social niceties aren't my strong suit and I never have got used to women officers."

"So you're just a typical male chauvinist?"

"Maybe I am, but I want to talk to you about Friday night. Just remember that we might as well be in some dive in Belfast."

"You don't need to worry about me, I can look after myself."

"I'm sure you can, but I'm more worried about me. If you give the game away it's most likely me who gets the kicking."

"And I thought that you were concerned for my safety."

"I want to see us both walk away from "The National" in one piece. And to that end I want to run through the details just so there's no confusion."

"Let's have a seat in my office and you can take me through your ideas step by step."

Crawford took the coffee Ellison had poured for him and followed her down the corridor to the cramped cupboard she called an office. She lifted a sheaf of airline documents off the only other seat, putting them on top of the filing cabinet, and motioned for him to sit down.

"So what's our approach going to be on Friday night? Same as the other day?"

"Same sort of idea but a little different."

"But we might be remembered from Monday, so shouldn't we look the same?"

"I'm not saying that we adopt a different identity, after all I'm known at "The National", but Friday's a social affair and even by the standards of a sympathizers' pub a little effort will need to be made for the *ceilidh*."

"Effort?"

"Yeah, bit of make-up for you and best bib and tucker for us both. Well, maybe not best, but have you got an outfit that is a bit, oh I don't know, let's say a bit tarty?"

"Not really."

Crawford could tell from her tone that Ellison thought he was deliberately trying to irritate her so he tried a conciliatory approach.

"It's not personal, it's just that this is what I know from experience. There are plenty of charity shops that you could get something from."

"OK, I know where to go. Something that a tart might consider to be sophisticated?"

"Yeah, that's the idea, and when it comes to make-up lay it on a bit thick. If we are remembered from Monday it'll just look as if we've tidied ourselves up for the night. The important thing to appreciate is that this is all going to be an act. If you believe in the character hopefully everyone else will."

"You'll be recommending acting classes next."

"Now there's an idea."

"Oh come on!"

"I'm serious. If you're comfortable with your persona nobody will give you a second thought. "Showing out" will get you in all sorts of trouble."

"I understand. Don't worry, I'll fit in on the looks side of things, but what if someone starts asking me questions?"

"Now you're thinking. Right, the best thing is to keep the "legend" simple. You're my girlfriend and you're a secretary in a small transport firm. It's all my idea to go to the *ceilidh* so you can get an idea of what I'm like as we haven't been going out together for that long. How's that?"

"So if anyone gets curious they'll talk to you, is that it?"

"Exactly."

"But what about my name?"

"OK, keep Jenny and let's say "Elliot". That'll be an easy one to remember, although to be honest I don't think you'll be a regular fixture in "The National", this job isn't going to last too long."

"What makes you say that?"

"Well, this whole "let's do something about Airey Neave's murderers" attitude is something of a pose. Don't you see it?"

"I think there's a chance of a result."

"You've just hit the nail on the head. Chance, the department never puts anything to chance. Haven't you noticed that Lynch only likes working on sure things?"

"But you have to take risks once in a while."

"In this line of work taking risks will get you killed, leave risks to amateurs."

"So why take a chance on walking into "The National" on Friday night?"

"Because it's not a risk as long as you remember your "legend" and make the effort with your appearance. What it comes down to is that we're professionals and the opposition isn't used to dealing with quality."

"You're very sure of your abilities."

"I have to be and I have to be sure of your's, which is why I want to see you in character this time tomorrow."

"OK, I'll go shopping and bring everything here so you can have a look."

"Good, well, I'll bring my outfit in so you can see what I'm getting at. But for now I've had enough pen pushing for one day so I'm off home. Do you want a lift?"

"Give me ten minutes and I'll be right with you."

"OK. In the meantime I'll take these mugs back to the kitchen."

The mindless task of washing their coffee mugs gave Crawford the chance to run through the discussion he'd just had with Ellison; he was pleased that she'd been receptive to his outline and ideas on this sort of close surveillance, if she kept this up she had the makings of a good operative, then again he'd see just how receptive tomorrow when she paraded her purchases from the charity shops.

* * *

The call was answered on the fourth ring and Jones instantly regretted not contacting Lynch yesterday.

"When I leave an urgent reply message for you Jonesy I expect action."

"I'm sorry sir, but there's an awful lot happening here with a lot of extra duties…"

"Don't give me that crap Jones. You're at Curzon Street for something specific. You could tell just about anybody to "piss off" and you'd get away with it, so don't tell me you've got caught up in the Neave investigation because I won't believe it."

"I'll bear that in mind."

"Don't get sarcy with me sonny boy. Just remember who you're talking to."

"Yes sir. I'm sorry sir."

"Good, OK, write this down", and Lynch proceeded to give Jones the "Cummings" account details and the instructions, "You've got today and tomorrow to make the transfer, and as I said before it's £107,000 that you're to transfer. After that forget about everything. I'm sure the two thousand will help."

"And what about the account in Dundalk?"

"That's my concern – you can forget it too. Everything clear?"

"Yes sir."

"Then I suggest you get on with your little task. The sooner it's complete the sooner I'll be off your back."

The line went dead and Jones cursed the day he'd ever come to the attention of Harry Lynch; he was going to take him at his word however and complete the transaction as quickly as possible, and for that he had to go home.

At ten to twelve a man known to the teller as Mr. Joe Mullan walked into the National Westminster Bank on Edgware Road. He had recently opened a substantial deposit account, just the sort of business that the bank wished to attract, so it was with regret that she made the fund transfer to the Manx Depository, but who was she to argue with the investment opportunity that the Irishman talked of, it sounded like the chance of a lifetime. The necessary phone call lengthened the process by about twenty minutes, but Mr. Mullan seemed happy enough to wait for the transfer to go through, so it was nearly half past when he was given confirmation that the transaction was complete. The final aspect of the business was the acknowledgement that she told him would be forwarded from the Isle of Man. He told her that he would drop by the branch at the end of next week to collect the confirmation if he had time and with that he was gone.

Jones arrived home at quarter past one having taken his time getting from the bank to the Tube and from the station at Finchley Road to his flat on Nutley Terrace. He took off his jacket and threw it over the back of a chair before pouring himself a Johnny Walker. The whisky blazed a trail down his throat on the first sip, but he needed the drink; strange how even the simplest of jobs could get the adrenalin pumping. Thankfully it had gone smoothly and with the transfer complete his interest in the affair was nearly over; all he had to do now was close the account and enjoy his fee but not just yet, he'd let things lie for a couple of weeks.

Ellison had worn the scruffiest clothes she possessed to go shopping for her outfit for tomorrow night's job; she'd thought it prudent to get into character as it were. War on Want and Oxfam had proved the best sources for clothes and she'd been lucky enough to get a pair of boots that almost fit from Action Cancer. She'd checked the contents of her make-up bag before she'd gone out that morning and was happy to see that she only really needed some garish lipstick and some blue eye-shadow. Those items she could pick up in any chemists so with her clothes bought she had time on her hands as a return to Leinster Gardens really wouldn't serve any purpose as she had little or nothing to do – the suspect lists hadn't been forwarded from Curzon Street, if in fact they'd been passed on from the British and Irish passport offices.

Her shopping trip had taken her to Covent Garden and the surrounding streets; fortunately there were no end of coffee shops that allowed her somewhere to take a break. As she sat enjoying a coffee and *pain au chocolat* she was able to give Crawford's words on the surveillance task some thought. The whole package of the physical portrayal and the "legend" of a character was something that she was familiar with but her duties within the department had never called for her to actually put her knowledge into practice. Jenny Elliot's basic "legend" called for her to be a secretary in a haulage firm, leastways that was what Crawford had suggested, but there were a lot of blanks that needed filling in. He had told her that keeping things simple was the best idea under the circumstances, but even a simple persona had some depth so she started to put a little flesh on the bones.

A waitress came and asked Ellison if she wanted another coffee, although it was clear from her tone that it was more a veiled "I think it's time you were leaving" than an offer for a refill. Jenny looked at her watch and was surprised to see that it was nearly four o'clock. She declined the offer, which was probably just as well, and made a speedy exit. Once on the street she quickly found a cab for hire and returned to her flat to collect her make-up bag. With that done she caught a bus that would take her to Bayswater Road where she hoped to find a chemist's for the last of her purchases.

Crawford wished he had brought his clothing for "Crossan" to Leinster Gardens that morning, instead he'd thought he would save time by taking the Ford Escort and had gone home at lunchtime. There had been no warning of any impending roadworks when he drove around the roundabout earlier but when he approached the major junction at the Elephant and Castle on his return he became caught up in a traffic jam that took the best part of an hour to untangle. As if that hadn't been bad enough he got caught in another jam at Grosvenor Place thanks to an accident. It was approaching six o'clock when he parked the car outside the department's building; so much for the convenience of making the journey by car, he'd have been quicker using the Tube.

As he made his way along the first floor corridor he was almost knocked off his feet by Ellison as she ran out of the kitchen. She was wearing the outfit that she had bought earlier in the day and judging from her expression she wasn't pleased to see him.

"Something the matter?"

"Damn! I was hoping to surprise you."

"Oh you did, you really did. It's a good effort on first impressions. Now let me take a real look."

Crawford started scrutinising her from head to toe. The boots looked cheap with synthetic soles but were polished and looked well cared for, the long tan corduroy skirt matched the boots, and the outfit was topped off with a light pink blouse. He kept quiet as he checked over her appearance making mental notes as he went. Next he turned his attention to Ellison's hair and make-up and was pleased to see that she had taken on board what he had said. She had let her hair down and had changed the style from being quite severely pulled back and pinned to a softer centre parting which let her hair frame her face. The make-up was the biggest change – too much of just about everything with electric blue eye-shadow and deep red lipstick dominating the overall effect. He nodded as he took in the complete package, but still said nothing, much to Ellison's annoyance.

"Oh for God's sake. What do you think?"

"Do you want a coffee?"

"No I don't, but I suppose you do."

"First thing in this job that you must always remember, be patient."

Crawford went into the kitchen and poured himself a mug and then gave Ellison his appraisal.

"All in all a good effort. The outfit is good – nothing fancy but reasonable quality and even the boots which aren't of the best show care and attention which fits the character. Hair and make-up are absolutely spot on, so nothing to improve on there. One question – what make is your watch?"

"It's an Omega, it was a 21st birthday present."

"Well get rid of it. You wear that tomorrow night and you'll show out. You're a secretary with a small haulage firm in the East end, not a secretary with some financial house in the City. And that's another thing, if you speak as you do normally you'll show out too, so lose that accent."

"Any other suggestions?"

"If you have problems with the accent chew some gum – you'd be amazed the difference it can make. And lastly, as you're meant to be a bit on the tarty side, undo a couple of the buttons on your blouse and show a bit of cleavage."

"You're enjoying this aren't you?"

"I just want your character to be believable that's all."

"So far all I've heard about is me, what about "Gerry Crossan", who's he?"

"OK, I'm a building contractor, strictly small scale. I met you when I came to complain about a discrepancy in a shipment of building supplies being delivered by the firm you work for. We've been going out for about six weeks and I've brought you to "The National" because my family originally come from Newry and I want you to enjoy a *ceilidh*."

"Why not Belfast?"

"Because I know Newry and I don't want to run into some smart arse who can tell me the times the buses run to the New Lodge. Fair enough?"

"Point taken."

"Look, if I'm being hard on you it's for your own good. We could run up against some wannabe professionals on Friday and I want us to be as good, actually, I want us to be better."

"I thought you said that that was unlikely?"

"I did, but you never know. Anyway it'll be good training, particularly for you."

"So show me "Gerry Crossan", let's see what he looks like."

Crawford lifted his grip and went down the corridor to his office. It took him less than ten minutes to make the change and when he returned Ellison was impressed by the subtle differences that now made Crawford "Crossan". When he spoke to her the accent was pure Essex and the whole man seemed much more animated than the impassive character she expected with Crawford.

"Just remember what I said darlin' and you'll be fine."

Robinson read through his finished paper and was satisfied that the small number of errors that he had marked yesterday were now eradicated. The content of the document was another matter – taken as a whole the proposals were something that had never been tried or even suggested as a way forward – Robinson was aware of the brave stance he was taking, but he was also aware that the climate within the group had changed. The next step was to put the paper into Phillips' hands. This was actually harder than it first appeared; Robinson did not have a secure route for any communications, his elevation to the position of special adviser had been so swift that no measures had been put in place. That was a detail that would have to be addressed the next time he spoke with Phillips. After some thought he concluded that the Royal Mail would have to suffice, in fact there was something rather amusing in the notion that the future of British affairs in Northern Ireland was being carried in the ordinary post.

He looked at the old clock that sat on his desk and realised that he'd missed the last post in Newcastle by a couple of hours. Phillips had told him that his outline paper wouldn't be expected until the following week so he could afford to leave the postage until tomorrow or even Saturday. In the meantime he'd give the secure communications route some thought – it could prove difficult – to go through Belfast meant the Civil Service and ultimately his old employers – Lisburn meant the army and the chance of running into a friend of Lynch's – and that left Dublin, which meant the involvement of the Secret Intelligence Service, which in turn placed his operation on a foreign footing. Given that he'd suggested to Phillips that his security detail be handled by the SIS it made sense to have them act as couriers and that would mean treating Northern Ireland like a foreign entity in intelligence terms. All the pieces were falling conveniently into place; if his outline document for future policy was implemented it would have just that effect.

He pushed his chair back and walked out to the kitchen to get something to eat. Hervey barely lifted his head as Robinson made his way to the fridge, a sure sign that he was out of sorts. The mournful expression, a speciality of the labrador, made Robinson stop and bend over to rub the dog's ears.

"I'm sorry old boy, been neglecting you a bit these past few days. Tell you what, how about a nice long walk up at Tollymore tomorrow."

The word "walk" was in Hervey's vocabulary, and he responded enthusiastically by getting off his bed and wagging his tail. Robinson looked at the unquestioning devotion and knew he would keep his promise, the dog deserved a reward for his patience, and besides, it would give him the chance to call into the post office in Newcastle to send the policy proposal by special delivery before going up to the Mournes.

* * *

Harbinson was beginning to dread the morning meeting – the team's spirits were dipping day by day – too much hard work and nothing to show for it. It was less than two weeks since the beginning of the Mullan investigation and yet the drain on morale was obvious – the Neave murder and the new priorities it had brought hadn't helped. He watched the men file into the briefing room and take their seats and reckoned it was going to be another dispiriting session until he saw Bill Kirkpatrick. The man was positively beaming when he walked in so Harbinson thought it best to let him start proceedings.

"Bill this had better be some good news or a bloody good joke, so let's hear it."

"It's hard to say which John."

"Well either way we could all do with a laugh."

"Right, well I'm sure we all remember young Derek speculating that the Mullans had been taken out. Well it seems he's not the only one thinking along those lines, and it could all tie in rather neatly with our other investigation concerning the INLA."

"What have you heard?"

"It seems there have been a few get togethers over the past week or so and the main topic of conversation has been the whereabouts of the Mullans and a few other key players as well. The rumour is that the Mullans have either been taken out or scared off by McGlinchey & Co. as part of a turf war. Now we've all read the stories in The Starry Plough over the last couple of months, but it seems there might be something in it this time, about them making moves in South Armagh."

"Bill your making concrete out of thin air. This is all supposition."

"That's as maybe, but I've been told that the story has been doing the rounds and if it is all a load of nonsense where are the Mullans and at least ten others for that matter."

"And who's been telling you this?"

"Let's just say he's reliable. Oh and here's another thing that's interesting – he tells me that Dessie Grew has been making a few calls locally."

Harbinson looked at Patterson and could see him tense up at the mention of Grew's name. Now was not the time or place for the whole team to be brought up to speed regarding Grew, so he gently shook his head and fortunately Patterson picked up the signal and kept his mouth shut.

"Were you given any explanation of his presence?"

"Not really, just that he's been about."

Harbinson let the matter rest there and the meeting carried on as normal. When it concluded he looked at Patterson and Kirkpatrick and nodded to them indicating that he wanted a word.

"What's this about John?"

"You may as well know Bill, as the two things now seem to be connected. Derek's been keeping an eye on Maura O'Driscoll's house this week in case McGlinchey shows up to see her wee sister. To be brief he hasn't, and neither has Maura's fiance Sean McNellis, but who should turn up the other night?"

"Dessie Grew."

"Exactly. Now what would you say to the absence of McNellis, the McGlinchey connection and the appearance of Mr. Grew from East Tyrone?"

"I'd say that there was something very seriously wrong with the Provos."

"Could I say something sir?"

"Go ahead Derek."

"It's just that I've had plenty of time to think watching the back of Maura's house and I've got a few ideas."

"Well let's hear them."

"Suppose for one minute that McNellis has made a move to McGlinchey's group and has given them his former mates in the PIRA as proof of his goodwill. There's a shootout at Mullans, all the PIRA players are snuffed, and Grew gets sent in to recruit replacements."

"It's a nice idea Derek, but there's no evidence, and frankly the INLA may be able to plant a bomb at Westminster but I don't think they are good enough to take out the Mullans and the rest."

"But it makes sense sir."

"Aye, well it might make sense but prove it."

Patterson had to admit that he couldn't unless he managed to get a body or two and the history of the Troubles to date indicated that the chance of that happening was unlikely.

"Don't be too discouraged Derek, you've definitely got something, so I'm putting you with Bill on this. See if anything else crops up and let me know, in the meantime I'll pass this on to the boss and see what he has to say."

Aiken sat across the desk from Lynch as he flipped through the list of names that she and her team thought required additional scrutiny. Nearly all the details that they'd asked for had been forwarded from Curzon Street and the team had made such enquiries as they could. There were about a dozen names on Aiken's list that had possibilities but in all honesty none of them looked that promising.

"It's a good piece of work Karen, my compliments."

She felt like a schoolgirl called in to see the headmaster for some unspecified reason and her anxiety showed.

"But?"

"But what do you think of this line of enquiry?"

"Can I be blunt?"

"By all means."

"In that case I think we're barking up the wrong tree sir. By that I mean the flight manifest checks; there are too many people prepared to accept the "Paddy Factor" and frankly I don't think they're that stupid."

"Good. Then I'm not the only one who feels that way. Tell me, what do you see as the way forward?"

"I'd keep the surveillance tasks running locally. Other than that I think it best to back off and see what develops in Northern Ireland. The INLA will try to capitalise on the Neave murder and in their haste for success they might get careless. If that happens fall on them from a great height sir."

"I don't think there'll be any falling as you say for some time. This whole job is about being seen to be doing something to keep the public happy. It'll be a bloody wonder if we're allowed to take action for what's happened."

Aiken knew better than to push Lynch for an explanation of his last comment, but she could tell that for some reason he was unhappy with the brief he'd been given. In an effort to change the subject she asked him about the status of the local surveillance operation.

"So far nothing, although this should interest you – your replacement in Ulster is going out on a job tonight."

"She never said anything to me about it. She's not running it is she?"

"No, Gerry Crawford is, and he probably wanted to keep things quiet, it's his way. No, Jenny's going along as his "girlfriend" to "The National". It's a *ceilidh*, so there might be something of use to pick up. Why are you so concerned anyway?"

"It's just that she has no experience in this sort of job. I would have raised it before when she was going out on Monday, but then she joined my team going through the mandates and I thought she'd been pulled because of that lack of experience so I dropped it."

"Well don't worry, Crawford will make sure she comes through unscathed, he's good at this sort of thing, got a real eye for it."

Crawford had spent the previous evening in preparation for the trip to "The National". He'd checked through his clothes for any papers that would look out of place and then put the driving license in "Gerry Crossan's" name in the inside breast pocket of the old Donegal tweed jacket he'd be wearing. Other than that he wouldn't be carrying any additional documents; as he'd said to Ellison it was best to keep things simple. He had checked to see if either his trousers or shirt needed laundering, which they hadn't, or if his shoes needed a polish, which they had. He'd retrieved his cleaning kit from under the kitchen sink and given the old Hush

Puppy brogues a bit of a shine. With his outfit sorted he'd gone to bed allowing himself the luxury of a lie-in as he wasn't going in to Leinster Gardens until after lunchtime at the earliest.

When he woke that morning he showered but didn't shave and dressed in the clothes he was going to wear that evening -"Crossan" would never be as careful about his appearance as Crawford and the longer he could stay in character the more convincing he would be. He left his flat and bought a paper before having breakfast in the little cafe around the corner. He read as he ate and paid particular attention to the comment section which was speculating on the progress of the investigation into Airey Neave's murder. Not one aspect of the piece approached the truth, which on reflection was just as well, sometimes the truth could be unbearable.

"John I told you that you were to continue with the line of enquiry you'd been given and not to indulge your imagination. Now you come in here with another preposterous theory."

"It isn't my theory sir. Bill Kirkpatrick came in with this one, and when you add it to what we already know…"

"We don't know anything John. It might all be very neat to accept this one but I work on what I can prove and your flight of fancy doesn't offer me the chance. I want answers as much as you do but not when they have no basis in fact."

"Kirkpatrick believes his source on this."

"I've known Bill for years and I think you'll find that he thinks his source believes the story, and that's not the same thing. Drop it John, we've got enough on our plate without chasing our tails, and you can tell Kirkpatrick and Patterson the same thing."

"So what about the surveillance on Grew?"

"We don't seem to be getting anywhere with it so you can return Patterson to the McGlinchey job."

"He's only been covering it for four days, you can hardly expect a result this early. Why not…"

"I've got a direct order from headquarters, I'm short staffed and you making suggestions isn't helping. We concentrate on the INLA and that's final. Now if you don't mind John I've got some real work to do."

Harbinson left McCleary's office feeling let down; if anyone should have gone for Kirkpatrick's story he thought it would have been the boss. Clearly the pressure was intense from the big hats at headquarters, but they in turn were probably having to deal with political pressure coming from Whitehall. When would people stop playing politics and let him and those like him get on with the job? Probably never, but knowing that didn't make life any easier. He walked down the corridor to his own office but the thought of reading through reports with no real content only added to his depression so he went in search of Kirkpatrick and Patterson to pass along the good news, knowing that both men would be as overjoyed as he was.

Rather than risk another traffic jam at the Elephant and Castle, Crawford had crossed the Thames at London Bridge and then made his way along Victoria Embankment to Parliament Square, once there he was able to follow his usual route and made it to Leinster Gardens for quarter past two. He had to park the Escort about 150 yards from the department's building, but the walk back gave him the opportunity to have a good look about him, not that he thought for one minute that the opposition would be watching, but training was so deeply ingrained that he couldn't grow out of it.

Once inside he went up to the first floor and his office to see if there were any memos on his desk – there weren't any – so he went looking for Ellison. She wasn't in her cubby-hole or the kitchen; he should have checked with the front desk to see if she was in the building. He was making his way to the stairs when Karen Aiken emerged from the conference room and gestured to him.

"I've got a message for you from Jenny. She said you were to pick her up at her flat any time after five-thirty."

"That's a bit early."

"Yes, well she said that she wanted you to take her through the job, start to finish as it were."

"That makes sense. Thanks for passing it on. Tell me, is there any good news from the mandate checks?"

"Not really. The only information of any interest that we've picked up is on a salesman from Watford who's taken his secretary away for a week in the Bahamas."

"I take it she's not his wife?"

"No, his wife's just thrilled to bits though. She thought he was at a conference in Birmingham."

"Wouldn't she have thought it a bit odd that he didn't lift the phone?"

"Good point. Doesn't sound like much of a marriage, now that you mention it. Anyway that's all we've got for our efforts thus far."

"Well maybe Ellison and I will find something worthwhile tonight, although I wouldn't hold my breath."

"Your optimism is overwhelming. You could try being a bit more positive."

"Why should I? This whole job's a farce. We should be going after the bastards in Ulster not pissing about in London."

"I know what you mean. This may not be much of a consolation but you're not the only one who would like full freedom of action."

"Politics, it's always bloody politics!"

"I'm afraid so, anyway I've got things to do and I'm sure you have too, so good luck for tonight and I'll hear about the results tomorrow."

Aiken returned to her office leaving Crawford wondering what to do next – with Ellison out of reach until after half-five he had little to occupy himself with, so he went back to his own office and checked through his pockets and wallet one last time.

It was five-forty when Crawford pulled into a convenient parking space outside Ellison's flat. Before going up he had a look through the interior of the Escort just to be sure that nothing untoward had been left in the glove compartment or under the seats, lastly he took a look in the boot which was as clear as the rest of the car. Happy with the car he made his way to the front door, making sure to lift the plastic bag from the front seat. He was just about to push the buzzer on the intercom when a resident came out giving him the opportunity to slip in. The numbers on the intercom panel had identified Ellison's flat as number three so he climbed the stairs to the first floor and knocked on her door.

It was opened after a few seconds by a somewhat more brassy version of "Jenny Elliot" than the one he'd seen yesterday. The outfit was the same but she'd followed his advice and left the top three buttons on her blouse unfastened, just enough to put some cleavage on display. Her make-up was also a bit heavier and gave a distinctly "trying too hard" appearance.

"Tarty enough for you?"

"You'll do. A pity we haven't got more time and we could work on your accent – roughen it up a bit."

"I could drop my aitches if you like."

"It would only be a start, unless you can do more with your accent it's really not enough. Probably better to keep your mouth shout as much as possible."

"'onest guv, you'd think I were tryin' to drop us in it deliberate like."

"That's not bad. Have you been practising?"

"Just a bit."

"It's very good but remember you're a secretary and as such you're semi-literate, so tone it down."

"Anything else?"

"Yeah. are you bringing a handbag tonight?"

"Of course."

"Let's see it."

Ellison lifted a tan bag from the coffee table and handed it to Crawford. He gave it a good look over, shaking his head as he did so, causing Ellison yet more irritation.

"So what the hell's the matter with my handbag?"

"Too expensive. This is an Enny isn't it? Jenny Elliot would never have the taste for this."

Crawford lifted the plastic bag he'd brought from the car, opened it, and handed her the patchwork leather bag that he'd bought that afternoon in the Salvation Army thrift shop in Greenwich.

"You'll carry this."

"Very fashionable!"

"But of course, and better yet, I'm not even going to charge you for it."

"You're too kind."

Crawford then proceeded to rummage through Ellison's own bag, leaving some of the contents out as he went. When he had finished he held up the items he had left out and held them in front of Ellison.

"See these? All your play acting counts for nothing when you look at these. You've got personal mail here, and who's it addressed to? That's right, Miss Jeanette Ellison, and what's your name tonight? Correct, "Jenny Elliot". Someone nicks your bag and reads the envelopes they'll know that you're on a job. This whole thing is about attention to detail and you're only half right and that isn't bloody good enough."

"For God's sake, how likely is it that I lose my handbag?"

"That isn't the bloody point! You cover all eventualities – that way should something go wrong you're prepared."

"Alright, you're the expert…"

"Damn right, never forget that!"

The tensions of the past week were reaching their peak and Crawford knew that if he didn't calm down he'd say or do something he would regret at a later date. He closed his eyes, took a deep breath and exhaled slowly before addressing Ellison again.

"Look I'm sorry if I've come on a bit strong. This job isn't moving as fast or even in the direction I hoped it would; the whole bloody mess has left me in a foul mood and I suppose I'm taking it out on you. You've made a very good effort and you've obviously given the job some thought."

"Apology accepted and I'll try to be a bit more switched on. Look, do you want a tea or coffee or something?"

"Yeah, coffee would be great thanks, black no sugar."

With the coffee made they sat down and tried their best to relax. Ellison asked a few questions about the set-up for the night at the *ceilidh*, which clearly showed that she had been going over things in her head. Crawford answered her queries and made such contingency arrangements as were necessary. His experience in surveillance came out in the course of the discussion with talk of previous jobs in London and further afield. Ellison was impressed by his meticulous attention to detail and the way he had applied his thoroughness to a series of different tasks. She picked up the bag Crawford had bought for her and began transferring the contents from her own. She finished quickly and put the multi-coloured bag down with a frown of disdain and looked at her new Sekonda to check the time.

"Gerry, it's nearly seven, shouldn't we be thinking of making a move?"

"That's another thing you'll have to learn; you arrive at a public location for a job early and you stand out – there won't be a good crowd in "The National" until half-eight at the earliest – we get there before then and we only attract attention, maybe even find ourselves in a conversation and that is something we definitely don't want."

"So what do we do in the meantime?"

"Well to be honest I'm hungry so if you've got any food in the house, I suggest we get something to eat."

Ellison led the way out to the kitchen and after searching through her limited stock of provisions they settled on scrambled eggs on toast as the only quick thing they could make. They ate in silence with the radio playing in the background as a distraction. When they had finished Ellison stacked the dishes in the sink and would have left them if Crawford hadn't pointed out the fact that they had time to do the washing up. With all the domestic duties complete Crawford lifted his jacket and moved towards the door.

"Time to go."

The drive to "The National" had been uneventful and Crawford parked the car down the side street that led from the corner where the pub was located. It was just after half past eight when they walked into the bar and as had been predicted there was already a substantial crowd. On the small raised platform that passed for a stage the band were busy setting up – the posters had said that they would be starting at nine but judging from the disarray of instruments, cables and amplifiers it would be sometime after that before they could begin playing. Possibly because of the draft created by the frequent opening of the corner doors the tables near the entrance had not filled up as quickly as those in the rest of the bar, and it was here that Crawford motioned for Ellison to take a seat while he went to get them a drink. The staff were being kept busy with orders so it was a couple of minutes before he was served. In that time he'd taken a look around the pub, making use of the large mirror behind the bar, but wasn't surprised by the lack of any recognisable faces. It was early and he didn't foresee any real work for either Ellison or himself until the band took their first break which was the usual time for a "collection for the cause" – if there were any faces to be seen that would be the most likely occasion, and there might even be the possibility of somebody making a speech.

His drinks were set on the marble topped counter and he handed the barman a pound note. When the young man turned back from the till Crawford smiled as he pocketed his change.

"Good to see such a crowd in tonight."

"Oh it is, aye."

Before he could be drawn into a conversation the barman moved on to his next customer, but Crawford made a mental note as he lifted the pint and a half of Guinness and walked back to Ellison. "The National" was filling up quickly and the atmosphere was becoming smoky with an underlying smell of beer. The seats around Ellison had filled up, and as Crawford slipped in beside her it was obvious that any sort of discussion between the two could not touch on the reason for their presence.

The couple to their right had already exchanged some words with Jenny while he'd been at the bar and the talk continued when he'd sat down. Introductions were made and that was more or less the manner in which the evening progressed. The band started playing at half-nine after there had been a round of slow hand-clapping from the, by then, packed bar. The usual rebel songs were played but the band had shown themselves to be no mean musicians with some skilful playing of traditional Irish melodies. "The Green Bushes" and "Down by the Sally Gardens" were played well and the singer, whilst not possessing a great voice, had made a passable effort at singing them.

The notices for the *ceilidh* had said that it would run late, so it was clear that the pub was going to operate a lock-in policy; it was nearly eleven when the band finished their first set, and one of the barman took to the stage and told anyone who wanted to miss the rest of the evening's *craic* that they could go now before the doors were locked. He'd barely made a move back to the bar when right on cue a man stepped forward and took a microphone from one of the stands. If Crawford and Ellison had hoped for a leading republican they were sorely disappointed. The speech when it came was poorly delivered and offered nothing new; there was a brief mention of the "job at Westminster" and a pledge to continue "the struggle" against British imperialism. But struggle against superior forces required funds and at this point the collection was made. If Ellison was surprised to see Crawford put two pounds in the bucket, being carried through the crowd by the young barman who had served him earlier, she didn't show it.

The band came back on stage at about eleven-thirty and played more of the same. The crowd showed their appreciation by clapping and cheering loudly, and if it hadn't been for the short address and the collection earlier an outsider would have thought it was just a night of Irish music; the anti-British sentiment didn't seem too strong and would have been excused as understandable, but Crawford was well aware of the hatred that drove such gatherings.

By twelve-thirty people began to leave, although a hardened core of drinkers would be there until throwing-out time, so Crawford and Ellison took their chance and left. The couple they'd effectively spent the evening with, Pat and Sheila, suggested getting together again at the next *ceilidh* but Crawford was non-committal and merely said that they would probably see each other sometime. He took Jenny's arm and weaved somewhat unsteadily out of the pub and back to their parked car before handing her the keys. She didn't say anything until they were well away from Kilburn.

"Well other than see a side of London I didn't know existed, I'd say that that was pretty pointless."

"I wouldn't say that. You did very well; the way you played the conversation with Sheila was very natural and you stayed in character. So pretty pointless? No, absolutely not."

"That's as maybe but we didn't get anything worthwhile."

"Wrong. You didn't get anything worthwhile. I, on the other hand, got a possible."

"I didn't see anybody and I don't know how you could."

"The barman, definitely not local from his accent and he looks familiar. Anyway that's for tomorrow, in the meantime you did very well for a first night out, so you should be pleased."

"I can't tell you how thrilled that makes me feel."

"Well here's something else to lift your spirits, you're leaving me home."
"Great!"
"I knew that would please you."

* * *

Although he hadn't got to bed until after two, Crawford was in Leinster Gardens bright and early so he could go through the photo files before he made his report to Lynch. He was looking for a match to the face of the barman from "The National", but the best he could come up with was strikingly similar but not the same. He took station at the reception area on the first floor knowing that Lynch would have to pass him there. Just after nine the sound of footsteps on the stairs announced the arrival of the department's controller; when he came into view he acknowledged Crawford with a nod.

"Get me a coffee and bring it to my office – milk, two sugars."

Before he could say anything Lynch turned and made his way down the corridor. Fortunately someone had put the filter machine on earlier that morning so Crawford didn't have to keep the old man waiting and was sitting opposite him in a couple of minutes.

"Judging from your appearance you got away from "The National" without incident."

"Yes sir. By its standards it was a fairly civilized night."

"Did you get anything?"

"One possible, but I've been through the files and I haven't got a match. It could be a younger brother."

"Name?"

"McGuigan. He looked a lot like Gerard, but not old enough."

"Doesn't matter if there's a connection or not – our investigation is concerned with the INLA and McGuigan is the PIRA."

"But sir we could have a new player in town maybe even an ASU."

"I don't care Crawford, we're after the INLA for Neave, anything else is surplus to requirements. If that's all you have then you can go."

A somewhat bemused Crawford made his way out of Lynch's office – under normal circumstances the very mention of Provos in London would have got a rise out of the old man – there had been no enquiry into last night's job at all – he hadn't even asked about Ellison's performance – something wasn't right but Crawford couldn't figure out what it could be.

Lynch waited for several minutes before dialling Sir Alistair Johnson's London home number. Fortunately the civil servant hadn't yet gone down to the country for the weekend and the call was answered on the third ring.

"Hello?"

"It's Lynch sir."

"And?"

"And nothing sir. The "Department" has had people out all week and I've got nothing to show for it."

"So keep at it."

"What's the point sir, really? You've already told me that the climate has changed."

"That is only a temporary problem. Don't worry Lynch, you'll soon be running more jobs like the Mullan farm raid."

"So what? So I can stockpile more funds for future operations that may never happen?"

"So you got the funds transferred?"

"Yes I got notification yesterday. But that's not the point – the "Department" is not here to act as a hired gun."

"No Lynch, that's where you're wrong, you're there to do exactly what you're told to do."

Johnson hung up leaving Lynch to wonder at the excuses people made for their behaviour. He knew he had little to be thankful for, but at least he was consistent.

Part Three

The alarm started ringing and Crawford reached over to his bedside cabinet to switch it off, but he fumbled the clock on his first attempt and sent it falling to the floor. He sat up in bed and swung his feet on to the rug which covered the cold parquet floor, allowing him to bend over and retrieve the errant timepiece from beneath his bed. Once he'd stopped the annoying beeping he walked out of his bedroom, across the narrow corridor that ran the full length of his flat, and went into the bathroom. After a shower he stood in front of the wash-hand basin shaving, with the mirror of his medicine cabinet giving him a clear view of his face. It was a face that showed little change in terms of weight, but in other ways it betrayed his age – the care lines were somewhat deeper, there were traces of cracked blood vessels grouped on his cheek bones and the eyes, which although they had lost none of their colour, were even more flat and inexpressive. He made a final stroke with his razor and rinsed the last of the shaving gel from his face before cleaning his teeth – he may have recently turned fifty-one but his teeth were still all his own.

He walked back to his bedroom and lifted a dressing gown from the chair beside the wardrobe before going back down the corridor to the kitchen and breakfast. The black and white chessboard pattern tiles were cold under his bare feet and for the umpteenth time Crawford asked himself why he hadn't got round to asking the landlord about re-covering the kitchen floor; after all, he'd moved into the new flat nearly three years ago. His thoughts then made the natural progression to the series of moves from Hoskins Street in Greenwich to his present home in Holland Park Mews. Those thoughts in turn led to an inventory of his career since leaving the army in 1984 – all told not unsuccessful – a partnership in a small private security firm – a comfortable standard of living – money in the bank – no tiresome commitments – definitely an improvement on the failed marriages and subsequent descent into alcoholism that seemed to be the fate of so many of his peers. Yet, for all his blessings, Crawford felt unfulfilled; he'd hoped for something more and whatever it was had always been just beyond his grasp.

He stood in front of his built-in fridge lost in thought, unaware that several minutes had passed, before shaking himself out of his reverie and getting the Greek yoghurt that had been his original intent. He took the tub of yoghurt over to the counter and then set to work making his breakfast coffee. As he went through his usual morning routine he switched on the radio to catch the news headlines.

"…. from Capital Radio on Friday 16th October, it's eight o'clock. The main news this morning is the announcement from the Nobel Institute that the recipients of this year's Peace prize are John Hume and David Trimble for their work in securing the Northern Ireland peace process. In other news…."

Crawford first looked at the radio in disbelief and then gave vent to his feelings.

"Jesus Christ! Peace process? God, what are they doing?"

As soon as he said it he realised the foolishness of the remark; the politicians in Northern Ireland were doing what they saw as the right thing, God help them, they just couldn't see the manipulations that were being made by the government in London. And it wasn't just this government but successive administrations. He'd seen the changes, taken part in some of the "dirty tricks" operations, and ultimately been unable to swallow the expediency of it all, so he'd left. The last couple of years had seen the ceasefires, the negotiations, the Good Friday Agreement, and now a Nobel Peace Prize; every job he'd worked on in Northern Ireland had been, as he saw it, for nothing. The very men he'd operated against were now regarded as respectable, but he knew different. He poured himself a mug of coffee and very nearly threw it at the wall, but thought better of it and set it down. His emotions had however got the better of him and he noticed that he had spilt coffee over his hand. He closed his eyes and clenched his jaw, exhaling slowly through his nose as the pain subsided, it wasn't the start to the day that he would have hoped for.

The newsreader had finished his broadcast and the DJ returned to his play list with some seemingly clever remark. Crawford was irritated by the droning of what passed for music and switched the radio off. He sat staring into space, focusing on nothing in particular, as his mind tried to address the turmoil that he had been thrown into. What sort of man was he that he could find no comfort in the news of the morning? There was peace after a kind in Northern Ireland, surely that was something? He tried to reconcile those present realities with his past life in the army but he couldn't. He attempted to rationalise his state of mind by telling himself that many years had passed and that people could change but he didn't believe it. He had always adhered to the principal "to thine own self be true" and there was no way of doing this in mutely accepting what was happening.

The main difficulty that he faced was defining just what was happening – the feeling that he was being made a liar was not enough – he had to have some concrete foundation on which to base his sense of betrayal. Once he had formed an overview he would be able to decide on a course of action, because he was sure of one thing, he was going to do something, it may not amount to very much but he couldn't stand idly by and do nothing.

He walked out to the hall and lifted the Yellow Pages from the telephone stand – he'd start with newspapers. He took the book back out to the kitchen, opened it at the newspaper listings and began making phone calls. After an hour he realised that his efforts weren't going to bear fruit quickly and that he would have to re-consider his approach – the truth was that he couldn't find anyone who wanted to talk to him. From the London Evening Standard through to The Daily Telegraph not a spark. Even The Guardian, which he thought might, as an instrument of the Left, look favourably on an attack on the Establishment, had shown no interest. All he'd got was one big collective "So what?". He could see where he was going wrong, unrestrained indignation lacked coherence and he would need all the facts arranged in order to make any kind of an impact.

He was trying to bring his thoughts together when the telephone rang. He lifted the handset from its cradle hoping the call would prove a distraction because his present mood was anything but good.

"Crawford."

"Mr. Crawford, it's Maria. I was getting a little worried about you, what with you not showing up this morning."

"Oh Jesus, Maria I'm sorry. I should have called in."

"You're not sick are you?"

"No, nothing like that. Something's come up and I was taking care of it before I came in today."

"Well that's good, because you've got a two o'clock with Mr. Hanson about the assessment you did for his premises."

"Christ, bloody thing…."

"Do you want me to call him and re-schedule?"

"No, no. I'll be in directly, and thanks for calling. It had slipped my mind completely."

Crawford hung up and went back to his bedroom to get dressed. The meeting with Hanson called for a formal appearance – there was potentially a lot of money tied up in the contract for warehouse security and Crawford didn't want to lose it – so he selected a classic navy pinstripe by Boss, with a sky blue double cuff from Turnbull & Asser and striped Zegna tie.

One reason Sean Kavanagh had for being late that morning was the fact that he had slept in. He had woken with the last images of a dream receding from his mind's eye and the next thing he was aware of was the alarm clock on Angela's bedside table; it was quarter to one, there or thereabouts. Angela Fitzgerald lay on her side facing away from Kavanagh and was still, as far as he could tell, asleep. She was another reason he was late; they had been seeing each other for about six months, but with them both working strange hours, she as a staff nurse at Great Ormond Street Hospital, and he with the department, their meetings were very much on an *ad hoc* basis. Much as he would have liked to have stayed in bed with her he had to be at the Gardens for a meeting with the boss at half passed two, so he slid from beneath the covers in an attempt not to wake her. He walked into the bathroom to get washed up, leaving Angela still asleep. After a quick shower he was back in the bedroom, a towel wrapped around his waist, rummaging through the contents of his grip looking for his electric razor. Once he'd found it he took a seat at the dressing table and began to shave. The buzzing of the razor brought a response from Angela.

"Do you have to do that in here? Can't you see I'm trying to get some sleep?"

"I'm sorry Angie, but some of us have got work to go to." As soon as he said it he regretted it; Angela sat up in bed and fixed a glare on his reflection.

"Your work, as you call it, seems to be a rather cushy number. Since I've known you, your hours can hardly be called regular. At least I'm doing something important, so don't come round here and take me for granted."

"Perish the thought."

"And your sarcasm I can do without. Look Sean just take your stuff and go, because really this conversation isn't doing either of us any good."

He neither saw the point nor had the time for an argument so he finished dressing, packed his bag and left. He'd call Angela later and eat some humble pie which would hopefully placate her, but for now his main concern was making it to Leinster Gardens on time for his meeting with John Blackwell. There was no way that he would make the appointed time on foot and with the questionable regularity of the buses he decided to catch the Tube. The Underground was crowded and as usual Kavanagh found no pleasure in being crammed into the narrow steel tube with a group of taciturn Londoners. Fortunately the journey wasn't a long one and when he made his stop it was just after two o'clock. He joined the other Underground users on the escalator and made the slow progress towards the surface and the relatively fresh air. Despite the heavy rain that had begun to fall it was with a great sense of relief that he made his way from the Queensway station to the Gardens; truth be told, he was a little claustrophobic and normally hated the Underground.

Even though it was only a five minute walk from the station around the corner Kavanagh, not having an umbrella, managed to get soaked. He entered the Gardens and stood dripping on the carpet at reception cum security as the guard, a man he hadn't seen before, put the call announcing his arrival through to Blackwell's secretary at her desk on the first floor. The briefest of conversations ensued and with clearance granted the man gave the dripping form in front of him the curtest of nods towards the staircase – it was a mistake and Kavanagh made the most of it. He placed both hands on the desk, pushing a folded copy of The Sun out of his way, and leaned over the security guard with a look of disdain fixed on his face.

"I don't know who you are, and what's more I don't care, but I'll say this much to you, you will treat anyone coming through that door with respect. Do I make myself clear?"

"Yes sir."

"Very good. Now I suggest you tidy your desk and your appearance; this isn't the Civil Service you know, so do your top button up and fix your tie. I'll check on my way out and there had better be an improvement or I'll take it up with Blackwell. Has that registered?"

"Yes sir."

With no further comment necessary Kavanagh made his way upstairs and after a brief word to Blackwell's secretary took a seat in the reception area to await the call from his superior. He was just getting absorbed in an article from the previous month's issue of Country Life when a door opened down the corridor to be quickly followed by a shout from Blackwell for Kavanagh to join him. It just wasn't in Blackwell's nature to use his intercom or to come down to reception to beckon his subordinate in person – he liked the sound of his own voice and, more important, he liked everyone to know who was boss – fairly typical of a man new to the job and not sure of himself. Kavanagh got up, and as he made his way down the corridor he passed the secretary. She looked up at him with a look of understanding on her face – clearly Blackwell's peccadilloes were well known to "The Garden" staff. Kavanagh shrugged and walked on and into Blackwell's office where he remained standing until instructed to take a seat. While his superior continued to study whatever document had his undivided attention Kavanagh took the opportunity to look around the office that he had seen for the first time nearly twenty years before. Little had changed – the Regency motif from Lynch's day remained as did the heavyweight desk – the main differences were the pictures on the walls, and even they were only new reproductions of military scenes – Blackwell's ego thankfully didn't require personal photographs showing his connections or diplomas detailing his qualifications.

Blackwell finished reading, closed the file and looked up at Kavanagh.

"Tell me Sean, what have our friends from the South been up to?"

"If you've read my report sir you'll have seen that the present activities amount to very little. Frankly I'm finding it difficult to maintain any interest in the task."

"I sympathise; which is why I'm pulling you off the job and giving you a break."

"But I've got no leave due at the moment sir."

"I know, but it's not that kind of break. There's a new intake and some of them will be down at "The Fort" in need of your peculiar talents."

"A training job with a bunch of snotty children?"

"It's a mixed batch you'll be dealing with; some of ours and some from our friends at "Gloom Hall". I thought you'd appreciate the change and the opportunity to make some of the graduates look small."

"Well anything's better than sitting on my hands. When do you want me down there?"

"Beginning of next week will be fine. You can have the weekend off."

"Thank you sir. Next week it is then."

Blackwell lifted another file as Kavanagh got up to leave, but his curiosity got the better of him and he turned back just before he left the office.

"Just one thing sir?"

Blackwell never lifted his gaze from the file but Kavanagh asked the question anyway.

"Are you moving me down to Gosport because of the new circumstances in Ulster and the knock-on effects?"

Blackwell weighed his answer carefully, but the reply, when it came, was exactly what Kavanagh expected.

"What new circumstances?"

There was no need for a reply and he took his leave.

The meeting with Hanson had gone better than Crawford had expected, with the firm being awarded the contract for the warehouse security cover, and better yet, at the original price quoted. It was now nearly four o'clock and Crawford found himself inventing little tasks to occupy his time. He reached across his bleached oak desk and retrieved the letters that Maria had handed him on his arrival, he looked through them but found nothing of any real interest, he checked through his "in" and "pending" trays and made an effort to clear his desk before the weekend, but found that Maria had dealt with everything that might have been of concern. Try as he might he found that there was no avoiding the questions and doubts cast up by the news of that morning. He got up from behind his desk and paced around his office – the interior offered no distractions – the finish of his desk best summed up the impact of the room, nicely appointed but rather flat. There was no escaping the unease that he felt.

He contemplated the Peace Prize award with a feigned optimism – maybe everything would turn out for the best and Northern Ireland would move forward into a new period of prosperity and good relations. The falseness of such an attitude meant that such optimism was short-lived. A sardonic smile spread across Crawford's face as he realised that he couldn't lie to himself. The reality, for him, was that something monstrous was happening to the truth that had guided the actions of the policy makers in the past; this wasn't the first time that appeasement had been tried, but it was the first time it had been this public. If such a new policy was to succeed black would have to become white, night become day, and men such as Crawford would have to accept that their every previous action had been for nought – worse than that had been wrong. If this was the price he was expected to pay then he would have to be a cause of disappointment; it was just something he couldn't do. His mind was made up, all that was necessary now was to discover a suitable medium for his disclosures.

He took another look around his office and was reassured that there was nothing that required his further attention. Taking his raincoat from the stainless steel stand at the door he left with the briefest of farewells to Maria as he walked out of the office. His decision on action raised his spirits and the walk to the Tube and the subsequent train journey home passed without incident. By the time he had walked back to the Mews he had not only decided on action but had also formed an idea about the best course to follow. With that in mind he went to the bureau in his study and began leafing through old address books until he found what he wanted – Dave Beatty's most recent contact number.

* * *

Crawford sat in the kitchen reading through the unintended hyperbole that was to be found in the various morning newspapers concerning the Nobel award. The complete disregard of reality was something he found impossible to dismiss – the usually cynical hacks had jumped on the "Peace Process" bandwagon and had accepted the myth that leopards could change their spots. He read about the "courage" shown by the key figures in the negotiations but could not equate their behaviour with the courage he had seen exhibited by people wearing uniforms in Northern Ireland. The notion of politicians displaying courage, particularly in this instance, revolted him. The reports only made him more determined to follow the course of action he had settled on.

He set down his mug of coffee and went to the study to retrieve the old address book that he'd found the previous night. On his return he began the process of tracking down Dave Beatty; which as it turned out was not as easy a process as he had at first hoped. There were several postings to be dealt with and even more initial "never heard of hims" to overcome, but the British Army was thankfully like a big family and as long as Crawford didn't mind waiting somebody would eventually be found who could point him in the right direction.

Crawford's efforts to trace Beatty took up the whole morning and just when he was about to take a break for lunch he met with success. He had made a call to the Sergeants' Mess at Aldershot where he had been told Beatty could be found. The first person he spoke to was unsure as to Staff Beatty's whereabouts and left Crawford on hold as he went away to find somebody who did know. After waiting for nearly five minutes a new voice came on the line.

"Sorry to keep you sir. I believe you're looking for Staff Beatty."

"That's correct."

"I'm afraid he's not here at the moment and he won't be until Monday, but I can take a message if you wish sir."

"That would be a great help. Take this number, it's 0171 --- ----, and ask Staff Beatty to call Gerry Crawford as soon as he gets a chance."

"If it's an emergency sir, I can contact him on his mobile and pass your details along immediately."

"It is a matter of some urgency, so that would be excellent."

Crawford replaced the handset, finally happy with the results of his efforts. He was tempted to go out for lunch and leave the answering machine to take any message from Beatty, but he considered that it would be better to wait for the reply when it came; considering the time he had spent tracking Dave down in the first place the matter of an hour's wait was of no consequence. Even so, to merely wait for a call could be a frustrating business, so he occupied his time making lunch; a rather satisfying wild mushroom risotto. The preparation of lunch commanded his full attention, but as he sat down to eat he was able to give some thought to a question that had been raised during his final conversation – Staff Beatty? – Dave had stayed in the army all this time and had only risen to staff sergeant? – and what the hell was he doing at Aldershot? – these questions would require answers when he eventually spoke to staff sergeant Dave Beatty. In the meantime he addressed the issue of the washing up.

As it turned out Crawford had to wait until just after three for Beatty to make contact, and when he spoke it was clear to Crawford that a more guarded and suspicious quality had entered Dave's character. After the initial pleasantries had been exchanged the business of the call took over.

"So what can I do for you Gerry?"

"Can't an old friend make contact without ulterior motives?"

"Not when it's "a matter of some urgency", so I say again what can I do for you?"

"Fine, I'll get to the point. A few years back you were involved in a disinformation job that required the services of the press."

"True enough. What of it?"

"I require those same services."

"What are you up to Gerry?"

"Not on the phone Dave. I need to see you, how about me coming down to Aldershot?"

"No need, I'm local. Look, if this is so important I can give you an hour at "The Rodney" at six tonight, does that suit?"

"Certainly."

"Right, I'll see you then."

Beatty hung up and Crawford was left with the distinct impression that the meeting would be anything but convivial; that in itself didn't matter as long as he got the information he wanted, but he had hoped that a friendly exchange would make the meeting that bit easier. If it wasn't going to be easy then at least he would be in control of the initial exchange. To that end he walked down the hall to his bedroom and went into the walk-in wardrobe in search of one of his surveillance outfits that now lurked along with the other little used items. Once he had found the correct suit cover he began looking for the shoes to match; he found them at the rear of the storage space lurking amongst some other long-forgotten kit. With the outfit taken care of he now only needed to make sure that the wearer looked the part, so he went into the bathroom and made what changes he could.

Kavanagh's weekend off had started badly and got progressively worse; he had gone back to Angela's flat and attempted to make amends for his insensitive remarks but she was having none of it. He had tried bribery, but the peace offering of flowers had failed, flattery hadn't worked, and when he tried agreeing with her every objection she saw through his obsequiousness immediately and another row ensued. Again he left before something unforgivable was said but his action left him at something of a loose end. With nothing else to do he returned to his own flat, packed enough kit to last him a couple of weeks and set off for Gosport only to find a series of roadworks that had made the drive a real pain.

When he'd finally arrived at "The Fort" there had only been enough time to grab a quick bite of dinner and get sorted out with some accommodation. There had been no personnel, senior or otherwise, available with whom to discuss the possibility of making an early start to the training programme. So with no arrangements made Kavanagh decided on an early night. That had been yesterday.

A look out of his window on Saturday morning didn't give Kavanagh any comfort – a wet overcast October day greeted him, with a brisk wind blowing from the south-west making "The Fort" appear even more bleak than usual. Since the long overdue refit in the eighties the accommodation was more civilized; Kavanagh's room even had an en-suite shower, which allowed him to face the day fully prepared. If there was one thing he hated it was having to share ablutions, but this being a civilian facility his pet hate wasn't to be stirred. He went down to the canteen and got breakfast, checking with the staff to see if any of the administrative people had put in an appearance. Hide nor hair had been seen, but previous experience let him know where to go, so he finished a leisurely breakfast before going in search of the Director Training.

The administrative offices were housed in another building and Kavanagh had to brave the weather and make a quick dash across the car park to reach it. Once inside he made his way down the carpeted hallway to the Director's unmarked door and knocked. Without waiting for a reply, Kavanagh pushed open the door and walked into the office. The man sitting at the desk in front of him carried on with his paperwork – Kavanagh's intention had been to take control of the meeting, but the lack of response was somewhat disconcerting – one point to the civilian. Finally he set the file aside and looked up, motioning Kavanagh to the seat in front of the desk.

"You'll be Mr. Kavanagh…."

"Yes."

"….and you're early. You aren't expected until Monday."

"I thought I could get the range set up and check the condition and availability of kit at the armoury."

"How very enterprising of you, but I think you'll find that everything is in hand."

"I just like to be sure."

This was not going the way Kavanagh liked or intended – he had previous experience of this type of civil servant and had thought his approach would clearly mark their differences to his advantage but it wasn't working.

"I'm sure you do; over-confidence is such a tiresome quality."

"Very true, and in my experience it can lead to all sorts of unfortunate circumstances."

"Your sort of experience is not to my taste Mr. Kavanagh, but the need to teach how to deal with certain situations is still on the curriculum, so there it is."

"So I'm a necessary evil, as you see it?"

"Something like that."

An opportunity presented itself and Kavanagh gladly took it as he frankly didn't see another being offered.

"Understood. Let me just say that I know what I'm doing in this part of the curriculum and until such times as you can produce an instructor, if you'll pardon the pun, of my calibre, I would appreciate a certain freedom to do my job."

The director narrowed his eyes and exhaled forcefully through his nose, clearly unused to having his authority challenged – one point to Kavanagh.

"Very well. The range is yours to do with as you see fit; you'll not be disturbed."

"Thank you. I'll get started right away."

The encounter ended with no winner but Kavanagh didn't care as he made his way out of the administration block; he was merely glad that he had made his point and even happier that he would be left in peace. After a brief visit to his room to collect a small kitbag, he again braved the elements and ran across the parking area to the entrance for the range facility. During the war air-raid shelters had been a grim necessity and this particular one had been used in 1946 as the basis for the range when the staff had arrived down from the west of Scotland to help with the building of the training school for the SIS. As he carefully went down the rain-slicked steps Kavanagh marvelled, not for the first time, at the simple economy of the use of the existing underground structure, simple but very effective.

The first heavy steel door opened onto the waiting area which was unoccupied. He looked around the room taking in the fact that it had been given a fresh coat of the institutional green paint that was such a favourite. A few notices adorned the walls giving supposedly sound advice on range safety and some of the in vogue small arms manufacturers were represented with posters advertising their latest offerings. Kavanagh looked at the security light that showed if the range was in use and finding it switched off he opened the second armoured door and went through to the range itself. Most of the recessed lamps were off, with the only limited illumination being offered by the light above the entrance to the armoury, but from what Kavanagh could see the range had a disused look to it. Several small piles of shot-out targets littered the floorspace over to the left-hand side of the range and the atmosphere smelled damp, an indication that the heating hadn't been on for a while. He shook his head in disgust; a first-rate facility like this lying dormant, not only dormant but also neglected, times really had changed and in his view not for the better.

He walked over to the protected control panel mounted beside the door that led to the armoury and lifted the cover, which gave him access to the lights and a bell switch which he pressed. His ring was answered with the door opening to be swiftly followed by the appearance of a small man wearing an oil stained apron. With all the unwelcome changes that Kavanagh had encountered since his arrival, he had almost expected to find the staff in the armoury replaced. Thankfully this was not the case and a broad smile split across his face.

"Mr. Curtis, am I ever glad to see you."

"Mr. Kavanagh, the feeling's mutual. I heard that you were coming down, so I've been on station getting your training battery prepared."

"And how would you know what I would want?"

"Because unless someone has re-invented the wheel it will be the same as the last time. Anyway come on in Sean and I'll show you what I've got ready."

Kavanagh followed the older man into the armoury and looked at the neat rows of pistols that lay on the oilcloth which covered the workbench. He nodded in appreciation.

"It's nice to know that some things are consistent. Change for the sake of it isn't a good thing. So, tell me what's the new director like?"

"Personally, I don't know. Professionally, he thinks that people like us should quietly pack up and return to the Ark where we belong."

"That's putting it diplomatically Jimmy. Between you and me, I thought him an arrogant, superior arsehole."

"Just about sums him up. If I wasn't in the process of securing my pension I'd tell him to stick this bloody job."

"And there was me thinking that you lived for your work!"

"Don't kid yourself. People like him take all the pleasure out of it. If the private sector wasn't totally knackered I'd have been out of here years ago."

"Don't remind me. It's crossed my mind more than once what I'll be doing when my time's up."

"I wouldn't worry, they'll always find something for you."

"Yeah, like coming down to "The Fort" to teach some beginners how not to shoot themselves in the foot."

"Don't knock it, it beats working for a living. Enough of that anyway, let's have a cuppa and then we'll see what needs doing."

"Sounds good to me."

At five twenty-five a distinctly unkempt Gerry Crawford walked into "The Rodney". With the redevelopment that was happening around Greenwich, courtesy to its proximity to the Millennium Dome, it came as something of a surprise to him that the pub hadn't really changed since he'd been a local resident. Certainly the decor was fresh but the layout was pretty much the same, so once he'd bought a Hennessy he took a seat in the booth that he and Beatty had occupied all those years before, the only difference being that he was facing the door this time.

He started reading the copy of The Mirror that he'd bought at the kiosk in the Underground to help pass the time, but hadn't progressed beyond page five when

Beatty came through the corner doors. He folded the paper and waved over to his old colleague who returned the wave and signalled that he was going to get a drink from the bar before joining him. Pint in hand, a slightly heavier set Beatty slid onto the seat opposite Crawford.

"Been a while Gerry."

"Aye a few years. You haven't changed much."

At this remark Beatty leaned back in the booth and patted his stomach.

"I don't know about that, I'm carrying a few extra pounds these days."

"That'll be the beer. You should stick to the shorts."

"This is all very interesting but my time's limited so what do you want Gerry?"

"Christ Dave! We don't see each other in ten years and you want to get down to business without any questions about what I've been up to."

"Well to tell you the truth Gerry I don't think you'll like what I have to say; I mean physically you look fine, but where's the man who was always so careful about his appearance? You look as if you're trying very hard but not quite making it. And that says you want something, probably money."

"Yeah, well, maybe so, but not from you Dave. Look let's just slow down a bit – how's things with you?"

"Never mind that Gerry. We both know that you aren't really interested, so what is it you want?"

"OK, I'm not going to waste time explaining but I need the name of one of your contacts in the press."

"And what makes you think that I know anybody?"

"It was common knowledge at the time that you were used to put the word about on occasions."

"Like when?"

"Like during the Stevens enquiry."

"That's not common knowledge and it would be wise of you to forget it."

"Done, just give me a name."

"OK, but before I give you the contact tell me what this is all about."

"You know the line of work I'm in now. Well, let's just say that a piece of information has come my way which could make me some much needed money."

"What have you been up to – fiddling the books or something?"

"Call it expensive habits."

"So it's either women or gambling. I would've thought that you of all people would have known better."

"Look Dave, I'm desperate."

"OK, OK. I'll give you a name, but I'll have to call you with it."

"When?"

"Probably tomorrow."

"Thanks Dave. You don't know how important this is to me."

"Look, I've got to run so I'll call you with that name, OK?"

"That'll be great."

Beatty finished his pint and left, with the look of a man glad to be leaving a situation not to his liking. Crawford stayed on and thought about the meeting; if there were any holes in his performance, he couldn't see them. Beatty had accepted the whole package of a man down on his luck and desperate for cash, without a second thought. Now it only remained to be seen if the name that was coming his way would prove to be of any use.

Kavanagh had spent a productive afternoon clearing the debris from the range while Curtis went through the final checks and preparations of the training inventory. By six-thirty they had both had enough for one day and at Kavanagh's suggestion they both went into Gosport for a drink and a meal away from the atmosphere of "The Fort". The conversation ran back to the topic of the afternoon – the arrogance and short-sightedness of their masters. It would have been a cause of some surprise to them both if they could have heard the duration of the attack and indeed the venom with which they assaulted officialdom. There was a bitterness in their mutual perspective that clearly showed two men who felt that their expertise had been all too often overlooked. With the bill paid and their drinks finished Kavanagh drove them back to "The Fort". As the two men parted company Kavanagh made arrangements with Curtis to meet on the range tomorrow so that he could draw some ammunition for practice just to make sure that he was performing up to scratch. Both men returned to their respective accommodation and went straight to bed although sleep did not come easily to either of them; the stormy nature of the evening's conversation was matched by the weather as a gale blew through the English Channel.

Crawford had made his way home from Greenwich by a reversal of the route and method he had followed to "The Rodney". The Tube had been filled with members of the younger generation embarking on whatever adventures passed for entertainment on a wet Saturday night. The "old man" tag that had been pinned to him years ago had never felt more appropriate as the disillusionment weighed ever heavier on his mind and drained him physically. His settlement on action had done little to raise his spirits and his despondency was almost made complete by the time he had walked back to the flat through the rain. He took off his overcoat and hung it on the stand in the hall before going into the kitchen to make a cup of coffee. With a mug of freshly filtered Jamaican in hand he retreated to his study and sat massaging his temples in an effort to dispel the headache that was building. He found no relief in his decision, only questions; questions about his actions, about his motives and about the possible outcomes.

He thought one way he could blot out the images cast up by his doubts was to put all the details of his proposed disclosure on paper, so he retrieved a block of A4 from his desk and spent the next two hours writing down everything he could think of. When he saw them starkly listed on the page his questions found their answer. Principles that he had held as irrefutable and the rightness of his actions in the past had not diminished, and the expediency of others was not going to make him a liar to himself or anyone else for that matter. The grandfather clock in the hall chimed midnight and Crawford went to bed exhausted by his trip across town to Greenwich and by the strain of noting his involvement in the past. With luck Beatty would contact him with a name and then he'd see if what he had to say really counted for anything.

* * *

After a good breakfast, and it was regarded as the only meal at Monckton that was consistently edible, Kavanagh made his way to the range to find that Curtis had arrived before him. He lifted the same kitbag that he'd brought with him the previous day onto the workbench.

"Morning Jimmy."

"Morning Sean. Any interesting kit in that bag of yours?"

"Just the one thing", and he opened the bag to retrieve a sealed plastic pouch, the contents of which he passed to Curtis, "A friend of mine made it up for me."

Curtis examined the irregular shaped piece of leather and reached behind him to pick up a small case which contained the pistol he wanted. Taking the Walther from the box he slid it into the holster – with the pistol in place the whole rig was generally speaking rectangular. He drew the PPK a couple of times, put the pistol back in its case and handed the holster back to Kavanagh.

"Bit on the loose side."

"It needs to be, otherwise it gets too cramped in the pocket. That's another thing, I had to have the pockets altered on some of my trousers to give a bit more clearance. Have a look."

With that he retrieved his own PPK from the holdall, put it in the holster and placed the whole rig in his right trouser pocket. The overall effect was that of a large wallet causing a bulge – it certainly didn't look like a holstered pistol. Curtis nodded in admiration.

"Impressive, but is it fast?"

"Only one way to find out. I don't want to use my own rounds, so if you can give me some .32 to be getting on with, I'll make a start."

While Kavanagh unloaded his Walther, Curtis pulled a box from beneath the workbench and put it on the oilcloth.

"There's a little of everything in there. There's Winchester, Federal, S&B, IMI and some really old Waffenfabrik. I thought I'd keep the new stuff for the students."

"Good idea, they'd only get the impression that this was some kind of Heath Robinson effort if we gave them that. Well let's see how it goes; I'll start with a double at three quarter-hip from about nine feet, and you might want to bring a set of ear defenders with you."

The two men walked out of the armoury with Kavanagh leading. He moved toward the far end of the range at a normal pace, his right hand casually placed in his pocket. A row of three targets were grouped slightly to his left hand side and it was as he came within about four yards that he engaged the target closest to him. Nothing dramatic happened, no exaggerated poses were struck, no apparent adjustment of his stance was made, he merely took his hand out of his pocket, turned slightly to his left, crouched, and brought the PPK to waist level before opening fire twice. It was all very relaxed and if Curtis hadn't been paying attention he'd have missed it.

Kavanagh re-holstered his pistol and turned to face his friend.

"Not bad at all. The K came out of the rig well", he cocked a thumb at the target, "Let's see if I can still shoot!"

On examination the target showed two holes about five inches apart, the first two inches left of the sternum and two inches below the clavicle, the second was in the centre of the throat at the Adam's apple. Kavanagh seemed pleased with the results if the look on his face was anything to go by.

"Well that's a good start. I shouldn't need much more to bring me up to speed."

"You are kidding aren't you?"

"No. What makes you say that?"

"Oh come on Sean, that was bloody fast."

Kavanagh took the whole rig out of his pocket and held it up for Curtis to take a closer look.

"It's really a case of what the eye doesn't see. The hand's got a proper grip on the weapon and the fact is I've got the draw about half-way complete. Watch."

With that, he showed Curtis the way in which his right thumb pushed against the outside of the holster which in turn lifted the PPK part way clear.

"See what I mean Jimmy? This all happens in the pocket, out of sight. After that it's just a question of hand speed."

"Let me have another look and I'll tell you if there are any tell-tale signs."

Kavanagh replaced the rig in his pocket and took position opposite the middle target. Curtis stood to his right and watched intently as Kavanagh repeated the practice. Again the hand cleared the pocket and two rounds were fired, impacting the target in the upper chest and neck. Curtis looked at the results and shook his head.

"Nothing to see Sean. It just looks as if you're fiddling with your change or something. All pretty innocent and it's still bloody fast."

"If you say so then I'll agree, but I want to finish this magazine and then I'll try out something else."

"It's your range Sean, you can please yourself."

Crawford had not enjoyed a restful night's sleep, the thoughts of the day had spilled over into his dreams and, while they had made little sense, certain episodes from his past had loomed large causing him upset. He woke with the image of a running figure pursued by shadows playing through his mind. The fact that his subconscious was causing such disquiet annoyed him; he'd made a decision, taken definite action and he shouldn't be making difficulties for himself. The only conclusion that made any sense was that he was replaying some of the concerns that he had already dealt with and that his subconscious hadn't caught up yet.

He stood in the shower and tried to blank out the shapeless anxieties that were trying to take form; over the years he had found the bathroom to be a great place to empty the mind. By the time he was washed and dressed the concerns of the night had been replaced with thoughts about how best to make an approach to the name that Beatty would hopefully supply today.

He retrieved his notes from the study and read through them as he had breakfast. From time to time he picked up a pen and either scored out a section or added one. When he had completed his amendments, he poured himself some more coffee and then thought about the nature of discretion and how his planned disclosures could impact on the public. He gave his mind free rein and he had run off to the realms of fantasy when his telephone rang. Such was his sense of displacement that he couldn't answer it immediately, he merely looked at it as if it were something alien. After maybe eight rings he pulled himself together and lifted the handset. Beatty sounded irritated as Crawford brought the receiver to his ear.

"I thought I'd missed you. What were you doing anyway? No – never mind – doesn't matter. Have you got a pen?"

"Yeah."

"Good. Then take this down. 07880 ------. Got that? The name is Alain Williams. That's A-L-A-I-N Williams."

"That's French."

"Well he isn't. It's a long story and he'll tell you if he's in the mood. Look, I've got to run."

And with that the line was broken. Crawford hung up and looked at the name and mobile phone number that Beatty had given him. The name meant nothing, which in itself didn't create any problem. Crawford only took an interest in the press when it could help him professionally; nonetheless, he hoped that Beatty had given him someone competent to work with. He looked at the kitchen clock to see if it was too early to place a call – it was just after ten-thirty – he decided to wait until the afternoon; the extra time would afford him the opportunity to go through his notes again.

Before he settled down to the task of reviewing his notes he took a walk to buy the heavyweight Sunday papers. On his return he went into the study and began working his way through the reports on the Nobel award and the specific events leading up to it. Several of the papers carried potted histories of the Northern Ireland Troubles which were little more than thumbnail sketches. When Crawford looked at his tale beside the apparent action that led up to the present circumstances he knew that it was impossible to reconcile the two. His success or failure would be in communicating this contradiction and it was to this end that he now addressed his thoughts. Taking his notes in hand he considered how best to array his story against the undoubted feel good factor that was covering reality like a blanket. He knew it was going to be difficult but for his own peace of mind he knew he had to try.

By midday Kavanagh had covered all the practices he thought were necessary; the pocket rig had performed beyond expectations and the shoulder harness and his belt scabbard had produced no difficulties. When he'd finished he patched out all the holes in the targets he'd fired on and then he picked up all the empty cases he could find. With the range clean he went into the armoury and deposited his brass in the large bin that stood by the door for that purpose. Curtis had left Kavanagh alone on the range after he had seen the pocket rig in action; he now stood in front of his lathe turning a length of case hardened steel rod. He turned the lathe off and looked over at Kavanagh as the younger man replaced his various rigs in his kitbag.

"All done Sean?"

"Oh, I think so."

"Really? It's just that you didn't seem to fire that much, not from what I could hear anyway."

"The quantity is not important Jimmy. It's what you do with it that counts, and I would've been wasting rounds if I'd carried on. So yes, I'm all done."

"Well so am I for the moment. Do you want a cuppa?"

"Yeah, why not."

Curtis went and put the kettle on to boil as Kavanagh finished stowing his gear; he looked at the loose rounds in the box that Curtis had given him and thought better of just taking them.

"Jimmy, the buckshee rounds, can I have them?"

"By all means, help yourself, and I meant to ask, any problems?"

"None. The IMI and particularly that wartime German stuff really packed a punch, should make useful carry ammunition."

Curtis finished making the tea and handed Kavanagh a mug; as he did so he furrowed his brow and shook his head.

"Sean, you should know better. That Waffenfabrik is old, very old, and I wouldn't want to rely on it."

"New rounds can malfunction too, you know."

"And I've seen them do it, but the older the ammunition the greater the chance."

"OK. So I'll only train with it."

The armourer smiled when he heard the younger man bow to his greater experience.

"Glad to hear it."

By one o'clock Crawford was sure of his approach and felt that the story he had to tell would whet any journalist's appetite. He was sitting at his desk in the study with his notes placed in order in front of him; all he had to do was make the call and yet he was making excuses not to. He questioned his motives, invented reasons for a lack of interest on the journalist's part, even decided that he was wasting his time as the call wouldn't be answered. He drummed his fingers on the desktop, took several deep breaths and lifted the handset before dialling the number Beatty had given him. When a voice came on the line Crawford, nearly dropped the telephone in surprise. Luckily for him he was saved the problem of an introduction that would, no matter how many times he had played it through in his mind, prove awkward. The voice at the end of the line clearly expected someone else.

"That had better be you Phil. I've been waiting for your call all bloody weekend. Do you not think I haven't got better things to do? Let's hear it, what's the excuse this time?"

Try as he might Crawford couldn't place the accent; the speaker was no stranger to English but he betrayed no regional affiliation. He covered the length of his pause with apparent disorientation at the case of mistaken identity.

"I'm sorry but this isn't Phil."

"Oh Christ! I'm sorry. I thought it was someone else, I've been waiting for a call and I'm getting a little hacked off.... and this is of absolutely no interest to you, so what can I do for you?"

There was still no clue as to the origins of the speaker, but in the meantime Crawford decided to let the matter lie. "That is Alain Williams, I hope?"

"Oh yeah, yeah. And who's this?"

At least he'd got the right man – better to get to the point before the curiosity disappeared.

"My name is Crawford and to establish my *bona fides* I'd better tell you that I got your name from Dave Beatty."

"Did you now, and how is Beatty?"

"He's well, but that has little to do with why I'm contacting you."

"And what has it to do with?"

"Let me just say that I used to be in the same line of work that you know Beatty to be involved in, and I have certain information that would prove interesting to you."

"And what might that be?"

"Not over the telephone."

"It never bloody is. Let me guess, you'd like to meet?"

"At your earliest convenience, that's right."

"Well here's the problem – I'm in Belfast...."

"And I'm not. But it's only geography and it can be overcome."

"That's as maybe but I've got some checking of my own to do before I'm prepared to carry this any further than this conversation."

"I fully understand. What do you suggest?"

"Well firstly I'll need to contact Beatty to hear his word on you and I'll take it from there. Give me your number and I'll get back to you."

"No, but I'll tell you what – I'll call you tomorrow morning. That should give you enough time to track Beatty down, and for your information he's working out of Aldershot at present, but you might find that it's easier to get him on his mobile and I'm sure you have the number."

"Fine, tomorrow it is then. I hope this isn't going to be a waste of time."

"You needn't worry about that. This story is bigger than anything you've seen before."

"I hope so. 'Til tomorrow then."

Crawford returned the handset to the cradle and thought about the man he'd just spoken to; the mention of a check with Beatty showed a certain discretion that pleased him, but it was all that he could deduce from the conversation. The man's background was important, but any speculation without definite information would only prove redundant. If Williams managed to contact Beatty, he knew he had nothing to fear from their talking, so with luck he'd be able to start adding to the bait that was already on the hook. As he looked at his notes again he realised that he was calmer than he would have expected. The first step had been taken and he could only assume that, if Williams was interested, it would be relatively easy to pass on the details.

* * *

The trainees had arrived seperately, the men from "Gloom Hall" had come in their own cars and the group of four from Ashford in a requisitioned mini-bus. The class, which comprised eight men in all, had been directed to the range and it was there that Kavanagh found them just before ten o'clock when he strolled over from the canteen following breakfast. They had all made the effort to be punctual which was gratifying but the way in which they had split up showed Kavanagh a certain independence that he'd have to deal with immediately.

Two of the class had gone to the side of the range where he had practised the day before. The other six had grouped together, watching the master-class being conducted over by the targets. The taller of the two men had brought his issue pistol with him and was demonstrating the finer points of his draw to his companion. Kavanagh quietly walked across the range, as he went he raised an index finger to his lips to silence the remaining six. He came to a halt about five yards behind the pair and looked with a growing sense of amusement at the careful foot placement of the taller man, obviously to ensure a stable stance. The next thing he saw was the demonstrator make a text-book draw that brought the pistol to a perfect two-handed, so-called, "Weaver" position. As he watched, he listened and heard a description of the necessity of a good "sight picture". He'd seen and heard enough.

"Let me interrupt gentlemen", at which both men turned around, "As an instructor once said to me in the States, "If you see your sights in a gunfight, they'll be the last thing you'll ever see". Now that's good advice and here's some more – I'm running this course and you will listen to me and me alone. This is the only occasion I'll indulge you, so don't push your luck. Now go and join the rest."

Kavanagh led the class into the armoury and lined them up in front of the workbench; Curtis had already placed eight Browning Hi-Powers neatly on the oilcloth, each with two magazines.

"OK gentlemen, my name is Kavanagh and I'll be your instructor for this course. You will start with the Browning and when I'm satisfied with your abilities you will move on to the Walther PPK."

The mention of the two pistols seemed to cause the tall young man whose lesson Kavanagh had interrupted a degree of irritation.

"You, Mr. Expert, name?"

"Robertson."

"Well Robertson, tell me what's wrong with the Hi-Power and the PPK?"

"They're old hat. I'm going to be using the 228 so I brought it with me for the course."

"What did I tell you on the range? I said you will listen to me and me alone, so if I tell you that you will be using the Hi-Power and the PPK that is what you'll be using."

"But...."

Kavanagh could see his authority was being challenged and fixed Robertson with a look of complete disdain.

"Mr. Robertson, I also said not to push your luck and you are pushing very hard. What it comes down to is this, men of infinite experience, experience I hope none of you ever have, have used these weapons effectively, they trained me and I'm here to train you, and you are going to be trained with the Hi-Power and the PPK. So Mr. Robertson you can take the 228 off and leave it with Mr. Curtis, I'm sure he won't break it."

Something about the way in which Kavanagh had looked at Robertson throughout the monologue told the younger man that compliance was the best way forward. He took the Sig-Sauer out of the new Galco holster he'd bought and handed it to Curtis, who dropped the magazine and checked the chamber to make sure the pistol was unloaded before placing it on one of the shelves behind the workbench. Robertson looked at Kavanagh to see if his acquiescence had softened the instructor's expression but was not rewarded with any change; he decided that Kavanagh would be a tougher nut to crack than that and he realised that his best course of action would be to do exactly as he was told.

Since he had got up that morning he'd been anxious to call Williams and by eleven-thirty Crawford could contain himself no longer. He sat in his study and dialled the mobile number. This time the phone had barely rung once when Williams' voice answered.

"Yes?"

"This is Gerry Crawford. Have you managed to contact Beatty?"

"I have and he gave you the all clear."

"So what does that mean?"

"It means that I may be interested to hear your story but I want to know what you have before I commit myself."

"I see. Well, like I said yesterday this cannot be discussed over the telephone, so may I suggest a meet?"

"I'm freelance Mr. Crawford and expenses are just that, expensive."

"OK. You said you were in Belfast. I can meet you there, there're plenty of flights, what do you say to later today?"

"I'd say you're in one hell of a hurry, but if you can afford it then by all means."

"Fine. I'll call you with a where and a when."

This time Crawford hung up before there was a chance for Williams to change his mind. Before he allowed any reservations of his own to take a hold and put him off acting he lifted the handset again and called the number of the travel agents that his firm used and booked himself on the evening flight from Gatwick to Belfast City Airport. He also asked for accommodation to be arranged at the Europa Hotel; it was there that he planned to hold his meeting with Williams. With his travel plans made it only remained for him to call Maria at the office. Should any effort be made to check his motives the only information forthcoming would be that Mr. Crawford was away for personal reasons and that, yes, he did seem to be somewhat preoccupied. If Beatty was careful and called the office he'd only hear what Crawford wanted him to hear, if he wasn't then so much the better.

The flight was at 1650 which gave Crawford plenty of time to prepare for his overnight stay in Belfast. He walked from the study to his bedroom and, as he began packing his grip, memories of previous trips filled his mind but none of them had had the obvious potential importance of this one, and besides, he was setting the agenda this time. Yet again he asked himself if he was doing the right thing and yet again his answer came back that he was.

Kavanagh had split the eight man class into two groups of four but he was still finding the progress slow. It wasn't that they were bad students, it was just the constraints placed on him as a solo instructor made for a rather deliberate approach. The discipline he was teaching could require a lot of hands on treatment unless there were more than the fair share of naturals and although they were attentive and obedient there weren't any born gunfighters amongst them. The fact that all the men had gone through a military training regime at some stage didn't help his emphasis on the use of only one hand when firing – most of them responded to a learned procedure of using both hands rather than giving into instinct and pointing with one hand. For most of the morning he'd made the class point their right index fingers at various points around the range. Once they had actually started to trust their instincts he felt able to allow the live fire practices to begin with rigidly controlled single shots at ranges of no more than three yards. It came as something of a surprise to most that shots began to hit targets in the desired place without the use of two hands and more importantly sights.

It pleased Kavanagh that the class was making progress and the fact that he had split them into two groups was proving a positive help; the weaker elements were benefitting from the encouragement of those making headway and the pointers that were being offered showed that they were really thinking about the mechanics of what they were doing. As these truths began to sink in, then the faster the class would move to the more advanced aspects of the syllabus.

He had offered the men the opportunity to break for lunch but none of them had been interested, preferring instead to continue with the practices. By three o'clock he was happy that all of them had grasped the basic principle of instinctive shooting – the use of the centre line of the body as an index – so it was time to move on to the practice of the two round burst.

"OK gentlemen, you're going to be moving on to the two round burst. Just remember that you will maintain the centre line and will not be shooting from the hip. I want to start you all at two yards and then I'll move you back when I think you're ready. Any questions?"

It was a measure both of the attention they had been paying and Kavanagh's ability as an instructor that meant that no-one felt the need to ask for clarification. The lead shooter from each group stepped forward and took position opposite a target. Each man held his pistol at roughly 45 degrees pointed down range; as yet no holsters were being used so no attempt at a draw was being made. Kavanagh handed each man a magazine and told them to load and make ready. Magazines were placed into the wells and firmly locked in place before slides were racked and a round was chambered. The looks of concentration and tension were obvious so it came as a complete anti-climax when Kavanagh gave the order to engage to shooter number one – his arm came up parallel with the ground and the hammer fell as he pulled the trigger and nothing happened. A rather bemused shooter stood and looked at his pistol unable to comprehend why it had failed to go off. Kavanagh stepped forward and took the pistol, dropping the magazine and racking the slide to the rear, extracting the round from the chamber as he did so.

"Mr. Maxwell has just had a stoppage and because he didn't deal with it, has, to all intents and purposes, died. You've all practised stoppage drills before, so you can use them now", Kavanagh held up the round he'd extracted, "This is a drill round gentlemen. Bear in mind that I've loaded the magazines so you may or may not encounter one of these which will simulate a stoppage. OK, let's start again."

The practice resumed and as the afternoon progressed the class as a whole encountered and dealt with such stoppages as Kavanagh manufactured. Initially the speed and success of the clearances varied but by the end of the afternoon Kavanagh was happy with the standard that the class had attained. By six he'd had enough for one day and called a halt so that weapons could be signed in once they'd been cleaned. Half an hour later the class left the range and headed back to their accommodation leaving Kavanagh with Curtis.

"How'd the first day go?"

"Some of the cockiness has gone, all in all they're not a bad group, but that said I'm still glad I've got two weeks to work with them."

There had been a fifteen minute delay with the flight so it was nearly quarter to seven by the time that Crawford managed to leave the small terminal at the Harbour Airport and get a taxi that would take him along the Sydenham bypass into the city centre. As he was driven into Belfast he took a look around the eastern side of the city; the depressed air that always permeated the Belfast of his memory had lifted somewhat; there was a lot of building work ongoing and the city seemed to be growing. This apparent confidence did nothing to raise Crawford's spirits; if anything the fact that optimism had superseded reality only brought him lower, that and the fact that he was back in Belfast.

The Europa had been remodelled yet again; after all it was the most bombed hotel in western Europe but this most recent renovation had nothing to do with terrorism – President Clinton had stayed in it as a means of showing confidence in the new-found peace. Crawford took a look at the new found opulence and the confidence that went with it, took a deep breath and made his way across the polished stone floor of the central lobby to the reception desk to check in. With that task complete he took his bag and his electronic key-card to the lift and rode up to his room on the seventh floor. Once he had unpacked he walked to the window and looked down on Great Victoria Street. The wet autumn evening kept pedestrians to a minimum with the most obvious signs of life coming from the traffic that moved to and fro along Belfast's "Golden Mile". Even his limited night-time view from the seventh floor showed a brighter, cleaner Belfast than the town he remembered. Across the street he could see the "Crown Bar", one of Belfast's most famous landmarks; he'd never been a customer and wondered if he'd get the chance before he returned to London. Knowing his time was limited and that Williams was waiting for his call he reached for the telephone by his bedside and began to dial the mobile number he'd been given but hung up before he'd completed it. Hotels would maintain records of all outgoing calls as would his own mobile phone company – best to find a payphone and set up the meeting that way.

Having taken the lift back down to the lobby he declined the payphones beside reception and walked out onto Great Victoria Street to use a phone box outside the new Great Northern shopping centre. The phone booth provided shelter against the rain as Crawford keyed in the number; he stood listening to the ringing tone, wondering if Williams was available and was almost taken by surprise when the mobile was answered on the fifth ring.

"Alain Williams, can I help you?"

"Mr. Williams, it's Gerry Crawford. I'm in Belfast and as we discussed earlier I think a meeting would be mutually beneficial."

"Well you don't waste any time, I'll give you that. Where are you and when do you want to meet?"

"I'm staying at the Europa and I'll be in the residents bar on the first floor until nine-thirty."

"How will I know you?"

"You won't. Just tell me what you look like and what you're wearing and I'll pick you out. I'll buy you a drink, we'll have a chat and then we'll see whether my story interests you or not."

Crawford had been sitting in the lounge nursing a Hennessy for the best part of an hour when the journalist arrived. As he'd said he was easy to spot – the motorcyclist's crash helmet was a dead giveaway. Other than that he was rather undistinguished, being in all ways, as he had said, average – average height, average build, with a face that wouldn't stand out in a crowd, nothing about him to attract the eye and nothing in fact that was memorable. Crawford watched as Williams looked around the bar paying particular attention to the few people sitting on their own. The few single drinkers all looked like business men having a nightcap; so with nobody seeming to live up to his expectations a look of irritation spread across his face and he made his way toward the bar. Not wishing to prolong Williams's obvious discomfort Crawford got up from his seat and walked over to where he stood.

"Glad you could make it. Can I get you a drink?"

Williams looked Crawford up and down, taking in the well polished shoes, the freshly pressed slacks, the tie and blazer, and his surprise was clear. He seemed a bit caught out and it was several seconds before he could make a reply.

"Well, I'm on the bike so I'd better stick to something soft, a Coke'll do."

"As you wish."

Crawford directed Williams to his table and then went up to the bar. After a couple of minutes he returned and placed a glass in front of Williams before sitting down. Williams was looking at him intently with narrowed eyes and shook his head before opening the conversation.

"You're not what I expected from the chat I had with Beatty, you know?"

"I'm sorry to disappoint you."

"I wouldn't worry about that, no. It's just that he painted a picture of a man somewhat down on his luck, and that's not what I'm seeing."

"Well, Dave never was the most observant of people."

"And here was me thinking that he was. I thought in your line of business it was paramount."

"So he told you what I was and am?"

"Not exactly but he did mention something about an indiscretion that you are party to and the need, as you see it, to expose it. It sounded interesting, so here I am."

"Something of the sex'n'drugs'n'rock'n'roll variety?"

"He didn't specify, but he did tell me that you work in the private security sector. I put two and two together and assumed you had some information to sell."

"Something that would make both of us rich and would attract all the right sort of attention.?"

"I suppose so, yes."

Crawford leaned forward and picked up his glass. He took his time before taking a sip of brandy and spent yet more time staring into space – apparently deep in thought. Williams, to his credit, made no effort to interrupt the older man's reverie, he occupied himself by taking a packet of cigarettes from his jacket and lighting one. He sat and smoked allowing Crawford the time to make whatever decision was necessary. After a couple of minutes Crawford set his glass down and continued where he had left off.

"Before we go any further, did Dave tell you anything about my background?"

"He said that you had served together but nothing more than that."

"I see."

"Yeah, and I think I do too. This story you have isn't about some clients bad habits is it?"

"No it's not. But this bar isn't the place for it. Let's finish these drinks and then we can go to my room to take things further."

Both men had taken seats over at the window; Crawford sat with his fingers laced together, staring into space, Williams placed his cigarettes beside the ashtray on the table but turned to Crawford before lighting one.

"So what is this all about?"

"I haven't decided whether or not I'm going to give you the story."

Williams shrugged his shoulders and got up from the table in the corner of the hotel room. He picked up his crash helmet and cigarettes before making for the door, turning to Crawford before he opened it.

"I just love wasting my time with some old git who has an inflated view of his own importance. I'm sure your story is fascinating but you'll just have to find someone else to tell it to. I'm off."

Crawford knew his best chance was about to walk out on him so he threw out a baited line that would keep Williams interested for the time being at least.

"South Armagh, March 1979. A raid was carried out on the local Provo Brigade."

As he'd hoped Williams left the bedroom door unopened and resumed his seat taking a small tape recorder from his waterproof jacket pocket which he set on the table.

"Tell me more."

"You'd better have plenty of tape because this could take some time."

"Don't worry about that."

"OK. Then I'll talk, you'll listen and no interruptions. You'd better start that thing recording."

Crawford spoke for nearly fifty minutes, only getting up once to retrieve the brief notes he had made back in London which were in his overnight bag. When he had finished he gestured towards the tape recorder indicating that Williams should switch it off. Neither man spoke for some time; Williams finished his fourth cigarette and ground it out in the ashtray sitting on the table in front of him. He looked through the questions he had listed in the reporter's notebook he had taken from another pocket on his biking waterproof, and shook his head as he flipped the pages back and forth. Crawford sat in silence, his eyes never leaving the younger man, as he waited for the inevitable questions to begin.

"It's a hell of a story, and I can see the potential impact such a thing would have, particularly now, but…."

"But what?"

"But nobody is going to believe it."

"Why not?"

"Well, for a start you've got twenty-one dead, two of them unspecified foreign nationals."

"And what is so fantastic about that?"

"This is the UK not some banana republic. Things like this don't happen here."

"And I've just told you that they do."

"But there's no evidence."

"Christ Almighty! Weren't you listening? There was never meant to be any. This whole job was planned with that in mind. Only a couple of people knew the full details then and those that I knew of are now dead."

"So how come you know?"

"Through another's indiscretion. I was never meant to know. Bury the kit and move on to the next job, that was how it was meant to be."

"This is too much. I can't corroborate any of this."

"I've given you some of the background and what happened in the aftermath. It won't confirm what I've said but it all fits together."

"Really? I can't believe you're being so calm about this. You've just told me about state sanctioned murder and you expect me to clarify a few points. It's not that easy."

"I think you need to face up to reality. These things happen, deal with what I've told you."

"But…."

"But nothing! Do you think it's been easy for me carrying this around for nearly twenty years? Do you think this kind of knowledge isn't dangerous? God, the number of times I've thought that my silence was worthwhile. Well, let me tell you those times are past. How can what I did be considered reasonable in light of the present actions in Ulster? The very people I fought against are being released from prison and are being given money by the state that employed me and others to take them out in the first place."

"So what is this all about then, revenge?"

"Maybe it is, maybe it isn't, but one thing's for sure I can't stomach the sickening hypocrisy any longer."

"You expect me to write this up and look for a publisher, well I can tell you nobody's going to touch this with a barge pole."

"I disagree. Think about it – you've got a government that has taken steps to end a conflict and everybody congratulates them – on the other hand that same government gave the go ahead for the job I've just told you about."

"It was nearly twenty years ago for Christ's Sake!"

"And it's still news. You can't ignore this now that you know, and there have to be means of checking the background. I can only leave it up to you."

"This isn't what I expected from the description Beatty gave me."

"Too bloody bad. I've given you a story that needs to be told."

"Don't tell me my job. It's just that this has all come as a bit of a surprise, so OK, I'm not promising you anything but I'll look into it."

"You're sure?"

"I said I'll look into it. Look, give me a ring in a week, by then I should have been able to access the archive material I need. I can't say fairer than that, can I?"

"I suppose so."

"Right then, well I'm off."

"OK. Look I'm sorry if I've come across a bit strong, it's been difficult to make this kind of disclosure and I hope you can see the trust I'm putting in you. Thanks for listening, but just make sure that you make the most of the information." "I told you that I'll look into it, and I'll see what I can come up with. Call me in a week and I'll tell you what I've done."

Williams left Crawford in his seventh floor room; one man relieved to have finally told his story, the other finding it almost impossible to come to terms with the knowledge he'd just been given.

* * *

Kavanagh assembled his class in the dining room on the ground floor of the accommodation block and gave them a briefing as they finished breakfast. The first hour of the morning session was to be little more than a refresher of yesterday's practises but after that he was going to issue them with their first holsters. He made sure to tell them to wear or bring the belts that they had been told to bring for the training course. Once that was covered Kavanagh gave them a start time of nine-thirty which gave him half an hour to check over the range and see if there was any need to re-set the targets from the previous day. He walked across the former parade square now a car park glad of the change in the weather, the blustery rain had been replaced with what passed for, in October, as warm sunshine. It was with definite regret that he made his way down the steps to the range; it promised to be a good day to be outside and he was going to stuck in a hole in the ground. He pushed open the door that led onto the range and found the lights switched on and the armoury open. A cursory inspection of the targets showed him that no rearrangement was necessary so he went into the armoury to see Curtis.

"Jesus Jimmy, haven't you got a home to go to?"

Curtis looked up from the frame he had fixed in a padded vice and put down his tools.

"Not when I have a job of work to do. You know the bean counters Sean, if there's any chance of prolonging the life of a piece of kit they'll ask it done. Take this old bugger here", and he pointed at the frame he'd been working on, "It's thirty years old and they want it and all the others serviceable rather than scrapped."

"If there's life in it why not?"

"Balls to that Sean. Some poor sod might need to depend on this some day and what if it doesn't perform?"

"Then it's your neck Jimmy."

"That's right and I don't like the responsibility. I tell you it's no way to run this business."

"You're right Jimmy, but we won't be able to make a change, nobody'll listen to us. Anyway, take a break and help me get the kit set out for my lot."

For the next twenty minutes the two men set the training battery out on the armoury work bench and loaded magazines with an assortment of live and drill rounds. No sooner had they finished than the sound of footsteps heralded the arrival of the class. Kavanagh called them into the armoury and weapons were distributed before he led them out onto the range.

"OK gentlemen, divide yourselves up as you were. Mr. Robertson you're first, now let me see what you've managed to forget since yesterday."

A rather disgruntled Robertson stepped forward and took the magazine Kavanagh proffered. He loaded it into the Browning and racked the slide chambering a round.

"Right I want two rounds on the target directly in front of you on the command 'Now'."

Robertson took up a ready position and visibly tensed up in anticipation.

"NOW!"

The crouch he had adopted became even more pronounced as he brought the pistol up to the classic three quarter hip position and squeezed the trigger. The first round went off and hit the target above the sternum. On the second squeeze, however, the hammer fell making no more than a dull click. With commendable speed Robertson racked the slide again, thus clearing the stoppage. He successfully fired a second round to be rewarded with another hit, this time below the right clavicle. Kavanagh looked at the result and then turned to the younger man who had returned to his ready position.

"Well done Mr. Robertson. That was almost good."

He'd had a troubled night's sleep and it had nothing to do with the hotel bed; Crawford had never been one to have difficulty sleeping in a new location, no, what had upset him was a dream which re-ran the story he had told Williams. His imagination had filled in the blanks of what must have been a bloody scene and it had become a nightmare. Five minutes in the shower did nothing to settle his mind and it was with little appetite that he sat down to a late breakfast. He looked through the Daily Telegraph that he had lifted on his way into the dining room but none of the headlines interested him. He mechanically made his way through some coffee and toast having declined the Ulster fry that would have frankly lain in his stomach like lead. The last vestiges of his nightmare had gone only to be replaced with old questions about his motives and new ones about the wisdom of involving Alain Williams.

His flight back to London was not scheduled until one-thirty but any ideas he might have had about taking a walk around the city centre as a means of killing time did not appeal to him – his memories of Belfast were not particularly happy and he had no wish to re-visit old haunts. After breakfast he returned to his room and retrieved his bag before he settled his bill at reception. With that done he decided to sit and watch the world go by from one of the sofas in the main lobby.

Crawford hadn't been the only one to spend a restless night; Williams had sat in his bedroom listening to the measured words of the recording he had made, finding it increasingly difficult to reconcile Crawford's matter-of-fact delivery with the enormity of the disclosure. He'd listened to the tape twice before he'd fallen asleep – a clear indication of his troubled dreams was the knotted state of the duvet when he awoke – normally he slept peacefully. He crawled out of bed and into the kitchen; he simply wouldn't function without his customary breakfast of coffee and a Marlboro. As the kettle boiled he smoked his first of the day and looked out the kitchen window onto the small yard behind his house on Pretoria Street; it had rained during the night and the cement paving was slick with rainwater, things looked clean but the underlying dirt hadn't been washed away. It was as good a metaphor for what he had heard last night as any he could think of.

He sipped at his coffee and lit another cigarette as he contemplated his next step. Crawford would undoubtedly expect action but that was easier said than done; Williams could hardly walk up to Connolly House, Sinn Fein's headquarters, and ask if a complete PIRA brigade had been wiped out in 1979. Documentary evidence simply didn't exist, so the best he could hope for was some corroborative details that, on the face of it, had little or nothing to do with events in late March '79. Newspaper archives seemed to be his best bet and the best specific collection resided in the political archive held by the Linenhall Library in Belfast.

Taken as a whole the class was performing well, some members better than others but Kavanagh was pleased with their progress. The one difficulty was not so much a lack of ability as one of a lack of instructors; he'd hoped to be making faster progress but as a one-man-band he had to be satisfied with the standard they had achieved. That said he was a little annoyed that he hadn't been able to move them onto the use of the holster, so with a degree of disappointment he called a halt for lunch at twelve-thirty, giving the class the chance to wind down and him the opportunity to check through the Len Dixon holsters that he had left in the armoury that morning. By the time he dismissed the class Jimmy Curtis had also gone for lunch which left Kavanagh on his own as he examined the eight rigs. The Dixon model 55s were all at least fifteen years old but they were in good order. Those individuals who had had possession over the years had listened to their instructors and taken care of the rigs. There was certainly the odd scuff mark on the leather but the stitching was uniformly in good order and the belt-loops showed no evidence of stretching that would lead to slippage on the belt with potentially fatal consequences.

He was looking at the interior of each holster to see if there was any evidence of wear and tear when the class members began to arrive back from lunch. They quietly formed up in the armoury waiting for Kavanagh to issue them with instructions. He put the last of the model 55s back on the bench and turned to face his students.

"I hope you're all well fed and watered gentlemen?"

There were nods of assent throughout the group.

"Good. Well, you've all made reasonable progress so I believe it's time to move you on to carry in and the draw from the holster. I want to fit each of you individually before we go out onto the range and that will take a little time so you'll have to bear with me. If you haven't got your belts on now would be a good time to get them."

Kavanagh went from man to man and fitted the holsters to each of the assorted inch and a half belts that they had brought with them. Not surprisingly not one of them was really appropriate – not even Robertson's fancy Galco came up to Kavanagh's exacting standards.

"You'll all have to get a proper belt. Not one of the things you've brought comes close; none of them have the necessary strength and rigidity. Here, take a look at this."

He passed Maxwell the belt that had been sitting on the bench.

"Now that's a special order from a friend of mine up north and as you can see it's very different from anything you have. That's the sort of belt that you need – something that gives your holster something to hold onto. I leave it up to you to acquire the right sort of kit when you finish the course. OK let's get started."

Weapons were issued and loaded magazines distributed before they moved out to the range. As he watched the men file out of the armoury one thing impressed Kavanagh and that was the fact that they had all paid attention and no-one, not even Robertson, had questioned a word he had said – there was definite hope to be had for this class.

It was nearly five o'clock by the time Crawford managed to get to the flat in Holland Park Mews from Gatwick. His mind had been occupied with only one thing all the way from Belfast, and no matter what excuses he had made about his disclosure he could take no comfort from his actions. There was no certainty regarding the outcome and that was something he craved more than anything else. He had put his trust in a man he did not know – only time would tell if that trust was well placed.

He had dropped his bag in the hall and brought a glass from the kitchen to the lounge where he had poured himself a large Hennessy. He now sat with his drink and tried to empty his mind to the strains of Bach's Partita No. 2, but the music of the violin only reminded him of how very much alone he was. With the acceptance of his solitary way of life came more questions, principally what was he going to do in the aftermath of his revelation – it wasn't that he had given it no consideration but the most important thing had been to make it – now the possible consequences made their presence felt and none of them were particularly comforting. Yet even the worst of them didn't give him cause for regret, after all any punitive action against him would be an admission and his former masters couldn't afford to admit to the truth of his story. Certainly he would be a great cause of irritation but it would probably be little more than a nine days wonder. That in itself saddened him but he wasn't conceited enough to exaggerate the long-term importance of his disclosure, in reality all that mattered was that the truth be in the public domain. It would be for the public to make something or nothing of the events in South Armagh. He had done his part and it remained to be seen if they would come up to his expectations.

Williams had spent a frustrating afternoon getting clearance to use the archive on the third floor of the Linenhall Library. He'd made a call to the archive custodian in the morning hoping that it would be nothing but a formality for him to gain access. Sadly this was not the case – the rules had changed and he needed a letter of endorsement for research purposes. Initially he thought that his freelance status would prove adequate but he had been informed that research on a commissioned basis was preferred, therefore an official communication seemed necessary.

Knowing the habits of his fellow journalists all too well he knew it was pointless to make calls at lunchtime so he had made himself a sandwich and coffee. Nothing of any great moment was happening in the world but the one o'clock news had helped pass the time. He had waited for an hour before returning to the task of gaining clearance. He had looked through his contact numbers hoping that he would find a name he could attach a favour to. He'd called a couple of the most likely people only to be disappointed – everyone was seemingly out on a job and wouldn't be available for several days at least. It wasn't proving as easy as he'd hoped. Eventually, after being kept on hold for ages, he'd managed to speak to a magazine editor who'd published a series of articles Williams had written about drug smuggling. After the usual "How are yous" and "What have you been up tos" he was able to ask for the favour. Happily this provided no difficulties, all the editor asked for was first refusal on the resultant piece. Williams accepted without question and was told that a letter would be dispatched stating that he had been commissioned to write an article that required the services of the Northern Ireland Political Archive. He was in. All he had to do now was prepare some brief notes that would detail the barest bones of the story Crawford had told and then see what the newspaper cuttings would or wouldn't tell him to hopefully add some flesh to the skeleton.

The afternoon had progressed smoothly with the whole class of eight quickly coming to terms with the physical change of drawing a weapon from the holster. Initially there had been a few hang-ups with pistols being held tight in the rigs which made draws anything but swift. Fortunately continuous use softened the contours of the model 55s a bit and the Hi-Powers began to come out of the holsters with reasonable speed. Kavanagh was at pains to tell his class that speed was not of the utmost importance, not at the moment anyway, and that it was more desirable to get the draw right.

Kavanagh had a surprise in store for his class at the end of the day's instruction; he could see that some of the men were beginning to wind down as their minds drifted towards the canteen and dinner so he gave them something else to think about.

"Gentlemen, I think we can call it quits for the day, on the range at least, but I want you to take your pistols with you."

There were questioning looks from the men.

"I can see that you are a bit concerned at this prospect but let me remind you that you are here to learn the use of the pistol and part of the lesson is to become familiar with carrying a weapon. Remember I said carrying; you'll be wearing the pistols at all times but I don't want to hear about anyone playing with them. Get used to the weapon being on your person but leave the handling for the range."

Robertson put his hand up to attract Kavanagh's attention; it was clear that he had become the unofficial spokesman for the class even though he had got off to a bad start.

"Mr. Kavanagh, are we to unload our pistols before we take them off the range?"

Kavanagh could see the point of the question – it was one thing to have a weapon on a range under controlled circumstances another entirely to be walking around in public with it.

"Now what would be the point of that? No, you will be carrying the weapons with a fully loaded magazine, condition three, and for those of you who have forgotten that means hammer down on an empty chamber. If anybody shows up tomorrow with their pistol in any other condition I'll crucify him."

With the training over for that day the class filed into the armoury where they unloaded their pistols and made safe before reloading with a full magazine. Some of the group looked far from happy as they prepared to leave for dinner. Kavanagh looked at the obvious concern etched on their faces but knew that they would have to learn.

"You'll get used to it, just don't ever get complacent."

The resigned shrugs that some of them gave showed that his words were of scant comfort but they were better than nothing.

Bach had been replaced by Rachmaninov and the brandy glass had been refilled several times while Crawford sat overcome by a self-indulgent melancholia. He had spent the evening examining his life in minute detail, from his decision to enter the army to his subsequent career in private security. The failures far outweighed the successes as he saw it – fifty-one years of age and nothing to show for his efforts – what kind of life did that add up to? Not one that he was proud of, that was for sure. His better judgement had been replaced by an alcohol sustained self pity which justified his present actions. A certain logic explained why he had behaved the way he had – the expediency of the whole sorry mess that he saw happening in Northern Ireland – the spineless behaviour of the politicians and the acquiescence of the soldiers – all these things excused him. He was right and nothing could remove that conviction, even the fact that it brought him no comfort.

The sense of being alone returned and Crawford surrendered to self-righteous indignation – everyone else was wrong – only he was right – no matter what the consequences he would have his say. He poured one last drink and tried to blank out the evening's conclusions about his own shortcomings. He gave his full attention to the music but found no release there. He looked around the room, at the small collection of personal effects that gave the flat its personality and found it sorely lacking. He could find no evidence in the room to show his positive affect. A new thought managed to raise itself above the morass of doubt and reproach and if anything it was more uncomfortable to live with – if he had been careless and done nothing – if he had been thoughtless – if he had not been consumed by a sense of guilt – if he had been none of these things then he wouldn't be in the mess he was in now. The realisation came to him that it was only he who was responsible for his actions and no-one else, and now more than ever, with no-one else to blame he felt truly alone.

* * *

Williams stood in the kitchen, mug of coffee in one hand and a cigarette in the other. The first post of the day had not brought the promised letter from his editor friend but in reality he hadn't expected it, not until tomorrow anyway. Nonetheless his patience was suffering as a result; after his success in securing the letter of introduction he had spent the evening making notes about the Mullan case. Now he had nothing to do other than speculate on what he would or wouldn't find in the archive and in truth he knew that such activity was pointless. He thought of listening to Crawford's tape once more but decided against it. He couldn't settle on anything and therefore did what he had invariably done in similar circumstances – he left the terrace on Pretoria Street and walked up to the newsagents on Stranmillis Road and bought copies of all the broadsheet newspapers and the better quality tabloids as well. On his return to the house he began reading, hoping and, to a greater degree, succeeding in putting Crawford and the archive job to one side.

The first thing Kavanagh did when the class assembled on the range that morning was to inspect their pistols. Happily they were all in the condition that they had left in yesterday but realistically he hadn't expected anybody to be stupid enough to leave a round chambered even if they had been mucking about.

"No crucifixions today, you'll be glad to hear. Mr. Maxwell, tell me, as you are one of the gentlemen without the benefit of regimental service, how did you find carrying the Hi-Power away from the range?"

"I didn't like it."

"And you aren't meant to. All of you, remember what Maxwell said and don't ever get to liking the feeling. If you do that you'll get careless and if you get careless you'll only do it once."

He looked around the faces and saw that his words had produced the desired result; it was always a concern – would some member of the class adopt a macho attitude to weapons? From what he saw he had no "wannabes" on his hands and that was good. Being capable out of necessity was one thing but actively pursuing the opportunity was at best foolhardy; Kavanagh didn't like heroes but then there were a lot of types he didn't care for.

"OK gentlemen, now that that's settled we can move on to the next practice. Let's see what difference a little movement makes to your shot placement."

It was lunchtime before Crawford surfaced. Somehow he'd managed to make his way to bed and he'd been lucky enough to have had an uninterrupted night's sleep. That, however, was the only good news – the hangover was just terrible – when he stumbled into the bathroom and saw his bleary eyed reflection in the medicine cabinet mirror it looked awful – and worst of all the doubts and fears from the night before hadn't diminished one bit. The hard lesson that he had to accept was that drink was not going to make his problems go away, no matter how much he would have liked it to.

After a shower, which did little to clear his head, and breakfast, which did nothing to settle his stomach, Crawford sat in the kitchen wondering what to do. Thankfully he was clear from work until tomorrow, because even freshly shaved and well dressed he couldn't disguise the fact that he was looking far from his usual self – a boozed up security consultant wouldn't inspire confidence in anybody. He had to do something though, even if it was only menial; he knew that another day contemplating the situation, second guessing the actions of others and reviewing his own, would only lead to another destructive bout with the brandy bottle. There was nothing to tempt him out of the flat so he settled on menial. He began with the mindless task of cleaning every piece of china he possessed – the repetitive nature of the task was surprisingly relaxing and with that came a calmer state of mind. When he finished the china he moved on to cutlery and then pots and pans and the day passed by without him once indulging in the negativity that had nearly claimed him yesterday.

"No, you're swinging your arm as you turn, that's why you're pulling your shots left."

"But...."

"But nothing. Look I've been doing this a hell of a lot longer than you, so if I say you're swinging your arm then that's what you're doing."

Kavanagh was indicating the hits on the five targets that had made up the practice for the last of the second group of four, a young man by the name of Fielding, another of the chosen ones from the SIS. As he had been walking from left to right his abrupt quarter turn to the left had in effect thrown his gun hand, his right hand, across the target as he'd engaged it. The result was that he'd either missed the target altogether or he'd made hits on the periphery of the left-hand side. Although he didn't say it Kavanagh was in fact pleased at the hits that Fielding had made; he was in truth one of the weaker links in the class and thus far had been the slowest student to get a grasp of the basic principles of instinctive shooting, but he would still have to do better.

"OK Mr. Fielding, we're going to try again, only this time I want you to keep the pistol locked into the centre-line of your body and I want you to keep it in the firing position. It may seem a bit awkward and artificial but I want you to get the feel of making good hits and the position that you have to be in. Right let's go again, and the rest of you keep a close eye on proceedings because I'll be asking questions afterwards."

Fielding moved forward and on Kavanagh's command he turned to his left and fired a two round burst. Kavanagh was right, the practice had taken on a distinctly awkward appearance, yet when he had finished on all five targets Fielding had two holes on each and most of them were centre-line hits.

"Big improvement Mr. Fielding. Now I want you to remember how that felt and I want you to go again, this time drawing from the holster and trying to keep your position. Do you think you can do that?"

"I think so."

"Good man. Well let's see it."

Fielding went through the practice again and it was quite obvious when he followed Kavanagh's instruction and when he didn't; when he did the hits were in the middle of the target and when he didn't he either missed entirely or put them on the left-hand side. As he looked at the results the disappointment that showed on his face was clear for all to see. As Fielding patched out the target Kavanagh turned to the rest of the class.

"Mr. Maxwell why did he miss?"

"His turn was too fast and he swung his pistol across the target making him miss or put the rounds on the left."

"You're half right. The speed of the turn is irrelevant if he remembers to keep the pistol centre-line. It's a simple case of anatomy – if you turn your whole body to face a target and look at it then your eyes are facing straight ahead – you will be keeping the pistol fixed on your own centre-line which lies between your eyes – so in effect, if you're facing a target and looking at it with your pistol centre-line and you then open fire, at this range, you'll hit the target. Simple, but it takes practice. Any questions?"

Again Robertson took it upon himself to act as unofficial spokesman and raised a hand.

"Mr. Robertson, what can I do for you?"

"You mentioned range. I was thinking that with the hand positions that you've been teaching us, well, the range for this sort of thing must be pretty limited."

"It is pretty limited Mr. Robertson, but then so is the range of the average gunfight. With handguns you're looking at twelve feet or less and what I'm teaching covers you out to five or six yards."

"What if they're further away than that?"

"Then you will use a quick aimed shot and you will be taught that in the next few days."

While it certainly passed the time, Williams found the hyperbole of some of the so-called journalists writing in the nationals hard to stomach. The masses, God help them, took these people at their word and formed opinions based on the distorted views of a few hacks. He considered his opinion of his fellow writers and smiled – with an outlook such as his it was small wonder that he was a freelance – he knew he'd never have survived at a paper for very long – his colleagues would have killed him. In fact, he had tried stringing for a while at Reuters but had found little satisfaction in that – he'd wanted to write the big story and he had never got the opportunity picking through snippets of information which were subsequently passed along to established journalists before he'd got the chance to make something of them anyway – no, all in all, he was better off freelancing.

Of all the stories carried in the papers the one he regarded with most disdain was the optimism displayed over the award of the Nobel Peace Prize. He had taken a cynic's perspective at news of the award and that view had been reinforced by Crawford's disclosure. The award in itself wasn't necessarily objectionable but the hypocrisy surrounding the events leading up to it was a different story. Williams was aware that he was in danger of becoming a crusader – prove Crawford's story – expose the lies – slay the dragon – win the girl. He'd seen people turn into zealots before with that wild-eyed "you've got to believe me because it's true" attitude and he wasn't prepared to go the same way. No, he was purely in this game for the money and there was definitely money in this story if the research didn't disprove it.

Kavanagh found Jimmy Curtis sitting in the dining room reading a training manual as he finished the coffee that concluded his evening meal. As he took a seat he saw the first members of the class file in for their dinner; they all looked anything but relaxed – whether they realised it or not the day's training was replaying itself through their minds. Another detail that he picked up was the fact that they were all carrying their Hi-Powers – another reason for their obvious discomfort. Curtis put down his book and gestured towards the young men as they sat down.

"If the boss hears about those chaps carrying away from the range he'll do two things Sean."

"And they are?"

"One; he'll flip his lid. Two; he'll have your head on a stick."

"Do I look worried?"

"Not particularly, but I've got news for you, you should be."

"Oh Sweet Jesus. How am I to teach the course if I don't get them carrying?"

"I know, I know, but he's a new broom and he intends to make a clean sweep."

"Then why keep this section of the training curriculum? For Christ's sake Jimmy, these lads may be out in the field and need to know what I'm telling them."

"You don't have to convert me, I know you're right. All I'm saying is that subtlety may be the order of the day."

"I know what you mean, but I'm not going to be lectured to by the likes of him. My course and my schedule."

"I don't like it any more than you do, but nothing's happened yet, maybe I shouldn't have mentioned it."

"Balls to that Jimmy, forewarned is forearmed. Anyway, let's not dwell on this, what's for dinner?"

"The fish isn't good tonight as I was told, so I had the chicken, which was pretty reasonable."

"Chicken it is then. I'll be back in a minute."

Kavanagh got up from the table and joined the short queue at the canteen servery. It hadn't always been like this, there used to be waiter service in the dining-room, the thought of which led him back to new brooms and cost cutting. As he made his way back to Curtis he concluded that change for the sake of it was a bad thing.

* * *

Williams had made the mistake of getting up early in anticipation of the post and when it hadn't arrived on time he had sat watching the minute hand on his mantle clock moving with what appeared to be incredible slowness. He thought of repeating yesterday's tactic of reading through the papers but the prospect of reading page upon page of journalese didn't enthuse him. The one thing that occurred to him was to contact Beatty to let him know that contact had been made and that a story was a possibility. He retrieved his personal directory and looked for the mobile number Beatty had given him. His first attempt was unsuccessful with an engaged signal but after several pushes of the redial button Williams was rewarded with a ringing tone. His call was answered on the third ring.

"Staff Beatty."

"Dave, it's Alain Williams."

"What can I do for you?"

"No, it's not a request, I just wanted to let you know that your friend Crawford has made contact."

"That's good. I hope that the story was worth your while."

The dismissive tone of voice intrigued Williams – what sort of story did Beatty think Crawford had to tell?

"Oh I think it will prove lucrative."

"So which of Crawford's charges is screwing who?"

Now he really was intrigued.

"It's not that kind of story Dave."

"From what he told me it was a celebrity piece. So what is it?"

Crawford had clearly not given Beatty the details of what he had in mind and Williams was now feeling unsure of how to break the news.

"He really didn't tell you?"

"Like I said he made it sound like some sort of kiss and tell. If it isn't that, what's he told you?"

"It's something of an old war story and…."

"So what's in it for you?"

"Well, it's…."

"Don't bullshit me Williams. What's he told you?"

He could see that Beatty would spot any attempt at subterfuge so he came clean.

"Crawford told me about a secret operation in South Armagh in March of 1979."

"What was the operation?"

"It was the complete annihilation of a full Provo Brigade."

"And who carried out this operation?"

"It was a mixed special forces team, mostly 22, but it was controlled by something I've never heard of before, something called the "Department". It's a hell of a story Dave."

"And if you want my opinion that's all it is. I'm surprised that a professional like you would be suckered in by a lot of nonsense like this."

"It's worth checking out."

"You're wasting your time. There is no story Alain."

Beatty had moved from "Williams" to "Alain", from ordering to cajoling; something was up.

"Are you warning me off Dave?"

"Not at all Alain. It's just that I know Gerry Crawford and he's feeding you a line."

"It doesn't look that way to me. There's too much detail Dave, it's all too plausible."

"Have it your own way but I'm telling you Crawford is having you on. There's no way that a story like this could be kept quiet, no way at all."

"We'll see. I'm going to check this one out anyway."

"Well I wish you luck because you're going to need it."

The connection was broken at Beatty's end leaving Williams with a new set of unanswered questions – why was Beatty behaving as he had? – was there something in Crawford's story? – was he being warned off? As he sat wondering about the conversation with Beatty the sound of envelopes landing on the hall carpet came through to the lounge. When he had separated the usual junk from the post that counted he was pleased to see the letter he had been waiting for. He'd be down at the Linenhall Library later today, he was in business.

A very nervous Beatty replayed the exchange with Williams but no matter what favourable gloss he tried to place on it the conclusion was always the same – there was definite trouble ahead and he didn't want to be caught in the middle. This was not how he had expected his Thursday morning to be; he was back in Aldershot drumming his heels with nothing to worry about and now the bloody journalist had called to serve him up with a king-sized disaster. It never occurred to him that it had been his quickness to believe a sob story from Crawford and his willingness to provide Williams's name that had brought matters to a head. All that concerned him was that he should look as blameless as possible. Wishing it and making it so were two entirely different things and what troubled Beatty was the best course of action. He initially thought of doing nothing – the story was nearly twenty years old so who would really care – maybe it was best to keep his head down and let the fallout pass him by. Attractive as that was he knew that it wouldn't take somebody long to add two and two and make four. Williams had mentioned the "Department" and for its very existence to come into the public domain was unacceptable. He would have to call Leinster Gardens and explain what had happened.

A curt order from the Director Training was delivered to Kavanagh as he sat at breakfast. The brief note called for his immediate presence so he took his time, enjoying a second cup of coffee and even taking the time to give instructions to his class concerning the necessity of cleaning their weapons in preparation for the day. When he felt he had made his point about orders from civilians he walked over to the administration building and instead of waiting for the secretary to announce him walked straight into the Director's office. The SIS man attempted the same tactic of addressing his paperwork before condescending to talk to Kavanagh but it wasn't going to work this time.

"I don't appreciate little notes at breakfast. If you want to see me either do it in person or have a subordinate make the request."

The audacity of Kavanagh's approach brought colour to the Director's face but with a credible effort he managed to keep his tone even.

"You have a very high opinion of yourself Mr. Kavanagh."

"That's as maybe, but what's for sure is that I'm here to do a job and you're stopping me, so what's this all about?"

"What this is all about is the fact that you've seen fit to turn a group of untrained men loose with firearms."

"And?"

"And I will not have my authority usurped by anyone, not even you."

"With all due respect, how in God's name do you expect me to train these men if I'm not allowed autonomy for fear of upsetting someone?"

"Just remember who you're talking to."

"How could I forget."

"One more comment like that and you are…."

"Spare me the rhetoric. If you wanted rid of me you'd have done it already. I've got work to do and doubtless you've got calls to make of which I'm sure to hear the results. In the meantime I bid you good day."

The Directors face was by now purple and Kavanagh considered the possibility of a heart attack as he left the office and made his way back to the range.

The single-decker Citybus made its final stop in Wellington Place leaving Williams a walk of less than a hundred yards to Donegall Square North and the entrance to the Linenhall Library. He pushed the well-used front-door open and stopped at the security desk to show his library card; he had never used the Linenhall much in the past but membership had its uses. With that formality dealt with he made his way up the steep stone steps to the first floor and then up the sweeping wooden staircase to the second floor where he talked with one of the librarians and signed in the archive attendance register after his *bona fides* had been established. The librarian made a call to the archive and Williams was told that someone would be down shortly to guide him up to the third floor. He took a seat and reflected on the apparent secrecy, the hushed tones and the fact that the archivists were probably part mountain goat what with all the stairs they had to negotiate.

After about five minutes his guide arrived, and Williams had to dismiss all the notions he had had with regard to bookish, dried-up librarians. The assistant archivist was young, blonde and very talkative, so much so that Williams found it hard to keep pace with all her questions as they made their way through the reference collection and then up the back stairs to the attic space that housed the Northern Ireland Political Archive.

"As you can see we're a bit limited when it comes to space but you'll doubtless make yourself at home."

There were only four seats available at a bench with a computer keyboard and

VDU positioned at one end. Williams hung his jacket over the chair nearest the computer terminal and placed his soft briefcase on the desk.

"What records have you got on the computer?"

"It's not complete by a long chalk but there's a lot of the Northern Ireland Office stuff on the hard-drive. Otherwise it will be a case of ploughing through the paper archive. Everything you see on the shelves is open to access, but if you can't find something just ask – that's what I'm here for."

"Well now that you mention it where do I find the back issues for local newspapers?"

"Could you be a bit more specific?"

"Any of the Armagh papers March, April and May 1979."

"I'll show you."

Williams spent the rest of the afternoon examining microfiche reproductions of the relevant copies of the Armagh Observer, Down Recorder, The Examiner and *An Phoblacht*. The only direct detail that corroborated Crawford's story was the report he found in the Armagh Observer concerning the fire at the Mullan farm. The story covered the "mysterious" aspects of the fire, the fact that no-one was in residence, the fact that there was no obvious cause. Yet it wasn't so much what the article said that interested Williams, it was the fact that there was no follow up, the "mysterious" fire was covered and there it ended. If nothing else it showed a lamentable lack of curiosity. He read through every copy of the Armagh Observer covering the period up until the end of May and found no further reference to the fire.

He turned his attention to the other local papers and found no material whatsoever that referred to the fire. He went back to the Observer and began looking for stories that, while not obviously connected, showed certain links to the fundamental change in the power structure along the Armagh border. Nothing really sparked his interest except a story in *An Phoblacht* from the third April issue which gave a thinly veiled warning from the Provisionals to the INLA, to the effect that any attempts to usurp control of South Armagh would result in serious "military repercussions". There had obviously been difficulties locally – Williams considered the possibility that it was merely sour grapes because of the INLA success with the Neave murder but dismissed this as being too flimsy a reason – what seemed more likely to him was that the PIRA was stamping its authority on the area hoping that nobody would realise just how weak it really was. He knew there was a danger in making connections where they didn't exist but the story of the Mullan farmhouse raid was too big to be ignored without proper research. If he had to join the dots then he only hoped that the picture he drew was believable.

Dave Beatty had sat in the office he'd been allocated on the base in Aldershot all morning and right through lunch deliberating the situation that Williams had outlined to him. He reckoned that he'd covered every angle and their possible outcomes should the "Department" decide to act. All had the potential to damage him personally but he'd settled on being honest, to a degree anyway, and to that end he now sat at his desk listening to the ringing tone of the telephone. He didn't have to wait long for an answer as a cautious female voice came on line.

"Hello."

"Good afternoon. This is Dave Beatty. I'd like a word with Mr. Blackwell, if he's available, please."

"I'll just see if he's in the office."

He was placed in limbo on hold as the secretary began the charade of checking for Blackwell – of course he was in the bloody office – the whole act was simply another way of making people uncomfortable as they waited to speak to the head of the "Department". A minute passed before her voice came back on the line.

"Mr. Blackwell is very busy but he'll speak to you briefly, I'll just put you through."

Another tactic – make Blackwell sound important and instill a sense of gratitude in anyone contacting him – another way of putting people on the back foot. The problem was, Beatty had to admit, that it worked – so much so that he was completely thrown off guard when Blackwell spoke.

"Mr. Beatty, it's been a while, this office has had no word from you since the Stevens business I believe. What can I do for you?"

Old memories of a previous disinformation job interrupted Beatty's train of thought and he was lost for words, barely managing an acknowledgement.

"For goodness sake man, spit it out, I haven't got all day."

"I'm sorry sir. I was rehearsing my best approach for delivery and I couldn't really come up with one."

"It might be best if you just keep to the facts."

"Yes sir. Well then, we have a problem."

"And what might that be, pray tell."

"The results of an old job have come back to haunt us – Gerry Crawford, you may be familiar with the name, has decided to spill the beans on the South Armagh raid in March of '79."

"He's what?"

"He's given the story, chapter and verse, to a journalist."

"Sweet Jesus!"

Now it was Beatty's turn to listen to an uncomfortable silence as Blackwell tried to collect his thoughts. When the man came back on line the patronising smugness was all gone.

"I want when and where and most importantly who. After that you can tell me how you managed to get wind of this particular nugget before we did. I'm taping this so begin."

"He had a meeting sometime on Monday evening in Belfast. I'm not sure of the location but the journalist's name is Alain Williams, that's Alain, A-L-A-I-N."

"Who does he work for?"

"He's a freelance."

"And how do you know about this?"

"I gave Crawford his name because he might…."

"You did what? Christ Almighty! You fucking idiot!"

"Sir, I didn't know what Crawford had in mind – he met me last week and he looked down on his luck…."

"And you like a good Samaritan gave him a contact name."

"He looked like he needed the money…."

"Oh, he'll get money all right for this one. A body count like this and an organisation that doesn't exist running the show? Yes, I should think any newspaper would love the chance to run this story."

"I didn't think he had this sort of thing…."

"Correct, you didn't think."

"Look I'm sorry this has happened but after all I didn't have to come to you with this."

"Don't come all indignant with me Beatty. This mess is of your making, the only good thing about it is that you were involved in the first place."

"Well, I thought that I could bring this information to you and it would give you the opportunity to clear up any problems before they arose."

"Almost smart, but not quite. If you'd really thought that, you'd have contacted me as soon as Crawford spoke to you regardless of the apparent direction he was moving in. No, the truth is you made a real hash of things and tried to make amends by telling me."

"I only did what I thought was right, sir, and I'm sorry for the trouble I've caused."

"Not as sorry as you will be if this gets plastered all over the front pages of the national press."

"Sir, I'll do anything to help."

"You've done enough already. No, you just sit tight in Aldershot and pray that the problem can be solved. Thanks to you I've really got some work to do."

Without any attempt at social niceties Blackwell hung up and Beatty was left under no illusions that his potential troubles were of huge proportions. He could only hope and pray that he'd done the right thing by contacting Blackwell, but the "Department" wasn't famous for its forgiving nature. Only time would tell if he would suffer for his actions, but still, he had to consider just how much worse it would have been if he had kept his mouth shut and been found out anyway.

Blackwell was finding it hard to get over the stupidity of Beatty's behaviour. The whole ethos of the "Department" was based on discretion, putting it bluntly "keep your bloody mouth shut". Yet, here was Beatty, who should have known better, giving information to a suspect figure like Crawford. The only saving grace was the fact that he had volunteered the details before the situation was critical.

First things first, he would need full background biographies on Crawford and Williams. In the time it would take for that information to be accumulated he would have time to plan the best form of action to deal with the problem. What that might be he had no idea at present. He had already reached one conclusion however, for good or ill, he was going to keep this an "in house" job so to speak.

Crawford's first day at work that week had been not so much a waste of time as uneventful. No new work had come into the office during his absence but rosters for the Hanson security job were only partly drawn so he gave his attention to their completion. He'd spent the day going through personnel lists, checking the suitability of his staff for the warehouse security detail. He knew it wouldn't be the most exciting job but he made sure that nobody would be bored rigid, boredom bred complacency and that led to expensive mistakes. One thing had to be said in favour of Hanson's acceptance of the original terms – the money was good – and that should mean a professional and secure result.

By late afternoon he was happy with the manpower schedule he had drawn up; none of his personnel had to come off existing jobs, the short-term Docklands contract had just ended so he was able the juggle staff with no great difficulty, and most important of all the necessary expertise for the installation of the electronics package was available. Everything was now timetabled and he was satisfied that the whole job could be started next week; all that remained was for the men to be informed of their new duties and a final word to the Hanson people to say that coverage would begin next Monday.

By the time he'd negotiated the rush-hour on the Underground it was after six-thirty when he opened the door to his flat. It was only when he saw the flashing red light which indicated a message on his answering machine that he gave any thought to his business with Williams. He marvelled at the fact that he'd got through a day's work without once succumbing to the temptation of losing himself in speculation. As he pressed the "play" button all manner of possibilities crowded his mind but it came as something of a disappointment when the message turned out to be nothing more than an advertisement for double glazing. He erased the message and went through to the kitchen to prepare a light dinner. All he could think of was the phone call he expected from Williams and the hoped for response.

He went through the motions of preparing a meal but by the time it was ready his appetite had left him. He sat at the kitchen table, his Spanish omelette forgotten, and looked at the bottle of Hennessy that sat on the work top. It would be all too easy to pour a glass and try to forget the mess that he'd got himself into. The temptation almost proved too much for him, but just as he got up to get a glass, he remembered the sad failures from his army days who had hit the bottle when their marriages had fallen apart, and he realised that he wouldn't find solutions or escape at the bottom of a glass.

* * *

Blackwell had uncharacteristically spent the night at the Gardens, normally he made a point of going home, but Beatty's call had left him with a thorny problem and some background reading. Not surprisingly he had found nothing in the files covering the year of 1979 – Lynch had been too careful to leave any evidence of the Mullan farmhouse assault – but there had been copies of the personnel files on both Crawford and Beatty. He'd never met Crawford even though there had been a brief period of contiguous service but the file gave a rounded appraisal of the man that indicated potential for difficulties based on Crawford's free-thinking character, something that had made him an extremely useful individual operator but far from a team player.

Beatty on the other hand had shown himself to be malleable but limited by a lack of imagination. It was this lack of imagination that had been his downfall; he'd seen an opportunity to make some money from, as he saw it, cleverly defrauding a "Department" account. The only thing clever about his little scam had been the fact that he had been stealing money from an organisation that didn't officially exist, so any sanctions taken against him would be strictly unofficial. Those sanctions were still in place so at least Blackwell didn't have to worry about Beatty having a sudden attack of conscience leading to a press disclosure. But that was small comfort – how best to deal with Crawford?

He picked up Crawford's file again, hoping to find a possible answer in the section covering his present career in private security. The firm had been established in the late sixties by former Intelligence Corps people. Crawford had come along in the mid eighties and had used his savings to buy in to what was a stable business. With an injection of capital and his fresh ideas the firm had prospered taking on new personnel and some very lucrative contracts. There had been one approach from the "Department", asking for assistance in a surveillance job which had been politely rejected. The "Department" was not in the habit of asking twice, but there had been no direct evidence linking Crawford to the refusal so he had not been blackballed personally. After the initial approach interest in Crawford and his firm was strictly a matter of housekeeping. Nothing in the recent entries gave any possible leverage against Crawford – the man appeared a cipher.

Blackwell dismissed thoughts of appealing to Crawford's better nature almost as soon as they came to him; some sort of threat looked a much more likely option. The problem that he faced was finding an angle of attack – how could he threaten somebody as one dimensional as Crawford? He looked back at the file and checked the list of associates – maybe there would be an answer there. The list of names was short and most of them were long gone from the "Department", in fact the only one still serving other than Beatty was Sean Kavanagh; perhaps it would be productive to give him a call down at Monckton to see if he could offer any suggestions.

Kavanagh had expected a call from Blackwell yesterday after his *contretemps* with the director training, so it came as something of a surprise that he had had to wait until this morning. It came as even more of a surprise that the call had nothing to do with the feathers he had ruffled.

"….and I wondered if you had any ideas as to how we should best approach this problem?"

"To be honest sir I haven't seen Crawford in, well, it must be getting on for eight years. I'd need to know what he's been up to and have a full appraisal of his present circumstances before I'd make any call on the best way forward. It's funny though."

"What makes you say that?"

"I once told him that he was in the wrong job to be an idealist something he disagreed with at the time and here he is behaving like one."

"Well, his idealism could be bloody inconvenient."

"I think you might be over-estimating the impact that such a disclosure could make, if you don't mind me saying so sir. I mean politically, really who's going to believe Crawford's story in the first place?"

"Don't bloody patronise me, Kavanagh. For your information this "Department" will not stand any disloyalty and that is all that counts. If the politicians want to play games in Ireland they're welcome, but we keep our own house in order."

Kavanagh decided that an apology was called for, after all he needed Blackwell on his side when the director training called for his head.

"I'm sorry if I overstepped the mark sir. If I could have all the necessary material I'll provide you with my thoughts in due course."

"His file will be with you later today and I expect to hear from you within twenty-four hours, is that clear?"

"Absolutely sir. There is one thing, however, before you break lines."

"What is it?"

"A difference of opinion with the pacifist in charge down here."

"No doubt I'll hear about it. Leave it with me, Sean. Just be sure to give the file your full attention."

"Yes sir."

He replaced the handset but rather than return to his students on the range he sat at Curtis's desk in the armoury and went over the brief facts that Blackwell had given him. Try as he might he couldn't really fault Crawford for blowing the whistle; it had always been something of a surprise to him that no-one had done it before. There could be little doubt that Crawford's sense of honour was being insulted by present circumstances and it was that insult that had made him take the steps that he had. Kavanagh reflected on his own possible actions if he was in a similar position, but he knew that would never be the case – his only guiding principle was to look out for number one – a sense of honour looked, in this case anyway, to be far too expensive.

Three hours and not a thing to show for his efforts – reading newsprint from the microfiche monitor had begun to give him a headache. He leaned back from the desk and massaged his temples, quickly realising that he needed a break. He lifted his notes and made his way out of the archive, telling the librarian, as he left, that he would be back in about an hour. After leaving the Linenhall he had made his way to a coffee shop where he now sat with a large cup of very strong arabica and his usual Marlboro on the go. He scanned the brief scribbles in his notebook and saw that the lack of hard evidence to the contrary was making Crawford's story more than just a rather nasty possibility. He sipped his coffee and took a look around the other customers in the cafe; mostly shoppers taking a break from the travails of bargain hunting, if only they knew what he did. He reflected on the privileged position that he occupied as a journalist and realised that there were times when ignorance was preferable.

He returned to the details that made the thin covering story outlined in his notes – an internal Republican power struggle – the INLA success – the rise of Dominic McGlinchey within the INLA – his apparent command of the border area. Those facts might point to a lack of PIRA strength on the ground but it was too great a leap of faith to explain that weakness with Crawford's story; he needed something else, but what? He knew that the answer to that question did not lie at the bottom of a coffee cup, so he drank up and went back to the archive.

After another two hours of research he thought he had corroborative evidence that, while it didn't exactly prove the facts of the farmhouse raid, at least showed that there had been a change of personnel in the South Armagh Brigade. A speculative piece in the Belfast Telegraph from mid May talked about the arrival of a senior figure from the East Tyrone Brigade of the PIRA and how he was making sweeping changes in Armagh. The final warning in the piece was that the security forces were placing themselves on a higher state of alert due to the increased threat that this so-called "hard man" was bringing to the area. Williams re-read the article to be sure of the details – yes, it was all there. He started making a diagram that showed the way in which these facts could be joined together: the INLA make their presence felt – coincidentally South Armagh Brigade PIRA is wiped out – Provisionals issue a statement in *An Phoblacht* warning the INLA to back off – a "hard-man" from East Tyrone is sent in, and here was where he made a speculative judgement, to recruit and train new PIRA members. He looked at the flow-chart he had drawn and nodded in satisfaction – all the details fit. On Monday or Tuesday he would be able to contact Crawford and tell him that he was satisfied with the truth of his disclosure.

Crawford's day had been a busy one with the implementation of the personnel schedule that he had drawn up for the Hanson contract. He had to admit that it wasn't the most taxing of jobs but it was time consuming and with his present state of mind the distraction of overcoming the minor difficulties that always seemed to present themselves at the last minute was desirable. By three o'clock he was satisfied that the job could be started in all respects next Monday. He had just poured himself a cup of coffee when the phone rang; it was Maria to say that there was a

Mr. Beatty on the line and did he want to take the call. Crawford had expected to hear from him and was in fact surprised that it had taken so long. He told Maria to put Mr. Beatty through.

"Dave, what can I do for you?"

"Don't Dave me, you bastard!"

"OK, let's slow it down and try and keep things civil."

"I gave you Williams as a favour. I thought you were down on your luck. And now it turns out that you want to drop everyone in the shit."

"It's not like that. This is a matter of right."

"Oh you think so. Bollocks! This is about you turning into some sort of bleeding heart."

Crawford sensed that there was little hope of placating Beatty, so he fell back on attack, after all it was supposed to be the best form of defence.

"Dave you and I were both involved in some pretty shitty little jobs in our time...."

"Some of us still are, you self righteous bastard! Do you realise what could happen to me if this gets out?"

"Who have you told?"

"I'm not stupid. So far this is between you and me."

"So why don't we just keep it that way?"

"How the fuck do you expect this to remain quiet? Williams is positively drooling over this one and if previous experience is anything to go by he'll make the most of it."

"Well, you've obviously given this some thought, what do you suggest?"

"I don't fucking know. Jesus, is this ever a mess! Why did you do it Gerry, why?"

"Like I said, it's a matter of right."

"Easy for you to say. When Williams puts his story out it won't take long for the trail to lead back to me."

"Deny it."

"It's not that simple. I've used Williams before on orders – he comes up with a story like this and it won't take a genius to figure out where he got it from."

"It's old news Dave. It won't even make the front page."

"Williams told me that you gave him chapter and verse on the "Department", that's not old news."

"Who's going to believe it?"

"It doesn't matter what the masses think of this one – there'll be enough people in the community who'll be more than a little pissed off and it's them that I'm afraid of. I can't believe you've done this. Jesus, you're meant to be smart!"

"Nothing will come of this."

"So why tell it? Answer me that!"

He considered Beatty's question and in truth he couldn't think of an answer so instead he tried to gain a little time.

"Leave it with me Dave and I'll speak with Williams."

"And what fucking good'll that do? You flew to Belfast to tell him the story in the first place! Liars just don't do that kind of thing."

"I promise I'll sort something out."

"You'd better or we're both buggered and I tell you now I won't be long in passing on your details. Understand?"

"I understand. Just leave it with me."

"That's all very well, but get it sorted and quick."

Beatty broke lines and Crawford sat wondering where all the good work he'd done had gone. A couple of minutes on the telephone had destroyed the positive efforts of the last couple of days. All the successful attempts at distraction that he'd made had been shown to be pointless, Beatty had seen to that. How could he have deluded himself about the possible outcomes stemming from his actions? There was no escaping the ultimate responsibility for his predicament – it was simply his fault. He sat lost in thought for over an hour; he wasn't aware of how much time had passed until Maria came into the office to retrieve his coffee cup and to say that she hoped he had a good weekend. A good weekend? There seemed little prospect of that, he'd have his work cut out trying to decide his best way forward out of the dreadful tangle he'd created.

After leaving the Linenhall, Williams had gone straight home and begun putting flesh on the bones of the research he'd done. He looked through the transcript he'd made of Crawford's tape recording and inserted some of the information he'd acquired. By the time he'd completed his first draft the pack of cigarettes that he'd bought that morning was finished and with no smokes in the house he went up to the small Chinese owned store that seemed to cater for the student population of Stranmillis. With a new pack in hand he was able to sit back and read through the tale of March '79. He spent about twenty minutes applying as much objectivity as he could but with honest reflection there was something that even his enthusiasm couldn't bring to the narrative. He put the draft down and got up to make himself a coffee.

As he stood in the kitchen waiting for the kettle to boil he considered the impact of the piece; it certainly grabbed the attention but what worried him was the balance – there was plenty of detail concerning the job itself but virtually none when it came to the organisation that oversaw the commission. If he wanted to do the facts justice he'd have to get more information from Crawford and that meant that either Crawford would have to come back to Belfast or that he would have to go to London. He thought about contacting Crawford right away but dismissed the idea as it looked too keen; better to let matters lie for a few days by which time he'd be able to give Crawford a full draft of what he had in mind along with the questions he needed answers to. When that had been dealt with there could be some discussion on the necessity of travel. He hoped that Crawford would agree to return to Belfast, his finances were pretty tight at the moment and he wasn't sure if he could afford the flight to London; he hadn't lied when he'd said that a freelance's position was at times precarious. That would hopefully change with this story – some paper would undoubtedly want his services when the quality of his work became apparent.

"How did that feel Mr. Robertson?"

"The draw felt a bit awkward."

"Why?"

"It felt as if I fumbled the butt of the gun. I'm finding my jacket a bit of a distraction."

The class had progressed to drawing from concealment and it was to this that Robertson was referring. Kavanagh asked Robertson to re-holster his pistol and then took centre stage so he could address the whole class.

"Mr. Robertson has raised a point which concerns us all and that is how everyday clothing while it doesn't draw attention to us can and very often does get in the way. Watch."

With that he unbuttoned his jacket and showed the class how he swept it to one side as he moved his right hand towards the place that his pistol would have been. He returned to a relaxed standing position and repeated the action, this time making the movements with an exaggerated slowness clearly showing the manner in which his right hand pushed the jacket aside.

"Some people recommend having your jacket weighted at the hem so that it can be flicked open with a twist of the hips. Personally I wouldn't endorse that – in my view it upsets the balance and such a movement attracts the eye, anyway it affects the cut of your jacket. OK, I want you all to face off against a target and practice the draw, and for the meantime unload and do it dry."

Kavanagh watched as the men made their draws and offered such criticisms or words of encouragement as were necessary. There were a few miscues, accompanied with some softly spoken oaths but they were to be expected; it had been a long day and Kavanagh had worked them hard. After they'd spent about ten minutes drawing from concealment he called a halt and brought each man to the front of the range and had them engage a pair of targets as a final practice for the day. Robertson was the last man to come forward and Kavanagh watched with approval as the Hi-Power was drawn, loaded and made ready for the practice. In less than a week the movements were swift and expert, Robertson and the rest of the group, even the weakest of them, had reached a level of competence that pleased Kavanagh, for it not only spoke well of them as a class but of him as an instructor.

Kavanagh gave the order and Robertson moved his right hand to the centre of his body with his fingers spread. As his little finger made contact with his belt buckle he moved it to the right opening his jacket and allowing him to access the pistol that rode in the holster located on his right hip. The hand took a positive grip on the pistol and drew it from the holster, as it started to come level the thumb knocked off the safety catch and the last action Robertson made was to pull the trigger. After he'd placed two rounds on the first target he turned to his right and engaged the second with a further two rounds. With that the practice ended and Robertson reapplied the safety catch and re-holstered his pistol. He turned to face Kavanagh.

"So how did that feel this time?"

"Much better, I'd say good."

"Oh you would, would you?"

"I didn't mean to...."

"Shut up Mr. Robertson, for your information it was good. You've got four good hits, your hand speed was acceptable and you looked like you meant it."

"But I did mean it."

"Good. Then you've stopped thinking like a target shooter. And that goes for the rest of you – you're all starting to take this seriously. OK, you've worked well today, when you've cleared the range that'll do you."

The group split the tasks amongst themselves without any direction from Kavanagh – empty cases were swept up and binned, targets were taken off the frames and replaced with clean ones for the next day. The range was tidied in under ten minutes and the last man out of the facility turned off the lights leaving it clear by six-thirty.

Blackwell put down the file that had occupied his attention for most of the afternoon. He couldn't help but admire the clarity of thought shown in the document. The general outline for deniable operations and the reasons for their very existence and desirability had an incisiveness that any graduate of staff college would have felt proud to produce. When the outline became policy and was applied to operations in Northern Ireland it had yielded some notable successes, but none so notable as the raid on the Mullan farmhouse. Sadly, for good or ill, that success had proved to be the nail in the coffin for large scale takedowns. Never again would his organisation be involved in operations like it – it wasn't that such jobs had ceased in Ulster but the manpower had changed – Loughgall, for example, had been a "hooligan" job from start to finish. Spectacular body counts were the order of the day – something had to be seen to be done.

So much for that; now he found himself trying to cover up what had previously been a great success because the climate had changed, but that was only part of the truth, if he was being really honest he would have said that the primary reason for the cover up was the protection of the "Department". There were rules about discretion; Crawford had broken them and right and wrong didn't enter into it. The question was to what degree should he be punished? Blackwell pulled a pad of blank A4 paper to him and began a flow-chart by writing CRAWFORD at the centre of the page. This he followed with the consequences not only for Crawford but also for the "Department" should certain sanctions be applied. The diagram expanded and Blackwell found that further sheets of paper were required to include the host of possibilities. He spent over half an hour filling a total of five sheets with his tightly spaced block capitals and when he'd finished the conclusions were the same as his initial thoughts on hearing the bad news from Beatty – either ignore the disclosure and hope that there was no fall-out or nip it in the bud before it became a problem. He favoured the latter course of action but theory was one thing, practical application another entirely.

When Crawford got back to his flat he'd checked his answering machine hoping for a call from Williams. In the absence of such a contact he'd dialled the mobile number he'd been given only to be informed that "the Vodafone you have called may be switched off, please try again later". After that initial disappointment he tried to make contact every ten minutes for the next hour, and each time the call went unconnected his disappointment grew. He became more frustrated with every attempt, but not only that, his mind began inventing reasons for Williams being unobtainable. Each possibility seemed even more negative than the last and by nine o'clock as his frustration peaked his self-pity returned with a vengeance.

Crawford succumbed to a host of negative emotions, none more so than a sense of persecution. If he had only considered his position rationally he would have realised that his greatest difficulty was his solitude, but lacking anyone to voice his fears to, he sought solace in the one place guaranteed to numb those fears – the brandy bottle. As he poured his first drink he justified it with the thought that he deserved it – all the trials, real or imagined, that he faced were the fault of others and if he couldn't find support anywhere else then the bottle would just have to do. The strength that he'd managed to array against the temptation of drinking deserted him now. He looked at the glass and briefly thought about the contempt with which he regarded those former associates who had allowed drink to take control of their lives. He shook his head and took a drink quite secure in his feeling of natural superiority. The failures who had tried to disguise their shortcomings with alcohol had failed in their careers, their marriages, their responsibilities, everything! That wasn't him, he was different, but what he couldn't see was that he was running away from the consequences of his own actions, and it was that blindness to present reality that would make the discovery of a solution virtually impossible.

As the glass emptied any chance of rational thought disappeared; the only thing that he gave consideration to was his sense of right. He dredged up episodes from his past career that had called his judgement into play and at every memory he made another decision. With as much impartiality as he could muster he questioned his motivations and the consequences of his actions, and try as he might to put himself in the wrong, all he felt was vindicated. He let his feeling of persecution envelope him completely and he thought about the way he'd been changed by his actions within the "Department". He tried to look at his own character before he'd been inducted but he found it impossible to be sure of anything that far back so he turned his attention to the present. What had he done that was so wrong? Why should he be loyal to an organisation that showed no consistency? When had right become wrong? He couldn't answer any of these questions either and that failure returned him to his position of superiority and the men he viewed as inadequate. What gave him the right to feel better than anyone in the first place? Questions, questions, questions – he couldn't offer any answers to make them go away. The drinking wasn't helping – how could he have been stupid enough to think that it would? Another question – all the certainties had gone and now everything was mounting up against him or so it seemed.

He wasn't reaching any favourable conclusions and he felt the beginnings of a headache as the tension increased. He got up, leaving his drink unfinished, and walked down the hall to the bathroom. As he stood cleaning his teeth he looked at the reflection in the medicine cabinet mirror. A sad, confused face looked back at him and he could clearly see the great weariness that was dragging him down. He moved into his bedroom and after leaving his clothes in an untidy pile he climbed into bed and let the weariness take hold – in five minutes he was asleep.

* * *

The knock at Kavanagh's door was not unexpected but that didn't soften the impact of being disturbed at ten to seven. He'd just finished his morning shower so he was still wrapped in a towel and dripping wet when he opened the door. Blackwell had been good to his word and had Crawford's file sent down to "The Fort" by dispatch rider – the delivery was brought up by the leather clad biker who had made the early morning run from London. With the unnecessary efficiency that seemed to mark the day to day running of just about everything a signature was required as a declaration of receipt. With that formality settled the delivery man left, allowing Kavanagh to dry himself off and get changed. After he had laced up his shoes he lifted the file from the bed and as he had time on his hands took the opportunity to have a brief glance at it before going down for breakfast. He took the buff coloured file over to the small desk in front of the one window that overlooked the old parade ground and sat down.

In the manner of all "Department" files the most recent additions were at the front so Kavanagh began his search in the middle. It didn't take him long to locate the discharge papers that marked the end of Crawford's military career and the beginning of his life on civvy street – the life that was of most interest to Kavanagh. The details had been accrued methodically – Crawford's efforts and eventual success in becoming established in private security were meticulously documented as were his domestic moves that had seen him finally take up residence in Holland Park Mews. The mention of the prestigious West-end address caused Kavanagh to raise his eyebrows – there must be really good money in the security racket, even if Crawford was only leasing the flat. The overall picture was of a quietly successful man who gave the appearance of being the last person to be found grinding an axe.

Kavanagh glanced at his watch and seeing that it was just after eight put the file down so he could make a move to the dining room for breakfast. What he had seen of Crawford's life, post-army, led him to suspect that the disclosure could prove harder to deal with than he had originally thought. Clearly Crawford was not acting out of desperation, at least not financially, and made him potentially more dangerous – cool heads were less likely to make mistakes. For the meantime though he had sustenance to think of and then the class – Crawford could wait, but come the evening he would study the file start to finish and see if there was a simple solution to the problem of the "old man".

For the second night in succession Blackwell had slept at the Gardens, not so much by design, but rather, due to his having become immersed in the problem that was Crawford and his lack of discretion. He'd managed to get to bed at around two – there was now a bedroom for the Controller, things had moved on a bit from Lynch's day – and after a fitful night's sleep he found himself back at his desk using his electric razor to give himself a reasonably kempt appearance. With his shave finished and the razor back in the desk drawer, he was just about to go down to the canteen to see if he could get a bite to eat when the phone rang. He lifted the receiver and was given the good news by his secretary that the Director Training down at "The Fort" wanted a word. There was only one way to find out what was wanted so he accepted the call.

"Blackwell."

"Blackwell, this is Pelham. I don't know if you've spoken with your man Kavanagh or not and frankly I don't care. The truth of the matter...."

"Can I stop you there. Look, I spoke with him yesterday and he mentioned some sort of difficulty but he didn't go into specifics. What's he done?"

"Firstly, he has seen fit to let his training group wander around armed. Secondly, when I voiced my displeasure and told him that it was against my wishes he became, to say the least, insubordinate. What have you to say to that?"

"You do understand that he's at your establishment to run a firearms course?"

"Absolutely."

"Then I suggest that you let him get on with it."

"You shouldn't adopt that tone with me, Blackwell. You described "The Fort" as my establishment and as long as that is the case I will run it as I, and not somebody else, see fit."

Blackwell leaned back and shook his head in disbelief. God preserve the community from peaceniks like Pelham. He tried to be diplomatic.

"I understand Pelham, believe me, I do. Kavanagh can get up just about anybody's nose, but what you seem to have failed to grasp is that these men are going out in the field and the skills that Kavanagh is giving them could save their lives."

"I will not stand for insubordination."

"I know that, look I'll order him to make a full apology. Will that suffice?"

"It will do to begin with, but I don't want armed men walking around this facility."

Christ Almighty! Didn't the fool appreciate that national security relied on armed men? It was all he could do not to call Pelham a fucking idiot. He took a deep breath and continued with diplomacy.

"I understand your position, but I do feel that Kavanagh is correct in familiarising his group with carry techniques. I do regret his lack of courtesy and I will make sure that he apologises for the breach of protocol, and furthermore I'll offer you my personal assurance that there will be no further difficulties."

"I suppose I can excuse his somewhat over-zealous approach but his lack of basic good manners is most unfortunate."

"I agree, most definitely, but Kavanagh has his uses even if he does lack the most fundamental social skills."

"May I recommend that you give this particular dog of war a severe talking to. If nothing else it will remind him of his place."

"I'll bear that in mind. Well, I'm sure we both have much better things to do than waste any more time on Kavanagh."

"Yes indeed, anyway, I'm glad we've had this little talk and that we've settled matters. Well, good day."

"Indeed."

Jesus Christ! Where did they get them from? A "severe talking to"? He'd almost expected Pelham to ask him what school he'd gone to. He wondered how such a man could progress through the service to the rank that he had. On reflection though his progress had probably been by the same methods that Blackwell had used – "fundamental social skills"? who was kidding who, or should it be whom? but then again did it really matter? The problem with Kavanagh appeared to have been dealt with – if only the business with Crawford could be solved as easily.

Crawford had been woken by the insistent ringing of his alarm clock at six-thirty – he'd completely forgotten to reset it when he'd fallen into bed the previous night and now he was paying the price. Initially he was tempted to throw it across the room, either through the window or against the wall, but he'd relented, and merely switched it off before attempting to go back to sleep. He struggled for a quarter of an hour and managed to clear his mind and drift off. He went into a deep sleep almost immediately so it came as something of a surprise when he woke up again and found that the clock now said ten-fifteen. The extra few hours sleep didn't make him feel refreshed – quite the opposite. He decided that to stay in bed wasn't going serve any purpose so he got up and went into the bathroom for a shower. The powerful jets of hot water cleared his head of the brandy he'd drunk the night before but they were unable to clear away the mess of his present circumstances; it would take more than hot water to wash away the stain of his involvement in the Mullan farmhouse assault.

As he dressed in his bedroom he realised that he had to take some action – Williams had the story, and was trying his best to prove or disprove it – Beatty, if he hadn't passed on details of the imminent disclosure, was about to – and he was in the middle, not a good place to be. He walked through to the kitchen and contemplated breakfast but couldn't decide on anything. His listlessness was infecting every aspect of his routine; if he didn't reach a decision on a way forward soon he'd be fit for nothing. He made coffee before he sat down with a pad of A4 and a pen hoping that by committing all his problems and options to paper he'd arrive at a solution.

It was a surprisingly clear and sunny morning and that had a lot to do with Williams's decision to take a ride down to the border country of South Armagh and take a look at the area that formed the killing ground of Crawford's story. He'd taken a roundabout route by going up the M1 and then turned off for Craigavon and Armagh. His Yamaha hadn't had much to do in recent weeks and he took the opportunity to give it a thorough work-out as he rode up the motorway and then followed the dual carriageway to Armagh. After that the road had narrowed and become a little more demanding.

It was hard to tell how many times he'd crossed the border, but his presence in Castleblayney and then Glaslough, with returns to the North in between, told him it had been at least twice. It was approaching lunchtime when he came northwards out of Glaslough along the B210 which according to Crawford's statement brought him almost to the scene. To his right he could see the old railway embankment that marked the route that the assault team had followed nearly twenty years before, and as he came up a hill the access road that most likely lead to the Mullan farm appeared on his right. Slowing almost to a stop he made the turn and rode along the cement road as it made a sharp bend to the left and then moved up a hill to a farmyard.

The road terminated beside an assembly of varied farm buildings – on his left was an old barn that had been divided into various storage units – to his right was a large concrete and corrugated iron building that housed a milking parlour – in front of him was another corrugated iron shed that was used for storing livestock during the winter months. One thing was immediately apparent to him and that was the lack of any farmhouse. He levered the kickstand down with his left foot and dismounted so he could take a look around the place. He tried to superimpose the mental image he had of the site that Crawford had described to him. When he'd got his bearings he had to admit that this was probably the place.

He'd just slipped off his helmet when the noise of a tractor engine alerted him of imminent company. Sure enough a large Massey Ferguson came into the yard and stopped beside the old barn buildings. The driver switched off and got down from the cab never taking his eyes off the leather clad figure standing beside the motorbike. He walked straight towards the biker and only came to a halt when his considerable bulk was inches from the smaller man. Williams thought for a moment that the man in overalls and steel-capped boots was going to open proceedings by hitting him, but when he folded his arms and his face softened with a smile things looked safe, for the moment anyway.

"Is there somethin' I can do for you?"

Williams had thought about a reason for his presence since he'd heard the tractor. Fabrication or honesty? He decided on a small amount of the latter.

"Well, to be honest I'm looking for the Mullan farm and I'm not sure that I've got the right place."

"God! I haven't heard that name in a long time."

"So this is it then?"

"It used to be, but that was a good while back. Tell me this though, why are you lookin' for the Mullan place?"

"I'm a journalist and I'm doing some research for a piece on Armagh going back to the seventies. There was a mention of the farm and I thought I'd take a look."

"Oh there was, was there? And what would this mention be about?"

Williams got the definite impression that he had moved into dangerous territory, but he'd decided on the honest approach, so he pressed on.

"Look, I'm sorry if this causes offence but the piece is about paramilitaries."

"Doesn't bother me none, but you need to be careful who you talk to is all. What's your name anyway?"

This really wasn't going as he'd hoped. Then again, he was still on his feet so maybe his luck was in.

"My name's Alain Williams", and he held out his right hand, "And you are?"

"Declan Gormley", he too extended his hand to grip Williams's with a powerful shake, "And this is my farm."

"Oh, I'm sorry, it looks as if I'm trespassing."

"Never worry about that. To be honest this is still Mullan land but my grandfather got the lease about eighteen odd years ago. There was a fire and the house burned down, but sure you must've heard about that?"

"Well, yes, I have read the old reports."

"And do you know the stories that went around at the time?"

"No, but I'm sure you'd be glad to tell me."

"Like I said you ought to be careful who you talk to. A wise man wouldn't come sniffin' round here if he really knew what he could be gettin' into."

"I'm just doing some research, that's all."

"Aye, well maybe so, but research like that could land you right in it. You do know that the Mullans were big time Provos?"

"Would I be here otherwise?"

"And you still think it's OK to be askin' questions about folk like that?", Williams shrugged his shoulders by way of answer, "Well, you're a braver man than I."

"I doubt that. Look, I'm just writing a story and there are a few blanks that I can't fill other than by getting answers to questions, so what can you tell me about the Mullans?"

"The Mullans thought they were better than anybody else – always had, so Joe and Seamus were no different. God if they knew that my grandfather, old Dermot, had the run of their place they'd have a fit. Not much chance of that though."

"You said that the lease was secured over eighteen years ago, what happened?"

"Well there was the fire and about a year after it the cousins from Newtownhamilton dealt with things."

"How could they do that?"

"Well, at the time of the fire Joe and Seamus did a moonlit and nobody knew where they went. It was all legal like."

"I'm sure it was, but you mean they just disappeared?"

"Somethin' like that, though there were plenty of stories goin' round at the time."

"Like what?"

"Like there was maybe a big fight at the farm and the fire was used to cover it up."

Williams could barely contain himself; here was a local source that, while not confirming Crawford's story, was at least not rubbishing the claims. He tried very hard to make his next question sound casual.

"So who was involved in this big fight?"

"Sure it was just a story used to frighten weans at bedtime, but it was said that the Brits might have had a hand in it."

"Surely you don't believe that?"

"Who's to know. It was a long time ago and all that counts today is that nobody's sheddin' tears for those boys."

"Was there never any news about them?"

"Not a word. It was as if they'd never been born. I remember there was a lot of talk about their just disappearin' at the time but that dried up quick – people found somethin' else to blether about. And I'm thinkin' I've said enough. I've got to get back to work so I'd ask you to be on your way."

"Well, thanks for the information and the advice – I will be careful about who I ask questions of."

"You do that. It'll be safer for you all round."

Williams got back on his bike, started up and with a wave to Gormley as he rode back down the lane made his way back to the road that would lead him to Caledon. From there it was but a short ride to Dungannon and the M1. A couple of times on the motorway home he thought about opening the Yamaha up and letting the 600cc engine really rip but dismissed the idea. Now that he had definite support for Crawford's story it would be stupid to put matters at risk with some flashy riding.

Maxwell was the last man to attempt practice six from concealment and it was clear from the resulting hits of the three strings of two round bursts that he had mastered the drill. Kavanagh was more than happy at the advances that the men had made in just five days but the next week would show just how much potential they really had. It was time to move them on.

"OK gentlemen, so far this week you have covered practices one to six. What you will have noticed, I hope, is that these practices have not involved any great degree of movement. That is going to change as we progress to what is known as the advanced course or practices seven to fourteen. You will see a lot of movement and you will see how desirable it is. You will come to appreciate very quickly that when the unthinkable happens you will not only not have the opportunity to stand up and fight like gentlemen, but in reality you won't want to. Movement is distracting to the eye and the more distraction you can make the more confused your opponent will be. Furthermore, any movement you make will put distance between yourself and your opponent and that increased distance will give you time, and time is vital. Never forget that."

The class had assembled early that morning and gone through an intensive revision of all that they had learned that week. As was to be expected some of the men were better than others, but Kavanagh was happy with the overall standard and confident that they were capable of at least attempting the next stage. He now stood in front of them with his back to a couple of unmarked targets; his appearance was no different than it had been all week – roll-neck sweater, moleskin trousers and a pair of plain tan Oxfords. His right hand was casually placed in his trouser pocket and he was making gestures with his left hand that added a certain emphasis to his words.

"While I've been satisfied with your progress this week I must make the point again that these disciplines are not about target shooting, they are about keeping you alive. They are totally practical in their methods with no extraneous details, and perhaps most important of all, they are adaptable to any situation. I'll give you an example – the nearer of the two targets behind me – now watch."

Kavanagh turned to face the nearer target and his right hand came out of the pocket. Before the class could be sure if he had a pistol a shot was fired, Kavanagh then made a quarter turn to his right and executed a forward roll, breaking his fall with his right forearm. As he came back to a kneeling position, he brought the pistol back on target; which wasn't easy as he now faced to the right. To achieve this he pulled on his right hand with his left, which not only helped steady the small pistol, but also had the affect of twisting him to his rear so he could clearly see the target. As soon as the turn was made he fired a further two rounds. From there he stood up, de-cocking the Walther as he did so by securing the hammer with his thumb before squeezing the trigger. He then gently lowered the hammer making the PPK safe before returning it to his right trouser pocket. From a shots fired perspective the demonstration had taken under four seconds.

"And that gentlemen is the "floor roll" or practice seven."

To a man the class stood with their mouths agape; nothing they had done in the previous week had prepared them for what they had just witnessed. Kavanagh wasn't surprised by their reaction, after all, what he had just done must have looked very dangerous to their eyes, but it was crucial that they understood that it was well within their capabilities, and the sooner the better.

"OK gentlemen, show's over. I can see that you're just bursting with questions, so let's hear them."

Robertson, having looked among his fellow students and seeing that no-one was keen on speaking first, started the ball rolling.

"How long have you been carrying that Mr. Kavanagh?"

The Walther was removed from his pocket again and he held it up so that they could all see it.

"If you mean this particular one, about six years. If you mean PPKs in general, about twenty."

"No, I actually meant this week."

"Oh this week. Well, it's been all week."

"But none of us ever noticed…."

"And you weren't meant to. Look, I'll talk about concealment at much greater length later, but at the moment I want your questions on the drill you've just seen."

For the next quarter of an hour Kavanagh fielded questions about the physical side of the practice, the safety factors, and the possible variations of the drill. He was pleased by the content of the questions because they not only showed that the men were thinking but also showed that they had ceased to be over-awed by the practice and the fact that they would all be attempting it in the afternoon. As the questions became repetitive he looked at his watch and decided that there was no point in beginning the drill as he'd only have time to take one or two men through it, so he called a halt to proceedings and let the class take an early lunch.

Crawford rubbed at his forehead, trying to make the pressure that had been building for the last couple of hours go away. The headache was merely a symptom of the frustration that he felt – nearly three hours of careful consideration and all he had to show was one page of notes and no hint of a conclusion. He had looked at his circumstances from every which way, and all that he could say was that the future relied on the actions of others – it was all a question of "if". "If" he managed to persuade Williams to drop the story. "If" he was able to convince Dave Beatty that the story wasn't being pursued. "If" his conscience hadn't got the better of him in the first place. "If" the men of power hadn't been dragged into the mire of expediency.

He almost allowed himself the luxury of blaming somebody else for his predicament but that wouldn't offer any solutions. He had taken the initiative in calling Beatty and from that starting point everything would progress or not, it was as simple as that and just as simply out of his control. The fact that the men of power were a lot of gutless wonders, as he saw it, was of little consequence and of no comfort whatsoever. He realised that all he could do now was wait – wait for Williams to reply – wait for Beatty to lose his nerve and run to his controller – wait for the controller to sanction action – and wait for that action to be taken. All in all not a very happy state of affairs, and it all came down to "if".

Williams sat at his desk in the living room looking through the notes he had just made and the piece he had already written. Taken as a whole they formed a compelling narrative even though the story relied a lot on the correct interpretation of the facts. He knew from experience that editors wouldn't stand for something open-ended, so he went through the material again and made a few judicious cuts that left less room for uncertainty. There was still something missing – an angle. Telling the story was one thing but it wouldn't survive without a context. He went back to the notes he'd made specifically on Crawford – the impression he had formed of the man and his motivations. The notions of a man full of recriminations and self-loathing appealed to him and they lent a human quality to the story that had been missing. He opened a new file on his computer and started typing. After two hours work and several Marlboros he looked through the new section and then inserted it. He set the whole piece down and went out to the kitchen to make a cup of coffee; on his return he sat down and lit another cigarette before picking up the story for what he hoped was the final read through.

Using a red felt-tip he marked the errors that he would correct later, but taken as a whole he was more than pleased with the effort – it read well and the pace was steady rather than the break-neck that seemed to have become an industry standard. In this instance he felt that a slow build was desirable, in his opinion it allowed the reader time to assimilate all the facts and reach the conclusions that he wanted them to. The final section was undoubtedly the most problematic – up to that point he had been reporting, now he was calling on the reader to make a judgement. The difficulty was that from his own point of view he couldn't be sure if the farmhouse raid was really wrong. What if the assaults had kept happening? Would terrorism in Ulster have been defeated? He looked at the sheaf of papers in his hand and decided that questions like that were academic in the present climate, it was better to focus on reality. With the euphoria that was sweeping people along it wouldn't do to point out that a military victory had been possible, better to say that monstrous actions had been ordered, and that the efforts to secure peace were tainted by them.

He thought about the contradictions and was momentarily troubled by the possibility that he was in some way undermining the progress that had been made in Northern Ireland. Williams was no idealist so the thought was short-lived; after all he hadn't been responsible for actions in 1979, he was merely telling the story twenty years later and people could reach their own conclusions.

Blackwell had read every file that had even the remotest connection to events in South Armagh in March of '79 and as his knowledge grew so did his resolution to act. There was a problem however, he could not simply sanction action himself – times had changed since Harry Lynch had run the "Department" – everything had to go through the proper channels. The "old boy" network wasn't even what it had been, but Blackwell hoped to avoid unnecessary scrutiny by seeking the advice of one of the few remaining "old boys". He hoped that he'd be able to contact the man at home so he turned from his desk and retrieved the small leather-bound directory from his wall safe. He leafed through the list of numbers, those that he wouldn't trust to his desk directory, until he came to the letter R. He keyed the numbers and hoped that the man was home. After what must have been a dozen rings the call was answered.

"Redfern."

"Sir Giles, it's Blackwell, at the Gardens."

"And what can I do for you?"

"I have a problem that could be rather serious if it develops, and I need your advice."

"Give me the details and I'll have a think."

It only took Blackwell a couple of minutes to give an account of the nature of Crawford's disclosure but it seemed longer. He referred to his list of relevant material, leaving nothing out, knowing from experience that the old man from "Gloom Hall" would be jotting down his own notes.

"….and in a nutshell that's it, Sir Giles."

"Leave it with me and I'll call you back in an hour."

"Thank you."

"I wouldn't thank me just yet. Wait 'til you hear what I have to offer."

The older man hung up first leaving Blackwell with an hour to kill. There was nothing demanding his attention in the office so he went down to the kitchen at the end of the corridor and made himself a cup of coffee. Someone had left a copy of that morning's Times on the table so he looked through the various headlines to see what was wicked in the world.

Giles Redfern looked at the notes he'd taken down while he'd listened to Blackwell and slowly shook his head. He was overcome by a weariness that had nothing to do with his sixty-four years; the resurrection of affairs best forgotten was part and parcel of the secrets business but this was one secret that he had genuinely hoped was dead and buried. What was it that made a man betray the trust of others? Over the years he had seen men forsake their position for money, for ideals, and simply because they could. This man Crawford looked like an idealist – the worst possible scenario. He'd seen the results of inappropriate disclosures and while none of them had achieved much general recognition they had all damaged the community of which he was a senior member. What Blackwell had told him appeared to be potentially disastrous for several reasons – firstly, the "Department" didn't exist, not even unofficially – secondly, the policy regarding Northern Ireland was moving in a different direction, a direction that could be permanently changed by such a revelation – thirdly, the secondary damage to the intelligence services was incalculable, with the prospect of inquiries into all manner of sensitive activities the likely outcome.

In all his time with the service nothing he had seen could have the impact that a full account of March '79 was capable of having. The public would stand for a certain amount of "dirty tricks" but the idea of state sanctioned execution was more than most would accept. The bleeding hearts would have a field-day and the concessions that Irish Republicans would wring from the present peace process could make the British government's negotiating position untenable. He looked at the notes he had taken and then began a new sheet detailing the debit and credit sides of Blackwell's story, but it was all too apparent after only a couple of minutes that there were no credit aspects to the situation. Crawford would have to be silenced and the story nipped in the bud. But that was easier said than done; if the story had been told to a wider circle than Blackwell was aware of containment would be next to impossible. If, however, it was limited to the small number of individuals that Blackwell had described, action could be taken albeit with the utmost care. It all came down to numbers and a flexibility with defining what constituted the common good.

For nearly forty years Redfern had possessed the necessary flexibility but what he saw on the page saddened him – Crawford had been part of a justified action but he would now suffer because of the expediency of what could only be defined as cowardice. Much as he sympathised with Crawford he could not, however, condone his role of whistle blower. There had to be certain codes of behaviour; after all it would never do to have the very foundations of the state rocked every time an individual felt like it, no matter what the seeming justification. He didn't like the methods of his masters at times, but he accepted the fact that it was his responsibility to protect the institutions that they had at their disposal. That would be the basis of any advice he would give Blackwell; nothing specific but enough to let the younger man reach the right conclusions.

He considered what those right conclusions could lead to and realised that if he afforded himself the same self-righteous luxuries as Crawford he would be counselling a course of no action. To do so would be to sacrifice the *status quo* and without that there was no reason for the existence of the various security services and that would frankly never do. No, Crawford had overstepped the mark and would have to be dealt with accordingly. There were penalties for believing in ideals and Crawford was going to pay them. Better by far to be a realist – the disappointments could be explained away and accepted – realistic acceptance was potentially painful but not as painful as the alternative.

Robertson was the first member of the class to attempt practice seven and he made a real hash of it on his opening attempt. The element of movement was responsible for most of his failings with over-confidence adding to his problems. The only thing that Kavanagh could say in his defence was that he hadn't shot anybody, either himself, or any of his classmates.

"Not as easy as it looks, Mr. Robertson?"

"No it's not", and he blew out his cheeks as the tension began to leave him, "I'll tell you something, there's an awful lot to think about as you do this."

"I agree Mr. Robertson. Now that may have looked bad to the rest of you, but I assure you, you will all experience the same problems. OK, before we try that one live I want you all to practice your forward rolls, and let's keep it safe, so leave your weapons in the armoury."

Once they had left their pistols in Curtis's capable hands they began their dry runs; Kavanagh stood back and let them get on with it. Under normal circumstances he would have found the sight of eight grown men rolling on the ground making a pantomime of drawing and firing non-existent pistols a cause for amusement, but this was different, this was deadly serious. There was much bad language from the group, caused mainly by the unforgiving concrete floor and the heavy falls that some of the class took, but after five minutes every man had managed to complete several satisfactory rolls and they were all ready to move on. Without being told they filed back to the armoury and retrieved their Brownings before taking station in front of Kavanagh once again.

"OK, Mr. Robertson, you made a pig's ear of it first time around, let's see you make up for it. On my command…. GO!"

Robertson drew his pistol and fired a quick two round burst before making a quarter turn to his right allowing him to roll away from the target. When he came to rest he brought the Browning back on target by pulling on his right with his left hand. He fired another two rounds before he reapplied the safety and re-holstered. He stood and turned to face the class, a look of relief clearly showing that he was glad to have completed practice seven without mishap.

"How did that feel?"

"Better. I didn't feel under as much pressure to be honest."

"Well, let's take a look and see what you've done."

They dressed forward and looked at the target – Robertson had two good centre-line hits about three inches apart.

"Those two are your first burst, the second two you missed."

Robertson visibly deflated at the mention of misses so Kavanagh quickly tried to raise his morale.

"Don't worry about the misses for the time being – it's the movement that's important and yours was good", despite the encouragement Kavanagh could see that Robertson was annoyed at the results he had achieved, so he pressed the matter, "I'm serious, I was pleased with the practice and so should you. Look, the shooting will come so don't worry about it. If I was you, I'd be happy – overall, good effort."

The comments had their desired effect, and Robertson rejoined the group in a better frame of mind. For the rest of the afternoon the class made steady progress as they all successfully carried out practice seven. Once they had mastered the roll to the right, which was easier for the right handed class members, they all attempted a roll to the left. It never ceased to amuse Kavanagh the difficulties that a change of direction could produce, but after several attempts in some cases every member of the class managed at least one good roll in either direction. The standard of the shooting varied from man to man but everybody had managed hits which was more than satisfactory for the first day. By five Kavanagh was happy with the progress they had made and decided to call it a day. Once they had cleared the range he let them go before he returned to his room and the file which was going to occupy his mind for the rest of the evening.

Blackwell was beginning to wonder if Sir Giles had forgotten to reply when the telephone rang. Before he answered it he flipped to a clean sheet in his desk jotter in preparation for the hoped for advice and the possibility of note taking.

"Blackwell."

"It's Redfern."

"I was just about to call you…."

"And why would you do a thing like that?"

"I….I thought that maybe…."

"You thought that this old man had maybe forgotten about your little problem and that he maybe needed jogging along?"

"I wouldn't presume to…."

"Calm down Blackwell, I'm pulling your leg. Truth be told, this Crawford business has raised some interesting questions."

"And have you arrived at any answers, Sir Giles?"

"None which I fear you'll find attractive. It comes down to this – Crawford is a believer and a zealous one at that – he feels that the truth of his old endeavours has been betrayed and he has acted in a potentially damaging manner to the new order. A fair summary so far?"

"I agree totally."

"Good. Given that I am correct thus far I shall continue. In my experience men like Crawford cannot be bought. Fundamentally they aren't interested by money, their lives are governed by notions of honour and integrity. These commodities have their uses under the right circumstances but can be very dangerous if given free rein."

"Again I'm in complete agreement."

"So you can see where I'm leading you?"

"Well if money won't work I suppose I could always fall back on threat."

"That won't work either. A threat will only convince Crawford of the veracity of his cause and course of action. No, when faced with a problem like Crawford, removal is the only sensible answer."

"But I'll never get approval for that from committee."

"So don't ask for it. This is an internal matter – deal with it internally. You have people capable of this kind of action – leave it to them. Treat it as a live-fire exercise, if you will."

"And you think that is the best solution?"

"Sadly I do. Well, I think that pretty well covers everything….oh yes, I almost forgot, this conversation has been purely academic and I would be most displeased if mention of it were ever made again."

"I understand, Sir Giles, and you can rely on my discretion."

"I depend on it. Well, if there is nothing else, good day."

Blackwell was about to offer his thanks when the line was broken, Sir Giles clearly didn't want to prolong contact longer than was necessary. Blackwell looked at the notebook in front of him and the single word that he had written during his conversation with Redfern – REMOVAL.

By the time Williams had finished his re-draft it was early evening and too late to e-mail or fax a copy to anybody – it was Saturday after all and there would be precious few people at their desks he could send it to – furthermore he didn't trust either method as a means of maintaining security – in that respect he was somewhat old-fashioned, preferring to put his trust in the Royal Mail. The one printed copy he'd made of the finished article would go to Crawford, he owed him that courtesy at least. As he put the printed sheets in an envelope he wondered what the reaction would be to the description of the embittered veteran telling his war story – nobody liked a negative portrayal but after all it was accurate. Once he'd settled matters with Crawford he'd start looking for a suitable publisher.

The confines of the flat had absorbed the negative emotions that had possessed Crawford and while he couldn't escape his mind he could at least walk away from the four walls that were beginning to feel like a prison. He had walked out of the flat with no destination or particular aim in mind, all that truthfully worried him was a change of scenery. As he walked through the West-end he became aware of the transition from day to night. It wasn't just the change in the lighting and the atmosphere that it created but the inhabitants of the streets took on a different character as well. People were dressed for a night out, they were going to the theatre, the restaurant, the pub – all centres of social activity and all alien to Crawford's state of mind.

He walked through Knightsbridge towards theatre land and Soho. The numbers of people increased and the apparent determination to enjoy the night out touched Crawford but failed to affect him. He looked at the faces of the revellers as he passed by and could make no connection between them wrapped up as they were in their hedonism and himself plagued with doubts and self-recrimination. He moved on into Soho and the garish neon lights of the sex shows marked a change of mood – this was life at its most raw – all pretence stripped away and only the most basic elements left on view. There must have been something about his look because none of the door touts attempted an approach – clearly he wasn't a prospective customer. He made his way down through the Haymarket and thought of human nature; his ugly conclusions matching what he had seen on his walk through Soho. God, but he felt so tired.

Kavanagh sat at the small desk once more, the file lying open and a notebook bearing his neat script showing the various thoughts that had occurred to him as he had read and re-read the details of Crawford's life. The record of service showed no blemishes whatsoever – Crawford had been the most diligent of soldiers – obedient to authority and conscientious in commission of his duties – there were in effect no indications of the possibility of future problems save a degree of independence which was to be expected in the "Department". The career post-army was remarkable only for its success – all too often the grand schemes of ex-serviceman floundered on the realities of commercial enterprise. Crawford had avoided failure through prudence and an adherence to common sense and an awareness of his own limitations.

So why had this apparent bench-mark of probity acted in the way he had? Kavanagh couldn't make sense of the situation at all and was therefore having difficulties reaching a conclusion that would solve the present problem. Try as he might, he could not escape the fact that he had always liked Crawford and that attachment was clouding his judgement – he was letting his personal feelings enter the equation and that was wrong, worse than that it was unprofessional. The Crawford of twenty years ago would have told him to divorce himself from the circumstances and act, which was as it should be, but today's Crawford would advise caution and the application of conscience. Why? Why had he turned whistle blower after all these years? What did it really matter if a bunch of bone headed Ulstermen were cut loose from the mainland once and for all? How could Crawford be driven to act by something that had no immediate impact on him?

If he was pragmatic and gave Blackwell a straightforward answer, it would be to counsel the necessity of action, but that would be in direct opposition to his own feelings. Political minds were at work here and Kavanagh knew that he should keep things simple and effective, and to do that he'd have to divorce himself from the advice and the conclusions it would lead to. He knew that the sooner he talked to Blackwell the sooner he could start forgetting about his involvement – after all if he was unaware of the action and the consequences then nothing really happened. He got up from the table and went over to the bed and the bedside cabinet where the telephone sat. He lifted the handset and dialled the number for the Gardens from memory. Truthfully he hadn't expected Blackwell to be there on a Saturday evening so it came as a real surprise when the front desk put him through on the direct line.

"I hope you've got something for me Sean."

"Well, I've gone through the file a couple of times and, yes, I suppose I've drawn some conclusions, sir."

"OK. Let's hear them, and you can dispense with the formalities."

Kavanagh looked at his notes and tried to articulate them in a reasonable order. God, but he wished Blackwell hadn't been there. Now he had to speak off the cuff and the chance for mistakes made him wary.

"Right, well, it doesn't look as if his motivation is financial, so I don't think any efforts to buy him off will work. I think we should be looking at the journalist for success in that area…."

"I'll stop you there. If we do that, Crawford will only find somebody else and

"Department" funds are not a bottomless pit. In short, we can't be buying off every hack we come across. Carry on."

Blackwell's interruption threw him slightly but he thought that the next point would be better received.

"OK. If the story comes out a simple denial should be enough. I mean, look at what he's disclosing – it's sheer fantasy – nobody'll believe it."

"Somebody will believe it, I assure you, that's the way of conspiracy theories. Besides the "Department" is not a matter of public record and we can't have the press sticking its nose in where it doesn't belong."

"Well, then we threaten Crawford."

"You mean appeal to his better nature, as it were?"

"Maybe, I don't know...."

"Too thin Sean, way too thin."

Kavanagh didn't like the direction that this affair was taking, but he reckoned that his next suggestion would put paid to any extreme measures that Blackwell might have in mind.

"If that's the case why don't we just kill him."

"There are still loose ends after that."

Jesus! The man was serious!

"Like what for example?"

"Oh come on Sean! Like the journalist. Think, man, think! We can't have this story floating around somewhere. We have one chance and it must be exploited fully."

"It sounds like you've already decided."

"Not quite. I wanted to hear what you had to say."

"And that's made a difference?"

"You know the man, probably even like him, after all he more or less trained you, so I expected you to look at all the pain free alternatives first. You've done that and I can understand your reasoning, but it simply won't do."

"So you mean there's no alternative?"

"There's always an alternative, but in this case it's unacceptable."

"Then I don't see what further purpose this conversation has...."

"Oh I think there's a purpose, but I don't want to talk about it even on this line, so I want you at the Gardens first thing on Monday."

"What for?"

"No questions and no arguments, just be here."

The line was cut and Kavanagh was left wondering what Blackwell wanted him for; several possibilities sprang to mind and none of them was pleasant.

Crawford had walked down to the Thames and followed the road along the Embankment until he reached Tower Bridge. Feeling tired he sat down even though it had started to rain. His loden cloth overcoat kept him dry but, with neither hood nor hat, his head was soaked in no time and the water ran down the inside of his collar. He could feel the cold fingers of water trace their way down his back and chest, soaking into his shirt, and all he could do was sigh, physical discomfort seemed unimportant. The bench he occupied faced across the river and he focused on the lights, looking for something to divert him. A couple of small boats made their way upstream and he followed their lights until they disappeared from view. With the boats gone he found little to distract him – the headlights of passing cars were too transitory to hold his attention and there was no river traffic – so he turned his gaze inwards but found little to comfort him there.

He knew he should be getting back to the flat, there was no excuse for him sitting at Tower Bridge getting wet, but he was having difficulty thinking of a good reason to go home. Walking would take about an hour but a taxi ride would only occupy a matter of minutes; it should have been a simple decision yet he was finding it difficult to reach it. All the directions he had followed recently had led to conclusions that he didn't like; his judgement had been shown to be severely lacking in nearly everything so maybe it was better for him not to make any decisions. The rain got heavier and still he sat – his indecision almost a perverse reaction to recent events. He sat gripped by a feeling of helplessness for several minutes which was only overcome by the practical intrusion of his need to get dry and warm. He got up from the bench and walked along the Embankment for nearly a quarter of an hour before he managed to hail a black taxi with the "for hire" sign illuminated its distinctive yellow. The drive through central London was without incident or thankfully, despite cab-drivers reputation to the contrary, conversation and he was dropped off at the Mews flat just before midnight.

* * *

Kavanagh was in a foul mood despite the good night's sleep he'd enjoyed. On waking, he'd stalked around his room with no obvious target for his ill-temper. The normal early morning routine had been completely upset by thoughts of his conversation with Blackwell and the subsequent summons to Leinster Gardens. As before, all manner of possibilities had gone through his mind and, as before, none of them was pleasant. His mood didn't improve any when he made his way downstairs for breakfast. The normally appetizing fry seemed tasteless to him and he now sat with his second cup of coffee as the training class drifted in for their first meal of the day. He looked at the young men as they took their seats in the dining room and wondered if any of them would be faced with an unpleasant situation in need of resolution like the one that he knew was waiting for him at the Gardens. God alone knew, but as this was a rotten business at times, chances were that one of them at least would have to put the lessons into practice.

He walked over to the range himself and set about arranging the targets for the first practices of the day. His pupils began arriving just after nine-thirty and he waited until they had assembled at the armoury door before he passed on the news of his imminent departure.

"And just what are we meant to do while you're gone?"

"On the ball as usual, Mr. Robertson, and as it happens I was just coming to that. One of the areas that hasn't been addressed is the quick aimed shot. That changes today and you'll be continuing with that practice and those you have already covered until I return."

"And when will that be?"

"I'm not exactly sure, Mr. Robertson, but rest assured you'll be among the first to know. If there is any major change in my schedule the Director Training will be informed and the message will filter down to you. To be honest I don't think that I'll be away for more than three or four days, but by the time I get back I expect you all to dazzle me with your expertise. Now let's get cracking!"

Williams rose late as was his habit on a Sunday. He reached over from where he lay and pulled his jogging pants from the heap of clothes that covered the armchair in his bedroom. When he managed to unearth them, he rolled out of bed to find the matching sweatshirt. He finished dressing by lacing on the training shoes that completed the illusion of his fitness – a twenty a day Marlboro habit put paid to any ideas he might have had on that score – fit he wasn't, but appearances, as he well knew, could be deceptive. After putting the filter machine on he walked up to the newsagents to buy the Sunday papers; he was going to spend an indulgent morning drinking coffee and reading.

He'd just picked up The Observer when his mobile phone started ringing – he'd switched it on as a matter of course and now it was going to upset the lazy day he had planned – he sighed as he put the paper down and lifted it from the coffee table. He pushed the receive button to accept the call but before he could say anything a man's voice came on line.

"Williams, you know who this is so there's no point in my identifying myself. You will not use my name in the course of this conversation, is that clear?"

What the hell was the man up to? It sounded like too much cloak and dagger, but he thought it best to humour him.

"Absolutely, but what is this all about?"

"I've had a lot of time to consider our piece of business and I've decided to cancel it before any progress has been made."

"Not so fast! I've already made certain efforts and the job's more or less complete from my end. You can't pull the plug now!"

"When my safety becomes a factor I can do anything."

"Don't give me that. The story's a good one but it's old news."

"You've missed the point – this was never news in the first place, and the existence of the "Department" has never been out in the open. My old employers will do anything to avoid exposure."

"I can appreciate the measures you've taken up 'til now but I think you're starting to enter the realms of fantasy. This is all pure "it's so secret, if I told you, I'd have to kill you". I can't go along with this."

"For Christ's Sake! Can't you see what I'm driving at? If it was acceptable to raid that farmhouse then, it's acceptable to continue the cover up now, and it will be covered up."

"How can you be so sure?"

"Because Beatty knows, and if he knows then so will his boss."

"And you really think that there'll be some sort of action taken against you?"

"If this story gets out you can depend on it."

"So where does that leave me?"

"You are now party to the same secret – they may feel that the same sanctions apply."

"I don't see it that way, not in this day and age."

"People haven't changed that much, not in the "Department" anyway."

"You tell me this now, but it was carry on regardless when it came to your story. If you're right, then we're both in trouble. How could you be so bloody stupid?"

"I saw a wrong and thought that I could make a difference. I'll admit to conceit but my intentions were good."

"And the road to hell is paved with them."

"Look, if the story is kept out of the press it should be enough to placate these people. I haven't even been approached yet."

"So why trouble me with "what ifs"? There may never have been a need."

"Better to act now and show them that I now realise that I've made a mistake and that matters will go no further. I'll face some sort of disciplinary sanction and you should get away with a talking to."

"And you think that it shouldn't amount to more than that?"

"If action is taken now, yes, I feel that that's all they really could do."

"God, you know, none of this had crossed my mind and then you raise the possibilities and I don't know what to think."

"Well, as best as I can judge it's my problem and as long as you don't make an issue of it you should be OK."

"That's just great! First off you didn't tell me there might be a problem, then you tell me that the Establishment could come after me, and then you finish up by saying that there probably isn't anything to worry about. Your conscience has made a right bloody mess of things!"

"For what it's worth I'm sorry."

"Well it's not worth the effort I've put in on this one, that's for sure."

"And did the effort convince you of the truth?"

"It doesn't matter – if I do what you say nobody is going to read it anyway."

"It matters to me. Do you believe it?"

"It's plausible."

"Still not convinced then?"

"I'm pretty sure your story has foundations, but like I said does it matter?"

"Not a lot maybe, but at least you don't see me as a liar."

"Is this what this whole thing was about?"

"I had to tell this to someone…."

"You want a confessor, then find a priest. Trouble like this I don't need."

"There won't be any trouble if I can do anything about it."

"Don't you think you've done enough already?"

"So I went about things the wrong way, but at least I tried to do something."

"And there was me thinking this was a simple disclosure piece when all along it was about you seeking absolution."

"Maybe I am, but this isn't the right way to go about it."

"It's a bit bloody late in the day to be having second thoughts!"

"I know, believe me, I know."

"Good. Look, you came to me with this story and I accepted it, my involvement is purely second-hand, the least you can do is clear that up. I don't want to be part of your mess, is that clear?"

"OK, I'll take care of it. It'll take a couple of days, but I should be in contact by the end of the week."

"I'll expect a call by Friday."

"That should be enough time."

The line was broken and Williams was left with only his disbelief for company – how could Crawford have done this to him and how could he have been stupid enough to have gone along with it in the first place – and what was the point of asking damn fool questions now – he couldn't change events – it would be better to see what turned up on Friday.

Crawford returned to his seat in the cafe and considered the effect of the conversation he had just had with Williams. His request for anonymity and the implicit threats he had made appeared to have created the desired response, but he hadn't been making things up – truth be told – the "Department" was capable of taking extreme action if the provocation was appropriate, which it undoubtedly was in this case. Safeguarding Williams was only one part of the problem – his own security was altogether more important. He knew that he had acted foolishly and that in order to redress the balance he would have to eat a lot of humble pie. One thing that he was glad of was the return of the professionalism that had so much been a part of his career – the fact that he'd remembered to make the call to Williams from an outside line, hence his trip to the cafe and its useful but somewhat old-fashioned phone booth – a clear indication that he was thinking again. The waitress refilled his mug with coffee and he voiced his thanks as his gaze returned to the paper that he'd been reading before he'd made the call.

His mind wasn't on the headlines, rather he was considering his next move – should he go to Beatty with an appeal to the "Department" or should he go direct to the Gardens? There were proper channels and protocols to follow; the men at the Gardens could ignore a direct approach, after all there would be no record of his attempted contact, so they had nothing to lose. On reflection it was better to involve a third party, so, much as he had doubts about him, he'd use Beatty. He got up from the table and paid for his coffee before starting the walk back to his flat. The weak autumn sunshine mirrored the course he was going to follow – it didn't offer any strength, it could be short-lived, but it was all he had and better than the possible alternatives. After the desperation he had felt for his own position it almost felt good to have decided on a way forward. All he could do now was hope that his efforts would be enough.

"Mr. Robertson, is that really the best you can do? This is only fifteen yards, you should be getting hits."

The group had made satisfactory progress, in fact some of them showed a very pronounced ability when it came to the quick aimed shot, but Robertson, despite all his apparent experience, just couldn't come to terms with the drill. Kavanagh was running out of ideas and was in turn becoming frustrated.

"I tell you what, I know that this practice is the quick aimed shot, but in your case forget about that. I'll tell you why; you are wasting a lot of time trying to find your sights and in the effort to get a shot off quickly you're really yanking on the trigger and that's pulling your shot to the right. I want you to try something different, as soon as the pistol comes into your line of sight fire a two round burst and we'll see what happens. Just remember, never lose your focus on the target, in reality it could move and if you're not paying attention the price you could pay is permanent, understood? OK, carry on."

Kavanagh stepped back and with the rest of the class looking on, Robertson lifted the Browning with his right arm fully extended, fired and missed the target.

"No! What did I say about trying to find your sights? That's right, don't! Let the pistol come up into your line of sight and as soon as the bulk of it covers the target, fire. OK, try again."

Again the pistol came up from the ready position and two shots reverberated around the range. The plain buff target displayed two holes, one low on the left hand side, the other level with where the clavicle would have been on the right. Robertson raised his eyebrows as he looked at the results with something approaching satisfaction. Kavanagh too was pleased by the improvement but he knew from experience that one positive didn't mark a guaranteed change for the better – Robertson was going to have to build on it and to do that he'd have to practice – practice a lot.

"Remember how that felt and repeat it."

Another two shots rang out. This time only one marked the target.

"You're thinking too much again. Keep it going and don't think."

And so it continued for the afternoon – Robertson made progress with the occasional backward step, but there were no doubts in Kavanagh's mind, the young man was definitely better than when he'd started. As the group worked through different scenarios, he could see the changes that had been made over the past week – there was a confidence in their use of the weapon and that had effects on their whole demeanour – their self-confidence had grown and that would have positive benefits for their careers when they left "The Fort". He was pleased by what they had achieved and he hoped that his enforced absence would not cause any difficulties.

"OK gentlemen, I think we can rap it up for the day. I'm afraid that I've got things to do and, I know this will pain you deeply, but they'll take me away for three days, there or thereabouts."

The group began clearing the range; picking up empty cases, patching out targets and generally preparing it for the next day. When they had finished the tidy-up they all went into the armoury to clean their Hi-Powers before they left for the night. Jimmy Curtis was working on a Sterling trigger group as they trooped in with Kavanagh bringing up the rear. He set down his tools and the part he'd been working on and nodded towards the instructor.

"By the sounds of it you were putting them through the mill today."

"They worked hard today but they had to."

"Any particular reason for that?"

"I've a job on Jimmy and it'll take me away for a couple."

"Anything special?"

"Come off it, you know better than that. Anyway, I have a favour to ask regarding the class."

"Yeah, I'll keep an eye on them while you're away."

"Thanks. Now I don't want them to do anything new, just practice what they've learned. They were going through the quick aimed shot practices today and I've no objections to them working on that but I will be taking them through all the other practices when I get back. You hear that gentlemen?", and the group looked up from their cleaning duties as one and nodded, "Good, because you'll all have your classification when I get back, and I take failure very personally. Remember that."

There were a few grumbles from the class but they were careful to keep them under their breath. Kavanagh smiled at their resignation, briefly shook hands with Curtis and left the range complex. Back in his room it took him all of five minutes to assemble his kit, another couple of minutes and he was pulling the "Department" car away from the forbidding main gates of Fort Monckton over the drawbridge and across the track that linked the base to the golf course and the town of Gosport. After negotiating the town he was back on the A3 that had brought him down from London. He'd never enjoyed driving, and he was glad of that fact as it meant he had to stay focused on the road rather than on the reason for his return to the Gardens. The traffic was surprisingly heavy for a Sunday, it had been a good day and it appeared that people had taken advantage and gone down to the coast, whatever the reason Kavanagh made slow progress back to London. The A3 brought him to the south-west of the city and the same roadworks that he'd experienced on the way down to Gosport, so it wasn't until well after ten o'clock that he managed to park the car and return to his flat. It had been a long day but he felt the need of a nightcap just to make sure that he slept. Having put his grip and other assorted kit in the bedroom he walked through the kitchen where he poured himself a good measure of Hennessy – old habits died hard.

Crawford sat in the living room listening to Mozart's concerto for clarinet. He'd been listening to various recordings since he'd got back to the flat around lunchtime; sometimes the music had taken a hold of him and at others he'd contemplated his way forward. He was left in no doubt that the contact with Beatty was imperative and the more he thought about it the safer this course of action seemed. The recriminations were still there, and as they began to take control of his thoughts he succumbed to the temptation of a drink. So it was that by eleven he walked none too steadily to his room and bed. As he drifted off to sleep he contemplated the attempt at restitution using Beatty as an intermediary – the thoughts didn't occupy his mind for very long, they looked too much like hard work and the allure of sleep was undeniable. His last conscious thought was that this coming week would see an end to his troubles.

* * *

At eight-fifty on a dull and overcast Monday morning Kavanagh parked the "Department" car outside the Gardens; he'd wasted no time at his flat preparing for his meeting with Blackwell, having decided that it was better to get it over and done with. He walked briskly along Leinster Gardens and into the refurbished offices to find the same security guard on duty at the front desk. It was obvious from his whole demeanour that the curt lecture of two weeks ago had made a lasting impression.
"Good morning sir."
"Good morning."
"Could I ask who it is you wish to see?"
Kavanagh was in no mood to play along with this seemingly polite approach and made no effort to reciprocate.
"Blackwell."
"Mr. Blackwell isn't here at the moment, but I'm sure…."
"Then I'll wait.
"Oh, then you can…."
"Then I can go upstairs and get myself a coffee. I know the way."
"I need to sign you in sir."
"I didn't need to the last time I was here."
"It's just that there's no-one to check your clearance with at the moment sir."
"OK, give me the log and I'll fill it in myself."
The guard realised too late that he was beaten and handed the record over to Kavanagh, who filled in his details before making his way along the hall and up the stairs. As the guard had said nobody was at the secretary's station so he went

straight to the kitchen and set about brewing a pot of coffee. He hoped that Blackwell would show up soon because he wanted to have this business dealt with quickly – if it was done and dusted he would be able to return to "The Fort" and finish the course – he was aware that his response would probably mark him out as shallow but wasting time on reflection and recrimination was just that, a waste of time.

The gurgling noise from the filtering machine indicated the end of the brewing cycle and Kavanagh poured himself a mug. As he stood in the kitchen drinking he heard footsteps coming down the corridor towards him. They stopped short of the kitchen and he heard another door open just before the voice of the Controller called out.

"Bring me a cup of that coffee, spot of milk and no sugar."

Kavanagh nodded his head in recognition of Blackwell's usual approach of putting people ill at ease. He retrieved a cup and saucer from the cupboard above the filter machine; when Blackwell said cup he meant it, he'd been known to throw mugs at secretaries when he was in a foul mood, and the last thing Kavanagh needed was a confrontation, there was no need to get an unpleasant meeting off to a bad start. He walked back up the corridor and into Blackwell's office, leaving the cup on the desk before attempting any exchange.

"Good morning sir."

"Why does that sound insincere?"

"It wasn't meant to sir, if it did I apologise."

"And that wasn't much better. Anyway Kavanagh, sit down."

"Thank you sir."

As Kavanagh took a seat he considered that if Blackwell thought that he was going to be intimidated by this meeting he would give the opposite impression; too many times in the past the Controller thought he had gained the upper hand, well not today.

"Well, you've read the file, what's your view?"

"We've covered this territory before sir. I don't see the point of going over it again."

"I asked for your opinion and I suggest you offer it."

"You've already decided on the action you want taken, so I don't see what use my opinion could be, unless you want some sort of cushion for your conscience."

"This is not a matter of conscience...."

"I think Crawford would disagree with you sir."

"Crawford's a bloody fool...."

"If that's all he is then surely he can be left alone? I mean, as I said, who is going to believe him?"

"That's irrelevant. His disclosure brings too many aspects of past policy into the public domain; past policy that doesn't ride well with present circumstances."

"So he's to pay dearly for his honesty?"

"Oh for Christ's Sake grow up Sean! This isn't the bloody playground you know. There are rules and we are here to make sure they are enforced."

"Maybe so, but they seem to keep changing."

"That's not for us to consider, all that matters is that the "Department" continues."

"That's a nice way of saying that the job is all that counts and to Hell with reasons and methods."

"Let me make it clear Sean. Crawford has jeopardised our past, present and future operations. He has jeopardised a policy strategy that has taken years to develop and if we want to get personal, he has put our necks in the noose, and I for one will not be brought down by the likes of him!"

"At last, we come to the crux of the matter."

"Don't be so bloody smug. You might be right, but tell me this, are you prepared to see this whole organisation crash and burn? Are you prepared to go to prison? Because believe me this is what will happen in the aftermath. So let's hear it, the truth that you seem so fond of."

Kavanagh shifted in his chair, for the first time he felt uncomfortable, for the first time he had to agree with Blackwell.

"I hate to say it, but you're right sir. We'll always look after ourselves."

"And not after our own?"

"Not this time."

"So that's settled."

"I don't see that we've settled on anything."

"Oh I think we have. Let's be realistic, I seem to remember you suggesting that we get rid of Crawford…."

"I said why don't we just kill him."

"Exactly, and how would you suggest we go about it?"

Here it was at last, the reason why he'd been called up to London. Of all the possibilities that he'd played through in his mind since he'd first spoken with Blackwell about Crawford this was the nastiest.

"If this is to be pursued how much time do we have?"

"Let's work on the assumption that we don't have any."

"How deniable does it have to be?"

"Totally."

"No time and totally deniable? Christ Almighty! Then I suppose it'll have to be suicide."

"Why not an accident?"

"We haven't got the time and there are never any guarantees anyway."

"OK, suicide then, but what method?"

"A soldier's way out – gunshot, with a cold weapon, which gives a lot of scope for creating some nasty stories that keep the attention focused on Crawford."

"What's your aim there?"

"Think about it sir, a successful businessman kills himself, don't you think the press would be interested in a story like that?"

"Their interest would wane after a day or two."

"Maybe so, but this way the story would be under your control. If it was known that Crawford was skimming company funds, gambling, whoring, involved in drugs – pick your vice, it doesn't really matter, but what's important is that there seems to be a reason for his death. What I'm saying is that there is less likely to be an exhaustive investigation if he looks dirty."

"I see what you mean."

"It's been done before. We'll just have to be careful about the management of the aftermath. It's just a pity there isn't a close family connection.

"Why?"

"The press is less inclined to go muck-raking if there's a spotless family involved. They'd accept whatever they're told. Oh well, can't be helped."

"So you want him dirty then?"

"Yeah, we should be able to come up with something. Wait a minute, where'd you hear about this in the first place?"

"Dave Beatty."

"Perfect. Old service friend hears from Crawford that there's trouble and the next thing Crawford offs himself. I take it Beatty will go along with whatever story we give him?"

"He's still on the payroll, so he'll say whatever we want him to."

"OK, well that would seem to cover the general background – I reckon any problems can be dealt with on the hoof – so you've only got to worry about the actual commission itself."

"Which is why I called you back."

"Now wait a minute, the answer's no…."

"You've got no choice. You're a part of this, every bit as much as Crawford, your direct involvement is the only way of insuring that the story never gets out."

"You bastard, you rotten bastard."

"What did you expect Sean? We're hardly the Boy Scouts now are we? We both know what is necessary and you're the obvious candidate."

"Knowing isn't doing and I'm…."

"You'll do what you're ordered. This whole business is time critical and I'm not wasting any briefing a team who'll only represent another liability. You're it Sean, and I couldn't care less about your scruples, is that understood?"

"I don't see any alternatives."

"That's absolutely right."

"Well, as that's the case I want this to be run my way and there'll have to be some sort of recognition."

"Meaning what exactly?"

"Meaning some sort of *ex gratia* payment."

"We're not a charity Sean."

"No, you said we weren't the Boy Scouts. What you're asking is outside the bounds of normal operations and I want paid."

"So your scruples have a price?"

"I'm no saint, if that's what you mean."
"You'll get your payment but I can make no promises as to how much."
"I'm sure that there are funds available – my price won't be that high."
"Now that that's settled, I want details as to how you're going to do it."
"All in good time. First up, I want a floor plan of Crawford's flat."
"You'll have it by lunchtime. Anything else?"
"Is Beatty the last person that we know to have a face to face?"
"Yes."
"Then I'll need to talk to him. It may not be worth much but he may have something to offer."

Trying to pin Beatty down had taken the whole morning and he'd had to let Maria leave several messages rather than waste time with distractions. His frustration mounted and it wasn't until lunchtime that the effort had produced results. During what had seemed like an interminable wait on hold Crawford had been able to review his present position and consider the wisdom of involving Beatty. No new possibilities presented themselves and if he were to be honest he hadn't expected any – Beatty was his best chance of redemption, truthfully, he was his only chance.

When Beatty's voice came on line Crawford realised that the exchange was going to be short and none too sweet; the man was obviously in no conciliatory mood.

"This had better be good Crawford, otherwise I'm hanging up."
"Dave I need your help."
"That's what you said the last time and look at the trouble that's caused. Oh no, you're not going to sucker me in with that."
"I'm not trying anything. Look, I've made a mistake, a big mistake, and I can't make up for it myself. All I'm asking is that you make the initial contact."
"Why the hell should I?"
"Because you would be showing good faith in clearing things with the Gardens…."
"Don't put me on your hook Crawford."
"I'm not, honestly I'm not, but look at it from their point of view; when they find out that this has happened, and one way or another they will, it would be to your advantage to be seen as helpful in closing it down."
"Don't try and appeal to my better nature 'cause I haven't got one."
"Dave I'm not as stupid as all that. You'll only do this thing if it makes you look good."
"That's right."
"So you'll do it then?"
"Not so fast. You don't get me that easily. I'll give it some thought, I'm making no promises, remember that."
"I couldn't ask for more, but thanks for listening at least."

"You can keep your thanks."

"OK then, but let me say I'm sorry."

"Sorry for yourself more like it. Look, if I decide to do this thing I'll call you and give you any details I get, but you are not to call me under any circumstances, is that understood? This is as far as our contact goes."

"I understand and I...."

Beatty hung up before Crawford could elaborate, clearly he had heard enough. No matter, Crawford was fairly confident that Beatty would take the offer to the Gardens and that something could be worked out. He felt pleased with himself for the first time in longer than he could remember; he had taken a chance, made a decision and stuck to it. If he had analyzed his actions he would have seen that the last time he had behaved like this he'd made his disclosure in the first place – strange how self-preservation always superseded an honourable endeavour – stranger still the blind eye that Crawford brought to bear on his predicament.

Beatty sat in the small office he'd been given in Aldershot and stared at the telephone. He knew that he should be calling Blackwell but something in the tone of Crawford's voice prevented him; the man had sounded genuine – people did make mistakes and it was possible that Crawford was trying to make amends. What passed for a conscience in Beatty's case struggled with the question for all of fifteen minutes and then the answer came to him – his own safety was paramount and Crawford would just have to take his chances with the "Department". He lifted the handset from the cradle and keyed in the number of Blackwell's direct line. The call was answered after two rings and Beatty heard a muffled voice tell someone else to stay where they were while the call was taken, then Blackwell came on the line.

"Yes."

"Mr. Blackwell, it's Beatty. I've just had Gerry Crawford on the phone."

"And what did he want?"

"He wants me to act as a middle-man. He wants to make a clean breast of the mistake he's made."

"Does he now?"

"That's what he said to me, sir. He knows that he shouldn't have acted as he did and he seems to have taken steps to clean up the mess."

"So how does he envisage doing that?"

"To be honest he didn't really say, but I got the impression that he wanted to hear suggestions from the Gardens before he committed himself."

"To see the lay of the land, so to speak?"

"Yes sir, that's my reading of his position."

"I tell you what Beatty, I'm going to give this situation some consideration and if necessary I'll get back to you with instructions."

"I understand sir."

"Good."

Blackwell hung up leaving Beatty momentarily unsure of his next move until the earpiece amplifier broke his reverie with a continuous tone that made him replace the handset. He thought about Blackwell's deliberations and where they might lead but found himself unable to make a clear judgement – the only thing he could be sure of was the fact that he had done the right thing in taking the story of Crawford's betrayal to the Gardens in the first place. He thought of the tone of the exchange with Blackwell. Did it show that he was safe? He had made a grave error after all, but no, he didn't think he was at any risk, Blackwell had sounded too much in control, not like a man ready to tear strips off a subordinate. With a sense of relief he returned to the file and the investigation that should have been taking up his time – best to leave the Crawford business with the Gardens, he had his own job to do.

Kavanagh sat watching Blackwell with an air of expectation, he knew damn well that the short conversation had been with Beatty, Blackwell had deliberately used his name for no other reason than to stir his curiosity, but he wasn't going to give the younger man the satisfaction of asking the obvious question. Blackwell sat shuffling through various papers in front of him seemingly oblivious to Kavanagh's presence, but even he couldn't keep up the pretence indefinitely so he broke the silence.

"You may have gathered that that was Beatty on the line."

"Yes sir."

"Well don't you want to know what he had to say?"

"Only if it bears any relevance to the task in hand."

"It could do."

"I not going to sit here and play twenty questions with you sir, so if it is of no importance to me I'll be leaving."

"Don't be in such a hurry…."

"You're the one who made such an issue of time, so I've no choice but to hurry sir."

"OK, point taken. Beatty says that Crawford has seen the error of his ways and wants to make amends."

"And you believe that?"

"I believe that Beatty believes Crawford, as for myself I'm not so sure. You know the man, tell me, is he capable of a change of heart in this instance?"

"He always had strong beliefs, he wasn't prone to wavering, so I'd say that this is a change made purely for self-preservation. As for sincerity, I don't think so, and if he took this point of view and subsequent action once, well, he can take it again."

"So you think he's still a danger?"

"Without a doubt. I don't see that this changes anything. It does, however, present us with the opportunity we would have found difficult to manufacture."

"Explain?"

"Crawford wants a meeting and we want to meet him, under the circumstances everyone is satisfied."

"But he could pick any location he wishes for the meeting and if that's the case he'll control the ground, which you don't want."

"I'm fairly confident that he'll be happiest at home. He knows the environment intimately and he'll feel that it's well under his control. The expectation won't be for any action to take place there."

"What makes you so sure?"

"Because that's how I would feel in his position and he taught me if you remember."

"So you would suggest a meeting at his apartment?"

"No, no! I wouldn't suggest anything if I was you. Let him set the boundaries, don't force anything on him, very gentle handling is what's required, let him think that he's making all the rules. Most important of all don't even mention my name, if he wants me he'll ask for me."

"One thing came to mind during Beatty's call – do you think Crawford is aware that Beatty has made contact with me?"

"It doesn't really matter, but if I were to hazard a guess I would say yes. Crawford may have been out of the loop for a while, but he isn't stupid."

"Well, if that's the case does it make any difference to our approach?"

"I shouldn't think so. The end result is going to be the same. He wants matters dealt with quickly too, and that means his time for preparation is limited and the advantage we have over him is resources and access to them."

"Right, I'll get back to Beatty and have him set something up."

"I'd prefer it if you just tell him that things are a go, but nothing more than that. He can pass on the willingness for a meet to Crawford but no timetable; that'll give me the opportunity to take a look at the home territory area of Holland Park; the road network, other means of transport – that sort of thing."

"Just remember I want this business finished with this week."

"Don't worry about that, you just get me the floor plans I asked for and I'll take care of the rest."

As Williams sat in front of his lap-top scrolling through the story, his sense of disappointment grew, he knew the piece was a good one and it seemed such a waste to have it effectively destroyed with one telephone call. Damn Crawford for his lack of resolution! Did the man not understand what he'd done? He looked at the central theme of the disclosure and wondered if there was any way to make it without mentioning the "Department". It was tempting to simply erase the organisation from the piece, but to do so took the keystone from the story, and without it the whole edifice collapsed. Unsubstantiated stories just made for sensationalist pieces that only belonged in the red-top press and that was not where he wanted it to go.

It was too good to let slip, maybe a call to Crawford would do the trick – then again, maybe it wouldn't, the man had seemed more than determined when they had spoken yesterday. As he came to the final paragraph he reached a decision – let matters lie and see what news Crawford had to offer come Friday – speculation in the meantime would only drive him insane. Between now and then he'd have to occupy his time as best he could – the trouble was he couldn't think of anything to do other than take the bike out for a ride. He looked again at the screen of his lap-top before he shut the file. He got up from the desk and pulled his leathers on – if he sat any longer he'd just get exasperated – better to vent his ill humour with some hard riding.

As the rain fell on the car windscreen Kavanagh looked at the colonnaded entrance to the terrace conversion that was the main access point to Crawford's flat and wished that he was somewhere else. There could be little doubt, however, that there was money in private security, and yet again, he found himself comparing his own rented flat with the understated style of the Holland Park address. What could make a man risk this kind of lifestyle over the head of a story that in Kavanagh's view no-one would want to hear or even believe if they did? He couldn't think of an answer other than Crawford taking leave of his senses. He knew he would reach no conclusions if he continued speculating, so he returned to the certainties of the assessment he had completed on the roads around Holland Park and the availability of public transport.

There were buses galore and the Underground to chose from – transport was not a problem if he had to rely on the public sector – what would be important was scheduling. Tempting as the use of either a bus or train was, he didn't want to be left waiting for somebody else to fulfil a timetable. He considered and rejected taxis – cabbies had memories that were just too dangerous. No, the flexibility and control of his own car looked to be the best option, although there were, of course, potential problems with the use of a private car – he was planning on making an exit as the West End emptied of cinema and theatre goers – and that meant that there was always the chance of an accident.

He flicked his notebook shut and took a deep breath. No matter what the job there was always so much to think about, so many "what ifs?" In an ideal world there would be time to spare, there would be the opportunity to put a team of "watchers" on Crawford, there would be the time to organise a foolproof takedown, there would be a carefully orchestrated aftermath, there would be so many things. What did he have? A day and a half, his own abilities, and no alternative as far as the commission of the job went. He wasn't going to get any help and if he were to be objective he could understand Blackwell's view – there was no sense involving awkward third parties in a job like this. Being objective was all very well but it was scant comfort when it could be him paying the cost for failure. All he could do was cover as many eventualities as possible.

He looked again at the front entrance and as the rain had slackened to a light drizzle he decided to take a closer look – a doorman or concierge was unlikely but it was better to be safe than sorry; he wasn't disappointed, the front lobby had no desk for a member of staff and the only sign that the house had been converted into flats was the stand of post-boxes that were allocated to the residents. He checked the name-plates and saw Crawford's name as expected at number three. The last thing that he looked for was any evidence of closed circuit television cameras but wasn't surprised to see that there weren't any. It never ceased to amaze him that people who lived in expensive locations always skimped when it came to providing for security; the simple expedient of installing a camera system and paying the maintenance charges would do more than just give them piece of mind – it would save them money too. Surely Crawford had pointed this out to his fellow residents? Maybe they didn't like the idea of having a security professional living amongst them; after all, that made him a tradesman and, with snobbery alive and well, barely tolerable in Holland Park Mews. His irritation gave way to quiet satisfaction at the lack of security and the ease it lent to his forthcoming job, anyway, he'd seen enough to complete his assessment. He returned to his car and made the short journey along Hyde Park that brought him to Bayswater and Leinster Gardens.

Blackwell was fairly pleased by his management of events thus far – Beatty was on standby and Kavanagh was carrying out such surveillance of the target area as he deemed necessary. As for himself, he had managed to obtain floor plans of the townhouse conversion in Holland Park Mews from the planning offices in Knightsbridge. A courier had been sent from the Gardens to retrieve them and had returned over an hour ago by motorcycle. The stencilled copies of the architect's original plans showed the layout of the flat, with the locations of the kitchen and bathroom obvious from the location of the utilities. The use Crawford had put the other rooms to was unknown, but Kavanagh could doubtless deal with any eventuality when he got into the flat.

He considered the possible actions that Kavanagh might take but decided that such speculation was pointless – all that mattered was that the job was completed successfully. His experience was not in field operations anyway, and he wisely concluded that his time would be better spent planning the organisation of the aftermath. What concerned him more than anything else was the existence of documents and how to secure them. He knew that time would not be on Kavanagh's side and the idea of sending a cleaning team in simply wasn't practical. One possible solution was to throw the blanket of "national security" over events and that would effectively close Holland Park Mews, but he was unsure of the response from the likes of Sir Giles Redfern. If the response was negative – too bad – the suppression of the story was paramount and any inter-community back-biting would just have to be accepted. Such confrontation may never happen but he was at least aware of the possibility and awareness was everything in this business.

Crawford had spent an anxious afternoon waiting for a call from Dave Beatty that had never come. He couldn't understand the lack of contact, surely Beatty had been keeping the "Department" informed as soon as he had become aware of the potential problem, and if the "Department" was aware then surely they would want a meeting as soon as possible? The apparent silence didn't make any sense to him, unless, of course, the "Department didn't care, but that was not just unlikely it was impossible.

He sought diversion with work but as there was little that required his attention he found himself making jobs that didn't exist. When Maria had brought him his customary mid-afternoon coffee he had been brusque, and it was his uncharacteristic rudeness that showed him just how pre-occupied he was. He sat looking at projected manpower requirements that had no meaning and sipped at the coffee that had no taste. By five o'clock, with no contact from Beatty, he realised how futile the day had been and decided to go home early. The journey back to the Central Line station at Holland Park passed in an unpleasant damp blur; he paid no attention to the other passengers on the Tube or the wet autumnal day when he was above ground. As he walked back to his flat it came to him that Beatty may have called him at home so it was a great disappointment when he found no messages on his answering machine. His disappointment gave way to a bout of self-reproach, followed by self-pity and he fuelled his negativity with a couple of glasses of Hennessy. He tried his best to think of something else but found the effort too much for him. As he finished his second brandy he reflected that this evening and God alone knew how many others would be ruined until he knew his fate.

Kavanagh was back at the Gardens just after six, and being in no mood to talk over his preliminary surveillance with Blackwell, went to the kitchen in search of coffee. He was standing looking through his notes when his commander came into the kitchen, cup in hand, looking for the same thing. Blackwell went about the business of getting a refill without interrupting Kavanagh's concentration and stood sipping at his coffee waiting for any comments that might be forthcoming. Anybody observing their behaviour would have been reminded of two boys in a school playground determined not to lose face; Kavanagh was in a foul mood because he'd been out-manoeuvred and Blackwell was irritated by the time constraints of this particular job and the apparent petulance of his subordinate. Blackwell's heart wasn't in the game and broke the silence.

"OK Sean, what did you learn?"

"There was really very little that I could see, but I'll say this Crawford's done well for himself, it's a nice address, but he's gone soft, his professionalism's deserted him."

"How so?"

"Well from my point of view it's wide open – no overt security and I would doubt any covert. Basically it's easy."

"You sound disappointed."

"Not really, it's just that I expected more from the old man."

"Just don't get complacent."

"Oh I wouldn't worry about that sir, my professionalism isn't in question."

"What else did you see?"

"I covered the availability of public transport just to be sure, but I think realistically that I'll be going in and out by car, so I checked out the local parking situation...."

"All very interesting, but not much use to me."

"What did you expect me to find? A notice on his door saying "I'm a whistle blower". It doesn't work that way, all the background is mundane but it's necessary, so before I go home I want to look at the floor plans. You did get them OK?"

There was something about Kavanagh's tone that Blackwell didn't like, it sounded as if Kavanagh was giving the orders.

"They're in my office. I've been through them myself and I don't think you'll find any unpleasant surprises."

"I'll be the judge of that sir...."

"Just be careful Kavanagh, you are treading a very fine line and you're not far away from insubordination."

"With all due respect sir, spare me the bloody lecture...."

"That's it!"

Blackwell slammed his cup down on the kitchen table and stood pointing his right hand at Kavanagh, unsure of his next move.

"I've had enough of you and you're superiority. It's about time somebody taught you a lesson."

Kavanagh looked at the man bristling in front of him and came closer than he'd ever come in his career to hitting an officer, to do so would have meant more than just the end of his career, there was no telling what Blackwell was capable of, so instead he made an observation that couldn't be argued with.

"Sir, you've given me a shitty job with no alternatives – if my manner is offensive I think I have every right to be. If you don't like it, then that's too bad. If you want to transfer me when this is finished I won't argue or complain, but remember what I know and remember that I might require some careful handling."

Blackwell knew that he'd been bettered but was also aware that if he didn't make an effort at the last word he'd be finished in Kavanagh's eyes.

"Just remember what sort of handling you could be liable for."

"I think we understand each other sir. Now, you said something about the plans being in your office, may I suggest that we go and take a look at them."

Kavanagh's attempt at defusing the situation worked, Blackwell visibly relaxed and Kavanagh reflected on what had been a close call.

The plans only proved useful in giving the dimensions of the flat and the locations of the kitchen and bathroom. Kavanagh folded them up and put them back on the desk with a sigh and a shake of his head.

"Well, I've seen enough sir. I'll be in the Gardens first thing tomorrow to have a word with Harry Woodford."

"What do you want to see him for?"

"He should have some kit that I need. I take it he's still lurking in the basement?"

"That's where you'll find him."

"Good. Well good night sir, and if it's any consolation I'm sorry for the exchange."

Before Blackwell could reply Kavanagh was gone, and the "Department" head was left wondering why it was that the apology sounded more like an insult.

* * *

Beatty's morning routine was following the pattern that he'd set during his weeks at Aldershot; as usual he'd woken at 0630 and gone for his morning run which was more for appearance rather than any real fitness value, although it was better than nothing. By 0730 he was back at the sergeants' mess and in the shower and at 0800 he was in the canteen for breakfast. His normal working day was due to start at 0900 so it was rather annoying to have his read of the morning paper interrupted by the ringing of his mobile phone. It was even more annoying when he realised who was calling him and for what purpose.

"I'll get straight to the point, a meeting with Crawford is necessary and you're going to be the middleman."

Beatty knew better than to raise any objections so he went along with the order. That said, anybody observing him would have seen the colour drain from his face when he'd answered the call – clearly the news wasn't good.

"What do you want me to do?"

"Very simple so even you can't make a hash of this. I want you to give him this number and that's all. Get a pen and write this down, ----- --- ---, when you've given it to him destroy it. I'm going to assume that you are successful, so there is no need for you to contact me with confirmation. Is all that clear?"

"Yes sir."

The line was broken and Beatty was left with no chance to ask for clarification. It was a fine start to the day and he could only hope that it got no worse.

Kavanagh had looked out on a fine sunny morning from his bedroom window and had decided to leave the "Department" car in its precious parking space and take the bus to work. It was a decision that he came to regret as soon as he got up to the top deck. A mixed group of teenagers, some going to school, some not, had taken possession of the floor and were making a nuisance of themselves. An elderly couple in particular found the youngsters behaviour intimidating and tried their best to look small. Kavanagh found a seat three rows behind them near the front of the bus and watched the antics of the teenagers as they jeered at the pensioners. Ordinarily he would have offered some sage advice and if it were not listened to a couple of heads would have been cracked, but with the forthcoming job he couldn't afford to get involved and he felt awkward for not lending assistance.

Fortunately nothing but words were directed at the old couple and Kavanagh was able to get off the bus with his conscience intact although his mood was far from good, he'd have really liked to have given the youngsters a lesson in manners. His temper didn't improve any in the walk to the Gardens and it was with a certain disappointment that he found the security man attentive and courteous when he stopped to check in at reception. He could feel the pressure building and he knew that he'd have to release it soon or his judgement would suffer. At least Harry Woodford was in the building, he'd seen the name in the book, and the fact that he didn't have to wait was one less thing that could annoy him.

He made his way down the stairs to the basement and the little room that acted as the armoury. The light above the door was on, indicating that Harry was in residence so Kavanagh made no effort to herald his arrival but walked straight in. The slight figure of a man in his early sixties stood hunched over a lathe with his back to the door.

"Don't you buggers ever knock?"

"And good morning to you too, you grumpy old sod."

Woodford put down his tools and turned, a smile spreading over his face at the sight of Kavanagh.

"Well look what the cat dragged in. And how the hell are you Sean?"

"I could complain, but who would listen?"

"Yeah, I could too. They keep me down in this bloody hole and sometimes I feel they've forgotten I exist."

"Well I haven't."

"Yeah, I know, and I know too that you'll want something, so let's hear it."

"OK, I want something cold that can be left after a job."

Woodford dropped the air of congeniality and gave some thought to the request before answering.

"Are the plods going to get a look in?"

"Undoubtedly."

"So who's the target?"

"I can't tell you that. All I can say is that the item has to look like something picked up either as a trophy or as a hideaway acquisition."

"One of our lot by the sound of it. Don't worry, no more questions about that. With regard to the item, what sort of dimensions and calibre?"

At this point Kavanagh reached into his front right hand trouser pocket and retrieved his rig.

"This is for a PPK, if you've got one it would be ideal, failing that something pretty close to that size and shape. Calibre isn't a major factor, but again .32 would be spot on."

"Christ, you don't want much, do you Sean?"

"You did ask."

"Yeah I did. Well I've got no cold PPKs to give away", and Woodford pulled open a drawer to his right, bringing out a small bundle wrapped in grease-proof paper which he passed to his friend, "But how about this?"

The wrapping was quickly discarded and a small black pistol nestled in Kavanagh's hand. He looked at the markings and nodded his head with satisfaction.

".32 Beretta Model 90, not many of them about and pretty good from what I know."

"So you've used one before?"

"Yeah, I tried one out about five years ago but the lack of spares and the fact that it's discontinued put me off. Other than that it points well and the accuracy's more than acceptable. Where'd you get this one?"

"Some lad tried to bring it back from Cyprus, got caught and was charged for it. Some kind soul down at Warminster passed it on to me."

"If the School of Infantry have had their paws on it I'm not interested."

"Don't worry Sean. You said it had to be cold and there's no paperwork on this one. You have my word it's as cold as they come."

Kavanagh slipped the magazine from the well in the butt and examined the feed plate and lips for any tell-tale signs of wear – nothing was out of place and everything was in order. Next he stripped the pistol so he could examine the bore – again everything was clean and no signs of wear showed themselves.

"You know something Harry, it'll almost be a shame to leave this one behind. I mean, I doubt if its had more than a couple of magazines through it."

Having re-assembled the pistol he tried to slip it into the pocket rig and was pleasantly surprised when it slotted home with only a little difficulty. Woodford watched carefully and noting the problem reached around to the shelves behind him and lifted a small plastic bottle which he passed to Kavanagh.

"Try this. It's white graphite and should slick things up a bit."

Kavanagh un-capped the bottle and gave a couple of gentle squeezes into the rig, before gently rubbing the fine powder into the leather interior. A few draws from the holster and any apparent tightness was gone.

"Just the job, although I won't be needing a fast draw anyway, this rig's only for carriage, still it makes life a bit easier."

"Looks like you're ready to go. I take it that you're OK for rounds?"

"I've got a bag of buckshee from Jimmy Curtis down at "The Fort"."

"And how is Jimmy?"

"Like the rest of us, waiting for the new brooms to sweep us clean."

"The new brooms, as you call them, haven't got a clue. There'll always be a need for the likes of us Sean."

"True enough Harry, true enough. Look, before I go I want to try this one out – is the "box" still available?"

The reference to the steel bullet catcher brought an amused smile to Woodford's face and he gestured towards the door at the rear of the armoury.

"They couldn't sweep that aside, all that they could manage was to make sure the test room was sound-proofed. Come on, it's next door."

They went through a heavily padded door into a small room, barely six by eight, which had a steel box mounted on a frame standing at one end. Both men took a pair of ear defenders from the hooks on the back of the door and Woodford handed Kavanagh five loose rounds which he loaded. When he was ready he levelled the pistol at the cardboard target clipped on the frame and fired. The Beretta cycled the five rounds flawlessly and Kavanagh nodded with satisfaction.

"It'll do."

Crawford had none of Kavanagh's troubles getting to work, but if anything his frame of mind was worse – waiting for the call from Beatty was gnawing away at him. He sat in his office with nothing to do but watch the telephone and yet it still came as a surprise when it rang. He nearly dropped the handset when he lifted it from the cradle and his voice nearly failed him when he spoke.

"C-C-Crawford."

"You know who this is so I'll just tell you what I was told. You got a pen?"

"Yes."

"Your request for a meeting was accepted. You're to call this number, ----- --- ---, you got that?"

"----- --- ---."

"Yeah that's it. Anyway, call that number and you can set something up."

"Who am I going to be talking with?"

"He'll tell you if he wants to."

"But...."

"No more questions Gerry. I've done my bit."

"Hold on...."

The line was broken. Crawford looked at the number and considered dialling it straight away but decided not to – better to formulate an approach that would leave him secure – he'd call when he was ready.

Blackwell had arrived at the Gardens just after nine and had spent the whole morning going through the Crawford file again. It wasn't because he thought that there was some piece of information that he had missed that would excuse the man's behaviour, it was rather that he was just being thorough. He found nothing by way of explanation and nothing that would be of use to Kavanagh. In one of his more philosophical moments he reflected on how little a life amounted to when the facts were listed, but there was a coldness about Blackwell that could never let him empathise, certainly not with the likes of Crawford. An accepted code of conduct was what maintained the "Department" and the Crawfords of the world couldn't be allowed to upset years of sound practice.

By eleven Blackwell had exhausted every aspect of the file – there was nothing to fear from the course of action he had decided on. All that remained was for contact to be made, and if Beatty had followed orders that should come at any time. The thought of the impending call triggered what was an irrational response from Blackwell – the number Beatty had given to Crawford was for a mobile phone which now sat on his desk – he knew the battery was fully charged – he knew it was switched on, and he picked it up and checked it anyway. God! but he wanted something to happen. He almost gave in to the temptation of calling Crawford at his office but he knew that to do so would show the "Department" hand and that was something he couldn't afford. A knock at the door pulled Blackwell back from the brink of precipitate action. If nothing else it would act as a distraction so he acknowledged the knock and Kavanagh came in, taking the seat across the desk from Blackwell.

"I take it you saw Woodford?"

"Yes sir and I've got sorted out with the necessary tool for the job."

"I won't ask."

"And I wouldn't tell even if you did sir. The fewer people who know about this the better, as I'm sure you'd agree?"

"So you're ready to go?"

"I suppose so, although I must say I'd like more time, even if it was just to do a bit more surveillance."

"You haven't got that time, let's be clear on that. Besides, what good would do?"

"I know Crawford is a target for removal, but I would like to know all I can about the people living around him. I don't want to trip over somebody when I've other things on my mind, it just makes things a bit safer from my point of view."

"As I've said there simply isn't the time for that kind of operation. Anyway, do you really think that Holland Park Mews is the kind of neighbourhood where people watch out for each other?"

"Probably not, no."

"Well then...."

Before he could say anything else Blackwell was interrupted by the annoying electronic shrilling of the mobile phone. He signalled to Kavanagh to keep his mouth shut and picked up the phone.

"Yes."

"I was given this number by Dave Beatty, so you know who I am."

"I do, but I don't know what you want."

"Let's not be coy. You know damn well what I want – a meeting. Beatty's outlined the whole story to you – I want a face to face to see if I can make amends."

"You know where we are...."

"Not on your turf, I want to control the location."

"So what do you suggest?"

"My home address."

As soon as Crawford said it Blackwell scribbled "HOME" on the back of an envelope and held it up for Kavanagh to read. By way of reply Kavanagh took the envelope and wrote "WHO WITH?" which brought a nod of agreement from Blackwell.

"I can live with that...."

"Oh no, not you, I don't know you."

"Well, Beatty then."

"Not Beatty, he's just a messenger. I want someone I know, someone I can trust."

"Trust is somewhat subjective in this business."

"All too true, but I'll go with what I know, so you'll get Sean Kavanagh for me."

Blackwell pointed at Kavanagh and mouthed "YOU". Again Kavanagh wrote on the envelope – this time it read "OK – DONT MAKE IT EASY – HAVE TO FIND ME".

"I'm new in this post, he's not familiar to me. What if I can't find him?"

"If you can't find him then the "Department" has gone down hill since my day. You'll find him."

"He could be overseas, anything. I don't even know if he's still with us."

"Sean'll still be with you and you will find him."

"And then what?"

"I'll give a couple of hours to find him and then I'll ring you back with the when."

Crawford ended the call and Blackwell switched the mobile off before looking across the desk at Kavanagh.

"Well?"

"You played that very smart sir. No two ways about it, he'll be thinking he's in control and that's what we want him to think."

"Maybe I overdid it a bit about you."

"I don't think so, in fact it was a nice touch playing ignorance – he'll feel superior to the "Department" of today and the complacency that that'll hopefully produce will be to our advantage."

"I hope you're right."

"Trust me sir, I know this man."

Crawford sat reflecting on the conversation he'd just had with the "Department" – could it really have changed so much since he'd been a member? The whole approach had seemed amateurish – even allowing for the faltering steps of a new man. Then again, perhaps he was being a little too critical – priorities did change, even in the "Department". One thing seemed clear to him though, and that was the fact that he was running things. He'd deliberated over his approach all morning, ever since Beatty had given him the number and made contact a reality, and he'd concluded that resolution was the best way forward. He analyzed every response he'd got and could not see one instance of his coming off second best – he'd been in control throughout and that sense of control gave him a greater feeling of security than he'd had in weeks. His last demand – for Kavanagh's involvement – had been potentially risky, he didn't even know if Sean was still attached to the "Department" but it had been important to set guidelines of some description.

Thoughts of Kavanagh took him away from the dangers of the present; he wondered how the younger man had turned out, if they did meet it would be interesting to see what the years had done. After the job in South Armagh they had worked together on three further occasions, twice in Northern Ireland and once in Germany, and Kavanagh had made progress every time. If that progress had continued there was no doubt in Crawford's mind that the younger man had become a first class team member. That thought made him pause – interesting that he'd thought of Kavanagh as a team member and not a team player. That was how Crawford had always seen himself – an insider outside – able to follow the rules as long as the rules were acceptable to him – never able to offer blind devotion.

He was sitting, staring into space, focusing on nothing, and all he could think of was an individual who belonged and didn't at the same time. The image of himself was distracting, yet seductive – the crusader. And then the emptiness of his conceit hit him – who was he trying to kid? – nobody but himself. If he didn't get some sense of perspective soon he'd find dealing with anyone from the "Department", let alone Kavanagh, an impossibility.

Blackwell had given Kavanagh as much detail from his conversation with Crawford as he could remember, and they had then looked at the various possible cover stories that could be used to explain Kavanagh's location. Both men decided that the best explanation was to stick to the truth, that Kavanagh was down at "The Fort". Anything else was too complicated and both of them were well aware of the problems of inventing difficulties, even in a job like this. With the cover finalised Kavanagh excused himself and returned to the kitchen for another coffee. Truth be told, he was finding prolonged contact with Blackwell distasteful – the man was totally lacking in compassion, not necessarily a fault in this business but even a hint of it would have humanised him a little.

As always there was coffee brewed and Kavanagh tried his best to divorce himself from the ugliness of the job as he sipped at the mug full he'd just poured. The bitter tang almost took him away but the weight of the Beretta in his right hand trouser pocket was a constant reminder that wouldn't afford him the luxury of distraction. With the reality of the pistol came the rehearsals that had been running through his mind since he'd seen the floor plans. He knew that he had to have a sequence of events mapped out before he made the visit but his conscience was troubling him and if he was unsure of himself during the planning stage then what would he be like when he was on site? Damn Blackwell to hell! But he knew that such an emotional outburst was unprofessional and to follow that direction would make him no better than Crawford. Damn Blackwell anyway!

Damnation was the last thing on Blackwell's mind as he sat at his desk waiting for Crawford's call; he was going through the fundamentals of Kavanagh's proposed action and, as objectively as possible, he was trying to knock holes in them. Realistically the potential difficulties all existed outside the flat, whether it was going to or coming from was the question – in truth the seriousness of discovery before the action would be of little consequence, but the problems would be enormous if Kavanagh was apprehended after the job was done. There were no margins for error that Blackwell could see and that troubled him, he'd have to talk matters over with Kavanagh to see if there was some way to limit the chances of failure. He really wanted guarantees, but if he were to be realistic he knew that there were no certainties. He didn't need an old hand, like Kavanagh, to tell him that there was one commodity that couldn't be accounted for, and that was luck, no, you could never have enough of that.

Keeping manpower input to an absolute minimum was making his life almost impossible. His experience of this kind of job was second-hand at best and the temptation to involve others was almost overwhelming but for the knowledge of Redfern's reaction when he'd first sought advice. No, there was no help to be had from other quarters, he was on his own, and if he didn't like it then that was just too bad. One lesson that had never really been reinforced, as he'd worked his way up the ranks, was that any commander had to take responsibility for his orders and the actions that grew from them. That sort of acceptance was always going to be difficult, but what angered him more than anything else was the fact that he was having to take responsibility for actions that had taken place nearly twenty years ago.

He looked at notes that he'd jotted down as he'd thought about the Crawford situation and one remark in capitals stood out – THE BUCK STOPS HERE. All the efforts at apportioning blame immediately became weak and hollow – he'd worked hard to get this position and if he couldn't accept the unpleasant realities then he'd no business occupying this seat. A sense of realism would overcome any obstacle, all he had to do was accept that fact and behave accordingly. But if that was the case, why was there a problem with Crawford? If realism was the answer, why was an individual creating such a great difficulty at present? The stumbling block had to be free will and the unpredictability that it bred. He shook his head in an effort to clear the troubles from his mind – how could he have foreseen that running the "Department" would lead to a philosophical debate? Things were meant to be simple and he realised that he had to make them so, otherwise nothing would ever be achieved and the need for problem solvers, such as himself, would cease to exist. Before he could get deeper entrenched in the question of leadership the mobile rang again. There was no preamble this time, Crawford got straight to the point.

"Have you found Kavanagh?"

"I have."

"And?"

"He was at "The Fort" apparently, but I've spoken to the Director Training and he has been ordered to return to London."

"When?"

"He'll be with me tomorrow morning."

"Does he know what this is about?"

"I didn't speak to him myself, I just said it was an emergency as a means of getting him here, but I gave no details if that's what you mean."

"Time enough for that tomorrow."

"Well I have to tell the man something, so I want to hear what you have in mind."

"As I've said I want a meeting."

"I know, but I want specifics."

"OK. I want it on my terms, on my territory."

"So what do you suggest?"

"My home address, at Holland Park Mews."

"When?"

"We all want this over and done with as soon as possible, so I would suggest tomorrow evening at seven-thirty."

"That doesn't give me much time for preparation...."

"Exactly! I know how the "Department" works. The less time you have the better I like it. You don't need a lot of time to give Sean the necessary anyway, besides he only really needs to bring an open mind and his memory to hear what I have to say."

"I don't see why this couldn't all be handled over the phone."

"No, no, no. I need to see a face. I need to be sure,"

"You seem to need a lot of things, but let me remind you, it's all because you couldn't keep your mouth shut that there's a problem in the first place."

"Meaning?"

"Meaning don't expect too much from us unless you have a lot to offer."

"I just need guarantees."

"Well so do we."

"Look, I just want to...."

"I know what you want and the meeting tomorrow should give you the answers."

"OK , seven-thirty it is."

"Kavanagh will be there."

Whether Blackwell hung up first or not was of little consequence, there were no points to be scored on this occasion as neither man had wanted to prolong the conversation. He looked at the time he'd jotted down – seven-thirty pm Wednesday – and he thought about the way he'd manipulated Crawford, the meeting with Kavanagh, the meeting on Crawford's home turf, the attempt at a change of approach and Crawford's insistence on a face to face. He congratulated himself on his skilful handling – Crawford had always felt in control, when in fact he'd willingly assured his own destruction.

Crawford re-ran the exchange with the "Department" man with mixed feelings. On the plus side were the facts that Kavanagh was going to be the face of the opposition and that the meeting was going to take place where he could control it.

On the negative were niggling concerns about the tone that had been adopted. He thought the owner of the voice had sounded almost dismissive, even when he'd tried to change the rules with the suggestion of a settlement over the phone. The truth was that he didn't know the man and he could spend hours second guessing the motivations and reasons for his behaviour and be none the wiser. He dropped his head and massaged his temples with his thumbs, realising that he had a lot to thankful for and that there was no point creating difficulties that didn't have any foundation. At least he was in a position to negotiate and despite his lack of certainty it looked like a position of relative strength.

Kavanagh temporarily overcame his aversion to Blackwell and thought it best to return to the office with a peace offering of coffee. As he made his way down the corridor he tried to adopt a more conciliatory frame of mind, after all it was early days in his relationship with the new controller. He knocked respectfully rather than walking straight in and even waited for the command to enter. But he knew that he was never going to mesh with Blackwell when he noticed the self-satisfied look that the younger man wore as soon as he went in. The look told him that everything was a game to Blackwell, a game without consequences and he knew that Crawford had been in contact without having to be told. Blackwell stretched the silence out for effect and must have been disappointed when Kavanagh didn't ask the obvious. The best he could do under the circumstances was to state it with a degree of smugness.

"We've got him."

Ever since he'd been told of the problem with Crawford, Kavanagh had known that his involvement was inevitable, but hearing Blackwell confirm it did nothing to lessen the impact. He set the cup of coffee down on the desk and took his seat opposite Blackwell before making any comment.

"I'll need details sir."

It wasn't the expected reply – the way the eyes narrowed and the manner in which the lips tightened showed that Blackwell thought that some form of congratulation was in order, clearly he felt deserving of praise but Kavanagh wasn't going to oblige him. Rather than compromise himself further he assented to the request.

"OK, well he wants the meeting at his flat tomorrow at seven-thirty."

"That pretty well covers it then."

Kavanagh got up and made his way towards the office door.

"Now just a minute", Blackwell was wasn't finished with him and pointed to the chair he'd vacated, "There are aspects of this task that aren't finalised."

"Really, I thought it was fairly simple – you want Crawford out of the frame and you're in effect blackmailing me to do it...."

"I wont stand for any more of your insubordination!"

"Jesus Christ! You want to take a listen to yourself once in a while. You're talking about a "task", you dress things up in neat words and you avoid the truth at every opportunity. With all due respect sir, you're ordering me to commit murder. I don't like it but I'm enough of a realist to know that the alternative isn't in my interests. So I'll do your shitty job but don't think that the normal rules apply in this instance."

"Are you quite finished?"

The condescension was patently obvious but rather then embark on another tirade Kavanagh merely nodded his head.

"Right Mr. Kavanagh, let me remind you that you aren't indispensable. This particular task is, I'll admit, far from pleasant, but you will be well rewarded for your involvement. We will liaise on this job as we have been doing and if you don't like my methods, well, as you've said to me, that's too bad. Finally, I don't wish to hear any more dissent from you, is that understood?"

"Yes sir."

"Well, as you seem to have no further questions I'll let you go."

As Kavanagh made his way out of the chilly atmosphere of the Gardens into the relative warmth of a bitter October evening he reflected on his tussle with Blackwell; he was smart enough to know that there could be no winners and losers this time around, but the amount of ammunition he had given Blackwell was damaging and the best thing he could do was to keep his mouth shut. Then again, he'd always had difficulty when it came to holding his tongue.

Blackwell sat at his desk and finished the last of his coffee which was by now lukewarm. He was considering the present situation with Crawford and Kavanagh and none of his thoughts were particularly cheering. The axe was waiting to fall on Crawford, so he didn't present too great a concern, but Kavanagh was becoming a worry. His attitude towards authority went beyond the usual bolshiness that was encountered from time to time. Blackwell couldn't be sure if it was merely a problem with officers in general or something that went deeper. Was it a problem that could be solved with money? Maybe Kavanagh could be bought? That thought took Blackwell to the small wall safe at the rear of his office. After he'd successfully entered the combination he retrieved the small green bound lodgement book and returned to his seat. He opened the book at the final list of figures and as always took a sharp intake of breath. The "Cummings" account had grown over the years and the depository in Douglas now held in excess of five million sterling. There could be no doubt that Kavanagh would have to be paid for the Crawford job and taking funds from the unaccounted for Isle of Man account was the best solution. So he'd be paid for the job and his silence would be secured, the only question was how much?

* * *

Kavanagh had spent a restless evening in his flat, thoughts of the job ahead of him had made any normal activities impossible. He'd had to force himself into preparations. Initially he'd cleaned the Beretta, which had taken him longer than usual as he'd had to make sure that there were no fingerprints on any portion of the pistol. He'd even put the one round he'd need into the magazine with latex gloves on – how many times had people made certain of a weapon only to load it with their bare hands? The next thing he'd addressed was his clothing for the next day. Memories of a conversation in a Belfast B&B came back to him as he'd gone through his wardrobe; Crawford had always been fastidious about his clothing on or off the job and Kavanagh had only thought it but right to apply the lessons he'd learned from his old mentor. Initially he'd thought of something very sharp but on reflection he had decided on the same sort of outfit he'd worn nearly twenty ears ago. His reasoning was simple, Crawford would be given an instant feeling of superiority as it would be clear to him that he'd moved on from the hacking jacket and cords look while Kavanagh hadn't, any small detail that would put the man off his guard or give him a misconception would always be to Kavanagh's advantage. He even pulled the John Lobb brogues that Crawford had criticised from the back of his wardrobe – something else to draw the eye away from Kavanagh and his true purpose.

With his preparations complete he'd gone to bed but attempts at sleep had been fruitless, his mind wouldn't let go of the job and the countless possibilities that he could encounter the following day. The rehearsals that he'd replayed over and over had been like a game of chess, the outcome of which was never in dispute, but no less compelling because of that. The result relied on his skill and that was truly the only comfort he'd been able to take from the dark hours of contemplation, the fact that he was one of the best at what he did. It had been close to four in the morning when fatigue had finally overtaken him and he'd drifted into a dreamless sleep.

The telephone on his bedside table woke him and his effort to ignore it had no effect, it just kept on ringing. He was tempted to lift the handset and put it down again but the caller would only be alerted of his presence and ring back. He sat up in bed, reached over and answered the call.

"Kavanagh."

"Where the hell have you been?"

It was Blackwell and his mood clearly hadn't improved since yesterday, then again, neither had Kavanagh's.

"If you must know I was asleep."

"You were in bed! Jesus Christ! Do you know what time it is?"

"No, but I'm sure you're going to tell me sir."

"Look Kavanagh, I had enough of your mouth yesterday, just watch it."

"I'm sorry, I had a rough night and I didn't get my head down until after three."

"But you'll be OK for tonight?"

"You needn't worry about that, I'll be fine."

"Good, that's what I wanted to hear."

"If that's all I'd like to get a bit more sleep."

"Fair enough, but I want you at the Gardens after lunch."

"I don't think that that's wise sir."

"But there are final details to be gone over and…."

"Sir, I have all the information I need and you really don't want me connected to the Gardens today of all days."

"But…."

"Sir this isn't insubordination, believe me. The task, as you call it, will be completed this evening. I'll contact you on completion. All I want from you is the mobile number that the conduit gave our man."

"You're being very conscientious all of a sudden."

"I don't see the point of giving details away on the phone, that's all sir."

"If you think it's necessary, then OK. But you can reach me here, I'll be at the Gardens 'til all this is over."

"Not even on your secure line sir. I'd prefer the mobile, you'll be dumping it anyway, so it may as well be useful one last time."

"As you wish, the number's ----- --- ---. Got that?"

"----- --- ---, I think I can remember that."

"OK Kavanagh, I'll speak to you later. Good…."

"Don't say it sir. I don't need it."

Before Blackwell could say anything else he replaced the handset. How could anybody be that flippant under the circumstances? Try as he might he couldn't come to terms with that kind of stupidity, it was beyond him. He slowly shook his head and looked at his watch – nine thirty-seven, if he couldn't get back to sleep he'd at least try to relax. He lay back and made an effort to clear his mind of Blackwell, Crawford and the job, and surprisingly he managed to drift off.

Crawford leaned over his desk and pushed the intercom button on his telephone.

"Maria, could you bring me in a coffee please."

"Right away Mr. Crawford."

He'd risen early and taken a cab to work, allowing him to clear his desk of the morning post without interruption. When the post was dealt with he'd turned his attention to the messages on his answering machine and the two notes that had been taken for him after he'd left the office the previous day. There was nothing of any great consequence among them, so with the basic housekeeping duties taken care of he was able to turn his mind to the meeting tonight.

Interestingly the aspect that gave him most cause for concern was not the substance of what he had done but rather the meeting with Kavanagh. The details of his disclosure, the method and the commission, the halt he had put on events and the guarantees he would offer, all these things were arranged in his mind. They didn't offer him any difficulties whereas just talking with Kavanagh raised issues that Crawford hadn't initially considered – there was the difference in their present situations, with Kavanagh the career staffer in the "Department" and him in the private sector – the outlook on the actions of a whistle blower – the possible change in Kavanagh's view of the "old man" because of the disclosure. These were issues that concerned him, the fact that they had served together meant that he wanted some sort of vindication for his actions from the younger man. Ultimately he felt justified for what he had done and he wanted Kavanagh to appreciate it, more than that, he wanted him to accept and condone it.

It was just after midday when he woke for the second time and for the second time he wished he was somewhere else, anywhere rather than London. He was possessed of a weariness that had nothing to do with physical activity – he'd heard expressions like heart sore and world-weary, but never before had he felt their full impact. It wasn't as if there hadn't been firefights, or specific targets in the past, but this was the first time that he'd been given a mark known to him personally. That difference was proving the stumbling block to a successful completion, but more than that, it was causing Kavanagh doubts that he'd never had about his position in the "Department".

He got out of bed and made his way into the bathroom for a shower. As he switched it on, he caught his reflection in the mirror above the sink and didn't like what he saw. His reflection was that of a troubled, hunted individual. He found it very hard to look himself in the eye, there was a definite effort at avoidance. God! If he couldn't face himself now, how could he make any approach to Crawford? He opened the glass door to the shower and stepped inside before turning the water on. He kept the thermostat low and the cold jets stung him – he needed some sort of shock to take away the self-indulgence that was threatening to make his job impossible. He told himself how important a sense of realism was in this instance, and when he held up the alternative to compliance, he liked it even less than his reflection. As he rinsed away the shampoo suds he accepted the fact that he would feel guilty but to feel that he would at least have to be alive. His usual certainties were being tested and he didn't like it. Normally he thought of himself as separate from the thundering herd, the little people who lived oblivious lives. In a matter of days his superiority had been shattered and he was sure if he could join the herd he would do so gladly. But there was no room for a creature like him in the herd and so he would do this thing and carry on. All he could hope for was that he'd be able to accept his actions, he wasn't enough of a liar to think in terms of forgiveness.

When he'd been in the shower there had been no distractions from the present, the test would be putting the conclusions into action and maintaining them. As he stood shaving he was able to pay more scrutiny to his face, if anything was going to betray him it would be his physical expression. The reflection showed a certain change, a hardness around the eyes, and he knew that if he could keep that he would be OK for the evening. When he'd finished in the bathroom, rather than get dressed he pulled on his old towelling robe and walked through to the kitchen to make lunch. One look at the paltry contents of his fridge reminded him that he hadn't been grocery shopping since his return from Gosport, he'd had other things on his mind and somehow food hadn't seemed important. He looked in the freezer compartment and was rewarded with a "cook from frozen" travesty of lasagne which he put in the oven to heat.

He switched on the radio and tried to listen to the lunchtime news but heard nothing of interest so he tuned into some of the music channels, but the banal noise that passed for music was worse than the silence. He turned it off and returned to his game of mental chess. He poured himself a glass of water and looked out of the window on the street scene below. The water satisfied his thirst but little else – he could have done with something stronger but only an idiot would have done that. By the time the lasagne was cooked his appetite had nearly disappeared but he forced himself to eat. He couldn't afford the distraction of an empty stomach tonight and he would certainly be in no mood to eat after the job.

By mid-afternoon Crawford had had enough of the office, the coffee and his efforts to finalise a strategy for the evening meeting. He put every document that could possibly relate to his disclosure in his briefcase, another aspect of the goodwill he intended to show Kavanagh when he saw him at Holland Park Mews. It didn't amount to much – a few handwritten references to Dave Beatty, Alain Williams and their respective telephone numbers, but he had the feeling that the "Department" would appreciate the effort on his part to hand them over. The damage that such material could do, even when added to the notes that he had at home, was strictly limited, and that led him to conclude that he'd be viewed as a minor source of irritation by the "Department". It was the best he could hope for under the circumstances although that still left Kavanagh to deal with and he was still nervous about their meeting.

He picked up his briefcase and walked out to reception where Maria occupied her station at the front desk.

"I'm going home early Maria. If you would look after any calls I'd appreciate it."

"Everything OK Mr. Crawford?"

"I suppose so. Nothing much to keep me here, that's all."

"Is there anything I can do?"

"No, no, there's nothing you can do, thanks for asking."

"Well if you're sure you're alright."

But Crawford was out the door before he could make a reply, leaving Maria to wonder what was weighing on his mind. He walked through Greenwich to New Cross station which was his usual route, the Underground took him to Shadwell on the Docklands Light Railway which in turn took him to the Central Line and home. As it was mid-afternoon there were fewer people on the trains than the usual rush-hour crush and he was able to get a seat. The whole trip was occupied with more thoughts about the meeting, even when he was standing on platforms waiting for the next train his thoughts blanked out any appreciation of what was going on around him, it was like a form of tunnel vision. His mind cast up all sorts of details, some necessary, some extraneous, but fundamentally he just wanted to get things right, most of all he wanted it to be over.

He stood at the kitchen sink and finished rinsing the glass before he dried it and put it back in the cupboard with the rest of his glassware. Normally he'd have left things in the drainer getting water stained, but today he was looking for any excuse not to address the real business of the day. Kavanagh looked at the clock above the kitchen door and, even though it told him that it was after four, he felt no compulsion to go and change. As he hung his tea towel over the radiator he closed his eyes and rested both forearms against the wall – he felt so bloody tired! He straightened up, taking a few deep breaths and then banished the self-indulgence before making his way to his bedroom.

He dressed slowly, taking particular care with the pocket rig, making sure that the holster didn't stand out or "print". After examining it from every angle, the only conclusion that he felt Crawford could reach was that he had taken to carrying his wallet, albeit a large one, in his front pocket. With his jacket on the line of his pocket was covered completing the effect – unless somebody knew for a certainty Kavanagh didn't look as if he was carrying a pistol. Standing up was one thing, but now he had to try sitting down – he moved the only easy chair in the bedroom in front of the mirror and watched as he took his seat, scrutinising the way a change of position altered the shape of his trousers around the rig. He watched as he moved about in the chair, crossing and uncrossing his legs, doing all the things that anyone would do unconsciously and he was more than happy with what he saw, which was nothing to raise his suspicion.

He got up from the chair, again watching to see if there was any tell-tale sign at his pocket, which there wasn't, and went over to the bedroom window. He looked up at the dull flat sky, overcast with the promise of rain, a nondescript day that didn't match his mood. It was still a couple of hours before he had to make a move, but the tension was building to a near intolerable level. Kavanagh knew that if he didn't try to calm down all the efforts at apparent ease would be for nought – Crawford would see through the act immediately. He moved away from the window and lay down on the bed. Sleep was out of the question but he could at least try to relax.

Blackwell found waiting for the result of his first action as head of the "Department" to be worse than he'd expected. It wasn't any worry for Kavanagh that caused him anxiety, it was more a matter of selfish concern – a failure on Kavanagh's part would open a can of worms, the repercussions of which would be serious consequences not just for him and the "Department" but for the intelligence community as a whole. He knew that the steps he was taking in this situation were the right ones but the prospect of failure was almost enough to put him off. The memory of the conversation with Redfern acted as the necessary spur – ultimately he couldn't afford to make an enemy there – better to act and rely on a favourable result. If all went to plan he would have a success to bring before his superiors and his position would be secured. That success depended on Kavanagh and all Blackwell could do now was wait.

Kavanagh sat watching the seconds tick by on the dashboard clock. He'd made the drive in twenty-five minutes, never once exceeding the speed limit or doing anything that would draw the attention of the police. Now he was waiting to see if the light drizzle would stop before he walked the couple of hundred yards to Crawford's flat; there was no sense in him getting wet as he might leave some forensic traces behind in his dampened wake. He had plenty of time to spare because of his usual earliness, time that he would have normally spent checking the details of the operation on task, but not this time, this time he'd just had to get out of his flat, giving him a change of focus and emphasis, so that he couldn't look too closely at himself.

He switched the windscreen wipers on and saw that the rain had stopped for the moment. He looked at the dashboard clock and then his own watch as final confirmation – it was seven-twenty-six – time to go. Leaving the car safely locked, he made his way along Portland Road to the junction with Holland Park Avenue. Traffic was reasonably light and there were no pedestrians for Kavanagh to encounter; the recent rain and the still blowing breeze had obviously put people off venturing out of doors, so much the better for him – no people meant no chance meetings that could prove awkward at a later date. He crossed the Avenue and took the turn that led to the Mews. In under two minutes he was at the entrance to the town-house conversion and Crawford's flat. Rather than walk straight in he crossed the street and took a look at the windows facing the front of the terrace. The only lights showing were on the second floor and they belonged to Crawford's flat. Either the other occupants were trying to save electricity or Crawford was the only resident at home. Kavanagh recrossed the road but before he went in he closed his eyes and shook his head in a final effort to dispel the last of his doubts. Self-interest conquered scruple, and it was with a clear mind that he crossed the threshold.

Crawford's expectation didn't save him from the shock of hearing the doorbell. He glanced at his watch – seven-thirty-four, Kavanagh had arrived. He went out to the hall and opened the front door. The man in front of him was carrying maybe seven or eight pounds extra weight but it was solid muscle bulk, there were a few grey hairs at the temples and the lines at the corners of the eyes were more sharply defined but otherwise the tanned figure hadn't changed since he'd last seen him, even the dress sense was the same. Neither man changed expression, no nods of recognition, no smiles of welcome, nothing. The wariness was tangible and Crawford broke the silence to deflate the atmosphere.

"You'd better come in Sean."

Crawford stood to one side and let the younger man enter, never once taking his eyes off him. Kavanagh stopped in the hall, waited for the door to close behind him, before turning to face Crawford as he shrugged off his overcoat.

"Where to Gerry?"

Crawford pointed to the open lounge door and extended his right arm for Kavanagh's coat.

"I'll hang that up for you."

Kavanagh looked around him as he made his way into lounge, taking in the basic floorplan he noted a chair with its back to the door and took the seat opposite. Crawford obliged him by taking the seat he wanted him to. Again there was a potentially awkward silence as both men sized each other up, This time it was Kavanagh's turn to start proceedings.

"OK Gerry, suppose you begin by telling me what's so important to bring me back from "The Fort" with no notice?"

"You know why you're here."

"I want to hear it from you."

"I don't see what purpose this sort of game playing serves."

"Humour me."

"OK, I made an error of judgement and I was caught up by a misplaced enthusiasm for it."

"Those are just words Gerry, give me the specifics."

"Jesus! Sean I don't know why you want this."

"Your perspective on your own actions will give me a foundation, so just tell me."

"Right, I got a name from Dave Beatty, a journalist who might be interested in a disclosure…."

"And the disclosure was?"

"Events before, during and after the raid on the Mullan farmhouse, March 23rd 1979."

"What else?"

"I talked about the "Department", how it headed up the job and would have continued to do so if the will had been shown."

"So you went on a crusade?"

"If that's what you want to call it, then yes."

"No, you did more than that, you mentioned the "Department", and it's never been heard of before."

"So what! Twenty-one people died in that raid. Don't you see how that sits with the circumstances at present?"

"Gerry nobody is going to care about what happened to a bunch of hardcore Provos. What they will care about is the existence, as they see it, of a "death squad" operating secretly within the military establishment."

"They'll care about the duplicity of the politicians who've endorsed and promoted this bloody mess that we've got now!"

"Oh come on! You think that really matters?"

"What we did was right Sean! We were fighting a bloody war!"

"So you're standing by what you told this journalist?"

"No, you're twisting this around."

"I don't think so. If you believe what we did then was right, then it follows that you disagree with present strategy, therefore what you've done about disclosure is right. In other words, my being here is a waste of my time."

"No, Sean, no. I realise that I've behaved badly, as some would see it, but…."

"No buts, you were wrong."

"OK, I was wrong. Look I don't want this story to get out any more than you do."

"Really? So why tell it in the first place? I don't accept that Gerry. You wanted it all out in the open and then you wanted to sit back and watch the events unfold. This was all about ego, wasn't it?"

Crawford was struck by what Kavanagh had said and frowned as he searched for a reply.

"Hadn't considered that, had you? Well it was one of the first things I arrived at when I read the file. This is all about you Gerry, not what we did."

Uncertainty wasn't just creeping into his thinking, Kavanagh had smashed a wide breach in his defences and an overwhelming horde of possibilities were storming in. For the first time Crawford found it impossible to look Kavanagh in the eye.

Kavanagh was amazed how quickly he had managed to batter a hole in Crawford's beliefs. The man was weakened and his guard was down, but it wasn't the time to make a move, he wanted to soften him up a bit more yet.

"Gerry, you have to understand the brief I'm working on. What you've done is potentially damaging to a lot of people. I'm here to try to understand your motives and then put the best case I can in your defence."

"You make it sound like a court."

"Well it is in a manner of speaking. You wanted this meeting, which looks like an admission of something…."

"Don't call it guilt Sean. I don't accept guilt."

"Have it your way. Not guilt then, maybe an acceptance of culpability, how's that?"

"Where is all this leading? What do you want – a signed confession? I've done nothing wrong!"

"Then why am I here?"

Kavanagh watched as Crawford struggled to find an answer. There was no doubt that Crawford was beginning to fall apart and the more vulnerable he was the easier it would be for Kavanagh to do his job.

"Look Sean, I got you because I thought I could trust you."

"No Gerry, you got me because you thought you could push me around. Well I'm sorry to disappoint you but that's not going to happen."

Crawford couldn't understand how he'd lost the initiative so quickly – he'd meant to explain himself briefly, hand over what little material he had and then offer his assurance that the story would never see the light of day. But Kavanagh hadn't played by the rules, at no time had he felt in charge of the meeting, and it had all gone horribly wrong. Kavanagh was questioning his motives, not just for telling the story in the first place, but also for involving him. Did these things really matter? Was it not enough that he was trying to make amends without dragging up the reasons for his actions? Had he not put himself through enough self-doubt and self-deprecation over the last couple of weeks? He knew he had to take control, otherwise he could find himself agreeing to any suggestion Kavanagh might care to make.

"Sean, I never wanted you to think that I was using you."

"Oh come off it! If I was in your position I'd use anyone or anything to help me. Spare me the soft soap approach and don't appeal to my better nature Gerry, 'cause I haven't got one. You're just another job."

"I'd never do that. Look, I just want this thing to go away", and he leaned forward to lift a file from the coffee-table, "This is all the material I've got – it's yours."

"Pass it over and I'll take a look."

Crawford gave him the file and sat looking as the younger man leafed through the sparse contents. He remembered the inquisitive nature that Kavanagh had always displayed and found himself wondering what had changed it – in the past Kavanagh had posed as a bit of a cynic – now the pose was gone to be replaced by the real thing.

The notes told Kavanagh that Crawford had either retained most of the details of the raid mentally or that he was concealing them, possibly as insurance. Given the fact that there were no official documents all the evidence was anecdotal anyway and if that was all there was then the dangers lay in Crawford's mind. With it gone most of the apparent risk would disappear. That covered the disclosure of the raid, but much worse was the naming of the "Department" – Kavanagh could see that the South Armagh story could remove some of the gloss from the "peace in our time" Ulster story but the real damage was to the world of secrecy. It all came down to the breaking of confidence – if you couldn't trust your own, who could you trust?

"Is this all there is Gerry?"

"I didn't want to put too much on paper, so yes, that's everything."

"You made phone calls, what about records?"

"All I could have brought you would be the itemised bills for the office."

"What about the telephone here?"

"There might be one or two connected calls made from here, I'm not sure. To be honest I made most of my calls either at the office or from phone boxes."

"Did anybody call you here?"

"Dave Beatty may have, but you'll have him covered. As for Alain Williams I always contacted him. I don't see what difference who called who and from where really makes."

"I'm just being thorough. If Williams goes ahead with the story a lack of provable contact would work against him, you know the rules."

"And I've broken them I know, but if you give me a chance I'll make up for that."

"I'm just here to listen and see what efforts you've made."

"Well you've got the file and I did make the initial contact with the "Department"…."

"What about Williams?"

"Yes, I knew it would come round to him."

"So what have you done?"

"I've spoken with him and I think he'll drop the story."

"And why do you think that?"

"I told him about the attitude the "Department would take regarding me and that he'd faced the same sort of trouble."

"You did what?"

"I threatened him. You know, the danger of going ahead with the story, the OSA and court cases, that kind of thing."

"And that might just give him another angle on the story. "Journalist threatened by secret establishment", that kind of thing. Christ Almighty! What did you have to go and do that for?"

"I really don't think he'll go in that direction Sean."

"Think! You're in this bloody mess 'cause you didn't think. Why didn't you leave Williams to us?"

Crawford let his head drop forward as his eyes searched for somewhere other than Kavanagh to focus. He'd realised that his behaviour had been questionable but the sting of guilt, which he hadn't wanted to accept in the first place, was intensified with Kavanagh's words. He kept his eyes fixed on the floor, unable to face reality for the moment. Everything he had thought true and honourable looked tarnished and his actions had done nothing to restore their shine. The principles that he had held dear were starting to look like lies or, at best, excuses that absolved any kind of expedient act. A career in the service based entirely on falsehood, but if that was the case, what the hell was he being loyal to? He looked up at Kavanagh and saw that he'd returned to the notes in the file.

"Sean if what you say is true, this bloody mess, as you call it, isn't down to me."

"Well whose fault is it then?"

"The system that we've worked for, it's at fault."

"Gerry you knew the rules when you started and you've broken them. Don't try to excuse that by lying. The only person you're kidding is you."

"Think about it Sean. The rules are wrong, there are no certainties...."

"Gerry you can't justify your actions this way."

"And you can't change the rules just because they don't suit you. What we did was right and people need to know. What the hell does the "Department" know about right and wrong? Tell me that Sean."

Kavanagh could see from the progress of the interview that the action was the only way forward – one moment Crawford had accepted that he was wrong, the next he was back on his crusade and dangerously out of control. The last thing the "Department" needed was a zealot running loose. He'd needed to be sure that there was no alternative, and now he was.

"Gerry I can't offer any words of consolation...."

"Well then don't. You can go back to your masters and tell them that Gerry Crawford nearly succumbed but decided that the story needs to be told."

"This isn't going to do anyone any good."

"I don't care."

"I'm begging you to reconsider."

"No Sean, my mind's made up."

"Then there's nothing more I can do."

"No there isn't and you can tell the "Department" from me – go to hell!"

All the time he'd been sitting in Crawford's flat he'd been looking for an opportunity but none had appeared, now his hand was forced and he knew he'd have to make the best of it. He put the file down on the coffee table and got up, moving to his left. As he moved toward the hall Crawford leaned forward to retrieve his notes and in doing so he put himself off balance. Kavanagh saw his chance turning before he struck Crawford with the heel of his right hand. The blow landed on the nerve cluster on the left hand side of the neck, the brachial plexus, and the effect was instantaneous. Crawford slumped forward onto the table and would have fallen to the floor had Kavanagh not stopped him. As he held the body he quickly checked for signs of life, yes, quite unconscious but very much alive. He knew from his study of the floor plan that the bathroom was the last on the right down the hallway and he'd also observed that it was carpeted, therefore dragging Crawford down the corridor was out of the question, one way or another he'd leave marks on the carpet and his clothing would pick up tell-tale fibres. He knew that the stun wouldn't last more than a minute and the clock was ticking. He moved the body back into the chair, putting it into a more natural lifting position, before he took his stance in front of the seat and made a classic fireman's lift. The strain was considerable and Kavanagh had to be careful, as he made his way down the hall with his unconscious and unwilling load, in case Crawford knocked against furniture or pictures – an upset of his balance, such as it was, could prove disastrous

– the crucial thing was to leave no anomalous features in what would be treated as a crime scene.

The bathroom door wasn't closed and Kavanagh gratefully pushed it open before laying Crawford's limp form on the tiled floor. He checked the life signs again and nodded when he realised that Crawford was slowly coming to. Time was going by so quickly but not fast enough to make a difference for either man. Kavanagh would have enough time to get the job done but Crawford would never return to the full consciousness that might have given him a fighting chance. Kavanagh turned away from the crumpled heap on the floor and surveyed the bathroom. It was a small space, maybe ten by ten at the most, with a low ceiling that housed a built in ventilation system. He reached into his outside left hand jacket pocket and brought out the pair of latex gloves that he'd taken from the medicine cabinet back at his own flat. He'd given the interior of the gloves an extra dusting of talcum powder and accordingly they slipped on easily. Crawford was showing definite signs of life – his breathing was stronger as he cleared his air passages and there were obvious flickers at his eyes.

Kavanagh bent over and pulled Crawford into an upright sitting position and then stepped back to take a couple of deep breaths in preparation for the final physical effort. He didn't allow himself any time for thought, if he'd done so action would have been impossible. He bent over again and slid his hands under Crawford's arms, bending his legs as he did so. It was going to be a difficult lift but thankfully not impossible. He took the strain and blew out as he straightened up and pulled Crawford with him. He pushed in on Crawford's legs with his knees, with the effect of keeping them locked straight and held the upper body with his left hand while he took the Berreta from his trouser pocket. He knew that swabs could be taken from an apparent gunshot suicide's hands, so he had to get the pistol in Crawford's right hand thus making sure of a good coverage of any residues. The manoeuvre was far from easy, but he managed it by leaning his full weight against Crawford's chest while he dropped his left hand to grasp the right wrist. He took a secure grip and pulled upwards bringing the hand more or less to eye level allowing him to watch unobstructed as he folded the fingers around the Berreta's grip before turning the pistol around so that he could push it into Crawford's open mouth.

The moment had arrived and Kavanagh tried to concentrate on the pistol as he squeezed on the right index finger that rested on the trigger but the flicker of Crawford's eye distracted him. He looked at the older man just as the eyes opened fully.

The first thing Crawford was aware of was the dull throb in his head, quickly followed by the knowledge of something in his mouth. He slowly opened his eyes and saw Kavanagh's face inches from his own, but he couldn't focus and looked across the room at the mirror above the wash-hand basin. He saw the back of Kavanagh's head first and then as he moved slightly to his right Crawford could see what was happening.

Kavanagh watched as reality hit Crawford. The unfocussed look was replaced by total clarity and with it came understanding, resignation, terror and sadness. Kavanagh tried to hold his contact but couldn't bear the look in Crawford's eyes and dropped his gaze to the Beretta. He kept on repeating "the job", "the job", "the job", and the mantra worked, allowing him to do what he'd come for. As he pulled the trigger he felt a stirring in Crawford's body that signalled a final effort against him but it never came as the hammer fell. Kavanagh never heard the shot, his concentration shut down his hearing, in truth his sight was the only sense working, working too well as he took in every detail of the scene in the bathroom. He watched as the tension in the body was replaced once again by a limpness, only this time the body would never regain consciousness. He wanted to be somewhere else and he didn't want to accept responsibility for what he had done. The disgust he felt for himself was nearly overwhelming as he released Crawford and stepped to the left, letting the body drop to the floor.

His breathing was coming in short gasps, the sound of it the first thing he became aware of. He rubbed his forehead with his gloved hand and shielded his eyes from the sight of the body on the floor. He took several deep breaths and gradually got back some degree of self-control. He knew he had to get away from the scene but his guilt was making it hard to drag himself away. He started to repeat "the job" in an effort to restore his professionalism. He hit his forehead with the palm of his hand, and told himself that professionals didn't get caught, which was exactly what would happen if he didn't get a grip. He closed his eyes and took another deep breath to compose himself before he made a last check on the bathroom. He opened his eyes and began an assessment of the scene – Crawford's body lay on its left hand side with the left arm trapped under the torso and the right arm resting on the floor – a growing patch of blood stood out from the white tiles where Crawford had bled from the entry wound in his mouth – the pistol had fallen out of the right hand coming to rest beside the pedestal of the wash hand basin. The empty case had ended up on the floor after ejecting, landing beside Crawford's right hand, and it was this small detail that held Kavanagh's attention. He knew that the case would be dusted for fingerprints in the course of any investigation and that their absence might raise suspicions. There was nothing else for it. He took a pen from his inside breast pocket and laid it on the floor, using the corner of a tile as one index point and the tip of the pen as another. With the position of the case marked he was free to pick it up and press Crawford's right index finger and thumb on it. As he marked the case he thought about the magazine and knew that he'd have to mark it in the same way. With the empty case dealt with, he picked up his pen and marked the position of the Beretta, before lifting it to eject the magazine and press Crawford's fingers on to the exterior. Once he'd got the necessary prints he gently returned the arm to its recumbent position. He then stood up and took a last look around – the bathroom appeared as it should, the scene of a suicide – nothing was out of place and therefore nothing should spark the curiosity of an imaginative forensic officer. He turned and opened the door just wide enough to let him out into the hallway. The barrier of the door seemed to separate Kavanagh from the reality of his act, the pain from having to look at Crawford diminished and he was able to focus on the rest of his task.

He walked up the hall to where his overcoat hung and reaching into the inside pocket he brought out the bag of .32 rounds that Curtis had given him down at "The Fort". He retraced his steps and was just about to go into Crawford's bedroom when it occurred to him that the bag would probably be dusted for prints and Crawford's weren't on it. He opened the door and made his way inside again, the smell of burnt propellant was the dominant odour in the bathroom, with a faint aroma of blood underlining it. It was strange how his senses were returning to normal, previously he'd been unable to smell anything. He knelt and for the second time grasped Crawford's right hand as he applied fingerprints to the plastic bag. He knew that he should put prints from the left hand on the bag as well but with it pinned under the body it was inaccessible. He could only hope that no-one would wonder why Crawford had only handled the bag with his right hand. It was surprising to him that he was able to be so analytical; maybe it was the feeling of disassociation that made it easier for him to do what he had to. Even the short time he'd been away from the body had put some distance between him and the responsibility for his actions. Again he left the bathroom and made his way across to the bedroom.

He stood just inside the door, after he'd turned on the main light, and took in the details of the room before he settled on the walk-in wardrobe as the best hiding place for the spare rounds. Moving across the room he reached up and switched on the interior light before he opened the door. Suits, jackets, shirts and trousers hung neatly on rails that lined both sides of the closet space. There could be little doubt that Crawford had enjoyed spending money on clothes, but Kavanagh wasn't going to quickly stuff the rounds into a convenient pocket, it seemed so out of Crawford's character to him and it was important to make this appear natural. He turned to look above the door and his search was rewarded with a small space on the lintel that would serve as a shelf for the plastic bag – not an obvious hiding place nor a careless one, but a thorough search would find them, and that was what he wanted.

He went back to his overcoat and took a handkerchief from one of the outside pockets. He'd been careful to avoid too much contact with his ungloved hands and now he made his way through to the living room and wiped down the leather Chesterfield that he'd sat in. He looked at the coffee table but decided against wiping it down; in all honesty he couldn't remember touching the surface at any time, even when he'd lifted the file, besides too many totally clean surfaces would look suspicious. When he'd finished at the armchair and lifted the file containing Crawford's notes from the table he walked over to the doorway leading into the hall and looked down the corridor before turning to look back into living room – nothing he could see showed any evidence of third-party involvement – to all intents and purposes the flat was clean of his presence. He glanced at his watch

– nine twenty-five – and decided that there was nothing else to do. He folded the file and pushed it into the inside pocket of his coat before taking it down from the hook in the hall. He shrugged it on and stood listening at the door for any noise that would indicate signs of life outside. Thirty seconds went by before he gently opened the front door and was relieved to find nobody on the first floor landing. He made his way down the stairs and into the ground floor lobby, maintaining a steady, purposeful pace all the time, determined to bypass any possible contact. His concern was natural but as it turned out unnecessary, he didn't encounter anyone in the building.

He stopped on the front step and stood in the shadows as he made sure that the street was empty of either pedestrians or vehicles. Again he let half a minute go by as he scrutinised the street, and again nobody added their presence to the emptiness. He glanced down at the step and caught a glimpse of his shoes; there was a mark on the right toecap and he took the handkerchief from his coat pocket to wipe it away. He bent over and rubbed the spot before straightening up to examine the result under the glare of the hallway light. As he looked at the stain he was brought back to the reality of his action – it was blood and it was Crawford's. He wadded the cloth up and stuffed it back in his pocket. His self-control was stretched to breaking point as a wave of nausea swept over him and yet, if anybody had seen the grimace that flashed over his face, they would have thought nothing of it, it merely looked like the reaction of a man annoyed to find dirt on his shoe. He had to get away, but with none of the care he had shown earlier he stepped down onto the pavement and made his way towards Holland Park Avenue.

The first obvious signs of life came with the traffic; private cars, taxis, a fully laden double decker bus, just ordinary people going about their mundane business. He stood at the kerb and waited for a gap in the flow that would allow him across and as he waited he realised that he could never be a part of the ordinary, no matter how much he wanted to be. He missed his chance to cross a couple of times as he tried to rationalise his position. He'd willingly become an outsider, and now through his own actions he'd removed any chance of rejoining normality. The traffic thinned out and even in his state of mind Kavanagh couldn't ignore his chance to cross. He jogged to the opposite side of the Avenue and quickly made his way to Portland Road and his car. He nearly dropped his keys in his hurry to unlock the door – the need to get into a safe space was undeniable and he started to hyperventilate again – eventually he got the door open and collapsed onto the driver's seat. He was sprawled half in half out of the car, his breathing little more than ragged gasps. He knew that he had to get in properly and get a grip of himself – failure to do so would attract all the wrong sort of attention and he couldn't risk that. After dragging himself upright, using the steering wheel for support, he sat with his eyes closed trying to put together a course of action. It should have been simple, but every time he settled on something the image of Crawford lying on the bathroom floor filled his mind and blanked everything else out.

Time passed quickly as he struggled with his conscience. Part of him wanted to hand the responsibility over to someone else but he knew that was unrealistic – no matter what he did the truth would always be with him, and that was the most painful thing – there could be no escape from what he had done. The pain was unbearable and he had to open his eyes to find some diversion, self-indulgence wasn't solving anything. He looked at the dashboard clock – ten oh-six – and it shocked him that he'd been sitting for the best part of half an hour. He put the window down and let the cold November air blow into the car, clearing the muggy atmosphere and his head. Next he put the key in the ignition and started up. To stay in Portland Road would be to jeopardise everything and much as he hated it he began thinking in terms of "the job" again. He made a three point turn and rejoined the Avenue, turning left he drove back into the West End. The bright lights and the increased number of cars proved to be the distraction he'd needed – he was too busy avoiding an accident to think of anything else. His instinct was to make for home in the north of the city, so he joined the flow of traffic along Oxford Street and turned left up Tottenham Court Road. Another fifteen minutes saw him close to home but he knew he had one more task to complete before he could rest. He found a bank of three phone boxes on Pentonville Road and stopped to make his call.

Blackwell had tried to occupy his wait with various pieces of paperwork but he'd come to the conclusion that he was merely inventing work. He'd left his desk and gone in search of coffee but after three cups and a read through the Evening Standard all he'd done was put himself on edge. He returned to his office and sat with his scribble pad making notes about the various potential outcomes of tonight's task. Some of the consequences he'd noted were implausible, some outright freakish, but one thing was clear, irrespective of the possibilities, the job wouldn't end with Crawford's removal. He considered the deployment of manpower, the where and the who, and when he looked at all the various aspects of future tasks they added up to a significant commitment. The thought of having to embark on some sort of large-scale cover-up all because of one man's indiscretion angered him. The waiting, the speculation and the uncertainty had all taken their toll. He looked at his desk clock – ten thirty-three – where the hell was Kavanagh?

The interior of the middle box of the three was plastered with the business cards and fly sheets advertising numerous massage parlours and women promising "a good time". Kavanagh shook his head in sadness and keyed in the number of the mobile phone from memory. It only rang once, it seemed that no-one wanted to prolong this longer than necessary.
 "The job's done."
 "And the site's clean?"
 "The job's done."
 "Are you OK?"
 "Like you really give a shit, but no, I'm not."

"Well, I'd like to give you some time off but I need all the details and any recovered material. You'll have to come in tomorrow."

"OK, but after that I'm finished."

"You're finished when I say you're finished. This job isn't over yet."

"It is for me."

"I think you've forgotten our earlier conversations."

"Oh that's perfect! Are you threatening me?"

"The job's not over 'til I say so and 'til then you're a part of it."

"Fuck you!"

"I don't think so. Just be here at eleven tomorrow."

Before Kavanagh could think of anything else to say the line went dead.

ISBN 142515719-X

Printed in Great Britain
by Amazon